The Duncan Trilogy

By
SHELDON LYNNE

i

Riverhouse Publishing
St. Louis MO 63146
ISBN: 1-893892-08-5

© 2014 Sheldon Lynne

Book 1

THE FORGIVEN

By
 SHELDON LYNNE

The Forgiven

Riverhouse Publishing
St. Louis MO 63146
ISBN: 1-893892-05-0

© 2012 Sheldon Lynne

PROLOGUE

For someone to be forgiven, they must have done something bad first. Charlie and Donna were good people, but they had things happen to them that ultimately caused them to become murderers. Thus, they were placed in a position of needing forgiveness. It all started at a funeral in Thibodeaux, Louisiana.

Thibodaux, Louisiana - July 1972

It was a lazy Sunday afternoon in the bayou country about sixty miles south and west of New Orleans. A memorial service had just been held for Army First Lieutenant Charles A. Mackey III at the local Catholic Church in Thibodaux.

The temperature was in the mid-nineties and, even for this area, the humidity was extremely high with a heat index of 115 degrees. The sky was a beautiful blue with a few white puffy clouds floating along through the sky, but in spite of the fact that the clouds hid the sun ever so often the day was very hot. Other than that, the weather seemed to cooperate with the memorial service for Lieutenant Charles Allen Mackey III.

His parents were notified of his death almost a month before, but the cruelest part to them was that his body would not be returned to Thibodaux for burial since he was listed as "Missing In Action, Presumed Dead". This listing allowed his death benefit to be paid at once to his beneficiary, his sister Miriam. Since Charles was single and his parents were extremely wealthy, it made sense to him to make Miriam his beneficiary.

Earlier, Charles had received the Silver Star for heroism during one of the firefights in which he participated in Vietnam. He had sent the medal to his parents who framed it and placed it a prominent place in their home where anyone who came to visit would see it. They were very proud of their son and devastated by his death.

After the service, the Mackeys invited only their daughter, Miriam, some family members and a few close friends over to their house for refreshments. Miriam, who was much older than Charles, was now their only heir.

Finally, after about an hour of socializing and accepting condolences from everyone in their house and trying to be friendly, Mr. Mackey said, "Well, we have to get on with our lives. Thank you all for being here and especially you, Miriam, but I think your mother and I would like to be alone right now."

"I understand, papa. But before I go, I want you to know I sent Charles an expensive bracelet seven months ago with his blood type and everything on it. Maybe that will help someone find him."

Miriam kissed her father and mother, and then left their house to return to her home in New Orleans.

Slightly after 1:00 AM the next morning, two ordinary-looking men, one black and one white, holding shotguns approached the side of the Mackey house and found the sliding glass door on the side of the house unlocked. The white man opened the door silently, stepped inside. His friend then quickly and as silently stepped inside. They immediately began holding the shotguns at the ready – their left hand halfway up the barrel and their right hand holding the trigger guard. They pushed a button to turn off the safety and placed their index finger on the trigger. Now the men moved quietly, but quickly down a short hallway to the bedroom where the Mackeys slept.

The door was half-open. The black man stood in the hallway at the ready while the white man released his grip on the trigger and silently pushed the door open. They both stepped inside the room and looked at the Mackeys sleeping in the bed with Mr. Mackey's left arm resting over his wife. The two men stood at the foot of the bed for a moment, then raised their shotguns and on a signal from the black man, each man fired two shots into the sleeping Mackeys.

They died without moving a muscle. After killing the Mackeys, they ransacked the house and took a few things in order to make it appear like a burglary.

Carrying the few items they took from the house, the two men left by the same door they had entered the house. They walked about a quarter of a mile through two lines of oak trees to their car, got in and drove down the highway that ran in front of the Mackey house and beside a bayou to where an old railroad bridge had once stood. Only the concrete bridge abutments were left when the structure was removed some years before. The white man got out of the car and threw both guns into the bayou.

They continued on the highway until they reached the little town of Raceland where they stopped outside an all-night convenience store. The black man got out of the car and walked to a public telephone.

He dialed a number in New Orleans.

A voice answered, "Hello."

"It's done and we threw the guns you gave us in the water by the old railroad bridge."

The voice sighed, sniffled a little bit, and said, "Your checks will be coming to you as we agreed."

Both parties to the conversation then hung up.

Four days later, the Steven Funeral Home in Thibodaux was packed with mourners for the funeral of the Mackeys who had been well liked in Thibodaux and the surrounding area.

The police chief, Emile Gaspard had been a close friend of the Mackeys. He and Deputy George Fallow were talking near the door of the parlor where the bodies were being viewed.

"Chief, we got two sets of finger prints which have to be those of the killers. Do you want to announce that we have the prints?"

With a nod of his head indicating he was thinking about that possibility and the fact there were no leads said, "No... I think we should keep that our little secret so we don't tip our hand too soon. But, send the prints we have to the FBI and to all the police departments in Louisiana to have them checked."

Just as he finished, Chief Gaspard spotted Miriam and a man he didn't recognize walking into the parlor. He immediately walked over to her.

Miriam walked up to Gaspard and in a matter of fact tone of voice said, "Gaspard, this is Antoine Broussard, my attorney. I want you to know I have set up a reward for the conviction of the bastards who killed mama and papa. Antoine has handled the details. I hope the reward will bring those killers to justice."

Antoine Broussard added with some bravado, "Miss Mackey has put up two million dollars, one million for each of her parents."

"That's an awful lot of money, Miriam. I hope someone will come forward and be able to claim it. As you know, we have very little to go on."

About an hour later, just before the caskets were closed for the last time, Miriam reached into the coffins and hugged her mother's body and then still crying hysterically and very loud, she reached into her father's coffin and hugged him.

She was still screaming and crying excessively loud as Broussard helped her out of the parlor.

As she passed Gaspard who was looking at her in her distress, she sobbed, Gaspard, I'm going to raise the ante to twenty million - ten million for each my mother and father. Get those bastards."

Placing his arm around her, he replied, "We will, honey. We will."

CHAPTER 1

Somewhere in Laos, 1975

It was almost 4:00 PM on a hot, sweaty day in a Laotian village near the Plain of Jars. The temperature was approaching 100 degrees and the humidity made the heat almost unbearable. A narrow dirt road ran between two rows of foliage-thatched houses, which was the village except for police headquarters and the heroin factory. The fields just outside the village were very colorful being covered with poppies in full bloom. This meant an abundant and healthy crop would be harvested soon. This pleased the farmers and everyone concerned - which included virtually the entire village.

Just to the north, where a river becomes a waterfall, a relatively new hydroelectric generator hummed away beside the rusting hulk of its predecessor, which had been presented to the village by the French. The new and bigger generator came courtesy of the Americans who installed it as part of a deal that allowed them to build a clandestine airfield and supply base just outside the village for their operations in Laos and Vietnam.

The heroin trade was booming. Everyone knew it had been there before the supply base opened and would continue to be there after the base closed. Very little of the proceeds from the heroin trade trickled down to the farmers and field workers even though that was the sole source of income in the village before the American base was built. The American base became the only other real source of income available to the villagers whose manual labor was needed and well appreciated by base personnel.

About all that was left of French colonialism in the village was the old French uniform worn by the police chief. It was still a symbol of authority and he never let anyone see him without it. Just now, he was standing beside three men and a woman near the entrance to the heroin factory, which was located directly across the dirt road from the police station in the center of the village. They were discussing the eminent closing of the supply base in their Laotian dialect.

The woman, who ran the heroin factory, was speaking to the group in her native language, but mainly to the police chief.

"We must take the airfield and their planes. With them, we can increase our deliveries. We will prosper and be rich like the Americans. But we must do it quickly before they destroy the base. I tell you they will leave no evidence behind them. I know because one of the men who works for the Americans heard them talking. They will destroy it all if we do not act in time."

The police chief replied, *"I agree, I agree. But how and when? We must plan...."*

The roar of a cargo plane coming in for a landing interrupted the conversation and they turned to look in the direction from which the sound was coming, but they could not see the plane because of the dense jungle, which surrounded the village.

A C-130 was making its approach to the landing strip at the base, which lay less than 200 yards from the village, but could have been miles from the village since the base was concealed from the village by the all-consuming jungle.

The base was little more than a landing strip, which was barely able to accommodate the cargo planes and had only a few tin shacks and tents. This was all that served as the last supply depot for the remaining last two outlying posts in this area of Laos.

For a few years when the base was used extensively, the C-130

10

supply planes would take off from here and either airdrop supplies or land on small risky airfields to unload supplies at the outlying posts. The base was virtually invisible within the lush vegetation that engulfed, then swallowed it. The only sign that a camp was there was the small runway, which ended only a few yards from the jungle.

Lt. Col. Macintire was in charge of the base. Because the base was illegal and was supposed to be secret, all personnel went by their first names or nicknames. References to their military rank were forbidden. Col. Macintire was known simply as Mac.

Mac was standing in the communication shack, such that it was, looking out the window and watching the sky as he waited impatiently for his demolition team to return. He had sent them out to destroy "Valley" camp and wanted to know that the camp had indeed been destroyed. He also knew the next morning he would send them to destroy "Mountain Top" camp and after that, this base would be destroyed in a day or two. He also wanted to find out from George and Alan who had been with him several years just how good the new man was. He had confidence in them and their opinion.

The new man had arrived the day before and had only recently finished his Special Forces training stateside. Mac had not had time to get to know him before he sent him out with the demolition team to destroy Valley. All Mac knew about him was that his name was Charlie and that HQ said he was good with explosives. HQ sent him to help destroy the remaining bases in a way that would satisfy those in power who wanted to be very certain that no traceable remnant of them remained. Charlie's paper work and records got lost somewhere between there and here, but Mac estimated his age to be about twenty and his rank was Second Lieutenant.

The sound of the radio broke in on Mac's thoughts. "Base, this is Mountain Top. I need Mac - now! Over."

Mac turned to look at the radio, made a face and thought, this sounds bad. Mark wouldn't say he needed me now in that tone of voice if he wasn't in some sort of trouble.

Mac walked over to the radio and picked up the mike.

11

"Mountain Top, this is Mac. What's up?"

"Mac - We have big problems. Alpha and Bravo people just contacted me and said the bad guys can and will probably overrun them in a short time. This means they could be at Mountain Top in a couple of hours."

"Go on," Mac said quietly.

"It looks like they can take Mountain Top anytime they want after they arrive here - tonight, tomorrow morning or whenever they damn well feel like it. They've got more men than we thought and they're coming fast. We need out - now. What can you do?"

Mac stood there looking at the mike because he could not believe what Mark had just said. The reason it was hard to believe was he had just been told by his Laotian friends that the North Vietnamese irregulars were not close to Mountain Top, but he knew Mark was in trouble or he wouldn't ask to be taken out today if it weren't an emergency.

"Hang on. I'll get back to you in a minute"

Mac put the mike down and turned to another man standing beside him.

"Is the Flyer sober?"

The Flyer was the best C-130 pilot Mac had. He had plenty of experience and knew the short landing strip at Mountain Top better than anyone else. He was the logical choice to make the rescue run - especially since it had to be made at dusk.

"I think so. I'll get him and put him on alert," came the reply.

"Hell, get him ready to fly."

Now Mac turned to the person in charge of flight readiness of the C-130s.

"Old Man, can you get the other 130 ready to go in thirty minutes?"

"Yes sir," was the reply.

"Do it."

Mac walked back to the radio and picked up the mike.

"Mountain Top."

"This is Mountain Top. What can you do?"

"Mark, have your people ready to leave in one and a half hours.

12

It'll take us about thirty minutes to get the other 130 ready and about an hour for the Flyer to make the run. I still have to get the demolition team ready, but that won't take that long. I guess you can expect them about 6:00 or 6:15 tonight. Can you make it?"

"Mac, we can make it, but the Flyer might have to wait a few minutes for Alpha and Bravo people. They'll need about two hours to get here from their outposts. I think we can have everything else at the ready."

"Good - the demolition team is just landing. I'll have them out of here ASAP."

Mac got into his jeep and drove to where the C-130 that landed had just turned its engines off. Its passengers were leaving the plane as Mac drove up to the plane. The tires on Mac's jeep skidded on the loose dirt near the runway where the plane stood. Mac waived to Lloyd and his men from Valley, then waved to George, Alan and Charlie in a manner that meant - I want to talk to you - now!

As Charlie walked over to the supply area, Mac took George and Alan aside.

"Guys, you've got to go right out again. Mountain Top is in deep do-do. It seems the bad guys can take the camp anytime they want - as soon as a couple of hours from now. You two and Charlie will leave with the Flyer as soon as the Old Man gets the other 130 ready," as he pointed to the second C-130 being loaded with fuel and explosives.

George and Alan looked at Mac, then back at each other. "Can we go to camp and get a quickie?"

"No, you'll have to do without your beer for another several hours. Now, how did Charlie do?"

Alan looked at George before he responded.

"Mac, he's absolutely the best I've ever seen. Fast and clean. When he pressed the radio control switch to blow the camp, we had just left the ground and were about to make the turn around the mountain when the camp blew. You know that's a good way from the camp, but we still received a push from the explosion. He even brought some plastic home with him."

"Mac, the kid is really good. What he can't do with plastic

13

can't be done," added George.

"How fast is he?"

"He can set more plastic than both of us combined in less time."

"He'll need to from what Mark told me."

The Flyer started the engines at exactly 5:02 PM. The C-130 roared down the runway and was airborne heading for Mountain Top on time. Because of the urgency at Mountain Top, the flight would take only 52 minutes as the Flyer flew faster than cruising speed.

The landing field at Mountain Top was very short because of the terrain, but the Flyer landed the C-130 as if he needed only half of the runway. He taxied over to a sandbagged bunker and turned the plane around so it would be able to take off straight down the runway. Even though the Flyer didn't turn off the plane's engines, a jeep hooked on to the tail of the plane and pulled the 130 into the bunker in such a manner that the plane could still take off straight down the runway without assistance. The Flyer now turned off all the engines except one that he left running.

The door to the plane opened and George, Alan, and Charlie carried the explosives out of the plane towards Mark who was walking towards the bunker.

"You don't have much time before Alpha and Bravo come home. My guess is less than thirty minutes. I don't know how long after that the bad guys will be here."

Pointing to a number of natives who were taking guns, ammunition and other supplies, he continued, "Those are the friendlies. I told them they could have what they could carry. The guns are over there and the ammunition is over there covered with that tarp. It's all yours."

Charlie, George, and Alan ran over to the four piles of munitions and supplies and began laying plastic and primer cord. Twenty minutes later, they heard gunfire coming down the trail where Alpha would be coming.

With the sound of gunfire, the locals shouldered as much as they could carry and hurried off. Then gunfire sounded from the direction from which Bravo would come. All personnel stopped what they were doing and prepared to repel the attackers, except

14

Charlie who finished setting the plastic in another six minutes.

The Alpha people appeared running at the edge of the clearing on the side away from the runway. Camp personnel could see that people were shooting at them and began to offer covering gunfire, but it was too late. A barrage of AK-47 gunfire cut down all four of them.

By now, Bravo people had reached the clearing too. They got within 50 yards of the ammunition dump only because all Mountain Top personnel as well as George, Alan and Charlie were offering covering fire when a rocket hit one of the ammo dumps. The explosion rocked the area.

Charlie was blown nearly ten yards through the air and landed beside the severed hand of one of the camp's men. The rest of the man's body was nowhere to be seen. Unconscious, but still alive, Charlie still had the radio control switch for the explosives tied to his wrist.

When the gunfire began, the Flyer started all engines. Although he had the urge to leave immediately, he decided to remain in the bunker so those who were able could get on board. The bunker gave them some cover.

After the explosion, the only people left alive were two men from Bravo running towards the bunker and Charlie. While the two Bravo men ran towards the bunker, they quickly and nervously looked for survivors. They passed the bloody and dismembered bodies of Mark, George, and Alan. Everyone was dead except Charlie, who lay sprawled with one arm under his body and the other over his face. When one of the men kicked him, he groaned. Realizing the man he kicked was still alive, he immediately dropped his rifle, picked Charlie up, and threw him over his shoulders. As he lifted Charlie, he saw a broken gold bracelet next to Charlie's hand and scooped it up too. Together with his companion, the man ran to the safety of the bunker and struggled quickly onto the plane.

As Charlie was laid down in the plane, the second man shouted, "What's that on his wrist?"

The first man recognized what it was; then with a grin on his face, reached down, turned the device on, and pressed the detonator

15

button.

The following explosion was greater then the previous one that had rocked the area, but the plane was protected from the explosion by the bunker. After the concussion, debris rained down for what seemed several minutes; then a strange silence settled down over what was left of the camp. The Flyer pushed the throttle to full power and the motors roared as the plane raced down the runway. The C-130 was airborne before the attackers could regroup and continue the attack.

As the 130 was gaining altitude, the Flyer spoke to the two men from Bravo outpost.

"Damn, that was close. You boys don't know how close I was to going home alone. I don't want to be that close ever again. Are you guys okay? Did we leave anybody?"

The two men looked at each other. "Yeah, we're okay, but nobody else is. They're all dead as far as we could tell, except for this guy. I've never seen him before. He's the one who had the detonator."

Breathing hard, the second survivor added, "He's still out."

"I'll have to thank him when he wakes up. If the ammo dumps hadn't blown, those suckers would have eaten us alive," replied the Flyer.

After the 130 had been airborne a short time, the Flyer used the radio.

"Base, this is the Flyer. Over."

"Flyer, this is Mac. How did it go?"

"The bad guys got there too soon." He hesitated, then forced himself to continue. "They're all gone - the demo team, Mountain Top people - everyone except two people from Bravo and that new guy. He's unconscious, but still breathing. I don't know how bad he's hurt so get Doc to meet us. We'll be there in about twenty-five minutes. Over."

"Crap," was all that Mac said at first. After twenty seconds that seemed like an hour, he said, "We'll be ready for you. Out."

When the C-130 landed, a stretcher jeep was standing by waiting for the plane to stop. Two men put Charlie on a stretcher,

16

carried him to the jeep, and placed him on the jeep's stretcher holder. The jeep then drove to the make shift hospital.

The base hospital had only four beds and the doctor was actually a medic with experience in Korea and Vietnam. He examined the unconscious man carefully, then reported to Mac.

"I wish I could get some x-rays. He doesn't seem to be too seriously damaged physically. A little cut up from shrapnel, but there isn't a lot of bleeding. But he's definitely suffered a concussion and is in a coma. I don't know when or if he'll ever come out of it. How quick can you ship him to a real hospital?"

"Damn. I guess I can get a medivac plane in here tomorrow. This will delay blowing this place. HQ will just have to send me some people to blow this place."

"By the way Mac and for the record, what's this guy's name?" "Hell, the only name I know is Charlie. They picked up a gold bracelet lying next to him. Let's look at it. Maybe his name is on it."

Doc examined the bracelet, then said, "Nice gold bracelet and it's expensive too. It says his name is Charles A. Mackey III, blood type AB negative. I can check his blood type. If it is in fact AB negative, then I would guess that's his name since AB negative is a rare blood type."

"Good. Check his blood type while I get him a plane out of here."

Two hours later, Doc walked into Mac's office.

"AB negative. That has to be his bracelet. As I told you before, AB negative is a rare blood type. By the way, did you get him a plane out of here?"

"Yeah. He'll be out of here tomorrow morning on the supply plane and probably in Hawaii in a couple of days - lucky stiff."

The supply plane arrived on schedule – 9:00 AM the next morning. Charlie was carried on the twin-engine plane while the pilot was handing some papers to Mac.

The supply plane turned around and headed down the runway. Mac looked at the plane disappearing over the jungle before he looked at the stack of papers the pilot had left behind. As he looked at the papers, he discovered that some of the papers were Charlie's records.

Rubbing the bead of sweat on his face, he mused he would have to send them back to headquarters – what efficiency!

CHAPTER 2

The monument over the battleship Arizona in the Pearl Harbor
Naval Base was just bathed in the bright morning sunlight just as Dr.
Robert Grimes and Nurse Allison Ford were completing their
morning rounds at the Pacific Fleet Naval Hospital. Dr. Grimes was
about to enter the doctor's lounge and dictate his morning reports.

"Nurse, I want to speak to Dr. Fitzmorris about Charles in room
315. I received a strange answer to our inquiry from the Army about
him and I think Dennis and I need to talk about it."

"Yes sir. If I don't see Dr. Fitzmorris, I'll leave a note for him
and tell Mary about it."

Looking at her watch, Allison said, "I have to go with Mary on
our checkout round. She should be coming on duty anytime now."

Nurse Mary Lee got off the elevator, turned to the left and
walked down the corridor towards the nurse's station. She smiled at
an orderly, then saw Allison coming from the doctor's lounge
towards her. They waved to each other.

Nurses Mary Lee and Allison Ford had both graduated from
Montana State University's School of Nursing and were good
friends. Mary, however, entered nursing school the year Allison was
a senior and graduated a couple of years after Allison.

"Good morning, Allison."

"You only say that because you're just getting here! Is that Dr.
Fitzmorris I see down the hall?"

Mary turned to look. "Yes, do you want him?"

"No, Dr. Grimes does. He wants to talk to him about the patient in room 315. Before we start our checkout round, let me get him."

"Okay."

Allison caught Dr. Fitzmorris just as he was entering room 315 to check on Charles.

"Dr. Fitzmorris!"

"Yes."

"Dr. Grimes wants to talk to you about Charles in the doctor's lounge when you're finished here."

"Sure. Let me talk to you for a couple of minutes about this patient first."

"Yes sir."

Dr. Fitzmorris and Allison entered the room.

"Allison, has he shown any sign of coming out of the coma?"

"No sir."

"Well, let's get another EEG later today. Schedule it for 2:30 PM so I can be here when it's run."

"I'll put it on the chart and tell Mary about it."

"Good, now I'll see what Bob wants."

"I think it's about the packet of information he received from the Army about Charles."

"That'll be interesting."

Nurse Ford and Dr. Fitzmorris left the room and walked together down the hall. At the nurse's station, Allison left Dr. Fitzmorris and joined Mary there.

"Dr. Fitzmorris wants another EEG on Charles this afternoon at 2:30. He said to set it up for that time so he could be there when it's run."

Mary looked to see if Dr. Fitzmorris was within hearing range. When she saw he was not, she turned to Allison.

"That man. He always wants things done just at shift change time."

"Come on Mary, you know all he wants is to talk to you afterward."

As the two nurses started down the hall for their checkout

20

round, Mary responded, "I suppose so - and he's single and a nice guy - but shift change time is not the time to talk. At night, over dinner, at the club...." She grinned.

Both nurses laughed.

Dr. Dennis Fitzmorris found Dr. Grimes in the doctor's lounge.

"Hi Bob. What've you got?"

"Dennis, I received this packet of information in response to our inquiry about Charles. I gave them all the information we had on him, but I never expected a response like this."

"What did they say?"

"You can read the complete report later, but in a nut shell, they don't think Charles is who we think he is. Charles A. Mackey III would be about the correct age - 22 - and he was in the Special Forces in Vietnam, but they claim he was killed in the fighting fourteen months before we left Saigon. They have already paid the death benefit."

"Interesting. Can we contact the Special Forces men who sent Charles to us?"

"Well that's another kicker. They said their records show that Charles was picked up at a particular base camp in or near Laos, but the day after he was evacuated, the camp was overrun by the villagers who live near the camp. They killed everyone and destroyed all records. The Army thinks the people who were processing heroin in the village near the base did it so they could use the airstrip and, most of all, the C-130s they captured."

"You mean they think our so called friends killed our people."

"That's the general idea, but then we convinced the Thai government to make an air strike at the base to destroy the C-130s, the airstrip and the heroin factory. Goes to prove you can't trust anyone these days.

"However, the Army wants to know in a bad way how we got Mackey's name. I wonder why - but, anyway I sent them a letter explaining about the gold bracelet which was found next to him with that name engraved on it and it also had his blood type engraved on it."

It was almost 7:15 AM when Allison and Mary were finally

entering Charles' room.

"I wonder if this guy will ever wake up. He's been in a coma for...what, at least three months?"

"Mary I've seen situations like this before and I've never seen one who didn't eventually wake up. However, there's always a first."

A soft, grunting noise made them stop and turn to look at Charles. His eyes were open and he moved his arm.

"Mary, go get Fitzmorris and Grimes, I'll stay with Charles."

Mary left the room quickly and hurried down the hall. Both Dr. Fitzmorris and Dr. Grimes had left the doctor's lounge and were now elsewhere in the hospital. Mary called the public address operator.

A few moments later the public address system barked, "Drs. Grimes and Fitzmorris to room 315 stat - code red."

Meanwhile Allison went to the bed, took Charles' hand, and spoke in a calm voice, "Can you hear me?"

To her amazement, he nodded his head.

She asked, "Do you understand me?"

Again, Charles moved his head up and down. He took her hand, moved it to the tube in his nose, and indicated he wanted it out.

"I know. It's uncomfortable. We'll probably take it out soon, but not till the doctor orders it taken out."

He nodded again to indicate he understood and in a rasping voice, asked, "Where am I?"

Allison replied, "You are in Pacific Fleet Naval Hospital in Pearl Harbor - in Hawaii."

He moved his head as if he accepted that.

Dr. Fitzmorris came in the door with Mary and saw Allison holding Charles' hand as she talked to him. He immediately went to the other side of the bed.

"Charles, this is Dr. Fitzmorris. He is a neurologist and that is Dr. Grimes, your internist coming in the door. They are the doctors who are taking care of you."

Charles spoke to both doctors in a rasping voice, "When can I get this tube out of my nose?"

Dr. Fitzmorris looked at Dr. Grimes, who nodded.

Dr. Grimes turned to Allison and Mary. "Remove the tube."

22

Looking at Charles, he said, "We'll talk later." Turning back to the nurses, he said, "See if he can eat some soup and something light."

Allison answered, "Yes sir."

Dr. Fitzmorris said, "Mary, if he is able, bring him to my office for his EEG, but if not, have the EEG run up here at 2:30."

"Yes sir."

Allison removed the tube from Charles' nose and a weak smile crossed his face.

Dr. Grimes said, "Charles, I don't want you to get out of bed just yet. If you want to get up, call the nurse."

Charles nodded and said in a less rasping voice, "Yes sir."

Allison, Dr. Fitzmorris and Dr. Grimes left the room. Mary remained behind to help Charles.

Soon Charles asked, "How long have I been here?"

"A little over three months. You have been in a coma all that time."

Charles sighed, looked at Mary again, then asked, "What's my name?"

Mary looked at Charles in an odd manner. "Don't you know?"

He shook his head no.

They found a bracelet near you with the name Charles A. Mackey III on it."

"Nurse, I don't remember anything before waking up in this room. Can you tell me anything about myself or what happened to me?"

Mary looked at Charles. "I don't know any more than what I have told you, but Dr. Grimes probably does. I'm sure he'll talk to you later today and you can ask him your questions."

At noon, Allison brought Charles' lunch to his room. As she entered, She said, "Hi! I understand you don't remember anything until you saw my beautiful face this morning."

Charles replied in a weak voice, "That's right, but there were two beautiful faces, weren't there? Is that food?"

"It sure is. You know what they say - the way to a man's heart is through his stomach. That's the reason I'm bringing you your lunch - also, so you can forget the other beautiful face. All of us on the floor have planned to make your first day awake such a great one; you will never forget it or us."

Allison smiled and Charles smiled back at her.

In a subdued voice, which still was a little hoarse, he replied, "That's very kind of you."

Charles ate his lunch very slowly, consuming almost half the food. Then he turned to the window, as he had done many times that morning, asking himself many questions, but receiving no answers.

After the EEG was run, Dr. Grimes returned to the room with another doctor.

"Charles, this is Dr. Ronald Moore. He's the hospital psychiatrist. He'll try to help you remember your past. I understand you have some questions about how you got here and other things."

"Yes sir." Reaching out his hand to Dr. Moore, Charles said, "I hope you can help me remember...my past. The only thing I seem to remember is my name isn't Charles, it's Charlie. But that's all I remember."

"Of course I can't promise anything," Dr. Moore replied, "But we'll certainly try to help you regain your memory."

"Dr. Grimes, can you tell me anything about how I came to be here?"

"Well, Charles, you were in a clandestine base in Laos that was closing after we pulled out of Vietnam...."

"We pulled out of Vietnam? What was going on in Vietnam?"

You don't remember the war?"

"No sir."

"Well, there's more history there than I can give you in an afternoon. You'll have to read up on most of that yourself. But you were a soldier with Special Forces at one of their camps when it was overrun by the North Vietnamese irregulars and you were injured in the firefight that erupted. Apparently, when you were injured, the shock of your injury or something associated with your injury caused you to lapse into a coma and it seems to have caused you to have amnesia. You were comatose from that time until this morning - some three months. Whoever rescued you sent us a bracelet that was supposed to be yours, but now there's some doubt about that. So we

24

aren't sure what your name is."

Dr. Moore interrupted, "The idea that you remember your name as Charlie does lend some credence to your being Charles A. Mackey III, but it may be a long time before that can be established beyond doubt."

Dr. Grimes continued, "Charles, you had only superficial physical wounds, but obviously you have some other wounds which are more serious, judging by your memory loss and the length of time you were comatose."

Charles nodded and looked at his feet.

"I think I would like to be called Charlie. Is that all right?"

Dr. Moore nodded and Dr. Grimes said, "Sure. Dr. Moore and I will look in on you tomorrow. This has been a very hectic day for you. I think you should try to get up and walk if you can, but don't forget to ask the nurses for help."

Charlie now asked, "When will Nurse Ford be here?"

Dr. Grimes replied, "I think she has the eleven to seven shift. Is that right, Mary?"

"Yes sir."

Charlie turned toward Mary. "Can you help me sit up and walk?"

"I sure can, but I'll have to do it after I check in my replacement for the three to eleven shift."

"That'll be fine."

The next day when Dr. Grimes saw Charlie, he was surprised to find him sitting in a chair and smiling broadly.

"Good morning, Dr. Grimes."

"Good morning Charlie. How do you feel today? You ought to be well rested, especially after your three month nap."

They laughed.

"I feel fine. I've been taking inventory - trying to see exactly what I do remember. Most of it is a blank, but I've figured out that I seem to know a lot of stuff - math, spelling, how to fire a gun, and so on. I also feel that I can speak two or three languages, but I just don't know. There are some other things, just below the surface, but I can't quite get a hold on them yet. Maybe in time they'll come back to

25

me."

"That's good. I have prescribed exercise for you. This will help you to recover your physical abilities, to walk for example, and get along by yourself. I've also prescribed dexterity exercises for you to help you do things with your hands. In short, rehabilitation of all your motor skills. This will all take time, but after seeing you now, it may not take as long as I originally thought."

"That'll be good. When is Dr. Moore coming?"

"I don't know exactly, but it will probably be this afternoon."

"Thanks for everything."

"You bet. See you tomorrow."

Drs. Grimes, Fitzmorris and Moore met in the doctor's conference room on the second floor early one morning to discuss the status and treatment of their common patients.

"Now we come to Charlie," Dr. Grimes said at last. "Guys it has been five - no six weeks since he woke up and started to exercise, but he participated in the "Iron Man" race two days ago - on Sunday. He finished last, but he did finish. I think he's in great shape physically even though he still doesn't know or remember anything that happened before he woke up, though."

"It may take a long time for him to recover his memory. What do you think, Ron?" asked Dr. Fitzmorris.

"I don't know what can be done right now. It sometimes helps if we take an amnesia patient back to the place where he was when he developed amnesia. But in this case, that will be impossible. Maybe we can get him to go to this Charles Mackey's hometown and see if that jars any memories, but nothing is certain. We know he's highly educated by the way he speaks and he was in very good physical condition when he was hurt."

Dr. Grimes added, "Well, I have to discharge him to your care because he is in great physical shape and there's nothing else I can do for him."

"I agree. Ron, he's all yours," added Dr. Fitzmorris.

"Bob, would you please keep him on your floor. I think it would be better if he stayed there for a while, primarily because it's familiar surroundings," replied Dr. Moore.

"Sure Ron."

Early that afternoon Charlie was walking in the hall towards the nurse's station when he overheard Mary talking to a foreign naval officer. He was speaking French to Mary, who obviously did not understand him, though she made a valiant effort to overcome the language barrier. The officer was inquiring about one of his sailors who had just had an emergency operation.

The officer asked in French, *"How is sailor Pierre doing? Is he alive? When may I see him?"*

Mary answered in a very patient manner, "I'm sorry. I do not understand you. Perhaps someone at the main desk...."

Charlie stepped up and asked in French, *"May I help you?"*

The officer turned toward him with obvious pleasure and relief. *"I must know how my sailor is doing after his operation and when can I see him. Can you ask her for me, please?"*

"Yes," Charlie replied and he turned to Mary and repeated the man's question in English.

Mary was surprised that Charlie could speak French so well and took a little time before she answered.

"Oh, his sailor is Dr. Rosenfield's patient. The surgeon removed his appendix just before it ruptured, but he's doing fine now. He can see him in about an hour when he comes out of recovery. Charlie, could you stay with him and act as translator?"

"Sure."

Charlie turned back to the French officer and told him what Mary had said. *"Let's go to the waiting room down the hall and wait for him. The room is just outside of surgery. I'll keep you company for a while."*

As Charlie and the French officer walked toward the waiting room, Mary dialed a number.

"May I talk to Dr. Moore?"

"One minute," came the response.

A voice came over the telephone, "Dr. Moore."

"Dr. Moore, this is Mary. I just found out Charlie can speak French very well - he may even be fluent in French."

27

"Fluent in French!"

"Yes sir."

"I wonder what else he can do? Enter that fact in his record."

"Yes sir."

As he hung up the telephone, Dr. Moore thought, they have better facilities on the mainland where they can find out what Charlie's capabilities are and can also treat his amnesia better. He'd have a better chance to recover his memory there. I'm going to recommend he be transferred there ASAP.

The next day Dr. Moore spoke with Charlie, "I understand you can speak French. Do you know any other languages?"

"I think so, but I won't really know how thorough my knowledge is until I get to give it a real test. I seem to know some other languages, but I'm not quite sure."

Dr. Moore responded, "That's reasonable. I think you should be transferred to a hospital on the mainland for further treatment. They should be able to help you better than we can. I'm going to make the arrangements later today."

"If you think that's what I need, then that's fine with me."

When Mary and Allison heard that Charlie was being transferred to the mainland, both were sorry to see him leave. They both had become quite fond of Charlie. When orders came for him to leave and go to the Army hospital in San Francisco, Mary and Allison planned a going away party.

The morning before he was to leave, Mary walked with Charlie down to the exercise room as she usually did. When he opened the door, a chorus greeted him, "For he's a jolly good fellow..."

Charlie was definitely surprised. All the medical personnel who had treated him, as well as a number of patients with whom Charlie had become friendly were there. Charlie was told at least a dozen times how happy they all were that he had recovered enough to leave and how sad they were that he was leaving.

The next morning, Allison and Mary took him to the airport.

As Charlie's plane was called, Allison reached over, put her arms around him, gave him a hard hug, and gave him a genuine kiss. Not to be outdone, Mary did the same.

Charlie said, "I'll never forget you two. You're the greatest."

As Allison and Mary were walking back to the staff car, Allison said, "I could have gone for him in a big way."

Mary nodded and said quietly, "I think I did."

CHAPTER 3

As Charlie was walking down the jet way to board Delta
Airlines Flight 896, he realized that he was no longer looking
forward to the long flight. There wasn't a cloud in the sky, the
temperature was in the high seventies or low eighties, and it was just
too beautiful a day to be cooped up inside a plane.

The flight attendant checked his boarding pass and he went to
his seat. He was in luck - it was by a window. In a short time, the
door to the jet closed and a flight attendant came on the public
address system, giving instructions as to what to do in an emergency.
Charlie realized to his surprise that the instructions somehow seemed
familiar, even though he had no conscious memory of ever traveling
by air before. When the emergency instructions were completed, the
plane was pushed back from the gate, the engines started, and the
huge machine taxied to the end of the runway. It turned to position
itself for takeoff and without ever coming to a complete stop started
to accelerate again. This time Charlie felt himself being forced back
into his seat as the engines roared to full power. The plane raced
down the runway until the front of the plane tilted upward and he felt
himself, and the plane suddenly lifted as the plane became airborne.
The plane then climbed to its cruise altitude of 36,000 feet. All this,
too, had a strange familiarity to it.

Looking out his window, he could see Diamond Head disappear
in the distance, then nothing but water. He began to think about
what awaited him. Would they really be able to do anything to help
him remember his past? As on so many earlier occasions, his

thoughts were full of questions, but few answers.

The only time the vast blue canvas of the ocean was broken during the long flight was when he saw several ships moving towards Hawaii; at least he presumed that was their destination. One was a very large ship, accompanied by several smaller vessels. He made out a flight deck and decided the largest ship must be an aircraft carrier and the others escort ships.

The flight attendant served him a meal. He ate, then leaned his seat back and closed his eyes. Listening to the whine of the engines lulled him to sleep.

Sometime later, the flight attendant woke him.

"We'll be landing in San Francisco shortly. We've been cleared for immediate landing. Please put up your tray and place your seat in an upright position."

Charlie responded, "Sure."

The jet way bumped the plane and the passengers crowded the aisle to get off the plane. As Charlie walked out to the concourse, he spotted an Army private holding a sign, which read, "Charlie, Charles A. Mackey, III."

Charlie walked up to the private.

"Hi! I'm Charlie."

The private replied, "Let me carry your luggage, sir. The baggage area is this way."

The private reached for Charlie's carry-on luggage.

As Charlie swung his duffel bag over his shoulder, he said, "That's okay. I didn't check any luggage. This is all I have and I can carry it."

The private shrugged his shoulders, then walked with Charlie down the concourse towards the baggage area. After leaving the terminal, the private led him to a staff car parked in an area reserved for the military.

Charlie threw his duffel bag in the rear seat and climbed into the passenger seat. The private looked at Charlie and shrugged his shoulders as if to say, "Wherever you want to sit is okay with me." The private maneuvered the car around the access roads then left the airport via an expressway.

Charlie asked, "Is it always this overcast in San Francisco?"

"No sir. It's mostly nice and warm, but occasionally we get some bad weather."

"That's good to know. How far is it to the hospital?"

"About ten or eleven miles. We should be there in about twenty minutes, depending on traffic."

Charlie was looking out the window at the bay bridge when he saw a building ahead of them, around a curve in the road. It faced the ocean and had a tall center section with shorter wings on the right and left. He estimated the tall section to be about twenty-five stories high and the smaller sections perhaps seventeen or eighteen stories.

As Charlie was looking at the building, the driver pointed to it.

"That's the hospital. I'll let you off at the main entrance. Admit is on the left as you enter. They're expecting you."

"Good. By the way what time is it here?"

Looking at his watch, he responded, "It's 4:07. Incidentally, dinner is served from 5:00 to 7:30. Don't get their stew if you can help it. It's the worst excuse for stew you can imagine."

"Thanks, I'll remember that."

Charlie found the admit desk without difficulty. The receptionist was a woman in an Army uniform.

"You must be Charlie. Welcome to San Francisco. You've been assigned room 1642. Please sign here and an orderly will help you with your luggage. Your nurse will explain what you are to do and when you are to meet with your doctor - I think it will be Dr. Marian Wells."

"Thank you."

By this time, the orderly had already taken his duffel bag and was heading for the elevators. Charlie and the orderly rode the elevator to the sixteenth floor then walked down what appeared to be a long hallway to room 1642.

Charlie noted it was a private room - something he did not expect. Almost as soon as the orderly put his duffel bag down, Nurse Lisa Giaventi walked through the door.

"Hi. My name is Lisa and I'll be your nurse. You must be someone special to rate this room and a staff car. Not too many people get that kind of treatment around here."

"I didn't know I was so special."

"We don't get many amnesia cases here - especially a Special Forces guy. Anyway, you have the rest of the day to get settled. Tomorrow morning you have an appointment with Dr. Marian Wells. She's real good."

"I have a woman doctor?"

"Yes, and she's one of the best."

"I need the best. It's really hell not to know anything about yourself."

"I bet it is. Wow, I guess I won't have to ask about you." Lisa smiled.

Charlie returned the smile and asked, "Would you like to have dinner with me in the cafeteria. You can even show me where it is?"

Lisa hesitated, scrutinizing this young, but handsomely, rugged face. Normally she never would have accepted such an invitation from someone, especially a patient she had just met, but there was something about him that made her want to know him better.

Finally, she grinned and said, "You don't let too much grass grow under your feet, do you. Okay, this once, just to show you where the cafeteria is."

Charlie and Lisa had a quiet meal. Lisa listened attentively as Charlie talked, moved by the plight of the good-looking young man. Her heart went out to him. He might not know very much about himself, but she couldn't help feeling that she had learned a good deal about him.

After dinner, as they were leaving the cafeteria, Lisa said, "You look like a good listener. I need someone to talk to about my love life and you seem to be just the right kind of person. Could I bend your ear for a while?"

Charlie was surprised by Lisa's openness, but at the same time flattered, that she would talk to him about such a personal subject. "Sure."

They went to the hospital lobby and found a quiet corner where they could sit down and talk without being disturbed.

"This gets complicated," Lisa began, starting to feel very

awkward. "I graduated from nursing school about two years ago and I got this job here at the hospital. I really like it here, so I moved from north San Francisco where my Uncle Frank lives to an apartment close to the hospital. My father died when I was five years old and my uncle took care of us all - my mother, my sisters, and me. Uncle Frank helped me an awful lot and he even bought my car, but I insisted I buy most of my furniture on time like everyone else.

"After a couple of weeks, I went to this church, The Ocean View Christian Church. I became involved in its activities. One night at a potluck supper, I met Mike. We hit it off right away. He told me he was a sergeant in the San Francisco Police Department and I told him my name. For whatever the reason, I didn't think to tell him I was the niece of Frank Giaventi. I just didn't think to tell him. You do know who Frank Giaventi is, don't you?"

Charlie shook his head no.

Lisa leaned closer to Charlie, grasping his arm as she continued. "I guess you'd say he's San Francisco's godfather - you know, like in the movies. He's a Mafia boss - Don Frank Giaventi. I don't see him that often now, but he is my uncle, he helped raise me, and I love him as I'd have loved my father. And no, I don't have any dealings with my uncle's people, and neither do my mother or sisters, even though they live with him.

"Anyway, I didn't tell Mike until several weeks later. Then I told Uncle Frank about Mike a week or so after that. All he said was not to talk about any family business with him. Two weeks ago, Mike called and said we had to talk. I was elated because I thought he was going to propose to me. We sat on a bench in the park on the hill and he said he had just received a big promotion to lieutenant. He was put in charge of the organized crime unit in the S.F.P.D.

"That hit hard. He also told me he was promoted three days before, and while he was reading the file on my uncle, he came across my name. Reading my name jogged his memory and he immediately went into his chief's office and told him who his girlfriend was. He said he didn't think that would make any difference, but he thought the powers that be should know. If they

35

had any reservations, he wouldn't take the job. If they had no objections, then he would want them to sign a statement to that effect.

"The chief said he would get back to Mike and let him know. That morning the chief had given Mike three letters, all supporting his appointment from the powers that be, including the mayor of San Francisco. So he asked me to talk to Uncle Frank. He also suggested we not see each other for a couple of weeks. I talked to Uncle Frank, and he said the same thing as before - just don't talk to Mike about family business. He also said he had Mike investigated and he found out he was an honest cop, a God- fearing man and in general a good man."

Lisa sighed softly. "What I'm getting at is this - what do you think I should do? I love Uncle Frank and I love Mike. But I don't want to cause any problems. I want Mike and Uncle Frank to like each other. I must tell you, if Mike asked me to go away with him, I wouldn't even take time to pack my clothes."

Charlie looked at Lisa, then responded, "You have a king - sized problem. I'll tell you what I'd do. I'd continue to see Mike and I'd introduce Mike to your uncle at an appropriate time. Also, don't talk to him about your uncle's business and don't talk to your uncle about Mike's business. I'd also postpone any decision about getting married for about a year. You'd have that long to see if your relationship works. If you and Mike still feel the same about each other then, get married. By the way, what is Mike's full name? You never said."

"Michael Gerad Forester. Why?"

Charlie grinned. "I just wondered what your name would be like - Lisa Forester.

"Mrs. Michael Forester," she said with an even bigger grin.

Lisa and Charlie got up from the sofa and Lisa kissed him on the cheek.

"Thanks. I think that's a good idea."

Charlie went to the elevators as Lisa left the hospital through the main lobby door. He looked back to watch her, realizing he liked her a lot, but only as he would like his sister, if he had one...which, for all he knew, he did.

At ten minutes to nine the next morning, Charlie entered Dr. Wells' office.

The receptionist said, "You must be Charlie? Have a seat and Dr. Wells will be with you in a little while. She's running a little late this morning."

Charlie sat in a chair and began to read an old U. S. News and World Report magazine. He became interested in it because it mentioned the U.S. withdrawal from Saigon in 1975.

At 9:23 AM, the door to Dr. Wells's office opened and a nice looking woman in her late twenties or early thirties came out of the office.

"Charlie, I'm Dr. Wells. Come on in."

Charlie put the magazine down and entered her office. Dr. Wells motioned for him to sit on a sofa. She sat in a chair near the sofa.

As Dr. Wells looked at Charlie, she began, "Charlie, you have what is described as partial amnesia. The part you don't remember is mainly determined by which part of the brain is affected. The treatment of choice in such cases is to find out where you were when this occurred and return you to that place. Often that will cause other memories to return. That isn't possible because of the war that's still raging in Southeast Asia and what occurred there after you left. The next best thing is to find the place where you grew up and take you there. We have a chance at that.

"In the meantime there are some other things we can do here. We can build on what we know about you. For example, we know you speak French as well as English. We also know you are well educated by the way you speak; therefore, you may speak other languages. We'll attempt to find out what other languages you know. Working towards that end, I have several linguists who will see you over the next few days.

"Next, we know you were with the Special Forces. To determine what you know and your abilities in that area, I'll arrange for you to visit a military base that trains Special Forces personnel and, at the same time, has someone who is familiar with amnesia and its treatment. Also, having you tested on what Special Forces personnel are required to know. Your memory might return.

"At any time when you are being seen by the linguists or being tested at the military base, you may begin to remember your past because you will be doing some of the things with which you are familiar. If this happens, you may experience some flashbacks first, then your memory may return slowly or suddenly. The flashbacks may frighten you, but don't be afraid. There is absolutely no way to tell how you will react if you get flashbacks or your memory suddenly returns. The only thing you must remember - and you must remember this - is not to become frantic or afraid of what you are experiencing.

"I might as well tell you this also - your memory may never return. However, we'll try everything we know to help you regain it.

"There is one more avenue we will try later. That is to contact one Mrs. Miriam M. Ward - she may be your sister. She lives in New Orleans. Do you have any memory of New Orleans?"

"No... I don't recall ever being there. Somehow, I know it's in the middle of swamps and they have a Mardi Gras carnival there once a year. But that's all I can say about New Orleans," came the reply.

"No matter, we will probably contact her in the future unless we find out you are not her brother. She may be the key to your memory recall. But before we contact her, I want to know more about you and your abilities. So, on Monday, you will begin your meetings with the linguists in the afternoon. If there are no problems, the week following those meetings, or as soon as I can arrange it, you will be temporarily transferred to a military base. Each morning, before your meetings with the linguists, you'll exercise. I believe that exercise is very helpful for you - both physically and mentally.

"I might add that each day I will receive a report on your progress and see you in your room or here about 4:30 PM. I'll tell the nurse where and what time we'll meet. Some days, I won't be able to see you, but for the most part, we'll get together every day.

"You basically have the weekend to acquaint yourself with the hospital. If you want to leave the building, you may, but only with a

38

member of the staff. You'll be given a little money in that case, so that you can eat out or catch a movie. Now, do you have any questions?"

"No ma'am. I think you've covered everything. I can't wait to get started."

Dr. Wells escorted Charlie to the door. After he left, he went to find the exercise room and do some jogging. Dr. Wells' optimistic prognosis left him pleased and encouraged.

Charlie was nervous as he sat in Dr. Wells's reception room. He had not seen her for a week and he didn't know what to expect.

Dr. Wells opened the door to her office. "Charlie, come on in. I'm sorry I wasn't able to see you as I said, but I was called out of town. My father became extremely ill and I had to leave to be with him. Thank God, he's better now and is expected to live."

She smiled and settled into a chair across from him.

"Now, let's look at how you did with our linguists. First, you are fluent in English, French, and Spanish, almost fluent in Arabic and Hebrew. You also have a working knowledge in German and in two dialects of Chinese. You are really an accomplished linguist.

"Because of your knowledge, you probably could get along in Italian, Portuguese, German, or even in any of the Balkan languages. The first tests showed us you are not only a highly educated individual, but extremely intelligent, maybe even on the so - called genius level. How that will help you or us in remembering your past, I don't know right now. Did you have any flashbacks during the sessions with the linguists?"

"No. I was hoping I would, but no. . . ."

"That's too bad, but hopefully you will have some next week when you go to San Diego. You will actually be at the Marine base there, Camp Pendleton. I won't see you next week until you get back here, but I am waiting for some additional information from the Department of the Army. After I get the information, I will be in touch with...Mrs. Ward in New Orleans and see what information she can give us."

"I want to thank you for all you have done for me. Can I treat you to lunch at the cafeteria?"

"Charlie, I'd love to eat with you, but I have too much work to do since this is my first day back. I'll take a rain check, though. Have a nice trip to San Diego."

Two days later on Sunday, Charlie boarded a U.S. Navy cargo plane for San Diego. Major Clarence Poter, a Marine physician at Camp Pendleton, met him at the naval airbase in San Diego.

"Hi, Charlie. Dr. Wells asked me to look after you. You seem to have made quite an impression on her. Since I am familiar with the treatment of amnesia patients, she asked me to talk with you and see if you begin to remember things or have flashbacks. Hope we can help you remember your past."

"I sure hope so, sir."

"First thing tomorrow we will test your hand-to-hand combat skills. Then you'll go the range and see how good you are with a rifle and pistol. Last, we'll see what you know about explosives and maybe some communication equipment. After we're through testing you, you and I will get together again and I'll tell you how you did. Then, if everything goes according to plan - and just to motivate you a bit - you'll get a day off for some R & R."

"Sounds good to me"

Dr. Poter's car stopped for Camp Pendleton's gate. The guard stepped out of the little white guardhouse and as he recognized Major Poter, he saluted and waved them through the gate. They stopped at the officer's club, where Major Poter registered Charlie to stay. The night went by very fast for Charlie.

The next morning, Charlie walked out of the club to find a Marine sergeant named Staples standing next to a jeep. Sgt. Staples drove him to a gym, where an oriental looking man in shorts, who was waiting for them, met them.

"Charlie, this is Sgt. Chen. He's our base expert on hand-to-hand combat."

"Welcome to Camp Pendleton, Charlie. You can change in the locker room over there. I'm supposed to grade you as to how much you know about hand-to-hand combat."

"Fine. I'll be right back."

Charlie went into the locker room and changed into shorts, then returned to Sgt. Chen.

Sgt. Chen walked over to Charlie.

"We'll start with the basics. Assume a position.

Charlie assumed a karate stance.

Sgt. Chen walked around Charlie, all the time looking at his stance, nodding his head approvingly.

"Good. Let me see your hands."

Charlie showed Chen his hands.

Chen looked at Charlie's face and then back at his hands.

Shaking his head, he asked, "How long have you been using karate?"

"I don't know if I've ever used karate. I can't remember a thing."

"I see. There's a punching bag over there. Give me a few kicks and punches. Do it in proper sequence."

Charlie went over to the bag, took a Karate stance, moved his right leg, and hit the bag with some force with his left leg. He then started to hit the bag often and hard. He continued for several minutes and after he had finished, returned to Sgt. Chen.

"Well how did I do?"

Sgt. Chen replied, "Not bad. Oh, you're not a tenth degree black belt, but possibly a sixth degree. I don't think I need to test you any more. I hope you regain your memory."

Sgt. Staples came over to talk to Charlie after he had finished in the gym.

"While you were hitting the bag, Chen said you're good."

"So he says. I wish I could remember where I learned karate."

"It'll come back to you - trust me. I'll be testing you tomorrow on the range and Lt. Tosca will test you with plastic the next day."

"Fine, what time tomorrow?"

"Eight thirty in the morning."

"Great."

The next morning, Charlie was up and waiting for Sgt. Staples in front of the club half an hour ahead of time. When Sgt. Staples drove up, Charlie jumped in the jeep next to him.

41

"Sergeant, I don't know why I'm excited, but I am sure hyper today. Let's go."

They drove to the rifle range. It was a clear day with no wind. Sgt. Staples stopped the jeep at the 200-yard firing line. He gave Charlie an M-16 with some ammunition and watched Charlie load the rifle. He handled the weapon like an expert.

He lifted the rifle and cradled it to his shoulder so that he could sight down the barrel, then lowered it and asked, "When may I fire?"

Sgt. Staples noted that his subject knew range procedure. "Whenever you're ready."

Charlie fired three times from the standing position. "Can the pit men mark the target so I can zero the rifle?"

Sgt. Staples made the call to the pit. The target came down, was marked, and then raised again. The bullets had hit the target so close together that a silver dollar would cover all holes, but they were grouped a little low and to the right.

Charlie adjusted the sights and fired another twelve rounds from the standing position. The target came down and the pit crew said, "They all hit in the 5 V circle in the tightest shot group I have ever seen."

Sgt. Staples thought for a second, then said, "Let's go to the 500 yard line."

Charlie took the prone position and fired three times. Again, the shot group was very tight, but slightly low. He adjusted the sights and fired another twelve rounds.

The pit crew called on the telephone. "Sarge, sign this guy up for our rifle team. We don't get many like him."

Sgt. Staples replied, "Thanks guys. We don't need you any more."

Sgt. Staples and Charlie returned to the jeep and drove to another range - the pistol range.

This time, Sgt. Staples gave Charlie a 45-caliber pistol with ammunition. Charlie again loaded the magazine as if he knew what he was doing, asked permission to fire, and then squeezed off six rounds at the fifteen-yard distance. His shot grouping was just as good as his shot groups on the rifle range.

Sgt. Staples shook his head and wondered how he could get Charlie to join the Marines and go to the Olympics as a Marine.

The next morning, Charlie was again waiting for Sgt. Staples in front of the club. He was just as excited as he had been the morning before. They drove to the explosive area.

After they arrived, Sgt. Staples introduced Lt. Tosca. "Charlie, he's our expert in plastic and other explosives."

Charlie extended his hand and Lt. Tosca grasped Charlie's hand firmly and gave it a hardy shake.

Two hours later, Lt. Tosca came over to Sgt. Staples who was sitting in his jeep reading a magazine waiting for Charlie.

"This guy knows more about plastic than I do. Radio controlled detonation, shape charges, the whole works. In short, he's good."

Sgt. Staples replied, "Major Poter will be interested in this."

Major Poter was in his office when Charlie walked into the reception area. As soon as he saw Charlie, he came out to greet him and took him inside his office. The major motioned Charlie into a chair, returned to his own seat behind his desk, and briefly glanced through Charlie's file again.

"Charlie, have you had any flashbacks? Did any of these tests awaken memories?"

"No sir."

"Not anything?"

"No sir."

"I have one more question. Why do you keep saying "sir"?"

"I don't know, sir. It just seems natural."

"Well, I guess that's all we can do here at Pendleton. I'll get you transportation back to San Francisco, maybe tomorrow. Until then, you're free to look about the base and do what you like. However, check with me or the orderly for your transportation schedule before 5:30 this afternoon."

"Yes, sir."

Charlie left Major Poter's office a little downhearted. He had expected this trip would accomplish much more.

After Dr. Poter had assembled all Charlie's data, he dialed Dr. Wells' number in San Francisco.

A voice answered, "Dr. Wells speaking."

"Marian, this is Clarence at Pendleton. We have the results. They're a mixed bag. He's definitely a special forces type, but we haven't done him any good as far as recovering his memory. He didn't have any flashbacks during the testing."

Dr. Wells made a low, exhaling noise, indicating her frustration. "Clarence, is that all you have?"

"Oh, there's a little more. This guy is one unusual person. He is good in self defense, possibly a sixth degree black belt. He's the best marksman this base has seen in a long time, maybe the absolute best, and he knows explosives quite well. We also found out he's knowledgeable about radios and telephones."

"I was hoping for more, but if that's what you found, that's what you found. Thanks for all your help. Next time you're in Frisco, let me know and I'll spring for lunch."

"You bet. Oh, Charlie will be arriving in San Francisco at 2:30 tomorrow."

"2:30 in the afternoon? Fine. I'll have someone meet the plane. Thanks again."

Dr. Wells pulled Charlie's record from the stack of manila folders on her desk and opened it. She found the name and phone number she was looking for, and then dialed Mrs. Miriam Mackey Ward in New Orleans.

The ringing of the telephone was stopped by a voice, "This is the Ward's residence."

Dr. Wells responded, "Mrs. Ward, please."

"One moment."

In a short time, another voice spoke. "This is Mrs. Ward. What can I do for you?"

Dr. Wells replied, "My name is Dr. Marian Wells. I am an Army psychiatrist in San Francisco and I've been informed that you are the sister of one Charles A. Mackey, III. Is that correct?"

"Yes. He died in Vietnam, but his body was never returned to us for burial."

"Mrs. Ward, I have reason to believe your brother is under my care in the Army Hospital here in San Francisco. The patient I'm

44

treating, and to whom I am referring, has amnesia and post-war traumatic shock; therefore, I am not certain if he is in fact your brother..."

Mrs. Ward interrupted, "My brother is dead and I doubt seriously you are a psychiatrist. You are just another hustler trying to get some money. I would appreciate it if you would call my attorney. He'll handle you."

"Mrs. Ward, I assure you I am a psychiatrist and I am calling from San Francisco. To verify what I have just said, let your attorney call information, and get the number of the Army Hospital in San Francisco. The hospital will verify the fact that I am a psychiatrist. He will then be connected to me. I can call him back so he doesn't have to pay for the long distance call. For your information, I do in fact have a patient who may be your brother."

Mrs. Ward hesitated, then said in a very controlled voice, "Dr. Wells, please forgive my outburst, but if you had gone through what I have, you'd understand. I'll contact my attorney immediately and have him call you. Please do not call again unless Mr. Broussard tells you to, or if he doesn't call you. Good-bye."

Mrs. Ward hung up without saying anything further.

Dr. Wells looked at the telephone in puzzlement. How could a sister be so unhappy at the news that her brother might be alive? She hung up the receiver.

Dr. Wells was walking out of her office fifteen minutes later when her phone rang.

"This is Antoine Broussard in New Orleans," the voice on the other end of the line said. "I am the attorney for Mrs. Ward. Did you just call her and tell her that her brother may be alive?"

"Yes, I did. Mr. Broussard, may I call you right back?"

Mr. Broussard replied, "That'll be fine."

Dr. Wells searched her desk quickly for a piece of scratch paper, then jotted down the number he gave her.

"Thank you," she said. "I'll get back to you in a few minutes."

She immediately dialed the number, which was answered by a cheery-voiced receptionist. A few moments later she was talking to Antoine Broussard again.

"What makes you believe that your patient is Mrs. Ward's brother?"

Dr. Wells briefly related to the man what she knew of Charlie, including the expensive gold bracelet with the name Charles A. Mackey, III on it that had been found near him when he was injured.

"That bracelet indicated that Mackey had a blood type of AB negative, which is a very rare blood type," she continued. "Army records confirm that information as factual. Charlie has the same blood type. We examined Mackey's service record and then tested Charlie's abilities to see if they match Mackey's. While not a perfect match, they're close.

"I feel there's a good chance that he is Charles Mackey. I'd like to take Charlie or send him to New Orleans to visit your client, so she can either identify him or tell us he is not her brother. The trip might help him recover his memory, too."

"Dr. Wells, I must say what you've said throws a complete new light on the picture. I'm sure Mrs. Ward will see Charlie under these circumstances. Let me know when he'll be in New Orleans."

"Thank you Mr. Broussard. I'll advise you before he leaves."

Antoine Broussard immediately called Mrs. Ward.

"Miriam, Dr. Wells is real. Your brother may very well be alive. The reason for this Charlie coming to New Orleans is to see if you can identify him because he has amnesia. I told her you would be happy to identify him if you can. Dr. Wells will call me back as soon as his travel arrangements are made. I'm going to get your parents' estate balance sheet ready."

"Antoine, I don't like this."

"Miriam, you have to see this guy. If he is your brother and his memory returns, he could cause you a lot of problems."

"Okay, but I don't like it."

46

CHAPTER 4

It was early on a Thursday morning one month later when Dr. Wells and Charlie boarded Continental Flight 1425 to New Orleans. Because Dr. Wells was nervous when she flew, she had checked the weather report and it was to be good flying weather except around the New Mexico - Texas border, but she hoped the jet could fly over whatever weather awaited them there.

The flight attendant asked the passengers to buckle their seat belts. Charlie and Dr. Wells finally buckled their seat belts by the time the plane taxied toward the runway to take off, where they were third in line.

While waiting for the plane to take off, Dr. Wells thought, it's been almost five months since Charlie came to San Francisco and I don't think we're any closer to finding out his past than we were when he first arrived. I just hope we'll discover he's Charles Mackey, III, but I am uneasy about this situation because of Mrs. Ward's reaction to the possibility that Charlie might be her brother was not what

I would expect from a sister.

She turned her head to Charlie.

"I don't know what to tell you to expect in New Orleans. When I talked to Mrs. Ward - who may be your sister - she acted as if she was anything but happy that her brother might be alive. Her attorney tried to explain her reaction. Her parents - maybe your parents too - were murdered about four years ago. After the Army declared her brother dead, several people showed up claiming to be her brother or wanting to tell her where her brother was, so they could get some of the money she inherited. He said that was the reason for her hostility. She thought we were more of the same. When I talked to her afterward she did seem different, but I am still not really convinced."

As the sound of the engines whirred to a higher pitch, the plane inched forward slowly and then stopped. They were now next in line to enter the runway.

Dr. Wells continued, "There must be a lot of money in her family."

The engines picked up again and the plane moved forward and turned to line itself on the runway. As soon as it straightened itself on the runway, the pilot gunned the engines to full power. The plane then roared down the smooth concrete pushing Charlie and Dr. Wells back in their seats and lifted off the ground. It began a sharp climb to its cruising altitude of 35,000 feet.

During that time, Dr. Wells and Charlie did not speak, but as soon as the plane was no longer climbing at a sharp angle, Charlie said, "Dr. Wells, I still want to meet her as soon as possible. I'd like you to be there with me, though. That would give me some reassurance."

"I'd like to be there, Charlie, but I have a problem. I have to meet with Dr. Sorrel tomorrow morning at the L.S.U. Medical School about your case. Unfortunately, that's when you're scheduled to see Mrs. Ward. As soon as your visit is over, you can meet me at the school and we'll go to Thibodaux together."

Charlie looked puzzled.

"Oh, I haven't told you about Thibodaux. When Mr. Broussard was telling me about the death of Mrs. Ward's parents, I asked where her brother grew up. He said he had grown up in Thibodaux. That's a small town close to New Orleans. Mr. Broussard referred me to the police chief there, a man named Gaspard. Apparently he knew the Mackey family quite well and might be able to help you. He also suggested we consult with their family doctor, a Dr. Blake.

"Thibodaux is about an hour and a half's drive from New

Orleans. We could make it tomorrow afternoon and be back in New Orleans hopefully by early evening. You may know by tomorrow if your name is Charles Mackey III."

"That'd be just great. I might even be rich!"

They both smiled and almost laughed.

After their meals, Charlie and Dr. Wells relaxed in their seats. Charlie was soon sleeping while Dr. Wells read up on the "Postwar Trauma Syndrome". She was combining in this one trip Charlie's search for information about his past, a two-week vacation in Florida, and the meeting of psychiatrists in New Orleans where she would hear more about the postwar syndrome and how to help those suffering from it.

Flight 1425 made an intermediate stop in Houston then it was just fifty minutes to New Orleans.

Dr. Wells and Charlie deplaned, picked up their baggage, and went to the Avis car rental counter where Dr. Wells rented a Chevrolet sedan. After they put their luggage in the car, they drove to the small town of Belle Chasse where Alvin Callender Airfield, the local Naval Air Station, is located. Dr. Wells pulled up to the gate and gave her name with her army officer's ID to the SP guard at the gate.

He consulted a sheet of paper, then said, "The officer's club is down this street, then turn to the left where the sign directs you to the club."

Dr. Wells returned his salute and drove through the gate.

While Dr. Wells went into the club to register for both of them, Charlie removed their luggage from the trunk. By the time he entered the club, Dr. Wells was walking back to find him.

"Charlie, the club manager gave me a note from Dr. Sorrel. He can't meet me tomorrow, so I'll go with you to see Mrs. Ward."

Charlie grinned. "That's great!"

"We have rooms across the hall from each other. Down this way. I'll meet you in the restaurant in thirty minutes for dinner. Okay?"

"Sure."

Charlie put Dr. Wells' suitcase in her room and crossed the hall to his.

As soon as Dr. Wells was situated in her room, she picked up the telephone and dialed a telephone number.

A voice she didn't recognize answered and said, "Mrs. Ward's residence." The maid had answered on previous calls, but this was someone different and her answer was also different.

"This is Dr. Wells. May I speak with Mrs. Ward?"

"Mrs. Ward has been expecting your call. One minute please."

"Hello, Dr. Wells? I've had so many things happen to me since we last talked, I might need counseling myself. Along with all the deaths in my family and this news that my brother may still be alive, I received word three days ago that my husband divorced me in Las Vegas and remarried his ex-wife. It's a good thing I had a prenuptial agreement signed, or I'd really be in a mess...but enough of my problems. What can I do for you and Charlie?"

"I'm sorry to hear about your marital problems. If you'd rather postpone meeting Charlie tomorrow, I'm sure he'll understand."

"No, I want to know if he is my brother even more than he does."

"That's good. I was just calling to tell you I'll be able to come with him. My meeting at LSU Medical School was canceled. Would 9:00 AM be too early?"

"No. - Oh, I've looked and I have only one picture of Charles with my parents...or maybe our parents. I must tell you, I'm much older than my brother and I didn't know him very well. I left home when he was only six and only saw him on rare occasions after that. Chief Gaspard and Dr. Blake in Thibodaux might help you more than I."

"Mr. Broussard told me that also and I've made appointments with them for the afternoon after our meeting."

"That's good. You'll find Gaspard to be just a little country policeman with very little on the ball. Dr. Blake is an old fashioned country doctor - a real gem!"

"We'll see you tomorrow morning."

Both women hung up their telephones.

At 8:30 AM, Dr. Wells was driving the Chevrolet across the

51

Greater New Orleans Mississippi River Bridge.

She told Charlie, "You have to tell me where to turn. You have the map of the city. Mrs. Ward lives on Prytania Street near Washington Avenue."

Pointing towards the Camp Street exit, Charlie said, "Get off the bridge there and turn right."

Soon the Chevrolet was on Prytania Street going towards Washington Avenue. By 8:47, Dr. Wells was pulling the car over to the curb and pointing to a very large house across the street.

"That's it. That place is a small mansion! I'll go up to the next corner, turn around, and park in front of the house."

Dr. Wells parked the car and both she and Charlie got out. Charlie opened the iron gate for her and they walked up to the front door. Even though it was obvious he was extremely nervous, Charlie rang the doorbell without hesitation. Dr. Wells was admiring the beautiful homes in the area and was extremely pleased that, in spite of the low hanging rain clouds, it wasn't raining. The television weather report had given an 80% chance of rain.

As she looked at Charlie, Dr. Wells noticed how nervous he was. In a quiet voice, she said, "She won't bite. The worst she can say is that you aren't her brother."

Mrs. Ward looked out the window at Charlie, became worried because Charlie looked like what she imagined her brother would look like. Then she saw a black man and a white man standing on the corner across the street. She smiled to herself, then went to the door and opened it.

"Come in. You must be Charlie."

"Yes ma'am."

"Please call me Miriam - both of you. Let me look at you. You're definitely the right age, build and looks, but I am not quite sure. Forgive me, how about some coffee?"

As the maid served the coffee, Miriam Ward said, "This is a New Orleans blend of coffee and chicory."

Dr. Wells replied, "It's very tasty, but you said you had an old picture of Charles. May we see it?"

"Of course, but I don't think it will be convincing either way. If

I had to make a decision, I'd say you're not my brother, but as I told Dr. Wells, I was not very close to Charles and I might not be able to make a positive identification either way."

Mrs. Ward handed the picture to Dr. Wells.

Dr. Wells looked at the picture.

"This could be you, but do you recognize the other two people in the picture?"

Shaking his head, Charlie dejectedly replied, "No."

Dr. Wells frowned, "Charlie, I think we'd better go to Thibodaux and see the Chief and the Doctor. Thanks for your effort and time, Mrs. Ward."

"I wish I could have helped you more. I wish you lots of luck in recovering your memory."

"Thank you, ma'am."

As Charlie and Dr. Wells walked out the door, they saw two men just outside the entrance gate to the property. As Charlie and Dr. Wells walked through the gate, the black man who was standing closest to Dr. Wells grabbed her and placed a knife at her throat.

"Doc, give me your purse."

She handed her purse to him.

At the same time, the white man flashed a knife at Charlie. "Your wallet, man, and hope you have enough money."

The black man dropped his knife for a couple of seconds from Dr. Wells's throat as he looked in her purse.

"Shit, for a shrink, you don't have much money."

The white man wasn't waiting for Charlie to get his wallet out - he went for Charlie about the time the black man had dropped his knife. In that moment, when there was no knife at Dr. Well's throat and before the white man's thrust could strike - Charlie reacted. Dr. Wells remembered it later as a blur of movement and action. A couple of karate kicks and punches were delivered so quickly that she couldn't really tell what happened, and then both of their attackers lay motionless and unconscious on the sidewalk.

Charlie spoke to Dr. Wells, "You okay?"

"Yes."

"Go to the house and call the police while I tie these two up with their shoelaces."

Just as Dr. Wells got to the door, she heard a police siren coming fast on Prytania Street. The car stopped in front of the house where Charlie was.

One policeman jumped out of the patrol car, pointed his gun at Charlie and yelled, "Police, face the fence - now!"

Charlie turned towards the fence and placed his hands on the fence.

Dr. Wells rushed back to Charlie's side.

"He's the one who was assaulted. The two men on the ground are the muggers."

The second officer looked at the men who were unconscious and spoke to the officer who had his gun drawn.

After the second officer spoke to the first officer, he holstered his pistol.

"Sorry, I thought you were the mugger. Now what happened?"

As Dr. Wells was explaining what had happened, Mrs. Ward came out of the house exclaiming, "I called the police when I saw what was happening. Are you all right? No one is safe anymore. Men like these should be put away."

Just then, the duty sergeant drove up in another squad car. Sgt. Cally stepped out of the car and walked up to the group. The two men had been placed in handcuffs by this time. They were awake, but groggy.

Sgt. Cally spoke to Dr. Wells and Charlie for a short time, and then turned to the other officers.

"Take these two to the station and book them with attempted robbery, assault, and murder."

With those instructions, the two men were placed in the police cruiser and driven away.

The officer turned back to Dr. Wells and Charlie.

"You'll have to come to headquarters and file charges tomorrow before 11:00 AM. Can you make it?"

Dr. Wells responded, "We'll be there. Give me the address. Here's my name. If you need to contact us, we are staying at the officer's club at Callender airfield."

"Just be at that address before 11:00 AM tomorrow morning."

The radio in Sgt. Cally's car barked, "Dead man found in St. Thomas project. Sgt. Cally, please respond."

As he was getting into his cruiser, he said, "Damn - another one."

It had started to rain heavily as Dr. Wells drove across the Huey P. Long Bridge over the Mississippi River on Highway 90 towards Boutte and Raceland. The rain slowed them down somewhat. As they passed through Boutte, it slacked off a bit and at Raceland where they turned north along Bayou Lafourche on highway LA 1 towards Thibodaux, the sun tried to peek through the dense rain clouds.

Charlie, who had been in deep thought finally said, "Dr. Wells, those two men were trying to kill us - maybe just me. They didn't care one twit about robbing us."

"I've been thinking the same thing. Did you hear what the black said to me?"

"Yes. He said 'Doc, give me your purse," and then he said, "Shit, for a shrink, you don't have much money'."

"Right. How did he know I was a physician? How did he know I was a psychiatrist? No one knew I was going to be with you - except Mrs. Ward, and I told her only last night. Besides us, she's the only person who knew both those things. Charlie, she wants you dead!"

Her companion's face became excited for the first time since they'd reached Louisiana. "That means she thinks I'm her brother."

"That's right, but let's not jump to conclusions so soon. Let's see what Chief Gaspard and Dr. Blake have to say."

"Right."

They passed a burned house just outside Thibodaux, a charred brick structure with large oaks in the front yard and a boat dock on a bayou at the front of the property.

They continued into Thibodaux, where they located the police station. After parking the car in the lot on the side of the station, they walked up the station steps and through the glass doors. One of the desks inside was occupied by what looked like a figure out of a bad movie - a stereotype, a fat southern sheriff.

The man behind the desk asked, "What can I do for you folks?"

Charlie answered, "We're looking for Chief Gaspard."

"You found him, boy."

Dr. Wells introduced herself and Charlie, and then explained that they wanted to talk about a private matter.

Remembering he had made an appointment to speak with them, he said, "Come on into my office and sit awhile. We can talk better in there - comfy chairs with arm rests and cushions."

Charlie's stomach growled and Chief Gaspard heard the sound.

"How about me ordering us some sandwiches - shrimp po'boys. They're really good. And Thibodaux will even spring for the tab."

Dr. Wells looked at Charlie, shrugged her shoulders.

"I don't think we can beat an offer like that."

"Good. Now one minute while I order them."

After Chief Gaspard finished ordering the shrimp po-boys, Dr. Wells started speaking. "Chief Gaspard, I was wondering if you could identify Charlie as Charles Mackey. In any case, do you have any pictures of Mr. and Mrs. Mackey?"

"To answer your first question, it's been a few years since I've seen Charles, but your friend here could be his twin, if he had a twin. To answer your second question, the only pictures of Mr. and Mrs. Mackey I got are from the murder scene. They aren't pretty. You can see them if you got the stomach. They're not exactly what I'd recommend around meal time."

"Would it be possible for us to see the Mackey home?

The man shook his head slowly. "No, I can't show you-all the house. Someone burned it down two days ago. Arson."

Charlie asked, "Did we pass it on the way here? Was that their house we saw on the bayou?"

Chief Gaspard nodded his head as he replied, "That was it, boy."

Dr. Wells frowned slightly, thinking. Then she said, "Yes, I think it would be good for Charlie to see the pictures, even if they are grisly. They may shock him enough to make him remember something."

With that, Chief Gaspard reached down in his desk drawer, but stopped when he saw a young black man coming into his office with the sandwiches.

"The pictures will just have to wait. In this area, food comes first. Thanks, George. Tell your mamma I'm gonna marry her for her cookin'."

"I don't know if she'll have you. You eat too much."

Pointing to the door, Chief Gaspard said in a laughing manner, "That's it. Out."

The young man left the room with both the young man and Chief Gaspard smiling.

"His mother's the best cook in these parts and I eat the most in these parts." He laughed and then added, "George is a good kid. He's going places. He even has an academic scholarship to Tulane, but his baby brother, Tyrone, may be getting himself in big trouble - he's hanging around with the wrong crowd. He's only twelve. Their mother, Emma, is really worried especially since their daddy, Tom, was killed in the line of duty – shot by a drug dealer. He was one of my best officers and a good friend, too. After they finished the sandwiches, Charlie put his hands on his stomach, then said, "In all seriousness, I've never had a better sandwich or tasted better food."

"Neither have I," agreed Dr. Wells.

"I told you two we have the best cookin' in the world right here. Now the pictures."

He withdrew the photographs from an envelope and showed them to his visitors.

As Dr. Wells looked at them, she asked, "What is supposed to have happened?"

Chief Gaspard replied, "Well there are several ideas. Most people think that one or more . . . "

Charlie interrupted, "Two."

Gaspard continued without commenting on what Charlie had said."...person or persons unknown broke into the house, went to the bedroom, killed Mr. and Mrs. Mackey in their sleep, then ransacked the house looking for money. Charlie, you said two people. Why did you say that?"

"Chief, I know quite a bit about guns." He pointed to one of the photographs. "This picture of the bodies has a couple of shotgun shells on the bed and a couple more over there on the floor. Semiautomatic guns quite often eject the shell casings to the front and right of the gun. The position of the two shell casings on the bed and the other casings on the floor could only happen if there were two of them and they both fired at the same time."

"Why couldn't one person have fired from two different positions?"

"If that were the case, one of the Mackeys would have moved. The hand of Mr. Mackey wouldn't be over his wife in that manner. Also, the shell casings would be in a slightly different position."

"Boy, either you are very observant and knowledgeable about guns, or you did it. Where were you on . . . "

Charlie interrupted, "Chief, I honestly don't know. Dr. Wells knows more about where I was and wasn't than I do."

"That's right, Chief. I don't think Charlie is your man or, I should say, one of the men who murdered the Mackeys."

"I don't think so either," Chief Gaspard said quietly.

As Dr. Wells looked Chief Gaspard straight in the eyes, she inquired, "You think you know who did this, don't you?"

Chief Gaspard leaned back in his chair, looked at his two visitors for a short time as if he were making a decision, got up and walked to the door.

He spoke to a woman in the outer office. "No one - and I mean no one - is to come near this door, open it, or listen to what is going on inside. Do you understand?"

The woman responded, "Yes Chief."

The Chief closed the door and returned to his chair. "One reason I wanted to see you was that I hoped you might be able to shed some light on the murders or cause the murderers to make a fatal mistake. The Mackeys were well liked in these parts. Their funeral was the event of the year. More people attended it than any other funeral I can remember. One thing that stuck in my mind was Miriam's reaction. She cried and carried on like crazy. After one of

58

her crying spells, she told me that she is posting a twenty million dollar reward for the arrest and conviction of the people who murdered her parents."

Charlie interrupted Chief Gaspard. "Did she ever withdraw the reward?"

"To her credit, she has not withdrawn the reward, but only limited recovery to five years."

"Chief, I think I know who the murderers are."

Dr. Wells looked at Charlie, "Of course, it's those two who attacked us and wanted to kill you this morning."

"Now wait a minute. You were attacked this morning before coming here?"

"Yes, sir. We have good reason to believe that all the men really wanted to do was kill me, or both of us, while making it look like a mugging. I think Mrs. Ward had something to do with it. It didn't work, and the men are now in custody in New Orleans - at least they were when we left to come here. A Sgt. Cally is our contact on the New Orleans Police Department."

Chief Gaspard looked astounded and leaned back in his chair, then said, "You'll get that reward if they are the men."

Charlie asked, "How are you going to prove they did it?"

"I didn't tell everything to the press or Miriam. I have two sets of fingerprints. If they match, I got 'em. Sgt. Cally, huh? I believe you wanted to talk to Doc Blake while you were here. Why don't you go see him? I need to make a few phone calls. Come on back here before you leave Thibodaux, okay?"

Charlie and Dr. Wells left the police station to go to Dr. Blake's office not knowing what to make of the turn of events. Dr. Blake's office was on the highway towards Chackbay on the outskirts of town. While driving to Dr. Blake's office, both Charlie and Dr. Wells were very quiet, but began to smile.

Charlie broke the silence, "Damn, even if I don't find out who I am, I will be a millionaire when I leave here if those two are arrested for Mackeys murders."

Dr. Wells continued to smile and nodded, "So will I" and being cautious said, "Maybe."

59

Dr. Blake was just what Mrs. Ward had described - a good, old-fashioned country doctor.

Shaking his head slowly, he said, "I can't tell if Charlie is Charles by just looking at him, but I can if I take a couple of X-rays...Charlie, go in that room and my technician will take a few x-rays for me. Charles Mackey broke both his legs about ten years ago. If you have no evidence of broken legs, then you are not him."

"Great."

Thirty minutes later, Dr. Blake returned to his office, turned on the view box, put Charles Mackey's x-rays on it alongside those that had just been taken. He studied them briefly, and then turned to confirm his opinion with Dr. Wells.

Dr. Wells nodded, and then said, "Charlie, I'm afraid you aren't Charles after all. There's no evidence of any breaks. Thank you for your time, doctor. Please send your bill to me at the San Francisco Army Hospital."

Shaking his head, he said, "There's no bill for the Army. Hope you recover your memory, son."

With those words, Charlie and Dr. Wells left his office. They drove back to the police station in silence.

It was 4:30 PM by the time they arrived. Chief Gaspard was walking impatiently up and down the sidewalk waiting for them on the curb. A Louisiana State Police car was waiting there also.

The Chief said, "If you don't mind me riding in your car, I'd like to talk to you while going to New Orleans. Just follow the State Police car as it goes to New Orleans. I want to know everything about what happened today. This may be my only chance to learn exactly what happened to you two and how this will help me in solving the Mackey murders. Is that okay with you?"

"Certainly," Dr. Wells replied. "Get in."

Chief Gaspard waved to the State Police car, and then got in the back seat. The State Police car pulled out and sped away at a brisk clip, sounding its siren when needed to move traffic out of the way. The two cars traveled toward Raceland. When the highway they were on crossed Highway 90, they turned left and crossed the drawbridge over the bayou, and now were headed toward New

Orleans.

Chief Gaspard had been silent since he got in the car.

Finally, he said, "We should be at parish prison by 6:15, the latest. I guess I owe you some answers to some obvious questions. If you tell anyone that I told you what I am going to say, I'll deny it and call you a liar. I'll also make your life as difficult as I can. Understand?"

Dr. Wells nodded.

Charlie said, "Understood."

"I began to suspect Miriam when I learned how much money was involved. You see Mr. and Mrs. Mackey owned some swampland. Oil was discovered there and there are now some 270 producing oil and/or gas wells on that land. The value of their estate was between 200 and 300 million. That's enough for motive."

Charlie whistled.

"The next thing that struck me as interesting was how much Miriam cried. It was a little...no; she overdid it by quite a bit. I thought it was just for show. She had already posted a two million dollar reward, but when she got finished hugging her father in his coffin, she upped the reward to twenty million. I just knew she had to be responsible. Call it a gut feeling or a hunch, I don't care, but I knew.

"I couldn't prove it because I didn't have the hit men. The one thing I've kept secret until I told you was that I have both of the killers' fingerprints. If they match the prints of those guys in New Orleans, I got 'em. And once I get them, I'll get Miriam.

"Now when you told me about what that mugger said and what happened, I knew she was responsible for the attack on you two, also. That also ties her into the Mackeys' murders, because she thinks you might be her brother and she doesn't want to share her parents' estate.

"Incidentally, Charlie, you're correct about the semiautomatic shotgun. I thought the same thing and tested several. A Remington, model 1100 gun kicked the shells out just about like you saw them in the picture. I reasoned the same as you did, that there were two gunmen because of how the bodies lay and where the shells were found. We tried to get the shells in those positions several times using only one man without him moving, but the only way we could do it was if we had two men firing the shotguns at the same time. I didn't think one man did it and fired from two positions because of the position of the Mackeys - especially Mr. Mackey's arm.

"To anyone who knows about break-ins, it would also be obvious that the trashing of the house was just to throw us off . . ."

Charlie interrupted, "The first and third shelves of books were not disturbed. Only the second shelf was thrown on the floor."

"Right. Not very thorough - just cosmetic. Now for the clincher. Those two jerks have the best criminal lawyer in New Orleans as their lawyer. His name is Evert Stedman. Those two just don't have enough money of their own or the connections to get someone like him to personally come to court with his staff and get them out on bail. But Evert himself was there in court with his staff this afternoon trying to get them out on bail. Fortunately, I called and requested they hold them until I got there and checked their fingerprints. The judge sided with the district attorney.

"There's the bridge. We'll cross it and be at the jail in maybe fifteen minutes. But to continue, the assistant district attorney was extremely surprised to see who his opponent was in court when Stedman showed up with his staff. He requested a short delay to talk to Sgt. Cally and I happened to be on the phone with him at that time. Cally told me to talk to the assistant DA about what I believed. After I did, he went back into court and won a four-day delay for the bond hearing.

"He called me back and was elated - he had beaten the great Evert Stedman in court. Now I only hope their fingerprints match those we got in the Mackey's house."

The State Police car double-parked on Tulane Avenue just outside of Orleans Parish prison. Dr. Wells parked in the space marked "Reserved for Police Cars." Chief Gaspard put a large card in the window identifying the car as there on police business. Charlie, Dr. Wells, and Chief Gaspard went into the building. Once inside, they were escorted to police headquarters and into the room where the fingerprints of the two muggers were being held for identification. It was now 6:32 PM.

Carl Henry, renowned throughout Louisiana as a fingerprint expert, welcomed them as they entered a room that looked like a chemistry laboratory.

"Hi! You must be Chief Gaspard, and you must be Charlie and Dr. Wells. Glad to be of some help. You got the prints?"

Chief Gaspard replied, "Sure do. Here they are."

Carl Henry moved his glasses up over his forehead, sat down in front of a microscope and began looking at the fingerprints that Chief Gaspard brought. He studied a set of fingerprints from one of the muggers, compared them with a set of prints Chief Gaspard had brought, nodded his head. Then he compared the second set of prints from Chief Gaspard with those of the second mugger.

Finally, he raised his head from the microscope, slid his glasses back down over his eyes, and turned to Chief Gaspard.

"They match."

Chief Gaspard smiled.

"Can I use your phone to call Thibodaux?"

Carl Henry motioned towards the telephone.

The Chief walked over to the telephone and dialed a number. "Let me talk to William Fisher." When Fisher came on the line, he continued, "Bill, we got a match. I want first-degree murder charges against Clay Young and Arthur Steiner. They actually did the shooting. And charges against Mrs. Miriam Mackey Ward for hiring them to murder her parents."

After a pause, the Chief continued, "Yes I'm sure. Also, get an order to seize the Mackey estate. I want you to tell Mr. and Mrs. Mackey's brothers and sister about these developments. Under no condition call Miriam. Understood?

"You'll be here around 9:00. Good. I'll see you then."

He took another deep breath. Another man came into the room - Donald Smith, assistant DA in charge of the mugging case.

"Now, we can't blow this," Gaspard explained to Smith. "We have them cold and all I need to have Miriam cold is just a little help from those two jerks. What do you think of this idea? We call Stedman in for a meeting about 9:30 tonight. Then we tell his two

63

clients and him most of what I have on them. Offer them . . ."

Charlie motioned to Dr. Wells to step outside the door. "You know, the more I see of this Gaspard, the more I believe he's really one smart dude."

Dr. Wells replied, "I completely agree with you. Won't Mrs. Ward be surprised?"

Donald Smith called Evert Stedman. "Mr. Stedman, your two clients, Mr. Young and Mr. Steiner, are going to be charged with first degree murder about 9:30 tonight. We would appreciate it very much if you were present when charges are filed."

"You'll be here? Good. I'll expect to see you then."

Smith turned to the group. "He'll be here," he said, grinning.

Dr. Wells asked Chief Gaspard, "Can we go back to our rooms now?"

Chief Gaspard replied, "If you must, I guess it's okay, but I planned to use you when I talk to those two jerks and Mr. Stedman. I want to let them see you for emphasis."

Charlie answered, "Then we'll stay. But, can you show us where the boy's and girl's rooms are?"

Carl Henry smiled, walked out to the hall, and pointed to the left down the hall.

Dr. Wells responded, "Thanks, with deep gratitude."

William Fisher arrived at 9:15 PM. Donald Smith and Chief Gaspard took him over to a corner and all three men began to talk.

After they had looked over the documents, Chief Gaspard asked, "Donald, can you have the seizure order delivered to Antoine Broussard tonight?"

"It'll be delivered within the hour."

"Then we'll follow the plan I outlined."

"Right."

William Fisher responded, "Agreed. Let's get the show on the road."

The three men together with Charlie and Dr. Wells walked to the holding area where they met Stedman. It was now 9:37 PM.

"Donald, this had better be good or I'll have your butt."

"Mr. Stedman, I'd like to introduce you to Chief Gaspard of the

Thibodaux Police Department and William Fisher of the Lafourche Parish District Attorney's office."

All four men shook hands.

Chief Gaspard looked into a holding room where he saw Young and Steiner, then led the others inside. Charlie and Dr. Wells remained outside but could see in and be seen through a window.

Chief Gaspard said, "Now boys, we have to do this thing legal, so would you do the honors Bill."

"Sure thing, Chief. Clay Young and Arthur Steiner, you are hereby charged with premeditated first-degree murder in the deaths of Mr. and Mrs. Charles Mackey, Jr. in Thibodaux, Louisiana. You have the right to remain silent. You have the right to an attorney. If you cannot afford one, the State will appoint one for you. You do not have to answer any questions, but if you choose to do so, anything you say may be used against you in a court of law. You have the right to have your attorney present during any questioning by authorities. Do you understand your rights?"

Stedman responded, "I can answer for them as I am representing them. They understand their rights."

After the legal ritual had been completed, Chief Gaspard began, "Boys, you're in a pack of trouble. I don't want you to answer any questions or say anything, but when I'm finished, I'll leave the room, then you and your attorney can discuss your options. I hope you understand what I've just said."

Both men nodded their heads.

Gaspard continued, "Now we got you both dead to rights for those murders. To tell you just one thing, we have your fingerprints all over the house and even in the bedroom where they were killed. There is only one way your prints could have gotten there and that is if you were the killers.

"We also know who hired you. She also hired you to kill a man who came to visit her this morning, but you two screwed up and were captured. Now, I'm here to tell you that Mr. and Mrs. Mackey's estate has been seized by the court until after the trial because in Louisiana a person can't profit from his crime."

Stedman broke in and said, "You mean Mrs. Ward can't write a check for anything?"

Gaspard smiled, "Why counselor, I didn't mention Mrs. Ward's name, but yes, if she owes any bills, they can't be paid by any funds in the estate - and, by the way, that's all she has. Or, I should say, had. She doesn't even have access to her recently divorced husband's money because she insisted on a prenuptial agreement. Interesting, isn't it?

"Now for the clincher. You see those two people out that window. That's Charlie and Doctor Wells. They were the people you two were hired to kill and tried to kill earlier today. They're prepared to testify that you, Clay Young, said she was a shrink. Except for Charlie, the only person who knew she was a psychiatrist was Mrs. Ward. No one even knew Dr. Wells was going to their meeting except Mrs. Ward, and she only learned that late last night.

"That's about all I am going to tell you right now, but I think that's enough to give you the idea. We've got a solid case against both of you and Mrs. Ward. We'll be transporting you back to bloody Thibodaux in the morning to stand trial for these murders. We have very few murder trials in Thibodaux - I guess the murderers rarely get to trial there."

Stedman exclaimed, "That's coercion."

"I apologize for the slip counselor, but you boys can ask around and see if what I just said isn't true. Now to the deal. We won't ask that you be toasted up crisp and dark at Angola - in other words we won't ask for the death penalty if you confess and tell us who paid you to murder the Mackeys and cooperate with us completely. Otherwise, we go for the death penalty. I think now is the time for us to leave so you can to talk to Mr. Stedman."

Everyone left the room except Stedman, Young, and Steiner. It was a short conversation. Stedman soon called Gaspard, Smith, and Fisher back into the room.

Stedman said, "Put what you said in writing and get a court reporter."

Chief Gaspard was at New Orleans International Airport at five in the morning, sitting in the reception area for Brazilian Airlines.

Mrs. Miriam Ward walked into the area fifteen minutes later and saw Gaspard sitting there, dozing with his eyes closed.

She hesitated, looked about uncertainly, and then walked directly over to him. "Gaspard, what on earth are you doing here?"

Gaspard opened his eyes with a jerk and answered, "I'm waiting to talk to you, Miriam."

Miriam snapped her reply, "Well make it quick. I have a plane to catch."

"I don't think you'll be catching any plane today...or for a long time. Come sit a spell with me. Before I begin to talk, I would like to introduce you to Donald Smith, Assistant District Attorney for Orleans Parish. You know William Fisher and Evert Stedman, don't you?'

"Yes. What's this all about?"

"I think we'd better do this thing just like we did Young and Steiner."

With those words, Donald Smith began, "Mrs. Mirriam Mackey Ward, you are charged with the murder of Mr. and Mrs. Charles Mackey, Jr. You have the right to . . . "

After she was read her rights, she turned to Gaspard and said, "You have gone mad, Gaspard."

"Miriam, I went to your house last night and you were not home. Your maid told us just after someone called, you immediately got dressed, hurriedly packed some clothes, then left the house. I wondered where you would fly the coop to. I remembered that Brazil didn't have any extradition treaty with the U.S. and that you've been there several times on vacation - seemed to like it a lot. So, I contacted the Brazilian Airlines and discovered you had just made a reservation.

"We have confessions from both Young and Steiner. They said you gave them the shotguns they used to kill your parents. We just recovered the guns from where they said they threw them - by the old railroad bridge abutments. It'll take about two weeks to find out who bought the guns, but we can and will trace the purchase through the serial numbers. Also, Miriam, Antoine Broussard was served a court order seizing the estate last night. You have no money to pay for anything."

Gaspard took a deep breath, and then continued. "The deal I am offering you is this. Confess and you don't sit in sparky - you know, the electric chair. In short, confess and we don't ask for the death penalty. Your two hired guns took our offer, 'fessed up, and told us all the details. They even told us how much you paid them back then and how much you're still paying them each month to keep quiet.

"Now, I'd like you to go over to that little room where the coke and candy machines are and discuss my deal with Mr. Stedman."

Again, it was a short conversation.

Stedman came back to Gaspard, "Put it in writing and we can go to the VIP lounge where the court reporter is."

Gaspard nodded his head.

He spoke to Miriam, "You had it made until you thought Charlie might be your brother. You should have considered sharing the estate if Charlie proved to be your brother, but you wanted him dead so you could still have it all. That's what did you in - greed. By the way, Doc Blake proved he isn't your brother."

Miriam Ward said one word, "Shit!"

Even though it was Saturday, Chief Gaspard authorized the release of the reward money to Charlie and Dr. Wells that same day. Charlie and Dr. Wells were now millionaires. Their money was placed in the Hibernia National Bank in New Orleans under each of their names. The name on Charlie's account read "Charlie." Both Charlie and Dr. Wells planned to transfer their money within the next couple of weeks to another bank, probably in San Francisco.

That night, Charlie and Dr. Wells celebrated the events of the day by having a quiet dinner at Commander's Palace.

CHAPTER 5

After the dinner at Commander's Palace, Charlie did not sleep very well. He went to the bar at the club and almost closed it, drinking cokes, and his new favorite, Barq's Root Beer. He had already had two glasses of wine, but he wanted to think clearly, so he limited himself to soft drinks after the wine. Just before getting in bed, he set the alarm clock for 6:00 AM.

It was Sunday, but Charlie was already up when the alarm clock went off. In fact, he had already brushed his teeth, combed his hair, and done several other things people do in the morning. However, he had not yet dressed to go jogging. He walked over to the alarm, shut it off, put on his jogging shorts, and went outside. He had measured his ten mile run the day before. He would jog to the street on which he and Dr. Wells entered the base, turn left towards the hangars, then past some buildings that appeared to be vacant, and finally back to the club. This was five miles and he would just repeat this route to finish his ten miles.

He was about to start, when a black man, taller than Charlie, but just as muscular, came out of the club in shorts.

He said, "Good morning. Great day for a run. No rain."

"Sure is. How about a run with me. My name is Charlie. I hope to do ten miles."

"That's better than I want to do. I only plan on five, but I'll jog with you that far. I'm Howard Browne."

The two men shook hands and began to jog. Both were in good shape and covered the first five miles in just under forty minutes. Howard stopped and went back into the club, but Charlie continued for the remaining five miles.

As he ran, Charlie thought of his situation. He was a millionaire without a name. What should he call himself? Charlie James? No, he didn't like that. Charlie Able? He didn't like that either. At last, he decided on Charlie Cain Duncan. He could call himself Charlie, Duncan, or C. C. Yes, Charlie Cain Duncan. He'd have to talk to Dr. Wells as soon as possible to see if she could get him a birth certificate and social security number with that name to make it official.

By 8:15 he returned to his room at the club. He showered, dressed, and went to call Dr. Wells. She was just about ready to leave her room when Charlie knocked on her door.

"Yes!"

"This is Charlie. You about ready for breakfast? And we have to talk."

Dr. Wells opened the door and smiled at him.

"Let's find a place where there's a breakfast bar," she suggested.

"Great idea."

They found a Shoney's restaurant not too far from the base that had a large breakfast bar. A strong mix of odors met them as they entered - fried bacon, sausage, eggs, grits, and the bar featured almost anything else a person could want for breakfast - most of it loaded with grease. Since neither one of them found greasy food appealing, they both selected the fruit and some grits to eat.

After they had finished their meal, Charlie told Dr. Wells what was on his mind.

"I have to get on with my life. It's been a long time since I woke up in Hawaii and I still have no idea or sign of who I am or where I came from, or anything else about me. You've tried everything you can, but I still don't know any more now than when we started. I just have to get on with my life."

"Charlie, I agree with you. However, if you ever have any flashbacks or remember your past, please call me so I can help you.

What are your plans?"

"First, I'd like you to get me a birth certificate. I've decided I'd like my name to be Charlie Cain Duncan. I like the possibility of being called C. C. Second, I'd appreciate it if you'd get me a social security number. With those two things, I think I can get along, especially with the ten million dollars I now have."

Both Dr. Wells and Charlie couldn't help giggling like children at their good fortune.

"Getting you a birth certificate and a social security number won't be a problem, but it will take some time. I'll call the hospital and get the paper work started now. As you know, I am leaving for Florida, but I will return in about a week. During that time, I can only suggest that you use some of your money to hire a driver and see the area until I return here. Keep the bill and I'll see if the Army will pick up the tab."

"Hell, I don't care. With all that money, the Army doesn't have to pay for anything."

After Charlie and Dr. Wells returned to the club, Dr. Wells left for the airport to catch her flight to Florida and Charlie called the United Taxicab Company.

"I need a driver and a car for about a week. The driver must be with me all day long. What are your charges?"

"We don't do that, but I have a part time driver who might be interested in such a job. Let me call him and he can get in touch with you."

"Fine. About how long will that take?"

"If he's home, five or ten minutes."

Charlie gave the man his telephone number. Less than five minutes later, the phone rang.

"Are you the person who wants a driver for a week?"

"Yes. What are your charges? Hell, would $1,000.00 for the week plus expenses be enough?"

An enthusiastic response came over the telephone, "Yes sir! And my name is Joe Catalano."

"Good. My name is Charlie. Pick me up in an hour at the officer's club at the Naval Air Station - you know, Alvin Callender

71

Airfield. I'll arrange for you to get a pass to enter the base."

"I can't make it that fast, but how about two hours?"

"That'll be fine."

At 1:26 in the afternoon, a black Ford sedan without any for hire markings on it pulled up in front of the club and a somewhat chubby man in a suit that did not quite fit him got out. Charlie was waiting for him at the door.

"Are you Joe?"

"Yes sir. Are you Charlie?"

"Right. Just to get off on the right foot, here's $500.00. You'll get the rest at the end of the week. I hope that's okay."

"Sure is."

"Fine. Then let's eat. Do you know of a good place?"

"Every place in New Orleans is a good place to eat. I think I'll take you to Mother's on Poydras Street."

"Okay. Let's go."

Charlie got in the car and they drove towards downtown New Orleans. At a traffic light in Belle Chasse, Joe turned right onto a highway marked LA 406. Charlie noted that the highway had what appeared to be a swamp on one side of the road and was mostly open ground on the other side, with a couple of radio towers situated in the open field. They drove about five miles, turned left over a drawbridge and onto a street with a median - a very wide median. Charlie saw a sign that read Gen. DeGaulle. This led to the bridge over the Mississippi River.

Charlie noticed it was the same bridge he and Dr. Wells had taken for their meeting with Mrs. Ward. After they ate at Mother's, they returned to the car for the drive back across the river.

Charlie started to loosen up. "Joe, I'm a tourist here in New Orleans. Show me the city and tell me a little about it."

"Well, I can't show you much this afternoon, but I can take you to where the battle of New Orleans took place - in a little town named Chalmette. It's not far from here - only a little down river. You know that was the battle that was fought after the peace treaty was signed to end the War of 1812."

After they arrived at the Battle of New Orleans park, Charlie and Joe looked over the area, went into the park headquarters building which was an antebellum house, heard the Park Service's version of how the battle unfolded, then they went outside and drove around the battlefield.

As they were leaving the park, Charlie remarked, "Joe, you know the British were really stupid to try to cross that open field as they did. They really got clobbered."

"They sure did. I like to come here because this battle changed the course of history here in the United States. I'm sort of a history buff. It sure changed the history of the United States, especially since I think the British wouldn't have honored the treaty if they had won the battle."

Charlie replied, "I think you're right. Now, Joe I want to tell you why I must hire you and who I am. I just came into a lot of money - the reward money from the Mackey case."

In a slightly exaggerated tone of voice Joe said, "You're the guy those two tried to kill and after you captured them, you and that police chief, what's his name - Gaspard - found out the muggers killed those people!"

"That I am. But, I'm here in New Orleans because I have amnesia. I don't know who I am or where I'm from, and neither does the government or anyone else. I know I was in the Special Forces in Southeast Asia, but that's all. Since I don't have any I.D., I can't do very much. I can't even get a driver's license, so you have to be my escort."

"Damn. It must be hard not knowing who you are."

"Sure is. I'd like you to take me back to the club, now. But to warn you, you might be going home late some nights."

"That's okay. The wife will understand. Say, how about you coming over for a good home cooked meal - how about Friday."

"I think I'd like that."

Joe dropped Charlie off at the club, then went home. Charlie went into the club restaurant and ordered dinner.

To his surprise, Howard, his jogging companion of that morning, came over to his table.

"May I join you? I hate to eat alone."

73

"Sure. Have a seat."

"Well, what have you been up to today, Charlie."

"I went to eat at Mother's, and let me tell you one thing - you stay in this town any length of time and you'll get fat. The cooking here is great."

Patting his stomach, Howard said, "Ah yes, I too have found that out."

"Next, I went to see Chalmette Battlefield - you know where the Battle of New Orleans was fought. It was an experience to see where the battle was fought that saved New Orleans and maybe the United States, especially because the battle was fought after the peace treaty was signed. You know, the British had beaten the Americans on the west bank of the Mississippi and if they had known that, we would have lost the battle."

"I've heard about the battlefield, but I don't think I'll get there this trip."

After both men finished dinner, Charlie suggested they go to the bar for a few drinks.

Howard nodded amiably. "Good idea."

At the bar Howard signaled the bartender. "Bloody Mary."

"Give me a Barq's," Charlie said.

"Root beer?" Howard asked in surprise.

"I hardly ever drink the hard stuff. I usually drink mostly Coke, but that was before I came to New Orleans. Now I think I'm hooked on root beer - Barq's."

Howard shook his head. "Damn. New Orleans does strange things to everyone."

The bartender served them their drinks.

Charlie asked, "What do you do Howard?"

"I'm a secret service agent - you know the guys who guard the president."

"And what is a secret service agent doing here in New Orleans?"

"Well, the service believes the President, or some other big shot politician we'll have to protect, will be coming here on a fairly regular basis over the next few years. That's because Louisiana has begun to vote different and can no longer be counted on to vote Democratic. So they sent me to look over the different ways the President may have to drive to the city and figure out what's the safest route."

Charlie thought for a minute, and then replied, "I think a pretty safe way would be to take Highway 23 to the intersection with Highway 406, turn and go to the draw bridge, then cross the Intracoastal Waterway to the Mississippi River Bridge. After that, it would depend on where in the city the President is going.

"The reason I'd pick that route is because it's the shortest and easiest route to temporarily close down to local traffic, not that anything the Secret Service could do would prevent the President from being killed if someone really wanted to get the President. You guys probably know this, but if anyone really wanted to get him, he could be killed very easily almost anywhere on any route, or while landing or taking off from just about anywhere."

Howard was looking at the television over the bar.

"Shush, I want to hear this. It's about the Mackey killings and how Chief Gaspard broke the case. I heard some of it at noon, but not all of it."

Charlie looked at the TV for a short time. He took a sip of his root beer, then got up and went to the men's room. He relieved himself of a significant amount of water, washed his hands, and returned to the bar just as the news broadcast was ending.

As Charlie returned to the bar, Howard mildly exclaimed, "You're the guy who got the reward for finding the killers, aren't you?"

Charlie settled back into his seat and replied, "Yeah, I'm the guy. Me and Dr. Wells. She's in Florida now, but she'll return in about a week."

Howard, now taking a greater interest in Charlie, asked, "What are you doing in New Orleans?"

"That's a long story, Howard. The best information I have is after the fall of Saigon, I was with the special forces in Southeast Asia and while closing some clandestine bases or something like that, I was wounded and in a coma for two, three or maybe even four

75

months. When I woke up in Hawaii, I had lost quite a lot of my memory. The doctors thought I might be related to the Mackey family, so I came to New Orleans to find out. This Mrs. Ward was the daughter of the Mackeys and she thought I would take half her money, so she hired those two to kill me.

"They didn't know I was a Special Forces guy. As you know, Special Forces type people have the reputation of being very good at taking care of themselves. I took care of them when they attempted to kill me. The rest you know from the TV."

Howard was extremely interested in Charlie's story, as he had never heard anything so bizarre from anyone - at least not something that was true.

After listening to Charlie's story, Howard was silent for several minutes.

"Charlie," he said finally, "If I could arrange it, would you be game for a little role playing? Do you think you could play an assassin who is trying to kill the President or some big shot politician coming to New Orleans as an exercise for the secret service?"

"Sure, but there would have to some rules, because I wouldn't want anyone to get hurt."

They discussed Howard's plan for several minutes. Then Howard said, "Good. I'll call Washington, talk to them, and see what they think."

On Monday, the next day, Charlie was doing his stretching exercises outside the club when Howard appeared.

Charlie said, "How about five miles, then my driver can take us both to see New Orleans."

Howard replied, "Can't see New Orleans. I have to leave tomorrow morning and I've got a few things to put together before then. Remember, I'll be talking to you probably no later than next Monday."

Charlie replied, "You bet."

Both men took off jogging. Again, after five miles, Howard stopped in front of the club. Charlie continued until he completed his ten miles.

After breakfast, he found Joe patiently waiting for him outside in his car. This morning he had been wearing a sport shirt with an open collar and dressed in clothes that fit his large chest and his enlarged abdomen, which protruded, slightly below his belt.

Charlie waved to him as he approached. "Good morning, Joe. Let's go somewhere else today - the zoo or the lake or anywhere you want to take me."

Joe hesitatingly replied, "Okayyy. Let's go to the zoo. It's first rate, or at least it's going to be when the renovations are complete."

Charlie got in the car.

Once outside the gate, Charlie asked, "Joe, how would you like to earn, let's say $5,000.00, and do it legally?"

"Keep talking."

"I might need help doing a job for the government. I won't know if I have the job for a couple of days, but I'll need someone who knows New Orleans and the local situation. I can't tell you more than that."

Joe looked at Charlie and nodded his head, a big smile indicating he would be very interested in such work. "If you get the job, sure."

Charlie and Joe walked around the zoo all day, looking at the animals. Charlie was most interested in the swamp exhibit with the alligators. When they had seen just about everything, Joe took Charlie back to the club, then left for the day.

The next morning, Charlie was ready to jog, but Howard was not there. Charlie wondered where he was; then he remembered Howard said he was leaving New Orleans this morning.

When Charlie returned to the club, he was surprised to find Howard waiting for him.

"Charlie, not only did my boss say my idea was good, but some other people thought they might offer you employment if you did a good job. It seems someone else has heard of you and your exploits here in New Orleans."

Howard looked around to see if anyone was listening, then continued, "That someone else is the CIA. Incidentally, Washington gave me a $50,000.00 budget for the project. I'm to talk to you about the rules and get back to them for their okay. I've been ordered to stay in New Orleans until the project's done. After that, I report the results to Washington and make any recommendations I think appropriate."

"Sounds good to me. Let's meet at ten o'clock in the bar - or better yet, in my room to set the rules."

"See you then."

It was a few minutes after 10:00 AM when Charlie heard a knock on his door. He opened the door to find Howard standing there with another man.

"Charlie, I want you to meet Morris Langley. His department would like to see what you can do in this exercise, so they sent him to observe."

"Glad to meet you, sir."

"What are the rules you want?"

"The one rule I insist on is if any damage or injury occurs, the government picks up the tab on all medical bills and any property damage, no matter how expensive. The reason for this is I will be handling some explosives and someone might get hurt or a good deal of property might be damaged or destroyed."

Howard turned to Morris. "That seems fine to me."

"Me too. Let's get it approved."

"Besides the rules, you must tell me when the president is to arrive and the route he is to take. I can fix the same events on any and all routes, but that would entail more than doubling the budget. If you guys want to do that, that's all right with me, but it would be cheaper if you would tell me the route and when he's to arrive."

"I'll check on that also. I'll get back to you as soon as I can, but no later than tomorrow."

Charlie was all smiles. As he was leaving the club about noon, he saw Joe in the parking lot waiting for him.

"Let's go. You know that job I talked to you about, well you have it. You may even be paid a little more than $5,000.00, but I don't know for sure. It all depends on how much it costs me. Now where can I buy some firecrackers and fireworks?"

"There is a fireworks stand on the West Bank Expressway."

"Then that's where I want to go."

The Ford pulled in the parking area for the fireworks stand. The stand was a long open building similar to a long trailer. Joe parked immediately in front of the stand. Charlie got out of the car and went to the counter. A middle-aged man and a young boy were seated behind the counter.

The young boy got up and asked, "Can I help you?"

Charlie replied, "First some information. Do you have any rockets that will go 500 feet in the air and then explode?"

"Sure do. There they are over on the corner shelf."

"How high will they go?"

The middle-aged man got up. "They are the best. They go up between 400 and 700 feet."

Charlie responded, "Good. I'll take thirty of them."

The man was surprised.

He said, "That will be $800.00 plus tax."

Charlie said, "I'll give you $700.00 and no tax."

The man frowned, but replied, "Deal."

The rockets were loaded in the trunk of the Ford.

As they drove off, Charlie told Joe, "I need a place to work. Where nobody will disturb me and it has to be reasonably isolated from people."

"I have a friend who has a place on the lower coast near the Coast Guard station. No one will disturb you there and the only people nearby are his family."

"Good. Let's go there. I'll pay for his family to move out for a few days to the Hilton or any other hotel in New Orleans."

After arriving at Joe's friend's house, Joe secured permission for Charlie to use his garage to work and store the fireworks. Joe's friend charged Charlie $200.00 to use his place and he and his family packed their car and left.

Now Charlie and Joe unloaded the fireworks. They placed them in the building that was used as a stable, garage, and workshop. It had a workbench along the back of the open area or garage, a chair, and good lighting over the workbench.

"Joe, do you know anyone who can get me five pounds of plastic and not ask any questions?"

"I think so. Give me a couple of hours."

By night, Charlie had five pounds of plastic explosive. He began to work on two rockets, disassembling the heads and reshaping them to accept the detonating device he set in each rocket.

When he finished, he placed the two rockets aside.

"Joe, no one - and I mean no one - is to touch these rockets. They could go off. You'd better tell your friend about them and reemphasize to him he is not to return to his home until after the test."

Charlie returned to the club to find Howard and Morris waiting for him.

"Where have you been?" Howard asked. "We got the okay to tell you the route, pay any damages, and even keep you out of trouble with the law. Here's a note saying you are part of an exercise working for us so you won't be arrested. As I said, we'll go to bat for you if you are arrested."

"That's fine. When will the President arrive?"

Howard smiled. "Friday at ten in the morning. You picked the route he'll take into the city. You have tomorrow and Thursday to work, plus up to 10:00 AM on Friday.

"Howard, could you arrange for a demonstration area where we can set off some explosives? I'll need a piece of steel at least two inches thick and some bullet-proof glass."

"Done."

"I won't be home until Thursday night. On Friday, all I want you to do is to be with me when the president arrives and to tell me when the President's plane is landing so I can do my thing."

Charlie called Joe. "Come back for me now. We have work to do tonight. I'll meet you at the gate to the base."

Charlie went to his room. He opened his window, climbed out, closed the window behind him, and ran quietly toward the shadows across a narrow alleyway. Once there, he turned and looked back. Two men had moved to the rear of the building and were now watching his window. He smiled.

Joe picked Charlie up just outside the gate and they went back to the garage where they had left the rockets. There they began painting some panels and aluminum pipes that had been used for downspouts on houses. After they were almost finished, they curled up on the floor and went to sleep.

Joe and Charlie spent the next morning until 9:00 finishing the painting of the downspouts. Now they spent the rest of the morning working very hard on the river side of the levee close to one end of the runway at Callender air force base. After they were finished there, they went to the other end of the runway and worked there for a couple more hours.

It was now almost 3:30 PM as they went to Highway 406 and immediately before a culvert installed a vehicle counter switch that could be activated by a radio signal. Next, they went to the drawbridge and parked near it. Darkness had settled in over the area.

The bridge had a large block of concrete on one end that hung over the roadway. It was the counterbalance for the other end of the bridge. That end of the bridge was resting on the other shore. When opened, that end of the bridge that rested on the other shore would be sent skyward, much like an alligator opening its jaw when the bridge opened. Charlie climbed the superstructure and placed some clay around the concrete then strung some rope to connect the clay.

After Charlie had placed the clay, he climbed down from the bridge. The bridge attendant was watching television in his little room. He wasn't even aware that Charlie was there.

Charlie then directed Joe to carry one end of the rope to the other side of the bridge while he ran the rope under the bridge, where it could not readily be seen. He pulled the rope up through the steel latticework of the roadway and put some clay in the latticework at that point.

Looking over what they had accomplished, Charlie said, "Good night's work. Now let's go back to the garage and get some rest. We'll complete the job tomorrow."

Howard looked for Charlie in the morning so he could go jogging with him, but when he could not find him, he thought, "Damn, he gave us the slip."

Thursday morning found Charlie stringing two sets of downspout pipes across DeGaulle so the open end of the pipes were pointed down at the roadway. They were painted black and yellow - the colors used by the Highway Department for safety equipment.

Next Charlie went to a gun shop Joe had recommended. It was in a house that was a shotgun double converted to gun shop. Joe had said the shop owner was not very reputable.

"I want to buy an M-16 with a silencer and no questions," he told the man behind the counter."

The owner stared at Charlie. "You got the wrong place, man. We don't sell to people like you and we especially don't sell silencers."

Charlie started to count hundred dollar bills. When the count reached $2,100, the owner placed his hand over Charlie's. He returned a few minutes later carrying an M-16 with an attached silencer and a box of ammunition.

Charlie said, "Thanks."

Charlie and Joe returned to the club at 4:15 PM.

Howard saw Charlie walking into the club and called to him. "Come over here. You really gave us the slip Tuesday night. Where'd you go?"

"You'll find out tomorrow. Is the demonstration area set?"

"It's set up in the old ammo dump."

"Good. Then tomorrow will be the day. By the way, I bought some illegal plastic just to show you how easily it can be done. The demonstration will be with the illegal plastic. I used clay or putty and ordinary rope as substitutes for plastic and primer cord. If you find that stuff, then you know that's supposed to be plastic."

That night, Charlie slipped out of his room and went to the hangar where the staircase the president would use to get off his plane was kept. He stood on a can and placed something in the rubber bumper that would hit the plane when the staircase was rolled up to it. He got down and returned to his room.

Friday morning was cloudy. There was a 40% chance for rain.

At ten the following morning, Charlie, Howard, Morris, Joe, the base commander, and the base security officer were standing just outside one of the hangars.

The base commander began the exercise as he said, "All air

traffic is to cease for ten minutes and the base is now closed."

Charlie took out a small radio device and pressed a button. Rockets at both ends of the runway shot skyward and exploded about 500 feet in the air.

Charlie smiled. "Note the President's plane has been shot down and has crashed. He is now dead."

The base commander turned to his security chief. "George, didn't your men check both ends of the runway?"

"Yes sir. There were only the markings for the runway - you know the ones which were just painted."

"George, we haven't painted anything there in over six months."

Morris smiled at what Charlie had obviously done.

Howard was frowning, but said, "Roll the steps out."

The steps were rolled out and placed in position. Joe climbed the steps to play the part of the President. When he waved, he grabbed his chest and turned around as if he had been shot. He did this several times, then dropped to the floor of the steps.

Charlie laughed. "Bad acting. The President has just been shot and killed. The second time the president has been killed."

George looked around, but didn't see anything.

Charlie walked to where the steps were. He pointed to a man walking over to them. He handed Charlie an M-16 with a silencer on it.

Charlie showed the gun to Howard and George.

George asked, "Where did he shoot from?"

Charlie pointed to a building about 350 yards from the tarmac. "Inside, on the second floor. You will find a barrel filled with sand and a shell casing on the floor. The M-16 was fired into the barrel when Joe waved his hand. You will find the bullet in the barrel."

Joe stood up and waved again. Charlie pressed a button on the device he held in his hand. Smoke poured from the rubber bumper.

Charlie shook his head. "I've just blown the President up. I've killed him three times and he hasn't even left the base!"

The base commander was now thinking, this base needs a new security chief or at least this exercise will get my security chief thinking.

Howard turned to Charlie, "What you did was on this base. Now the Secret Service will show you how it protects the President."

Charlie smiled. He joined Howard and Morris in a limo. The car left the base and turned left on Highway 23, then turned right on Highway 406. After they had gone about a mile, they passed over a vehicle counter. Joe pressed a button on a radio switch and two rockets fired and exploded in the air.

Howard said, "Damn. But those rockets couldn't damage the president's car."

Charlie responded, "Let's wait to see the demonstration before you say that. Anyway, the explosive charge was placed in the culvert under the road and was enough to blow a heavy tank into several pieces. The auto counter was the switch. The President has now been killed four times."

They continued on to the drawbridge.

As the car rolled onto the bridge, Charlie said, "The bridge has just been blown up and the President along with his car, is now in the water. The President has now been killed five times."

Howard smiled. "The president wasn't in this car, he was in the car that stopped just before it went onto the bridge so it could not have gone into the water."

"You mean the President was in the car that's under the concrete counterbalance?"

With some pride, Howard said, "You got it man."

Charlie pressed another button and two more rockets went skyward and exploded.

He turned to Howard. "The concrete counterbalance on the bridge to our rear and above the second car has been blown and has fallen on the second car. As I said, the President has now been killed five times, make that possibly six times. Incidentally, you may check each area and you will find putty to represent plastic and rope to represent primer cord placed appropriately in the different areas."

Howard was now getting frustrated. They continued towards the Mississippi River Bridge. The car went under the pipes hanging over the street.

Charlie again said, "This car has been destroyed by rockets. You know rockets can be fired from above just as well as from the ground.

"That's all I have prepared, but I could have prepared many more events if given the time and the inclination. Let's go to the demo area.

"By the way, the president has been killed at least six times, possibly seven if you include two times on the bridge."

Howard sat very quietly in the back seat as the car turned left to cross the wide median to return to the demonstration area where Charlie had the rockets.

The steel plate and the bulletproof glass were in place at the safe site. Charlie took ten minutes to arrange the demonstration area the way he wanted it. Everyone then took cover. He fired the two rockets he made by touching some wires to a couple of batteries.

Fire spit from the rear of the rockets and they sped forward towards the steel and bulletproof glass. The resulting explosions caused the steel plate to have a four-inch hole where each of the rockets hit. The bulletproof glass was nonexistent.

Howard looked at the damage resulting from the rockets. "Nobody can protect the President from guided missiles."

Again, Charlie smiled. "Howard, those rockets were purchased at the fireworks store on the West Bank Expressway and modified with plastic. Anyone can do that."

Morris shook his head in a surprised, but approving manner. He left the group, went to his car, drove from the area to a pay telephone where he dialed a number.

The telephone answered, "Central Intelligence Agency."

After dinner, Howard was talking to Charlie. "You really did a number on us. I've been in the base commander's office all afternoon discussing what can be done to avoid what you did. When my boss in Washington was told about what you did, he ordered a complete overhaul of our protocol for protecting the President. After the new protocol is in place, it will be harder to kill the President.

"You know, I never thought anyone could kill the president like you did, but you made a believer out of me. Anyone can be killed if

85

someone really wants him dead. The number you did on us will eventually help us to better protect the President. Damn, I never thought anyone could do what you did."

"Howard, if someone wants to kill someone bad enough, there's nothing anyone can do about it unless the assassin is caught before he kills that person. Trust me on that."

"I guess you're right."

Saturday morning started like any other morning. Charlie was up and running and back at the club by 7:30 AM. He showered, then came out to meet Joe at 8:30 AM. They drove off by 8:45 AM. Charlie handed Joe a check for his services.

He asked, "Joe I would like to know how you got that plastic. Can you tell me?"

"Charlie, my contact is that gun shop owner. He told me he gets the stuff he wants through a gun merchant in Switzerland. I'm trying to think of his name. Kozar - that's it. I think Kozar has dealings with the CIA and other governments in their secret operations."

"Thanks. I was just wondering. Are you sure we can be at the airport in time to pick up Dr. Wells?"

"I'm quite sure."

It was early afternoon when Dr. Wells' plane arrived. When Charlie made eye contact with Dr. Wells, she noticed that he had gained a great deal of confidence, or at least she thought he had. Joe picked up her luggage.

Charlie could hardly wait to tell Dr. Wells what happened while she was in Florida. He finished telling her about the time they arrived back at the club.

Dr. Wells spoke for the first time. "Charlie, that is an incredible story. By the way, have you heard anything from San Francisco about getting a birth certificate and a social security number?"

"No, I haven't."

"I'll try to find out something. They should still be at work because of the time difference."

As soon as she found a telephone, Dr. Wells called her office in

San Francisco. "Do you have Charlie's material ready?" she asked.

"Almost. All he has to do is sign a couple of forms, wait another couple of weeks. Then he'll have a birth certificate and a social security number. By the way, we've heard some real wild things about what you two did in New Orleans. What's the scoop?"

"What you heard about the Mackey murders is probably as complete a story as you'll get, but what happened to Charlie and what Charlie did after that is something else. He was employed by the Secret Service and he . . . "

The nurse in San Francisco exclaimed several times as Dr. Wells related the story: "He did that? My God, he's something else." Finally, she asked: "When will you two be getting back?"

"We'll arrive in San Francisco about 2:30 PM on Thursday on Continental flight number 1278. Have someone meet us."

"Sure will. And we'll all want to hear what happened to you two - first hand. Bye."

It was Monday night when Morris Langley knocked on Charlie's door.

Charlie opened it and invited him in.

"Charlie, I have an offer for you from the CIA, but because of the nature of the offer, no one will confirm that such an offer was ever made or that I was in your room tonight. Do you understand?"

"Understood."

"The company needs a man with your talents. We're willing to pay you $100,000 per year plus all expenses. No taxes would be taken from that money as it would be deposited in a Swiss bank account for you. For that money, you would be required to be on call all the time, but when not working, you could do anything you wanted. You might be required to silence someone, however."

Charlie looked Morris straight in the eye. "What you mean to say is I would be a hit man for the CIA."

"In a manner of speaking, yes."

"I have to think about it. I'll let you know in a couple of weeks. Give me your telephone number."

Morris handed Charlie a piece of paper with a number on it.

He said, "Ask for me by name. When someone answers, say

87

only 'This is New Orleans - yes.' Nothing else. If you say anything else, they'll know something is wrong. If you say yes, they will give you instructions. Don't call if your answer is no. You must call within thirty days. Understood?"

"Understood," came the reply.

CHAPTER 6

Lt. Michael Forester arrived at Lisa Giaventi's apartment at 6:45 PM on Wednesday. He rang the doorbell and impatiently waited for Lisa to answer the door, moving around the door in quick movements.

Lisa opened the door and kissed him and Mike responded with a kiss of his own, then they embraced.

Breaking the embrace, Lisa said, "I'll be just a minute, honey."

"Take your time, Lisa. I need to get my courage up for tonight."

When Lisa returned from her bedroom, she and Mike immediately left the apartment and went to Mike's car. She sat close to him on the front seat.

"Mike, are you carrying?"

"You know a policeman must carry his pistol everywhere he goes. And yes, I'll be careful not to spook anybody."

"I just don't want anything to happen."

As Mike drove towards Frank Giaventi's mansion, Lisa became silent - very silent. She was thinking about how she had met Mike. That reminded her of Charlie and what he had told her when she went to eat with him his first night in the hospital, almost nine months ago. She wished she could have spoken to him before they went to Uncle Frank's birthday party, but he was in New Orleans with Dr. Wells and he wouldn't be back until tomorrow. Anyway, this was the night - the night she'd tell Uncle Frank that they were getting married.

Mike observed that Lisa was preoccupied. "Penny for your thoughts."

"I was just thinking about Charlie, what he told me and about tonight...you know, telling everyone about our engagement and all."

"Think how I feel."

"I know darling, but we have to tell them. And you know I want Uncle Frank to walk me down the aisle."

Mike continued, "Our meeting each other must have been directed from heaven, or maybe hell."

"I choose heaven. How else could a cop marry into the Giaventi family?"

The car pulled up to the gate of a very large mansion and the gatekeeper came out to meet them.

"Hi Lisa. They're all here waiting for you two. Just a second while I open the gate."

As the gate swung open, Mike said, "Would you call the house and tell them I'm carrying? You know, police rules say I must."

"They know, but to be on the safe side, tell Jack and Donna when you get to the big house."

Mike replied, "Sure."

As Lisa looked at Mike, she added, "Look at it this way. It won't be long now. When we drive up, I bet the entire family will be looking through the window so they can get to see you. My entire family will be here tonight and most of them haven't met you yet."

She squeezed his arm.

Mike stopped the car in the front of the house and, true to what Lisa had said, he saw a number of faces peering out of the window to the right of the door.

Mike whispered, "Haven't they seen a man before?"

"You're special. They want to see the man I've selected to marry. And besides, you're a cop."

Smiling, Lisa continued, "Loosen up, you gorgeous hunk. It'll be over soon."

The front door opened and an attractive young woman stood in the doorway.

Mike looked at her and thought, Donna is certainly a good-looking woman.

Lisa whispered in Mike's ear, "Remember, I'm the one you're marrying."

Mike smiled. "How did you know what I was thinking?"

"Mike, remember - I know you."

The woman in the doorway was wearing almost skin-tight, sky-blue trousers with bell-bottoms. She was also wearing a loose fitting, bright yellow blouse with a high neck - almost a turtleneck.

She said, "Hi Mike. I believe you know Jack over there."

Mike replied, "Sure do. Hi, Jack, and it's a pleasure to see you again, Donna. I was told to remind you two that I'm carrying. It's in my belt in the middle of my back. And I've been warned not to make any sudden moves in that direction."

"We know you won't do anything foolish," Jack replied. This is supposed to a party. We're supposed to have fun here."

Frank Giaventi stood five feet nine inches tall, was a little overweight, had some gray hair and a receding hairline, and when he came to the door, he kissed Lisa and said, "My favorite. Hello Mike." Frank looked around for a moment, then continued, "Would you come into the library for a minute. I want Donna to show you something."

Mike looked at Frank, then to Donna, shrugged his shoulders, and then answered, "Sure."

The three of them went into the library. Mike noticed Jack came too.

Frank started the conversation. "Mike, I know you're armed, but I would like to ask a favor of you. Please remove your pistol. You may put it anywhere you like, take the magazine out - I don't care, but this is my birthday party and I'd like it very much if no guns were around."

Mike shook his head reluctantly.

"Before you decide, please look at Donna carefully."

Mike followed Frank's gaze to the well-shaped woman.

"Now," Frank continued, "while still looking at Donna, move your hand towards your back quickly."

Mike looked puzzled for a moment, shrugged his shoulders, and

91

then did as he had been asked.

It was quick - quicker than anything Mike had ever seen before - so quick that the weapon seemed to materialize out of thin air. Donna's right hand had lifted her blouse slightly, reached under it, and was now holding a 9 mm Luger pistol that was leveled at his gut, all before he could even reach his own hand under the rear of his jacket.

Mike was startled to say the least. "Donna, where did you get that, and so quick?"

Jack laughed, "She's quick, isn't she."

Mike whistled while responding, "The quickest I have ever seen."

Mike now realized what Frank was saying with this demonstration. "If you even seem like you're going for your gun, Donna will beat you, and she might shoot also. So you see, your gun is useless."

Mike shook his head. He realized Frank was right; his gun was indeed useless, so he slowly removed it from its holster, removed the magazine, and drew back the slide to eject the round in the chamber. He then set his pistol on the table.

Donna smiled and did the same, as did Jack. "I guess I won't need this either," she said.

She bent over and lifted the bell-bottom of her right trouser leg very slightly and removed a small gun strapped to her leg.

Mike looked at what he could see of Donna's legs; they were as worthy of admiration as the other parts of her body.

Frank noticed Mike's look. "You may look, but if you ever touch . . ."

"Frank, I can't promise anything, but the day I don't look, that'll be the day you know I'm dead."

Jack added, "Donna is my girl and I'm very jealous of her. I'm also proud of her good looks."

Mike swallowed and he bent over and removed his backup gun from its ankle holster.

Frank said, "Mike, I've told Lisa this on several occasions and so I now tell you the same thing - you keep your business on that side of the room and I keep my business on the other side. If we keep the family in the middle of the room, everything will be fine. Now, let's go eat. I had the cook prepare a special dish for tonight. I had lobster flown in from Maine this afternoon. The cook's pasta is very good. He takes the pasta, then he..."

Frank put his arm around Mike as he led him to the dinning room.

Frank looked at everybody standing around the table waiting for him to tell them where to sit. He motioned Louis, his nephew, Lisa's cousin, and heir apparent to the chair on his right, the place of highest honor. Then he looked over at Lisa and Mike and he motioned Mike to sit at his left.

Lisa gasped. "Mike, he's accepted you. You're sitting in the number two spot. Only Louis is sitting in a place of higher honor."

Mike knew instinctively that he must take the seat offered, but he also knew this would be his seat only in family matters, not business matters.

As the dinner was being served, Lisa said, "Uncle Frank, you know Charlie, the man I told you about. You know the one who has amnesia and was in the Special Forces in Southeast Asia."

As he ate some of his salad, Frank replied, "Yes, I vaguely remember you told me something about him."

"Well, he and Dr. Wells went to New Orleans to see if he was related to someone called Mackey."

Louis interrupted, "Do you mean the couple who was killed several years ago, but the police only discovered who killed them a week ago?"

"Yes that's the Mackeys. Well, Charlie found out who did the murders and received a very large reward. Dr. Wells received the same amount. But that's not all Charlie did in New Orleans."

Frank was looking at Lisa, listening to every word. He loved to hear Lisa talk enthusiastically.

Lisa continued, "He ran into some secret service guy and they struck a deal. Charlie would play assassin and try to kill the President in some sort of a game. Well Charlie ate their lunch. He "killed the President" at least six or maybe seven times. The Secret

Service was embarrassed to say the least."

Louis was now looking very interested in what Lisa was saying. He asked, "Didn't you say he went to Pendleton and was tested in military knowledge and abilities?"

Frank glared at Louis as much as to say, "Shut up!"

"Yes - he did exceedingly well."

About this time, the servants brought in the lobsters - one for each of the guests. Other servants brought in the pasta and garlic bread. Everybody began to eat. Mike ate heartily as a policeman hardly ever gets to eat this type of food.

After the meal, Frank said, "Let's all go out on the veranda. It is a beautiful night and we can see the lights in the bay."

Everyone got up and went to the veranda except Louis and Frank, who strolled into the library instead.

Frank closed the door, and then said to Louis, "Louis, it wouldn't take much to see you were interested in this Charlie for our purposes. Did you see me ask specific questions? No, but I am very interested in Charlie. I'll call New Orleans tomorrow and find out more. You contact someone and get his medical records. Understand?"

"Yes sir."

"Good. You must learn these things and not be too obvious when asking questions if you are going to take over in the future. Now let's return to the party."

Lisa and Mike were on the veranda with Lisa's mother and the other guests looking at the bay.

Lisa said, "Mike, it isn't going to get easier. We have to go in and talk to Uncle Frank."

Mike took another swallow of wine. "One more glass and we'll do it."

Lisa replied emphatically, "No more delays. Now."

Mike put the now empty glass down and the two of them strolled casually over to where Frank stood.

Lisa asked, "Uncle Frank, can we talk to you privately."

"Sure. Come into the library with me."

As they walked toward the library, Donna and Jack followed

very quietly. Mike did not notice them until they were in the room. He also knew it would be useless to ask them to leave.

Lisa began, "Almost a year ago when Mike and I realized about the conflict between Mike's job and the family, we were torn apart. I talked to Charlie and he suggested that . . . "

Uncle Frank interrupted, "This same Charlie who has amnesia?"

"Yes, the same. Anyway, he suggested we continue to go out together and see if it would work. He suggested I not talk about family business to Mike and not talk about Mike's business to the family."

Frank shook his head in an approving manner.

Lisa continued, "Well, we waited for almost a year and . . ."

••□Mike interrupted, "Frank, we want to - no, we are getting married and Lisa wants you to walk her down the aisle."

Frank smiled. "You know, my biggest fear was that Lisa would not ask me to give her away. Now Mike let me tell you something. I know more about you than even your own department. I have your police records or at least a copy of them, I know where you are most of the time, and I must tell you, you are a good man. I like you, and Lisa will make you a good wife. I'm pleased Lisa selected you."

Jack and Donna were grinning and in an obvious manner, whispering to each other.

"What's so funny?"

Donna replied, "Mr. Giaventi, Mike's a cop. He's marrying a Giaventi. Does that make us legit?"

Frank smiled as he saw some humor in what they said.

Mike started to laugh aloud.

Frank now looked at Mike.

He asked, "Now what's so funny with you."

"Uncle Frank - I hope I can call you that - think of the wedding. You walking down the aisle with Lisa. On one side of the aisle is the Giaventi family, and on the other, the San Francisco Police Department."

Frank looked at Mike and Lisa. He began to laugh too, as did Donna, Jack, and Lisa.

Frank added, "We might need a metal detector at the church

door."

The laughter only grew louder with that remark.

Frank continued, "Now let's go tell the others the good news."

All five of them walked out of the library. Lisa's mother was waiting just outside the door when they walked out. Everyone was smiling.

Lisa walked over to her mother and whispered in her ear, "Uncle Frank is going to give me away in my church. He gave us his blessing. He even seems to like Mike."

Mrs. Giaventi breathed deeply as she heard the news. After all, she was once married to Frank's brother, who had been a police officer, too.

She asked Frank, "Will you make the announcement for me?"

Frank looked at the other guests. "I don't have to make any announcement. They already know."

The twenty-eight guests all applauded.

Louis came over to Mike and said, "Congratulations. I know what your job is and you know our business. You dislike our business, but I tell you this - if you're in need, you have a good family here and we take care of our own. Remember that - we take care of family."

Mrs. Giaventi exclaimed, "Let's have another round and Frank, do you have some nice dancing music on records or tape?"

"I have just the music. Donna, go get those tapes I just bought and play them."

It was now a Mike and Lisa's wedding announcement party and not Frank's birthday party.

Mike realized no one had sung happy birthday to Frank and being so elated about the events of the evening, he started to sing, "Happy birthday to you . . ."

Upon hearing Mike starting to sing, the other guests joined in.

The party was still going strong at midnight when Mike and Lisa left. Mike was walking out of the door when Donna walked over to him.

"Mike, I think you forgot this." She handed him both of the pistols he had taken off earlier in the afternoon.

"Damn, I sure did forget them. Don't tell anybody."

"You mean you think I might blackmail you over this." And, in an exaggerated tone of voice said, "I wouldn't **d r e a m** of telling anyone." She smiled as did Mike and Lisa.

Mike drove Lisa back to her apartment, kissed her goodnight and left to go home.

The next morning, Frank was thinking about the previous night. Lisa getting engaged and knowing that he would walk her down the aisle was the best birthday present he had ever received. He just wished he could make Mike a real member of the family - even the Godfather. No, he thought, Louis is a good man too. It would be a tough decision.

Louis interrupted his thoughts. "Uncle Frank, what about trying to contact the Vancouver family and see if they can get us some supplies? Our last shipment from Mexico was confiscated and the feds are getting better at catching the guys bringing the stuff up here. The state police are doing a better job, too. I think we need another supply route."

"I agree. Go up to Vancouver and talk to...what's his name...Cleve Ronson? He's supposed to be a good man to do the kind of things we want done. By the grapevine, his position isn't as secure as ours, so be on your guard. Support him and deal with him only."

"I'll catch the morning flight to Vancouver on Monday."
"Good."

It was 2:25 PM and Continental Flight 1278 was approaching San Francisco International, about twenty minutes late because of the head wind it had encountered. However, the flight from Houston to San Francisco had been smooth as glass. Dr. Wells and Charlie slept most of the way, but now the flight attendants were walking the aisles waking people up and asking them to put their trays up and their seats in an upright position.

The plane was nearly empty - only thirty-three passengers in a Tri Star! They were sprawled all over the place and a child was running up and down the aisle, talking or screaming at the top of his

97

lungs. He had been doing this through most of the flight - in short, making the flight attendant's life as well as that of some of the passengers miserable. He was a pest.

Dr. Wells leaned over to Charlie.

"If that were my child, I know what I would do with him."

"What would you do? Remember, you're a psychiatrist and you're supposed to believe in Dr. Spock."

"I know, but if that child is five, he would not live to be six."

Charlie smiled and nodded in agreement. A bell rang in the cabin and Charlie noticed a flight attendant who had been walking the aisle as she sat down in a vacant seat and quickly buckled her seat belt. The other flight attendants were doing the same thing without even making an effort to return to their proper stations - they just sat down in the nearest available seat.

Then it happened. The plane hit an air pocket and must have dropped several hundred feet in an instant. The plane became absolutely quiet.

Charlie noticed that the flight attendants were remaining where they were, and he leaned toward Dr. Wells. "Brace yourself. There's more coming."

In less than two minutes, the plane hit another air pocket. This one was not as potent as the first one, but it quieted and frightened the passengers again.

When the flight attendants started to get up and move around the cabin again, he said, "Okay. You can relax now, I think."

Breaking the silence, the voice of the unruly child came loud and clear, "Is that wind shear, mommy?"

Charlie and Dr. Wells turned around to look at the boy, who was seated nearby. They saw his mother grab him and put him in his seat in a very stern fashion. The boy never said another word until the plane landed.

When the wheels touched the ground, all the passengers applauded.

The plane taxied up to the gate without any further incident. Dr. Wells and Charlie gathered their bags from the overhead bins and began to deplane.

Lisa was waiting with Mike at the gate to pick them up. She wanted to tell Dr. Wells and Charlie about their engagement.

Dr. Wells was the first to see Lisa, but she didn't know the person standing next to her. Smiling, she waved to Lisa, then nudged Charlie and pointed her out. He waved too as they walked toward her.

Lisa hugged Dr. Wells and kissed Charlie on the check. Then she said, "Dr. Wells, Charlie, I'd like to introduce Michael Forester, my fiancé." Then she held out her left hand toward them to display her engagement ring.

"Lisa, this is good news. What are your plans? I hope they include continuing to work at the hospital? We really need you. You're one good nurse."

Charlie was holding her hand, looking at the diamond. "This is a beautiful ring. What kind of cut is it?"

Mike answered, "The diamond was my mother's. She died a few years ago and she wanted me to have the ring. It's an emerald-cut diamond and - before you ask - almost three-quarters of a carat. Lisa chose the setting. I think it's beautiful - not too large, but large enough to be appropriately noticed."

"Mike, it's not beautiful, it's gorgeous!"

Charlie began thinking it would be nice to remember his mother.

Dr. Wells asked, "When is the wedding?"

"Mike and I haven't set the date yet, but we're considering sometime in late August or early September. We're waiting to see the pastor and find out when the church will be available. The reception will be at my Uncle Frank's house."

Charlie was still smiling when they entered the baggage area. As they waited for the luggage to show up, Charlie said, "How did your Uncle Frank take the news that you're marrying a police officer?"

Lisa responded, "You know, we took your advice...

Mike interrupted. "It was the best advice she had concerning us. Uncle Frank likes me and, so long as business isn't brought up, he said we'll get along fine. Louis even said I was a part of the family and as a member of the family, if I - er, we - ever need help, the family will be there. I think it's just great, but I admit to being a little nervous."

"If you weren't nervous, you wouldn't be human."

Mike continued, "My brother will be coming in from Washington. He's a FBI agent assigned to the D.C. office. He's one of the junior directors."

"That's a pretty high position for someone so young," Charlie said. "I assume he's around your age."

"Around it. He's four years older than I."

"The wedding will certainly be unusual," Charlie said, chuckling.

Dr. Wells asked, "What's funny?"

Charlie looked at Dr. Wells, then at Lisa. "Does Dr. Wells know who your Uncle Frank is?"

Lisa responded, "Yes, unless she forgot."

As she remembered, Dr. Wells began to laugh too.

"That will be funny or dangerous as the case will be. The police and FBI on one side of the aisle and the hospital staff and the Giaventi Family on the other. At least the hospital staff will be able to administer first aid if anything starts. But how are you two going to keep them separated?"

Mike looked at her and said in a joking manner, "There will be metal detectors at every door, with one guard from the police and one from the family to see no one is packing.

He laughed as he continued, "I don't see any problem. I told the chief this morning and I was assured by him that no police officer will screw up our day and Uncle Frank has said the same thing concerning the family."

Lisa turned toward Charlie, speaking more softly now that other people were standing nearby, "I heard you really ate the Secret Service's lunch. Was it fun?"

"Sure was. They were a cocky bunch when the exercise started, but when it ended they looked like poor, whipped puppy dogs. I bet some heads will roll, but I know there will be changes in the way they guard the President. In all seriousness, they were pretty nice guys and pretty intelligent, too."

Mike added, "They are nice guys, but a little too big for their boots."

It was August 29th when the chief called all the police officers from the division under him into the auditorium where he would talk to them. The room could seat almost 200 people and was built in a semicircle with all seats facing the podium.

All the officers in his division were assembled and seated when Chief Gene Caruth came into the room. The noise ceased as he began to speak.

"Gentlemen, you know Mike is getting married tomorrow at the Ocean View Christian Church. You're also aware that he is marrying Lisa Giaventi whose uncle is Frank Giaventi. The same Giaventi we would all like to see have a private room in San Quentin. We all know that Mike's been working diligently towards that end and that he would have succeeded a few months ago but for a search warrant.

"Now we'll be sitting on Mike's side of the church and the Giaventi family on the bride's side. I will not tolerate any badgering of the other guests. You must act like they are just another family at the church.

"After they're married, we'll give the bride and groom an escort to the reception, which will be at Frank Giaventi's mansion. Don't act like hoodlums. Act like refined police officers. Don't take the silverware or anything from the house. Be good for a change - for Mike's sake and for the sake of your job also.

"Now here are some additional instructions. When you're in the church, casually notice the people on the other side of the aisle. Distinguish between the hospital staff and the Giaventi family. Remember their faces - you may see them again on the street or in line-ups. When you are at the reception, don't drink too much and be friendly with the other guests and try to remember their faces. Remember we are there to have a good time, but we're still cops and we have a duty to remember their faces. Any questions?"

An officer in the back of the room stood up. "You previously said we are not to carry our guns. Will they be carrying?"

101

"Good question. From what Mike has told me, I'd think only one person might be packing. That's a gal named Donna. She has a permit, too. You guys probably know she has a clean record at this time even though she works for Frank Giaventi and we suspect she isn't as clean as she seems, but since we don't have anything on her, she has her permit. Mike also thinks she might not be packing, but don't get too close to her. She's good in self defense and she can hide things in a skin-tight dress that you wouldn't believe. We won't be carrying our guns. Do you understand that?"

Everyone nodded and muttered softly.

That night Mike invited the wedding party to a little Chinese restaurant for a small party.

As the after dinner party was beginning, Frank took Lisa's arm and moved her to a corner where Louis was.

He asked, "Where are you two going on your honeymoon?"

She looked at him, then smiled. "Several places and we don't want to be disturbed."

"You know I only want to help you. Now tell Uncle Frank where you're going. I promise not to tell a living soul or make any arrangements for you."

Louis looked behind Uncle Frank's back. He saw Uncle Frank had his fingers crossed.

Lisa looked him in the eye. "Okay. We're going to one of those plush hotels at Lake Tahoe. After a few days there, we'll go to Las Vegas, then we really don't know. Does that satisfy you."

"It sure does, honey. You can trust your uncle."

With a grin, Lisa answered, "I know I can."

As Lisa crossed the room back to the party, Louis came up close to Frank and said, "She knew what you were up to. She was lying to you."

"Louis, it's a game we play. She knew I had my fingers crossed behind my back. We used to play like that all the time when she was little. She plays the game with me, too. She'll tell me something that might be true or false and let me guess if she's telling the truth. We each win about half the time. By the way, did you fix up the place

102

where they're to spend their first night?"

"Of course, Uncle Frank."

Both men laughed softly.

August 30th began for Mike the same way as every other day. He got up, went to the bathroom, brushed his teeth, and took a bath, but this morning he was ecstatic. He was going to be married to Lisa in a few hours.

Lisa stayed at Uncle Frank's house over night for two reasons. First, the wedding was to be held mid-morning and the second reason was the limousines would not have to stop at her apartment. She was to ride in a stretch limo with her mother and Uncle Frank to the church and then she and Mike would get in a Rolls Royce and ride back to Uncle Frank's house. She was thrilled to say the least.

The police escort had arrived at the station early. They knew there would be hell to pay if they were the least little bit late. They checked their bikes and then went for their morning cups of coffee and doughnuts. They were ready.

Mike and his brother, Al, were putting on their tuxedos and would be ready slightly before 10:00 AM.

At precisely 10:15 AM, eight policemen on their motorcycles stopped at Frank Giaventi's gate. The man at the gate opened it immediately.

The sergeant in charge of the escort shook his head slowly, thinking this was a first - a police contingent welcomed at Frank Giaventi's mansion!

The motorcycles roared up to the house where several stretch limousines were parked.

Frank Giaventi walked over to the sergeant in command.

"Thank you for being so prompt. Lisa will be out in a moment."

The sergeant replied, "This is a big day for Mike and Lisa." The escort noticed a very attractive woman in the doorway. She walked out a few steps, then turned around to help Lisa with her dress as the bride came down the steps.

The sergeant shook his head again, admiring the young

woman's beauty and wondering who she was.

Frank Giaventi saw the sergeant looking at Donna, smiled, and then said, "Sergeant, you have excellent taste in women. The other woman is named Donna. She is special to me and Jack over there."

There was no more conversation. Lisa got into the limo with her mother and Uncle Frank while her family got into the other limos, and the signal was given to move out. With sirens shrieking, the police escorted the Giaventi family to the church.

Mike got into another stretch limo at his apartment. His groomsmen were already there, but there would be only a two motorcycle police to escort his vehicle. He arrived at the church at 10:45, went to the rear door and entered the pastor's office, then entered the room that led into the sanctuary where he would wait until the wedding started.

Finally, at 10:50 AM, the organ began to play. As the bride and her party arrived, the opera singer Pavlov sang "True Love" and "O Promise Me." Uncle Frank had made the proverbial offer Pavlov couldn't or would be a fool to refuse - so he sang for Lisa's wedding. Then the organ played music for the family as they were escorted down the aisle.

With the sound of the first notes of the wedding march, Mike and his groomsmen walked out of the room and into the sanctuary. Mike saw the bridesmaids walk down the aisle. Then the music rose to a new level and he saw Lisa as Uncle Frank escorted her down the aisle - God she was beautiful! Everyone in the church stood as Lisa entered the sanctuary.

Not so strangely, Mike was oblivious to who was sitting on either side of the aisle.

Lisa too was oblivious of her surroundings, except when she saw some of the hospital staff and Charlie. Charlie had positioned himself on the aisle. He really liked Lisa. He thought of her as family.

The service was short and soon over. Mike and Lisa turned to face the people in the church.

The minister said, "I would like to introduce to you, Mr. and Mrs. Michael Forester."

Everyone applauded.

Mike and Lisa walked out of the church and into the waiting Rolls Royce. The wedding party got in the limousines and the police escort started the trip to where the reception was to be held - Uncle Frank's mansion.

The reception was possibly the grandest San Francisco had seen in many years, or will see for many years to come. Both the police and the Giaventi family mingled together on a friendly basis. There was no turmoil. Even Gene Caruth and Frank Giaventi spoke of how good a match Mike and Lisa were.

The only problem was the news media. A couple of TV stations and the newspaper wanted to crash the party and ask penetrating questions about how a police officer could marry a Giaventi. It was a strange sight to see the police and the Giaventi guards at the gate banded together to keep the news media outside.

The cake was cut, Lisa threw her bouquet, and then Mike and Lisa hurriedly dressed to leave. When they were ready, Al drove Mike's car to the front of the house. Mike and Lisa got in and pulled away from the house and out the rear entrance. The police and guards had removed all the news media from the gate area and the couple sped away without anyone following them.

Gene, Louis, and Frank waved goodbye.

Gene asked, "Frank, do you know where they are going to spend tonight?"

Frank answered, "Seattle."

Louis continued, "It's a house overlooking a lake near Seattle called Sa..."

Gene added, "It's pronounced Sa mam ish."

"That's the lake," Louis said.

Frank asked Gene, "I would hope you arranged something for them to remember."

Gene said, "I went up to Seattle yesterday on business with a few friends and we sort of conditioned the house and left some appropriate signs on the front. Some of my friends who were with me even placed saran wrap on the toilet."

Louis asked, "Saran wrap on the toilet?"

"You know, if you place the wrap correctly on the bowl, you can't see it. So when the first person..."

Louis smiled. "You call us bad. The police are heathens."

All three men laughed.

Frank interrupted, "I forgot to ask this, but did you find the bottle of wine in the refrigerator when you decorated the house? It cost over a thousand dollars. I bought it a couple of years ago with four other bottles."

"Yes and we didn't even sample it!"

Louis added, "How could two intelligent people think they could hide where they were going to spend their first night together when it involved the police and the Giaventi Family."

The three men laughed like old buddies as they walked back to the party.

Mike and Lisa arrived at San Francisco International Airport in time to catch their flight to Seattle. They would spend their first night together in the house they had rented overlooking Sammamish Lake.

As Mike and Lisa drove up to the house, Mike said, "Honey, look at the door!"

"How could they...?"

"...know where we would be staying the first night?" he said, completing her thought.

"We were so careful."

"I know, but we were dealing with some unscrupulous people - your uncle and the department."

They kissed as they entered the house. There were roses everywhere. Lisa saw a note. It read, "Look in the refrigerator."

Lisa opened the refrigerator and saw the wine.

She exclaimed, "Mike, look what Uncle Frank gave us. It's his hundred-year-old wine. Open it while I go to the bathroom."

Mike was opening the wine when he thought of something. He yelled, "Lisa, don't sit on the toilet!"

Lisa looked up at him as he came into the bathroom. She had been brushing her teeth.

"What are you saying about the toilet?"

106

Mike was relieved. He said, "Lisa, put your hand through the toilet seat towards the water."

"What?"

"Just do it."

Trusting him, she moved her hand towards the water, and then exclaimed, "What's there? I can't...it's plastic wrap!"

"Tom is as good with the plastic wrap as anyone," Mike said. "They think that's funny."

Lisa answered, "I think it's funny, too...except if I was the one who got caught."

Laughing, they hugged each other and the night began.

This was a night of love - a night of ecstasy for both of them to remember.

It was just like any other Monday except this was Lisa's first day back to work since she and Mike had been married. She was still floating on air as she looked over the charts of her patients. She came to Charlie's record and noticed that his birth certificate and social security card were now in his record. She also noted Dr. Wells planned to discharge him on Wednesday.

Lisa walked down the hall to see Charlie. She found him sitting in a chair, looking out the window, thinking about only he knew what.

As soon as he saw her, he jumped to his feet. "Lisa, you're back!"

They embraced, then Lisa said, "It's good to be back. I also have a secret to tell you. I haven't even told Mike yet."

"You shouldn't keep any secrets from your husband - now that I have said that, what is it?"

"Well, either I'm late or...I think I'm pregnant."

"That's great. When is it due?"

"Charlie! About nine months from now, I guess."

"That's wonderful. I wish I could be here when the baby is born, but I don't know where I'll be."

"I understand, but we can keep in touch. Oh, I almost forgot - Uncle Frank said he would pick you up whenever you are discharged and give you a ride anywhere in San Francisco. He also said you could have one of his cars for a few days. I guess he thinks you deserve it because you agreed with him about Mike and me and business."

"I guess so. Would you mind telling your uncle that I'll leave the hospital about nine in the morning on Wednesday. I could use a ride to the Chrysler dealership. I bought a Chrysler last Saturday and they'll have it ready Wednesday. I'm going to drive to Seattle, then to Spokane. I hear it's beautiful up there. I don't know where I'll go after that, but I'll keep in touch."

Uncle Frank's green Cadillac was waiting for Charlie when he walked out of the hospital.

Frank Giaventi opened the door for Charlie. "Welcome to the real world, Charlie. Where can I take you?"

Charlie gave him the name and address of the dealership as he settled into the seat beside him. Frank signaled the driver and the Cadillac moved out onto the street.

"Lisa tells me you are going to Spokane and that you don't know where you're going after that."

"That's right."

"If you're in need of a job, I can use a person with your talents in my organization. You'd be well paid."

Charlie replied after taking a deep breath, "Are you offering me a job as the Giaventi hit man?"

Frank answered, "You are very direct. We prefer to call it 'enforcement'. But to answer your question, Mr. C. C. Duncan, yes. I rarely answer such questions directly, but somehow I think the direct approach is probably best with you."

All conversation stopped until the Chrysler dealership was reached. Charlie got out of the car.

Charlie said, "Thanks for the ride and the offer."

"If you wish the job, please get in touch with me, but not through Lisa."

"I understand."

Charlie began thinking - the CIA isn't any better than the

Giaventi family. They both hire killers - people call the Giaventi killers hit men and the CIA killers good guys who have a dirty job to do - killing the bad guys. But, killing is killing.

CHAPTER 7

Charlie, now C. C. Duncan, began his drive to Seattle as he entered Interstate 5. The next day as he was passing through Portland, he noticed on the map he would cross the Columbia River. Traveling towards Portland, he had seen a rather large snow covered mountain in the distance towards the east. At one stop he learned the mountain's name was Mount Hood. He would like to see that so he turned east on the interstate that went along the Columbia River.

As he traveled along the Columbia River, he took an exit to the south, which took him off the main highway and onto a scenic route south paralleling the main highway along the Columbia River. Soon he returned to the main highway. There were many points of interest including several waterfalls, some of which were tiered. One waterfall had two falls with each waterfall dropping maybe 200 feet or at least that's what he estimated. He was awestruck by the beauty of the area.

At the community of Hood River, he turned south towards Mount Hood. The Chrysler began to climb almost immediately after leaving the small town. The road went through a forest with many creeks along the road. Soon, he turned west and almost immediately saw the entrance to Mount Hood. He turned north and after a few miles began to see snow on the side of the road. Soon he saw the lodge at the foot of MT Hood. He thought he would stay the night there.

The next two days were beautiful. Clear blue sky and not a cloud anywhere. While there, he learned the lodge was open all year for snow skiing. He thought that was unique. He drove around the area and discovered a small lake about fifteen miles from the lodge. He would remember this lake because Mt. Hood was reflected in the calm waters of the lake.

The same day he left MT Hood, he arrived in Seattle where he stayed for several days, noting the concrete floating bridges, visiting the underground city, and seeing the Boeing museum. Getting a little bored and having seen most of the Seattle area, including Mt Rainier, he got on Interstate 90 and drove east towards Spokane. Time passed quickly on the interstate. After he passed the exit to the Spokane Airport, he found himself almost immediately in the heart of Spokane. Since he had not eaten since Seattle, he stopped at a cafe for dinner.

"This seems like a nice area," he told the waitress. "You have some industry and even an air force base. How are the schools?"

The waitress replied, "Spokane's really nice. You can find a job here pretty easy, and it's close to Idaho. Now that's really God's Country."

"Is that where you come from?"

"Yes. I grew up in Sand Point and Coeur d'Alene. Coeur d'Alene is only twenty-five or so miles east of here on the interstate. It has some beautiful lakes. But, if you want a much quieter town, try Sand Point. That's about fifty miles north on Highway 95."

C. C. thought this sounds like what I'm looking for, then he thought, I'll stay here for the night and go to Coeur D'Alene and Sand Point tomorrow. After ending his thought, he said and then asked, "I think I'll stay here in Spokane tonight. Can you recommend a motel?"

"There are some nice ones on the east side of town."

"A thought, can you get into Canada from Sand Point?"

"Sure, Canada is about seventy-five miles north of Sand Point on 95."

Charlie finished his meal, and then checked into a motel on the eastern edge of Spokane. He wasn't sure why, but he found himself interested in Sand Point.

The next morning, he drove east on the interstate and was in

112

Coeur d'Alene within thirty-five minutes. He cruised around the town to see what was there, then found U.S. Highway 95 and went north towards Sand Point where he ate lunch.

He was thinking the food wasn't as good as in New Orleans, but it was good. I think I'll look around and see if I can buy some property here. Maybe I'll settle down here. With those thoughts, C. C. looked for a real estate agency, found one by looking in the phone book, and then went to the real estate office.

At the Sand Point Real Estate office, a rather big man was seated behind a desk reading the morning Spokane newspaper. When C. C. entered the office, the man put the paper down.

"What can I do for you, friend?"

"My name is C. C. Duncan and I'd like to know if you have any property for sale in this area that I might be interested in. I'm looking for a nice, rustic house or log cabin near water and in the woods, but not too far in the woods, if you understand what I mean."

"I think I do. I just listed one this morning that matches what you want to a tee. Incidentally, my name is Terry Bracken. Everybody calls me Terry. What do people call you?"

"C. C., Charlie, or just Duncan. What's the asking price of this property?"

"$350,000.00, but I think you can get it for a lot less. The bank is almost ready to foreclose on it."

"Interesting. Can I see the place now?"

"Sure can. Let me call and tell Hank we're coming. Hank and Martha named the place 'Our Hideaway'."

C. C. and Terry got in Terry's jeep and drove for ten or eleven miles on a well-maintained black top highway, then turned off the highway onto a good gravel logging road. Just to the right of the road was a freshly painted white house with a red trim, a red barn, and a For Sale sign. The red barn could be seen behind the house nestled in some trees by the foot of a mountain next to a small river.

C. C. asked, "Is that the place?"

"No. This man died and his widow moved to Coeur d'Alene."

"What do they want for that place?"

"$65,000.00 and I don't think they'll settle for less. The widow

113

and the children believe they can sell it without any help. None of the real estate agents in Sand Point think so, though." He grinned. "I have a lot of other properties listed which are better buys than that one."

Terry continued on the logging road for a quarter mile, crossed an old bridge that needed a great deal of repair, turned left onto another well maintained gravel road, then rounded several bends in the road. Soon the road went straight for a short distance, and then started to climb up the side of a mountain.

Terry stopped the car just before the road started to climb up the side of the mountain and pointed to his left. "That's Hank's place on the southern end of the lake. The lake's shallow - about fifteen feet at the deepest or so I'm told. There are several creeks that empty into it. The main creek enters the lake from the north. It's beautiful, isn't it?"

"Sure is."

"There's Hank. Let's go and meet him."

Hank was waiting for them by the boat launch - a strong looking man, probably in his late fifties or early sixties. C. C. thought he would weigh in about 190 to 200 and noticed he stood erect and ramrod straight. C. C. continued to think he must be about six feet tall and didn't look like he had an ounce of fat on him.

Terry called to Hank as they walked towards him. "Henry Teller. This is Mr. C. C. Duncan. He's the guy I called about. He'd like to see your place. He might be interested in buying it."

Hank had a frown on his face and was obviously ill at ease.

After he had seen most of the property, Charlie said, "Terry, I'd like to talk with Hank alone - okay?"

Terry was obviously reluctant to do this, but Hank said, "Terry, have a seat in the house while we talk."

Hank and Charlie walked a short distance along the lake, not saying anything. Then Charlie pointed to a small cross on a little knoll overlooking the lake. "Who's buried there?"

"My wife, Martha. She died last year."

"Are you comfortable selling off the land where she's buried?"

Hank looked very uncomfortable. Finally he said, "Believe me, I wouldn't do it if I didn't have to. I sort of thought I'd be buried next to her some day."

"I was told the bank was foreclosing on you. How much do you owe?"

A look of suspicion followed by a severe expression of annoyance passed across Hank's face. He thought this SOB city slicker was trying to weasel down the price. But he answered anyway, "About $100,000.00."

Both men were quiet as they walked towards Martha's grave. C was thinking that he would need someone to help him with upkeep on the property. Hank looks like a good man and money wasn't a problem.

"Hank, I'm going to make you an offer I hope you won't turn down. I'll pay you $300,000.00 for your place with an agreement that you can be buried with your wife. And if I can buy the place up the road, you can live in the house for as long as you want, rent free. You know the one with the red barn.

"The only catch is you'll have to agree to stay close and more or less be my guide around here. Also, you'll have to keep the place up at no salary, but with me paying for all supplies needed. If you agree, let's go to the bank now."

Hank was very pleasantly surprised and not a man to delay making a decision, he replied, "C. C., you've just bought yourself a beautiful piece of property."

All three men went into town to the bank where C. C. met the bank president, Paul Croket.

"Hank and I have agreed to terms on buying his place," he told him. "I'd like to complete the sale as soon as possible. Can you recommend an attorney to handle it?"

Paul Croket looked surprised, glanced at Terry, then said, "You can use the bank's attorney, Sean Fuller. I'll make all the arrangements. I'll call him to set up a time."

Paul left the room and went to a phone on a secretary's desk. The three men could see Mr. Croket through the glass window as he picked up the phone and had an animated conversation. Finally, he returned to his office.

"People, Sean said he will set up the act of sale for December

20th. Is that all right with you two?"

C. C. looked at Hank, who even though he said, "Fine with me." noted Hank was visibly disturbed. C. C. nodded his agreement also.

"Then it's all settled. Be here at 10:00 AM December 20th."

"It's nice meeting you, C. C. You will have a certified check with you for the act of sale?"

C. C. replied, "Sure will."

Once they were outside together and alone, C. C. looked Hank straight in the eye. "You and I have been set up," he said. "I think that banker wants your place and he intends to get it for the mortgage."

Hank replied, "You saw it too. Paul didn't phone anyone. None of the lights lit up on his phone when he was using the one outside his office. What do you suggest?"

"Let's go to Coeur d'Alene and see an attorney there. Also, do you know the people who own the property with the red barn?"

"Sure do. Widow Mae was a friend of Martha's. She and her two boys moved last week to Coeur d'Alene. Let's get going and see what we can do."

Hank and C. C. arrived in Coeur d'Alene at twenty minutes past three. They entered the office of an attorney whose sign read "Specializing in Property Sales."

C. C. explained their problem, then asked, "How soon can you hold the act of sale?"

"One day after I find out you have enough money to pay for the properties. Of course, there will be an extra charge for processing the act of sale that quickly."

C. C. replied, "That's fine. Please call the Bank of America in San Francisco. If they need some ID, put me on the phone and I will give them all they need."

The next day at three in the afternoon, both properties were sold to C. C. Duncan. C. C. asked the attorney to contact Paul Croket to clear the mortgage and take care of Terry's real estate commission.

Hank and C. C. returned to Hank's place. In a mood that was anything but unhappy, Hank began to show C. C. around the property on foot and by jeep. He began by showing C. C. an old

116

mine shaft that had two entrances - one just behind the house in the tool shed and another entrance that looked like and doubled as a small bridge over the gravel logging road that led to the camp.

Two days later, Paul and Terry came to see Hank and C. C. They were angry and showed it.

Paul said, "Hank, what you did wasn't legal. The bank started foreclosure proceedings on this property three days ago and you can't sell the property while it's being foreclosed. So you and Mr. Duncan can get off the bank's property right now."

C. C. responded, "Mr. Croket, you know better. Mr. Teller can sell this property any time he wishes as long as the bank is paid the amount of the mortgage. Would you prefer I call the law or do you want to leave my property now?"

Paul Croket and Terry Bracken looked at C. C. for the first time in a realistic manner. They immediately came to the conclusion that he was not a man who could be pushed around. They left.

Their visit left C. C. in a thoughtful mood. These fine, upstanding citizens weren't anything but crooks. Because they couldn't be trusted, they were worse than the Giaventis. If these two jerks were fine, good, and upstanding citizens, then what would be wrong with being a hit man - an independent hit man? C. C. wondered. Why not? He began to wonder if that guy in Switzerland would be interested in getting him some work. What was his name...Kozar?

CHAPTER 8

Five years later---

It was like any other morning for a couple with children. Mike and Lisa were out of bed by 5:30 AM. Mike went to the master bathroom while Lisa used the spare one. After they finished, Mike went to wake up their four year old, Angela while Lisa dressed the twins, Mike and Al. The twins were not quite three. Mike left for his office at police headquarters in his police cruiser at 7:30 while Lisa followed him out fifteen minutes later in their Ford Van.

She dropped Angela off at pre-school kindergarten slightly before 8:00, then went to the hospital, and placed the twins in the day-care nursery where they would stay until she got off work at noon. She would pick up Angela from kindergarten on the way home. She only worked part time at the hospital, which made it possible for her to do the things she needed to do for her family.

Mike walked into his office expecting to see Gene, and when he did not see him there, he asked Tom where he was.

"He's with the commissioner. He called and wanted Gene ASAP."

"I wonder what's up. Doesn't matter right now. What's new with the wire taps?"

"I haven't gotten to all of them, but we recorded a funny conversation from the Giaventis. Someone, by his voice I think it

119

was Frank himself, called some number - let me find it - here it is 555-0187.

"Tom, for now, just tell me what was said."

"Well, a recorded message answered in English, then was repeated in other languages - French and Hebrew, I think. It said, and I quote, "If I can help you with a problem, please leave a message after the tone. You will have thirty seconds for your message." The caller said, "I have a problem, call me. This is Frank in San Francisco.""

"That's all?"

"Yeah, that's all, but you'll never guess whose telephone number it is."

"Okay, I give up, whose number is it?"

"The telephone booth right outside St. Mary's Hospital."

"Strange. Someone must have tapped the phone line, and then set up a recording machine with that message. Check it out."

"Right."

As Gene was walking through the door, he called to Mike, "I want to see you and Tom in my office – now!"

Mike and Tom looked at each other as if to say we haven't done anything lately – have we?

"I guess we'll find out what the chief heard in his meeting," Tom said.

"I guess we will."

Gene held the door open as both men entered his office, closing it after them.

"Mike, the commissioner received a telephone call from your brother. Al wanted to set up a meeting with you and Tom for about two weeks from now. He wants you two to give some big shot from Europe a briefing on organized crime in San Francisco. Al said this big shot specifically requested you two by name. What's going on, guys? Should I know something?"

Tom looked at Mike and Mike looked at Tom. They both shrugged their shoulders.

Finally, Mike said, "This is the first I've heard of this. Did Al say I could call him?"

"He said you would call him, but all he could tell you was the name of this guy because he doesn't know any more than what he told me. His name is Pierre Richard. Incidentally, he pronounces it like Re Chard. He's French and from Interpol."

"Mike, I wonder if it is t-h-e Pierre Richard - you know the one who gave the talk last year at the police convention about the new electronic equipment and how Interpol works."

"I think it is. Now, today is Tuesday. Two weeks from today is when I said you would be ready to give the briefing. Make it good, with slides and everything. Have the latest on your wire taps ready to share with him. Don't leave out anything. Pull out all the stops. Everything else put on temporary hold unless it's extremely urgent. Any questions?"

"I don't have any," Mike responded. "Do you, Tom?"

"No, I can't think of any right now. But Mike, please call Al just to satisfy both our curiosities."

"As soon as we leave this room."

"Good, then we understand the importance of this meeting. Oh, I forgot something. You two, and Al and Pierre, are the only people allowed in the briefing. Strange, isn't it?"

In Chinatown, a meeting of the heads of the Tong was about to take place in Lee Chen's house. Lou Chan walked into Lee Chen's office and Lee Chen motioned for the other people there to leave. Two out of the three people departed immediately, but Deng remained. Lou bowed to Lee Chen and sat down.

"Lee, Michael Forester is getting too close to our drug suppliers. We must silence him. I suggest we send Deng to take care of him."

Lee looked straight at Lou Chan. "That would be unwise from two aspects. First, he is the husband of Frank Giaventi's favorite niece and second, he is extremely well liked by the SFPD. If we kill him, we would have both the police and the Giaventi family looking for us. I believe it would be wiser if we did as before - establish another supply route."

"The Giaventis will not intercede and to hell with them if they do. We can take care of them as well as the police."

121

"Lou Chan, the answer is no. Do not order the assassination of Michael Forester."

Lou Chan rose and bowed his head, but his mind was far from changed. He had the telephone number of that special hit man. He would hire him to take care of Mike no matter what it cost and then, Lee Chen.

Almost two weeks had passed since Mike and Tom had been given instructions to brief Pierre Richard as they waited for the DC-10 to dock at the terminal. The passengers from the Delta flight from New York began coming down the jet way towards the concourse where Tom and Mike were waiting. Al and Pierre were not in the first group of people who deplaned, but were among the first to reach the concourse in the second group.

Mike waved to Al when he saw him.

Tom nudged Mike. "It is t-h-e Pierre Richard with Al. This must be big."

Mike nodded in agreement. He shook Al's hand and then embraced him.

Al said, "Mike, Tom, I'd like to introduce Pierre Richard of Interpol. He's the reason for the briefing."

The three men shook hands. They started down the concourse towards the baggage claim area, with Tom escorting Pierre while Al and Mike followed a short distance behind them.

After walking a short distance, Pierre spoke to Tom as he smiled, "Tom, you are a good team man. I would think you and Mike have been partners a long time."

"Sure have - over seven years. Why did you ask?"

"You skillfully led me away from Mike and Al so Mike could, what you say, pump Al concerning what he knows about my visit here. Am I correct?"

Tom sighed, "I didn't think it was that noticeable."

"It wasn't, but added to several other things I observed, that conclusion seemed likely. Mike will learn nothing from Al because he doesn't know anything. He may guess what it concerns because of my position in Interpol, but he would never guess what the full reasons are."

Meanwhile Mike asked, "Okay, brother, what's up?"

"Mike, I don't know anything except that Pierre is the head of Interpol's section on Assassinations and Terrorism. He became interested in San Francisco about six months ago. That's all I know, honest."

"Damn, I wonder what he thinks we have here - another Carlos or something."

"They've been trying to get Carlos for over ten years now. Pierre says they are close, but have to wait until the proper moment."

By this time, the four men were riding in Mike's car towards the downtown area.

Al said, "Mike, I'm supposed to show Pierre the local FBI office. Let us off there and I'll take him to the Hilton. Incidentally, that's where I'll be staying, too."

After Mike dropped off Al and Pierre, he and Tom returned to their office to get everything ready for the briefing the next day. Also, they would get the latest on the phone taps.

One of the officers who listened to the tapes from the phone taps called to them as they arrived. "Mike, Tom - come over here and listen to this crazy call."

"Is this the one with the answering machine message in different languages?"

The man nodded as he rewound the tape. "This just came in." He started the tape.

"Please call me - 555-0155. Ask for" and then a gong sounded.

"Where'd it come from?"

"It was made from Lou Chan's restaurant. That's his dinner gong we heard."

The officer continued, "And you will never guess where the call went."

Both Tom and Mike replied at the same time, "A telephone booth outside of St. Mary's Hospital."

"How'd you guys know that?"

"Tom, after the briefing, that will be job one - finding out about that telephone."

"I agree."

"Now, are we ready for the briefing tomorrow?"

"I think everything is in order - slides, projector, and blackboard. I guess we can go home now and wait for the big day - tomorrow."

"See you then, Tom."

Pierre and Al walked into the briefing room at 8:57 AM. Mike and Tom were already there, waiting for them. The men greeted each other as Tom closed the door. A uniformed police officer was stationed outside the door to insure no one would interrupt the briefing.

"Before I begin the briefing," Mike said, "I want to ask Pierre a question. Why only Tom, Al, and me?"

"Interpol has investigated the three of you and found you to be competent and honest police officers. You also know organized crime in San Francisco better than anyone else does and we need to know more about those organizations.

"We even know about your wife being the favorite niece to Frank Giaventi. We know a lot. But Mike, we have heard several stories about how Lisa came to live with her uncle. Some of these stories are, what you could say, wild? Would you mind telling me the complete story as to what really happened, if you know it?"

Mike looked surprised, but said, "I don't mind. It will take up a little time though."

Pierre responded, "Please, I'm interested."

"Lisa's father's name was Carlos and he was a policeman. He left San Francisco because he didn't want any conflict with his brother Frank. Frank had just made it to be the "godfather", if you understand what I mean."

"Yes, I understand."

"Carlos was the police chief of a small California town a few miles south of the Oregon border where nothing much happens. Then one day, two young punks who some say were high on drugs came to town and deliberately ran over Carlos several times with their car, laughing all the time they were doing it.

"As it turned out, someone in the street jumped the driver and tried to pull him out of the car, but was unsuccessful. The car sped out of town. However, two people recognized them as being from another town close by and gave the police their names.

"Frank heard about the incident and went immediately to his brother's side. Carlos lived about eight hours after the incident. When Frank saw his brother, legend has it Carlos said, 'Get the bastards' and Frank replied, 'Before I do another thing.' Frank left the hospital and went to his car.

"His organization had already found the punks near a small lake about thirty miles away. Frank arrived there just before dark. He had his men block the entrance to the lake and not to let anyone in the campground where the punks were. He walked in. He had his .357 drawn and cocked. He saw a car parked ahead and heard some loud laughter. He walked around the car and was literally shocked at what he saw.

"There was a girl they had kidnapped. She was about fifteen or sixteen and they had her staked out or a better description would be tied to the ground, stripped naked. She was crying her heart out and those two slobs were laughing and drinking only a few feet away. They were pulling their pants up when one of them said, "Let's switch next time" or something like that.

Frank stepped between the girl and the two men without either of them noticing Frank. The girl looked at Frank. Frank thought she wanted to scream, so he placed his finger to his mouth and mouthed be quiet.

"She kept quiet and forced a smile. In another instant, the two men turned around and saw Frank with his gun raised and cocked. He fired and the head of one of the men disappeared. I guess the other guy was too scared to move or something. He just stood still. Frank cocked his gun again and eliminated his face, too.

"He turned to the girl and cut her loose, wiped some of the blood and tears from her face, gave her a drink of water, and generally showed compassion for her. He told her to keep the blanket around her and he would send the police.

"Within an hour, the police were at the scene. The girl

happened to be the daughter of a sergeant in the California Highway Patrol. He took over the care of his daughter. At Carlos' funeral, this sergeant and his wife walked up to Frank and said, "Thanks," knowing full well who Frank was, but also knowing what he had done. Within a year, the sergeant and his family moved to somewhere in Canada, I believe.

"Frank offered his home to Lisa, her mother, and Carlos' family. About three or four months later, they moved in with him. That's the way I heard the story."

Pierre replied, "That's about what we were told, with some slight changes. By the way, the girl is now in her late thirties or early forties and is married to a RCMP sergeant. Her father is RCMP and stationed in Edmonton. He is head of that office.

"You see we investigated your situation in depth and we know you told your chief about Lisa. You also have in your possession several letters from the police leadership that state they wanted you to head the organized crime division in spite of the fact you were going to marry Lisa. Now, let's get on with the briefing."

As he looked at Mike, Tom quietly remarked, "And I thought we were good at getting information."

Mike nodded his head in agreement.

He began the briefing, "There are three gangs or families in the bay area. They are the Giaventi family, the Red Dragon Tong, and - for want of a better name - the Black/Latino gang. The Giaventi family and the Red Dragon Tong each have one leader and a second in command. After that, there is no leadership to speak of. The Black/Latino gang really has only one leader, who does not have anywhere near the control that his counterparts have, and there is no leadership structure beneath him.

"I will start the briefing with the Giaventi family. As you can see on the screen, the leadership is vested in Frank Giaventi. His second in command and heir apparent is Louis Giaventi, his nephew. Frank is 63 and Louis is 46. Frank has a loyal following in the family and has two very loyal individuals who, I guess, can be called his enforcers. Their names are Donna Weir and Jack Hall.

"The family business is gambling, drugs, prostitution, just what you would expect from an organized crime family. At this time, we know that Louis went to Vancouver, B.C., to talk with one Cleve Ronson, who is the leader of a Vancouver gang. We don't know much about him or his gang except they are not nearly as well organized as the Giaventi family or the Red Dragon Tong. His position is not as solid as those here in the bay area.

"Donna and Jack double as Frank's bodyguards. They also insure that no one attempts to take over Frank's job. They are very good at what they do. Jack Hall is good with a gun and is absolutely loyal. He does have a fault and that is he tries to skim money off everybody, including Frank. Frank knows this, but does nothing as long as he doesn't take too much, because he values his loyalty and the fact he can count on him when the chips are down.

"Jack dated Donna for a while, and eventually she moved in with him. She is better than Jack in all respects - self-defense, guns, etc. From experience, she has the ability to hide a 9 mm Luger in a tight fitting pair of trousers where you could see the outline of her panties, but not see the outline of the gun. She can draw the gun and fire it accurately faster than anyone I have ever seen - even in the movies."

Pierre remarked, "Could it be you did not see the gun because you were observing her feminine lines?"

"I thought of that the first time, but I have seen her on other occasions and it was extremely hard to spot her gun. Tom can vouch for that."

"I can, but I have to admit, I was looking at what you call her "feminine lines" and I could have been distracted."

"To continue, she is very loyal to Frank also. Why the fierce loyalty of these two, I don't really know. The remainder of the family is loyal only to a point. They would desert him if the price were right. Jack and Donna insure that they stay loyal.

"A little bit about Jack. He now plays around with other women, I guess because he and Donna had a falling out. She moved out of his apartment; however, she does stay overnight occasionally. He has very few interests outside of his job, which seems to be the only really important thing in his life.

"Donna, on the other hand and although she is not Jewish, goes to the Jewish Center and helps out with the disadvantaged children. She attends a little Christian church on the bay side of town. Donna helping out in the Jewish Center and going to church does not fit with her job, but that's what she does - strange. We feel she has killed about twenty to twenty-five people for the family, but we have no evidence to support this. She still has a gun permit."

Pierre interrupted, "Does she ever leave San Francisco for long periods of time - say five or six weeks?"

"No, not unless she is going with Frank or for a short time on a job. Now, a little about Louis. He is also very loyal and would never attempt to take control of the family. He is also very smart, and when Frank retires or dies, the family won't lose a step in their business.

"Do you have any questions about the Giaventi family?"

"I have one question. Does the family have an assassin on its, what you say, payroll, other than Jack and Donna?"

"Any member of the family would kill if ordered to do so, but as a regular job, no. They do not have any paid assassins on their payroll."

Pierre frowned. "Continue."

"I forgot to mention that none of the other two gangs will pick a fight with the Giaventi family. They are plainly just too strong.

"Now, for the Red Dragon Tong. The leader is a Chinese named Lee Chen and the number two man is Lou Chan. Like the Giaventi Family, these are the only two leaders. Unlike the Giaventi Family, the number two man is not that loyal to the number one man. There is little loyalty in the Red Dragon Tong. Lou Chan would try to oust Lee Chen except for the fact Lee Chen has some kind of hold over the enforcer squad and has another enforcer squad standing in the wings. However, the main enforcer squad would desert Lee Chen if the price were right.

"The enforcer squad is led by a man named Deng. While in the Giaventi family either Jack or Donna would, and probably do, go out on business alone, the enforcer squad only goes out as a group or team. There are five members in this squad.

"Lee Chen is very smart and also very adept at keeping his job. Just like Frank, he will only order a hit when no other means will work. The Tong's business is the same as the Giaventi family. The difference is the Tong does business principally in Chinatown and the Giaventi family does business in the middle to upper class neighborhoods.

"The big difference in the leadership is Lou Chan. He is out for himself and himself alone. He has tried to undermine Lee Chen's authority in the past, but has very little to show for his efforts. We think Lee Chen tolerates him because he is also very smart and helps him do certain things with drugs and prostitution. Lou Chan owns a restaurant that serves as a meeting place for the Tong.

"The head of the enforcer squad, Deng, has a problem. He likes women and he does not hide that fact."

Pierre smiled. "My friend, then I, too, have this problem. I like women too."

Everyone in the room laughed.

When the room quieted down, Mike continued, "I don't think you like them the way Deng does. If he is to kill a woman, he first has sex with her in as many different ways as he wants or wishes. Then he kills her. The hit squad is very good and to our knowledge has never missed the person they were sent to kill.

"That's about all on the Tong. Do you have any questions?"

"Do they have a special assassin on their payroll?"

"No."

"Then continue."

"Now the Black/Latino gang. As the name implies, most of the gang members are either blacks or latins, but they have members from all races. This gang has virtually no organization. It is composed of several street gangs with their own territory, which is basically the lower income areas. The so-called leader is one Mario Rodriguez. He really does not control the gang the way Frank or Lee Chen do, but he does have some control. It comes from one man, Maxwell Crown, known as Mad Max.

"Mad Max is just that - he is crazy, but he is extremely loyal to Mario. We guess the reason for this loyalty is that Mario furnishes him with anything he wants, from drugs to women. Max has the reputation of killing just for the enjoyment of it. He likes to torture people - and I don't mean small-time stuff, either - and likes to watch them die slowly. He sometimes cripples his victim for life and lets them live. In short, no one except Mario would mourn his death.

"Mad Max also has another bad trait. He likes to go off on his own and kill people. Mario keeps him on a tight leash, but sometimes he gets loose. We are trying to catch him when he is out on his own and put him out of circulation."

Pierre interrupted, "You know all these things about these killers, and you have not arrested them. Why?"

"Our legal system has made it extremely difficult to obtain a conviction on these people. No one will come forward and testify against them and they don't leave very much in the way of incriminating evidence - in short, no witnesses. Our information is always second hand and wouldn't hold up in court.

"To give you an example of what we're up against, we arrested one drug dealer two years ago, got a conviction. About a year later, a higher court ruled we obtained our evidence illegally. He returned to selling drugs again, but we have finally arrested him again. We hope to do better this time. I hope that explains our situation."

"I have heard of your situation here in America, but I do not understand how or why you put up with such things from your courts. But please continue."

"If Max were to die or become incapacitated in some way, Mario would lose all control. That might be real bad. We could have a big gang war between the rival groups in the Black/Latino gang.

"That's about all I have on the Black/Latinos. Do you have any questions? And before you ask if they have one paid assassin, the answer is no."

"Thank you for such a comprehensive briefing."

Mike now asked, "Pierre, I think we have a right to know why you wanted this briefing and why the question about a paid assassin. Would you please tell us why?"

Pierre rose from his chair and looked first at Al, then at Tom, and finally at Mike.

"Gentlemen, I planned to tell you the answer to your question so we - the San Francisco Police Department, the FBI, and Interpol - could work together and catch this assassin.

"To begin, Interpol has been watching a gun dealer in Geneva. He is reportedly used by many governments for secret operations. He does not go by his real name any more, but by the name Kozar. What he does skirts the hem of legality and we want to put him in jail, but we cannot use what we can prove because of political reasons."

Mike interrupted, "Same as over here, huh?"

"A little different. Our hands are tied in a different manner than yours. But to continue, about four, maybe five years ago, we noticed a change in his activities. He became a broker for assassins. He collected the money for the assassinations and paid the assassins for their work.

"At first, there were only three that he dealt with, Carlos, Miguel, and another named Klaus. These three are very good at what they do.

"Carlos is a terrorist. You must know of him. He does not hesitate to blow up people for no reason except to create terror and political gain for organizations such as the Irish Republican Army, the IRA. He uses explosives mostly, but has also employed automatic weapons, rifles, or pistols. He has an organization behind him and he uses it very skillfully.

"Klaus is more precise in what he does. While competent in the use of explosives also, he prefers automatic weapons for the most part. He has a smaller organization, but uses it skillfully also.

"Miguel is more of what you say, a loner, with a minimal organization. He is a very good marksman and almost always prefers a rifle. He is probably the most skillful of the three.

"However, about four to five years ago, we discovered that Kozar was working with a fourth assassin. For want of a better name, we called this person 'Iceman'. We had no leads as to his identity until recently - about eight months ago. We know Kozar calls 555-0187 number here in San Francisco to contact the Iceman.

That is why . . . "

Tom raised his head and shot a quick look at Mike. Mike was already staring at Pierre in a strange manner.

Pierre noticed the reaction of the two men. "Do you know of such a number which an assassin uses?"

Mike replied, "Maybe. Tom, go check it and bring back the tapes."

Tom immediately left the room.

Mike suggested, "Folks, it has been a long morning. Let's take a coffee break. I sense we're going to work through lunch and maybe even supper. During the break, I'm going to order lunch. How about Chinese?"

Al looked at Mike, then Pierre, who nodded.

Al said, "That'll be fine - if the SFPD is paying for it."

"Only if the FBI picks up the dinner tab," Mike replied, grinning back at him.

All the people in the room began to laugh.

Tom returned to the room to find the three men drinking coffee and having doughnuts. He asked, "Where's mine?"

"Your coffee was getting cold," Al replied as he poured Tom a cup of coffee, "So we drank it and split your doughnuts."

Pierre added, "Police are all the same, everywhere. We take everyone's coffee."

Tom grinned, accepted the fresh cup, took a sip, and said, "Mike, the number is the same."

"So you do know the Iceman?" Pierre asked.

Mike replied, "Not really. We just learned about that number within the last month. But please continue and we might be able to connect your information with what we have, or do some 'brainstorming' on the subject."

"Well, as I said, about four years ago, Kozar began using the Iceman. Because we know very little about him except what we have been told and that he is contacted by Kozar at this number, I came here to see if you could help us. I thought he might be associated with one of the crime families and, because of your knowledge about these families, you might be able to help us.

"The Iceman is by far the best assassin of those Kozar brokers for. He is knowledgeable in explosives, drugs that kill and probably the best marksman in the world today. He is an enigma, though, and even seems to have somewhat of a conscience. Unfortunately we know very little about him."

Mike interrupted. "You said you can't arrest the assassins and Kozar because of politics. What political pressures are protecting them?"

"I will deny that I said what you are about to hear. The government of France uses Kozar and on occasion uses the assassins Kozar brokers. The CIA, KGB, all Arab governments, Israel - in short, most of the governments in the world use them. They do not want them arrested at the present time. Israel uses the Iceman more than any other government. He is their favorite assassin. Do you understand what we are up against?"

Tom replied, "Damn. Maybe we should just lock up shop and go home. It seems we are destined to lose."

Pierre responded, "We must be ready to arrest these men when the political climate changes.

"When I said we know very little about the Iceman, that is slightly incorrect. We know that when Kozar calls this number, in two to three weeks, someone of importance dies.

"Permit me to illustrate what the Iceman has done. A very rich Greek shipping owner was offshore on his yacht. He was drinking a cup of coffee. The sea was very calm. Suddenly, his head jerked back and a little hole appeared in the side of his head. The other side of his head disappeared. The shot came from shore because there were no other boats around. We estimate the distance of the shot to be 800 to 1000 meters. One shot and he was dead. Our Iceman is a good marksman. On this occasion, he used a 7 mm magnum. According to our information, he was paid two million dollars for that job.

"Another time, a duchess was sleeping with her boyfriend. We found out what I am going to tell you after some extensive investigation and from an informant. The Iceman found out that the duchess was a very brittle diabetic. He gained access to her bedroom

133

and since they were sleeping nude, he could see she took her insulin injections in her thighs. He injected enough drugs into her thigh to kill her. Along with an excess of insulin, he injected an exotic drug that is very hard to detect. Her lover did not even wake up until the Iceman was out of the room. The duchess did wake up. She looked around and finally realized what had happened. She woke her lover up, went towards the door to call for help, but dropped to the floor unconscious as she reached it. She did not recover. It was very difficult to prove murder, but our toxicologist finally managed to prove it.

"Another time, an Arab who was opposing Israel got into his car and he was killed. How we know these things, I cannot say as it would place our source in a great deal of danger and he knows nothing beyond what I have just told you.

"Now, the Iceman did a few things for reasons we do not understand. One time, Carlos planted a bomb on a Jet going to Germany from France. We believe it was the Iceman who called us and told us a bomb was on the plane. We did not believe it, so he set a smoke bomb off in the lavatory, forcing the plane to land. When we searched all the luggage, we found the bomb. It was set to go off just after the plane took off for England. Again, our source must remain confidential.

"He also turned down an assassination because the person was a family man with several children. His name is Dr. Karl Schneider who is possibly the best cosmetic surgeon in the world today. We think he even contacted the surgeon and told him about the contract and he told Kozar he would take care of anyone who killed the surgeon. So you see gentlemen, he is an enigma. We know little and nothing else about him. Now what about the telephone number."

Tom answered, "About three weeks ago, Frank Giaventi called this number, and after the recorded message Frank said 'I have a problem, call Frank' and hung up. From what you have said, this Iceman should know that it is Frank who called and will get in touch with him sometime in the future.

"That number also received a call from another number we are tapping - Lou Chan's restaurant. The message left was to call a certain number and a Chinese gong sounded. That number is Lou Chan's private phone.

"It would appear that the Iceman does not know Lou Chan, but does know Frank Giaventi. Interesting. Do you have any idea who they want killed? If you do not know, you may expect someone to be assassinated in the next few weeks."

There was a knock on the door. Mike went to open it and found an officer standing outside holding some Chinese food.

"Here's your lunch, Mike," he said. "Hope you like it."

"Thanks." Mike closed the door and began handing out the meals.

After lunch, the four men again met in the briefing room.

Mike turned toward Pierre and Al. "Tom and I have to do some brainstorming now, so unless you wish to join us, we must leave."

Pierre asked, "What is this 'brainstorming'?"

Tom replied, "That's when we don't know what to expect and have to try to guess what's going to happen."

"Ah, yes. I might be able to help you with this because I think I have a feel for the Iceman."

"Mike, I would like to sit in also."

"Tom, why don't we do it in here?"

"Fine with me."

Pierre said, "I would like to start with the Giaventi call. I would think they have a problem with someone or some people and they do not want to be connected with their deaths. It could be here in San Francisco or elsewhere, but they definitely do not want to be associated with the kill."

"Good point," Mike replied. "If they didn't care, then they would have either Jack or Donna do the hit."

Al added, "Mike, Tom - I think it is an out of town hit because I don't think Frank would hesitate about using either Jack or Donna locally, or for that matter anywhere nearby in the U.S. Such a hit locally would only build up the family in the eyes of the other gangs and its own members."

Mike looked at the other men. Both Tom and Mike said at the same time, "Vancouver."

135

Mike added, "It has to be Vancouver. Tom, get on the phone, no, get on the next plane to Vancouver and talk to the chief up there personally."

"Right. I might be able to catch a plane this afternoon. Let me check and I'll be back as soon as I know something."

Tom left the room, leaving the other three men to talk about the other phone call.

Pierre again started, "I think Lou Chan might be making his move on Lee Chen. I don't know much about the Tong, but it would seem Lou Chan does not want Lee Chen to know about the assassination."

Mike replied, "That's possible, but I think it's more probable Lee Chen ordered the hit and Lou Chan is just following orders. Al, what do you think?"

"It could be either. Since I don't know these men nor have a feel for the situation, I would have to go with it being a fifty-fifty proposition. It might even be Lou Chan is going for Lee himself."

Pierre replied, "Could be."

"Pierre, when are you going back to Paris?"

"Al, I have to be in Washington to meet with your director next Tuesday. This gives me three days."

"Good. I would like you to be here when we look into that local number."

"Mike, don't do anything to that number. It's our only link to the Iceman and we need that link until we find out who he is."

"That's fine, but we can do things such as trace the calls placed to it and see where the recorder is located. Who knows, we might get lucky. If we don't get lucky, then this is where we need more intelligence."

CHAPTER 9

The day Pierre Richard was to be briefed, Frank Giaventi called Donna and Jack into his library to talk to them. They entered the library slightly after seven in the morning. Both Donna and Jack knew Frank had withdrawn a large sum of money from the bank the day before, but did not know how the money was to be used although they suspected it might be used to pay them for a hit.

Frank was looking out the French doors as the two stood by his desk. He turned toward them.

"I've hired a man to do a job for us," he said. "I warn both of you - and especially you Jack - don't skim any money from the package you're going to deliver to him. If you do, you'll pay for your greed with your life. Trust me. I know what I am talking about. The man you'll be paying is the best assassin in the world, and I mean the best. It's not an exaggeration. I've checked his credentials with Antonio in Italy.

"I decided with Louis that it would be better if we could get him to do the job for us - if, that is, we could afford him. His price was acceptable. He specified how the money is to be delivered and when. He said to follow the instructions to the letter. If there's any deviation at all, he said the person or persons delivering the money will die.

"Here are his instructions. Go on highway US 50 towards Lake Tahoe. About 32.4 miles from Sacramento and before you reach Lake Tahoe, you'll see a motel called Sleepy Rest. It is a nice motel - in the Holiday Inn class, he said. Enter by the main entrance and park in the space for room 102 or 104. Room 102 is at the corner on the ground floor. Walk up the stairs and go in room 202. The door will be unlocked and you won't be able to lock it. Go to the bed nearest the door and place the money on the bed. He said to have the money in $10,000 bundles of $100 bills. Put them on the bed separately so they can easily be counted. Then leave the room, go down to your car, and drive away."

Donna and Jack had been listening attentively.

"Do you both understand what I have just said?"

Jack replied, "Yes sir, Mr. Giaventi."

Donna nodded. "I understand."

"You are to be at the motel between 7:00 and 8:00 PM tonight or tomorrow night. If you leave now, you can easily make it tonight. If you do, you can stay at a luxury hotel in Lake Tahoe and I'll pay the bill. Any questions?"

Both Donna and Jack replied at the same time. "No."

Frank motioned to a briefcase on the sofa.

"The money is in the briefcase and has been counted several times. If you wish to count it, you may, but you'll find it's just as I described - $500,000 in bundles of $10,000 each. Be very careful with it. If you let it get away from you somehow, I'd have to find a couple people to take over your jobs, and I don't want to do that. Remember - no skimming."

Frank fished in his pocket, brought out the keys to his Cadillac, and tossed them to Donna, who caught them with ease. Then he turned away from Donna and Jack and said no more to them.

Donna went to the briefcase, opened it. She looked inside while Jack watched over her shoulder. They both saw a lot of money. Without counting it, Donna closed the briefcase. She carried it outside with Jack following right behind her. Frank's Cadillac was parked at the curb. It had front wheel drive, which gave it better control if they ran into some snow, and were forced to drive on snow-pack. The weather report was calling for a great deal of snow at the higher elevations later that night or early the next morning.

Donna sat in the driver's seat with Jack in the passenger seat. The briefcase was on the floor at his feet. Donna started the engine, pulled out of the estate, and drove straight towards Interstate 80. They followed Interstate 80 to Sacramento.

Jack edged closer to her, put his hand on her thigh, and squeezed it a little.

"We haven't been together for a couple of weeks now. Let's spend a couple of nights at Caesar's. That's a real fancy place."

"That would be a real nice way to end this trip," she said, glancing toward him with a smile and a twinkle in her eye. "I didn't bring a night gown. I hope you didn't bring any pajamas."

"Baby, you read my mind." His hand slipped up her thigh a little higher.

"Jack, that's for tonight, not now. Understand? I don't concentrate well when I'm distracted, and right now I want to concentrate on our job - and the road."

"Anything you say, baby."

The Cadillac passed through Sacramento and turned onto US 50 headed toward Lake Tahoe. The mountains were all snow capped and the road was filled with skiers going towards the Lake Tahoe ski slopes with their skis tied to the tops of their cars. Some of the ski slopes had just opened for the winter. After that night's expected snowfall, the remaining slopes would be open for the rest of the season.

Tom Buckley was reading some notes he had made for his meeting with the Vancouver police department when the flight attendant stopped by his seat.

"We'll be landing in Vancouver shortly. Please raise your tray and keep your seat in the upright position." As she moved on to the next row of seats and said the same thing, Tom watched her walk down the aisle with appreciation of the way her uniform accentuated her body, especially her backside.

Tom glanced back at his notes. The chief of detectives was coming to his office just to meet with him tomorrow, so he wanted to have all his notes in order. He still was uncertain about a few points, and decided as he gathered them up and started to put them away that he would call San Francisco and talk to Mike, Pierre, or Al after he got to his hotel.

He looked out his window and saw several islands off to the west. Then the plane banked and he could see the snow capped mountains on the mainland. It was a beautiful sight, just as pretty as the Bay area from the air. He noted the plane was dropping fast and soon he could see the edge of the runway where they were to land. The touchdown was bumpy, but then the plane settled in for a smooth taxi to the gate.

Tom got up from his seat, went to the attendant, retrieved his val pack before he walked out of the airplane. He was surprised to see a man holding a sign at the end of the jet way saying, TOM BUCKLEY.

He walked over to him. "I'm Tom Buckley."

"I'm Brice Hawkins. The chief asked me to meet you and bring you to the office. If you're up to it, he would like to meet with you now instead of tomorrow. What he really means," he went on, breaking into a wide grin, "is that he wants to go skiing with his kids tomorrow and meeting you tomorrow will get in the way."

"I completely understand, but what I have to say may get in the way of his ski trip anyway. Let's go to the office."

At police headquarters, Brice introduced Tom to a man in his early forties who jumped up from behind a desk to shake his hand.

"I'm Chief Richard Smith. I just talked to Mike and Pierre in San Francisco about what you're here to discuss. I must say you have one good man helping you out down there. We were working on an international terrorism gang last year when I met him. He's sharp. Now what can I do for the San Francisco police?"

"Well, I think it's what we can do for you first. Then, maybe, you can do something for us. We have reason to believe that one of our crime families, the Giaventi Family, has hired a hit man to come to Vancouver to take out someone. We don't know who is the hit, but we're quite certain he's coming to Vancouver.

"We know Louis Giaventi came to Vancouver some time ago," Tom continued. "He met with one Cleve Ronson, we think to establish a supply route for drugs. We're getting close to significantly interfering with their drug supply routes into the Bay

141

area."

"We know Cleve very well," Smith said. "He can't do what you think he is going to do for the Giaventis. He just doesn't have the support of his 'family,' as you call it. There are two men who would not permit that to happen, and they're strong enough to prevent any agreement. They may even be strong enough to replace Cleve! No, he wouldn't try that without their approval."

"Even with those two dead?"

Smith paused. "I see what you mean. Is that where you believe this contractor comes in? If he kills these two men, Cleve will reciprocate and begin a supply route for the Giaventi Family?"

Brice said, "That's possible. Maybe we should have Joseph look into it."

"Who is Joseph?"

"He's an informer," replied Brice.

Tom countered, "I don't think he'll know anything about the hit - er, the contractor. This contractor is supposed to be the best and nobody knows who he is. Pierre came to Frisco to see if we could help in identifying him, but we were of almost no help. Also, if what Pierre says about him is true, then those two men should get their wills in order quickly. Pierre, or I should say Interpol, has named him - the Iceman."

"We'll look into this from our end and if this Iceman comes here, we'll identify him for Pierre and you people - in our jail. Brice will take you to your hotel and to your flight tomorrow. Thanks again for the information."

Tom smiled and thought, this guy thinks we're nuts. Well, I think the Iceman will make a believer out of him.

"We'll appreciate any help you can offer," Tom said. "I hope this information will help you. Oh, did Mike tell you that Frank Giaventi withdrew $500,000 from his bank a few days ago - in cash?"

"No, but that could be for any illegal purpose. I suggest you look into that when you return."

"They are looking, now!" replied Tom.

With those words, Brice led Tom out of the office, but before they had gone very far he said, "I forgot my keys in the chief's office. Excuse me while I go get them."

"Okay," Tom said, grinning. He hoped he hadn't been as obvious when he got Pierre away from Al and Mike at the airport as Brice was now in returning to talk to Richard.

Back inside Smith's office, Brice closed the door and looked at his boss.

Chief Smith said, "If the San Francisco Police Department thinks they're going to scare me into believing a high priced contractor is coming to Vancouver, they're stupid. There is no such man as the 'Iceman.' I wonder what old movies they have been watching."

"Chief, I talked to Tom on the way here from the airport, and he seemed to know what he was doing. What he said does make sense."

"I'll think about it on Monday. Right now I'm going skiing."

Brice went back to rejoin Tom.

Tom said, "He doesn't think the Iceman will be coming here, does he?"

Brice took a deep breath, and then answered, "He doesn't know now. He's going to think about it on Monday."

"Monday may be too late. If it were up to me, I'd place a tail on the three men - Cleve and the other two. I doubt you'll prevent the hit, but you might be able to get an idea as to what the Iceman looks like or maybe even capture him. You might be interested in what Pierre said about him. Here's a transcript."

"Thanks. I'll read it tonight and we can talk about it tomorrow on the way to the airport."

The road sign said fifty miles to Lake Tahoe.

Donna said, "It's only a little after five. Let's stop for a burger. There's a Super Burger over there."

Jack agreed, so Donna pulled over to the burger stand. They ate in the car, and then continued on their way. In a very short time they saw the Sleepy Rest Motel. It was just as Frank had described it. They drove into the motel and parked in the parking spot for room 102. It was now 7:15 PM.

143

Donna and Jack went upstairs to room 202. Donna remained outside the door while Jack entered. Seven minutes later, Jack came out of the room and they returned to the car.

Jack pulled out ten $100 bills and showed them to Donna. "We've got a little more money to spend than what Frank knows about. In that much dough, nobody would ever miss it."

"Look, damn it. That's not our money," Donna said, her eyes flashing. "Give it to me and I am going to replace it now - or no tonight."

"Baby, if that's how you feel, here it is."

Donna got out of the car and went upstairs. She thought Jack had given her the money too easily, but she had it and that was all that mattered. As she went upstairs, she noticed a cleaning woman down by the car. She thought she was a little too lean and muscular looking for a maid. Also, she just didn't look like a woman, but she continued up the stairs. The weather was turning colder, much colder. She entered the room and placed the money in another stack.

As she turned to leave, she noticed a gun case on the other bed from where the money was placed. It was a beautiful case with brass corners and very highly finished wood. She fingered it appreciatively and discovered that it was made of oak. Then she opened it and found an M-16 inside. Separate from the assault gun, a silencer for the weapon that rested nearby in the foam rubber. The case also held the imprint of a pistol and smaller silencer. They were missing.

She now realized she had been in the room for almost fifteen minutes, so she closed the case and left quickly. Donna walked down the steps and slipped in the driver's seat.

She said, "Now Jack, let's do it up right."

She turned to kiss her companion. Only then did she notice the blood oozing from the little hole in his head. He had been shot with a small caliber pistol, perhaps a 22 she thought. She then noticed a note lying in his lap.

It was hand written and read, "He was a bad boy."

Donna quickly looked around the car, thought for a minute, then started the car and quickly pulled away from the motel. She

144

drove towards Lake Tahoe, and then turned north, traveling until she came to a pull out near a cliff. No one was around. She parked the car near the edge of the cliff and looked over the edge. There was a stream at the bottom of the cliff coming from a waterfall and several small snow banks at the bottom of the cliff next to the stream. She walked back to the car, opened the door on the passenger side. Jack fell out of the car. She dragged his body over to the cliff and pushed it over the edge, watching until it landed in a small snow bank.

Donna thought, if the weather predictions come true, his body would be covered with snow until spring. Good-bye, Jack. It was nice while it lasted.

Her eyes had tears in them. She dried her eyes, then after a few minutes, returned to the car, started the engine, turned the car around, and headed back to San Francisco.

The next morning, Brice was one hour early to pick up Tom and take him to the airport. Brice entered the hotel, went to the house phone, and dialed Tom's room number. However, as he waited for the telephone to ring, he saw Tom eating breakfast in the coffee shop. He hung the phone up and walked over to Tom's table.

"Brice, have a seat and order what you want," Tom said cheerfully. SFPD is paying."

"No thanks," he said as he settled into a chair across the table from Tom, "but I finished reading what you guys in San Francisco have. I think you're right. Those two men who oppose Cleve are as good as dead if this Iceman is for real. What do you think - is he for real?"

"Brice, we've been watching Frank Giaventi's bank account for several years now and he has never - not ever - withdrawn that much money, even when the family was buying a million dollar shipment of coke. We can think of no other reason for him to withdraw that much money. Our only question is why so little because Pierre thinks the Iceman works for nothing less than a million dollars, or close thereto."

"I'm going to see if this information will change Chief Smith's ideas," Brice said, "but I am not sure it will or even if I can convince

145

him. I'd like for you to do me a favor. When you get back to San Francisco, call Chief Smith, and ask what he plans to do. When the murders occur, call him again just to see if he has any leads . . . and to dig him a little."

"The pleasure will be all mine."

Donna turned west at the intersection of US 50 and the highway on the west side of Lake Tahoe. She traveled past the Sleepy Rest Motel and on to Sacramento.

She was thinking, that son of a bitch. If I ever meet that bastard, I'll kill him for killing Jack.

A few miles closer to Sacramento, she thought, it was really Jack's fault, but he got his money back. He didn't have to kill him.

The highway at Sacramento was almost deserted at this time of the morning. She drove around the bypass, then turned west on Interstate 80 and headed for San Francisco.

She continued to think. I guess if it were me, I'd have done the same thing. But he had all of his money. I wonder if Jack gave me all the money he skimmed.

Dawn was breaking behind her and the sun was reflecting in her rear view mirror. She adjusted it so it did not blind her. She still had a few tears in her eyes.

When she reached San Francisco, Donna drove up to the gate at Frank Giaventi's mansion. The guard called the house to announce her, then the gate swung open and he waved her through.

Frank Giaventi was dressed to play his Saturday golf game with Louis. He was at the door waiting for Donna when she drove up to the house. He walked around to the driver's door and opened it for her. She got out of the car and fell into his arms. They hugged each other.

She said, "The son of a bitch killed Jack."

Frank replied, "I know. Now come into the house and drink some hot cocoa."

They walked inside, holding each other's hands.

Frank Giaventi fixed Donna the hot cocoa. She sat on the sofa; head bowed and held the cup in both her hands for a long time before remembering to sip some of it.

"Donna, I found out yesterday that Interpol has a name for this hit man. They call him Iceman. They must have gotten the name from a B movie."

Donna was staring down into her cup of hot cocoa.

"He called me last night," Frank said. "He told me what happened and what you did. He said he watched you push Jack over the cliff. He was impressed by what he saw."

"You mean that bastard called you to tell you what happened?"

"That's right. He also apologized for what happened to Jack, but he had no choice. He said Jack had taken almost three thousand dollars and he gave you only one thousand to return. He couldn't let that pass."

"I wondered why Jack gave in so easily. That jerk knew I would return the money, so he told me he had only taken one thousand."

"What happened to Jack is tragic, but remember what I told both of you when I gave you the money - no skimming."

"That makes it a little better, but if I ever meet that bastard and he gives me the least reason, I'm gonna kill him."

"Donna, forget the Iceman. He was only doing what he had to do."

Donna became silent again. She finished her cocoa and went to her apartment for some sleep.

Tom came into the office Monday morning and found Mike at his desk. Pierre and Al were sitting nearby.

"Mike, did you see the morning headlines?"

"Yes. What did the Vancouver PD say they would do?"

"To tell you the truth, there was a guy named Brice who believed me, but his chief, Richard Smith, was more interested in going skiing with his children than in police work. He didn't believe me."

Pierre said, "I know that man. He is a fairly good police officer, but a little stubborn."

Al entered the conversation. "I guess he now realizes he's at

147

least one day late. Look at the morning paper. Two gangland leaders were killed on the ski slopes in Vancouver."

Tom smiled and added, "Brice asked me to call him today to ask what he plans to do about what I had told them. He also asked me to give him a little dig after the hit. He was convinced that what I said was correct.

The telephone on Mike's desk rang. Mike answered, "Mike Forester."

The voice on the other end of the phone replied, "This is Richard Smith in Vancouver. I want to apologize for not believing Tom. This contractor is really good. He killed each of his targets with one rifle shot each to the head. He must have been at least 500 meters away from the men as they were beginning to ski down the slope up here. We can add nothing to what you already know, but we're looking at these murders very closely. In short, Mike, I blew it. I hope you won't hold it against me."

Mike answered diplomatically, "Chief, if I was told what you were told, I probably wouldn't have believed it either. Keep looking and if you come up with something, let us know."

"I'll definitely let you know."

"Take care, Chief." Mike hung up the telephone.

"That was Richard Smith. He just called to apologize for not believing you, Tom. Pierre, when we find the answer phone hook up, we will disconnect it and tell you we found it and any other information we pick up."

"Mike, don't do anything like that. Remember, that is our only lead to the Iceman."

"That's right. You did say that. Okay, we won't disturb the machine."

Tuesday morning was like any other morning in Chinatown. Everyone was hurrying around to get to work. A Fed Ex courier came to an address and rang the bell.

When the door was opened, the courier said, "Fed Ex for Lee Chen. He must sign for this letter."

The woman replied, "Just a moment. I will get him."

148

She returned in three minutes.

"Please follow me."

She led the courier to the rear of the house and pointed to a man who was obviously an Oriental and was seated behind a desk.

The courier asked, "Are you Lee Chen?"

"I am Lee Chen."

"Would you please sign here for this letter?"

"Place it here, please." The courier set his log on the desk in front of the man, waited as he slowly traced out his name on it, and then left the house.

Lee Chen opened the letter and saw a computer-printed note. It read, "I hereby turn down the contract for Michael Forester. If any harm shall come to Mr. Forester or his family, the person or persons responsible will have to deal with me. Iceman."

Lee Chen frowned and called Deng.

"Get Lou Chan in here now."

An hour later, Lou Chan walked in with Deng.

He asked, "You wish to see me?"

"You attempted to hire the Iceman to kill Michael Forester after I told you not to harm him. I will not tolerate any more of your impertinence. One more disobedience like this and you will be removed from the Red Dragons."

Looking surprised, Lou Chan asked, "Who is this Iceman?"

"That is the name Interpol gave the man you tried to hire."

Lou Chan saw no use in denying the contract and he also knew what Lee Chen meant when he said he would not be a Red Dragon any more.

He responded, "You are correct. I will not defy your wishes any more."

Lou Chan left Lee Chen's office and went to his restaurant. He thought, now is the time to eliminate Lee Chen by showing the Tong membership he is weak and I am strong. He called Deng and asked him to come to his office.

"What can I do for you?" Deng asked when he arrived.

"I sense you believe as I do that Michael Forester must go. Do you think so?"

Deng thought for a moment, and then responded, "I think we would be better off without him."

"I would then suggest you see Mr. Forester and do what is necessary to eliminate the nuisance. After eliminating the problem, you and your men will receive $50,000."

Deng smiled. "Consider it done."

CHAPTER 10

One month later

It was a crisp, cool day in San Francisco, with a beautiful, cloudless sky in all its blue glory. The wind was blowing out of the west off the Pacific Ocean.

Mike and Lisa woke up earlier than usual. Mike left for work a little before 7:30 his usual time of departure. Lisa had the twins ready for nursery school and Angela ready for kindergarten a little earlier than usual. She was sitting in an easy chair reading the morning paper and taking time to relax with her second cup of coffee when the phone rang.

She got up and answered it. "Hello."

The voice on the other end said, "Hi, Lisa, this is Charlie. I'm in San Francisco now, but I won't be free until a little after noon."

"That's great. Can we expect you for dinner?"

"I was thinking of taking all five of you out to eat."

"Now you know Mike wouldn't stand for that. Be here about five. He should be home about that time."

"If you insist, but how about if I come over a little early, say about three, so we can talk about old times?"

"That's fine. By the way, where have you been this time?"

"Well, business took me to Australia, then to New Zealand. I took a few days off and went sight seeing - those are two beautiful

152

places. You and Mike should visit there some time. I had to come back through San Francisco, so I thought I'd stop and see how you two are doing. What's it been, seven, no eight months since I've seen you?"

"It's been too long. Seeing you will be just great. You have pictures of Australia and New Zealand don't you?"

"Sure do. I'll show them to you when I get there. I'm calling from a pay telephone in the airport. I still have to go through customs and do some other things, so it might be mid afternoon before I can get there."

"It'll be great to see you, Charlie. Come earlier if you can. Look at the time. Gotta go. See you this afternoon. Bye."

Deng called the other four men in his squad to his office, which was Lou Chan's Restaurant. Deng was eating breakfast when they walked up to his table.

As the remaining four members of the hit squad stood around him, Deng said, "We have a top secret job to do. We'll position ourselves at 2:00 PM and wait. This is the plan."

Pointing to a drawing on a piece of paper and addressing two of the men, he continued, "You two will be parked here, very near the driveway. You'll take the second shot if I miss."

Deng turned toward the other two men. "You're back up. If they miss, you must prevent him from escaping. I will be in the house. I will take the first shot. I will also insure that he is dead. Meet here at noon for lunch, and then we will go to his house."

One of the men asked, "What's his name?"

"None of your business. We get $50,000 for this job."

Another one of the group whistled. "For that kind of money, I don't care who it is."

They all nodded in agreement. The four men walked out of the restaurant while Deng finished his breakfast.

At noon, the five men of the hit squad again met in Lou Chan's Restaurant. They were in a festive mood, anticipating the $50,000. They ate a large lunch from the buffet and were finished by 1:00. They drove to the north side of San Francisco in two cars where

153

Deng directed them to turn onto a tree-lined street.

As they passed Mike and Lisa's house, Deng pointed to it, noting there were no cars in the drive indicating that probably no one was home. Then he signaled to the second car to position itself across the street and a little over 75 yards from the house.

The car Deng was riding in circled the block. Just before passing Mike and Lisa's house a second time, it stopped very close to the driveway and near a tree with a large trunk.

Deng got out, walked up to the door, and rang the doorbell. There was no answer. He then went to the rear of the house, where he found the back door unlocked. Entering, he moved slowly through the house, spending almost fifteen minutes there before returning to the car parked next to the driveway.

Lisa left her floor at noon and went to the hospital nursery school. When she walked into the nursery, two boys screamed happily from the back of the room and ran to their mother.

Lisa looked inquiringly at their teacher.

"They were very good today," the grandmotherly woman said with a smile. "Don't forget your drawings."

Mike, Jr. ran to get them and then ran to bring them back to his mother.

With the drawings safe in Mother's hands, the three left the hospital. Lisa now drove to the school where Angela was in kindergarten.

Angela was the last child to be picked up.

The teacher said, "Lisa, I wish you would be more punctual. The principal asked me to tell you that the next time you're late, she will charge you $10.00 for baby sitting service. You know she can do that."

"Yes, I know, but I come as quickly as I can. Today, Murphy's Law reigned at the hospital. But I'll try harder."

"I'll tell Mrs. Harris what you said," the teacher said with a shrug that indicated it wouldn't make any difference.

With Angela in the car, Lisa drove to the supermarket. With Charlie coming for dinner, she had to get additional food and other groceries.

She told the children, "Uncle Charlie is coming to dinner tonight and..."

The children all screamed with delight. They liked Charlie and besides, he always brought them a present.

After completing her shopping, Lisa returned to the car with her children and put them in the rear seat, making sure they were securely buckled up.

Lisa decided this was a good time to visit her mother and Uncle Frank. She couldn't stay long and neither her mother nor uncle Frank would feel hurt because she had a good excuse to leave early.

At Uncle Frank's the guard opened the gate and she drove up the driveway to the big house. Lisa's mother was waiting for them at the front door.

The visit was a little short, just as Lisa had planned. She headed home just before 3:00 in the afternoon.

Mike and Lisa's house was located in the middle of a long block and only a hundred yards from a small park. Passing the park, as he had on many other occasions, Charlie became excited because he would soon be visiting Lisa and her family. He turned onto Lisa's street and slowed as he neared their house. He noticed three Orientals in a Chevrolet sedan parked very near their driveway.

Two men sat in the front seat and one in the rear. The man in the rear seat seemed to be the boss judging by the way he was talking and the other two listening.

Because Charlie did not like the looks of the three Orientals sitting in the car, he speeded up to pass the house. As he continued down the street and passed the parked car, he saw another sedan parked across the street with two more oriental men in it.

He thought, "Damn, the Tong is going for Mike. I hope I can get to them before it's too late."

He speeded up, went around the block, and went to the park. The park was relatively small. But it had two softball diamonds, one at each end of the park, some swings and a jungle Jim in the middle with several picnic tables around the park. The grass looked as if it

155

needed some work on it.

He looked for, found the rest rooms, and pulled into a parking spot close to the men's room. He all but jumped out of the car and opened the trunk. From the trunk, he pulled out his make up kit and an old trench coat, and then carried them into the men's room.

He thought, "I'm in luck. No one is here."

He put on a red beard, put on some make up, then the old-looking trench coat. He now looked like he was in his sixties or seventies - in short, he looked old and homeless. Returning to his car, he opened the trunk again. However this time, he opened his gun case and put silencers on both the pistol and the M-16. The magazines were always kept loaded. He looked around the area and carefully strapped the M-16 on under his coat. The Ruger 9-mm went into his coat pocket. He looked up to make sure there was still no one was around to observe what he was doing, then began to walk towards Mike and Lisa's home as fast as he could while maintaining his impersonation of an old man. The time was now 3:35.

Lisa turned into her driveway at 3:10 PM. Her children had fallen asleep during the ride from Uncle Frank's house. She carried the twins into the house one at a time and put each in their own bed, still asleep. Angela was waking up when she returned to the car for her. Lisa picked her up also and carried her into the house. She laid her in her bed and left the bedroom door open. Angela turned over restlessly, but then went back to sleep. Lisa returned to the car for her groceries.

Deng was waiting for her. He was holding her groceries with one arm and a gun in his free hand.

He said, "Mrs. Forester, I will carry your groceries into your house. Please lead the way."

As Lisa saw the gun, she took a deep breath. She asked, "What do you want?"

Deng smiled and replied, "Walk or you die here in the driveway."

Lisa turned and walked into the house.

After Deng had placed the groceries on the table, he said,

156

"Please put the groceries away while I check on your children."

Lisa started for Deng, but he raised his gun and pointed it at her. She stopped and Deng went to look in on the twins and Angela.

When he returned to the kitchen, Lisa was half looking at him and half putting away the groceries.

Deng said, "Your children are sleeping and as long as you do what you are told, nothing will happen to them." Mentally, though, he added, maybe.

The time was now 3:45.

The driver of the car Deng had ridden in looked in the rear view mirror and saw an old man walking along the sidewalk just behind their car.

He said in Chinese, *"That old man better not be here when our man comes home, or he won't live too much longer."*

The second man answered in Chinese, *"The world wouldn't miss him very much. It has enough old, homeless bums. What he really needs is a grave."*

The driver thought for a minute, and then said, *"I agree - he needs a grave,"* and they both laughed at the comment."

The driver remarked again in Chinese, *"I wonder if Deng has had sex with the woman yet?"*

They both laughed again.

While they laughed, the old man had slipped behind the tree so that they could not see him. He was now holding a pistol with a silencer and moved to where he could see both men clearly.

There were two sharp, popping sounds, barely loud enough to be heard thirty feet away - one of the men in the car slumped over the steering wheel and the other man slumped over the dashboard, and then fell to the floor of the car. Blood and the men's brains were splattered over the windshield and the driver's window.

The old man picked up the two spent shell casings, then moved on to the rear of the house. Looking inside, he saw Lisa standing in front of Deng, who was sitting on the sofa.

Charlie thought for a moment. He did not want Lisa to recognize him, so he realized he would have to disguise his voice

157

and...use his ski mask so some of his red beard would show."

Deng said, "Your husband has upset many people. We are waiting for him to come home. He is the only one we want. We will not harm you."

Lisa thought, the bastard. He knows I can identify him. He's going to kill me. But maybe, if I do what he says, he might not hurt my children.

Deng looked at Lisa. "Mrs. Forester, remove your clothes. If you do it quickly your children will not be hurt, but..."

"You son of a bitch!"

Deng pointed his gun at the room where Angela was sleeping.

Lisa said, "You know you are as good as dead."

"Your uncle can't help you at this moment. Now, take your clothes off."

Lisa started to undress.

Deng was smiling, more of a smirk, as he looked her over.

Lisa had removed most of her clothes and as Deng was looking her over, she heard a sharp popping, yet exploding sound, somewhat like air being forced through a small opening just to the right of her. She then noticed Deng's legs flinched, then totally relaxed and remain still.

The four seconds Lisa waited before she really looked at Deng seemed like an eternity, but when she looked at Deng she saw his head resting on the back of the sofa, he had a small hole in the left side his head, and the right side of his head was missing.

Deng's blood and brains were all over the sofa and the wall. His body was resting on the rear of the sofa with his head, or what was left of it, lying on the top of the back of the sofa.

She backed away from Deng, losing her balance and falling to the floor. Then she stood up, trying to regain her composure. She looked toward the kitchen, expecting to see Donna, but instead she saw what appeared to be an old man wearing a ski mask and an old trench coat. Peaking out of the bottom of the ski mask was the edge of a red beard.

The old man swung an M-16 from under his coat as he walked past her as he placed his pistol in his belt.

With a heavy German accent the man ordered, "Get dressed. Call the police."

Next he went to the front window, opened it, moved the curtain aside so he wouldn't have the curtain interfering with his aiming the assault rifle.

Lisa sensed he would not harm her. She reached for her blouse, and began putting it on.

The old man did not look at Lisa at any time. About the time she was pulling the zipper up on her powder blue uniform blouse, he put the rifle up to his shoulder and fired twice. She heard the same sharp popping sounds that she now knew the sounds were the sounds of a gun being fired with a silencer, but this time she also heard the sounds of the bolt ejecting the shell casings. The old man quickly picked up the two spent casings and left the house as Lisa was calling the police.

She thought he was quite agile for an old man. I wish he would've stayed so I could've thanked him. I will just have to thank Uncle Frank when I see him.

The police operator answered. "Police. May we help you?"

In a controlled voice, she said, "Yes, this is Mrs. Michael Forester, Lt. Forester's wife. I have almost been raped. There is a dead man in my living room and I can see two more dead men in a car just outside my window. Please send help quickly. Please call Mike in the Organized Crime Unit. That's my husband."

The operator replied, "One minute" as he checked the special screen to determine the address from where the call was coming; then he dispatched patrol cars to Lisa's house.

He now continued to talk to Lisa, "Cars are on the way, Mrs. Forester. Remain calm. We'll be there as soon as possible. I'm transferring your call to Organized Crime."

A moment later another voice said, "Sergeant Tom Buckley."

"Tom, this is Lisa. Get Mike and tell him I'm okay, but I'd really appreciate it if he could come home right away. In a few minutes our house is going to be crawling with police." She told him briefly what had happened.

"We're on our way," he said.

Charlie was in the men's room at the park removing his make up when he heard police sirens coming from every direction. He returned to his car and placed his make up kit inside the trunk. After putting his pistol and rifle in their case, he closed the trunk.

He thought, if I go over there now and they find that stuff, Lisa will know who I am, and then

Mike will know. I better go to the bus station and place the stuff in a locker. Better yet, a storage facility.

It was almost 5:00 when Charlie finally returned to Mike and Lisa's house. Several police cars and the coroner's vehicle were parked along the two sides of the street. A uniformed police officer stopped him as he tried to go inside.

"You can't go in. This is a crime scene."

Charlie replied in a concerned manner, "My God, are Lisa and Mike okay? The kids?"

The officer was not expecting this answer, but he replied, "They're fine. What's your name?"

"Just tell either Mike or Lisa, Charlie is here."

The officer went into the house. In a short time, Mike came out.

"Charlie, come on in."

Charlie followed him inside.

Mike said, "Tom, I'd like you to meet Charlie - a real friend to Lisa and me. You met him at our wedding."

Tom shook Charlie's hand, but replied to Mike, "He's the one who told Lisa to stay with you and not mention family business. Right?"

"You certainly have a good memory, Tom. Now what happened, Mike?"

"As I see it, the Red Dragon Tong wanted me dead for some reason. Maybe we were getting too close for comfort. Anyway, the Tong hit squad was waiting for me to come home. During that time, the dead guy over there was forcing Lisa to undress. Just as she was about to do what the bastard wanted, someone killed him. He then killed two other members of the squad. He had already killed two of them.

160

"How's Lisa?"

"She's in the bedroom with the children. She's still shaky, but okay. I guess she'll be out soon."

"Mike, I wonder if Uncle Frank had something to do with this."

"I don't know, Charlie, but he's the only one I know who could do this."

Tom added, "He's my guess too."

As they talked, Charlie was looking around the floor for the 9-MM shell casing he had forgotten to pick up after shooting Deng. He spied it just slightly under the refrigerator.

He thought, if I make an attempt to recover the shell and I am spotted, I'll become a suspect, but if I tell Mike about it, I won't be. The chance of the police obtaining my Ruger is almost nil. I'll tell Mike.

"Mike, what's that under the fridge?"

"Where? Oh, I see it."

To Charlie's astonishment, Mike reached under the refrigerator and picked up the shell casing. He did not take photographs of the casing or lift it out in a way that would preserve possible fingerprints. He just picked it up and put it in his pocket.

Tom said, "I didn't see anything, did you?"

Charlie responded to Tom's question and statement with, "Huh? Did you say something?"

Both Mike and Tom smiled. Tom added, "He catches on fast."

Charlie realized that Mike would not want to turn in any evidence against the person who had saved his family and that Tom understood and respected that.

Lisa was coming through the door now, and Charlie went to greet her. As they embraced, Lisa started to sob.

Charlie patted her on the back.

"Lisa, it's over and everyone's okay. And most of all, nothing happened."

"I know, but my nerves are still shot."

Tom said, "Mike, we'll leave two cars parked in front tonight and for as long as it takes."

Lisa suggested, "Mike, let's go to Uncle Frank's house for a while. It'll be safe there."

Charlie looked at Mike and Lisa, and then interrupted, "Lisa, I don't think it would be too safe for Mike, you, and the children to stay there. Think about it. If the Tong made a contract on Mike's life, don't you think they would be going for your uncle too? After all, Mike and you are his favorites. The Tong would expect your uncle to go after the guys who killed you and Mike."

Tom interrupted, "Charlie's right, Mike."

Charlie continued, "I know where you two can stay and be as safe as you can be."

Lisa asked, "Where?"

"In the roof plaza suite of the Marriot. There is only one elevator to the suite and one set of stairs, and that's the fire escape. There is only one suite on the floor. Two officers could easily defend the floor and another two could check everyone who enters the elevator as it doesn't stop until it gets to the suite. Look, I'll spring for the rent for a week. How about it? Anyway, it would be an experience for you two lovebirds."

Mike and Lisa looked at each other. Mike answered, "Just for a week, Charlie."

"Now let me see if it's available."

Charlie dialed information and got the Marriot's telephone number. He then dialed the Marriot, spoke to the night manager, and made the arrangements.

"If we go to the Marriot now, they'll feed you for free. Tom, do you think you can arrange for police protection quickly?"

"It's done. Mike, get your clothes and let's go."

Mike and Lisa had just settled in at the suite when three waiters arrived at their door with dinner. The police guards inspected the food and opened the door to the suite. Lisa looked at the food and told the waiters to place it on the table.

Mike tried to tip them, but they refused, "The tip has been added to the bill already."

Lisa and Mike looked at Charlie. Mike said, "Thanks, but we should pay our way."

"Mike, you and Lisa are the only family I have. I can easily

162

afford everything. Remember, I'm a very rich man. Now let me have this pleasure."

Mike lowered his head.

"Okay, but next time you're in Frisco, you'll be our guest at any place you wish to eat."

"That's fine Mike. Now folks, I see it is a little after seven. I have a business appointment for 9:00. This appointment may take a long time, but I'll be here for breakfast at seven. Please excuse me, I must go."

Charlie went to his room and changed his clothes. He put on some blue jeans and a black sport shirt. This would make it harder to see him in the dark of night.

He walked out of the hotel, got into his car, and drove to the Day and Night storage facility where he retrieved what he had placed in the locker. He was satisfied with this storage facility since he knew no one would enter the storage room because it was locked and he had the only key. He didn't think anyone would break in either, and most of all, it would not be inspected by anyone.

Then he drove to Frank Giaventi's mansion and parked his car 150 yards from the front gate. If he had to protect Frank, he would. It was 9:02 PM - he waited.

Charlie did not have long to wait, but he did not expect what happened. A white Cadillac sedan drove up to the gate and Lee Chen got out of the car and went to the gate.

The guard was suspicious, but asked, "What do you want?"

"My name is Lee Chen and I would like to see Frank Giaventi. It is of the utmost importance."

"One minute." The guard disappeared into the guardhouse.

He spoke over the intercom to the house, "Mr. Giaventi, someone who says his name is Lee Chen wants to talk to you, and he says it's important."

The reply over the phone was, "Wait two minutes, and open the gate."

"Yes sir."

Frank Giaventi turned to Donna. "Be on your guard. It was his hit squad that was killed at Lisa's house. Louis, leave the room, but

163

be in a place where you can hear what is said and see us."

Lee Chen's car drove up to the house. Donna met the car and opened the door for Lee Chen.

"Mr. Chen, this way," she said pleasantly.

As she led him to the library, he passed through a metal detector that did not sound any alarm. Louis nodded his head.

Frank opened the door. Lee Chen bowed from the waist.

He said, "My sincere apologies for the events of this afternoon. I wanted you to know the Red Dragon Tong had nothing to do with ordering the squad to Mike and Lisa's house. I can only assume what happened. Lou Chan wanted Mike eliminated. I gave him a direct order not to harm Mike. He contacted the Iceman ..."

"The Iceman?"

"Frank, ignorance does not become you. You know as well as I do that Interpol has given that name to the assassin in San Francisco. But to continue, the Iceman wrote me a note in which he said 'I hereby turn down the contract for Michael Forester. If any harm shall come to Mr. Forester or his family, the person or persons who are responsible for the harm will have to deal with me. It is obvious that the Iceman keeps his word. He must have some connection to Lisa or Mike. Here is the note just as I received it.

"I again told Lou Chan not to do what he obviously did. He hired Deng to do the job. I found out about these things after I heard about the events of the afternoon. Lou Chan apologized in the proper manner. Either he will be found soon or he will be found by early morning. It is my hope you and the Iceman will accept my sincere apologies and Lou Chan's apologies."

"Lee, permit me to copy this note."

"Of course."

Frank signaled for another woman to come to them.

"Mona, please copy this."

"Yes sir."

A few minutes later, she returned.

"Here's the copy, Mr. Giaventi."

"Thank you, Mona."

Lee Chen bowed, turned to leave.

164

Frank called to him. "Lee, I believe you did not give the order, but I must say you may have to prove it to the Iceman."

"I hope I have proved it by Lou Chan's unfortunate circumstances. You must be aware of another possible threat to you - Max. If he thinks now is the right time to take you out, you could be on his list. I doubt Mario would do something so stupid."

Frank thought for a moment, and then replied, "I think you might be right."

Lee Chen walked out the door, got in his car, and drove out the gate past Charlie.

Lee Chen had been in the house only forty minutes. Charlie wondered what he had told Frank. Obviously, enough to get off the hook. Now he would go to see Lou Chan.

Charlie drove to the China Gate where a crowd had gathered. He got out of his car to see what everyone was looking at. He found Lou Chan's body lying on the bed of a Ford pickup truck with a note pinned to his chest. It read, "Our apologies."

Charlie understood what had happened. He took a deep breath, then went to an all night Quick Print Center. Charlie wrote a note to Lee Chen. He would deliver it himself so Lee Chen would have it in the morning.

Lee Chen was up at 5:00 the next morning. He could not sleep. He went to pick up the morning paper by his front door. It was still wrapped in plastic as it had been delivered. He slipped off the plastic bag that kept it from getting wet, unfolded it, and smiled. A note was pasted to the front page.

It read, "Apologies accepted."

It was 6:30 AM when the phone rang at Frank Giaventi's house. Donna answered.

"This is Lee Chen. I would like to speak to Frank. I believe he will want to know this."

"One minute and I will see if he is available."

A short time later, Lee Chen heard, "Lee, this is Frank."

"Frank, I received a note glued to my morning paper. It read "Apologies Accepted." I've sent you a copy by one of my men. He'll leave it at your gate."

165

"That will be fine and I thank you for this information. It seems you're off the hook."

"Yes, it does. We will have to meet again sometime under better circumstances."

"I agree."

Both men hung up their telephones.

Charlie was down at the suite elevator in the lobby. The police guards knew him as a close friend of Mike and Lisa's, but they still checked him with a metal detector. After being cleared, he went up to the plaza suite. Mike welcomed him at the elevator.

"This is some pad, Charlie. Do you stay in this type of room all the time?"

"Mike, I've never stayed in a suite like this. I go for the room to sleep, not to party. Anyhow, what's for breakfast?"

Lisa came in, walked over to Charlie, and kissed him on the check. "This is really nice. Thank you, Charlie."

Charlie responded, "I'm hungry. Let's eat!"

After breakfast, Charlie excused himself to return to his room. As he left the special suite elevator in the lobby, he saw Frank Giaventi coming towards him with Donna at his side. He also saw Tom entering the hotel door.

He thought, "He'll get Frank past the guards. I better leave."

Waving to both Frank and Tom, he got in the normal elevator to go to his room.

Donna found a comfortable chair in the lobby and settled into it as Frank continued on to the elevator. She had on another pair of close fitting trousers and a loose blouse.

Tom came up to her. "Are you carrying and do you have a permit to carry?"

Donna replied, "I bet you even know the permit number."

"Just checking."

The guards at the elevator did not want to let Frank go up to the suite.

Tom walked up to them. "He's okay. Let's go up."

Frank and Tom went up to the suite together. When the

166

elevator opened, Mike and Lisa were waiting. Lisa all but threw herself at Frank, kissing him.

"Thank you Uncle Frank," she said.

Mike added, "My thanks also. You might give this to one of your men. He dropped it," placing the spent shell casing in Frank's hand in such a way that no one could see.

Frank looked at Mike. The three children heard Frank's voice and ran out of the bedroom to hug him. They were only half dressed for the day.

Frank hugged all of them. "Now you run along and finish dressing. You have a big day ahead of you."

He turned back to Mike and Lisa.

"You think one of my men saved you. You're wrong. It was the Iceman."

Mike's face gave way to his astonishment.

Lisa asked, "Who is this Iceman?"

"I am breaking one of my rules. I am going to tell you some of the family's business. I'll be brief.

"Lou Chan hired this Iceman to kill Mike. The Iceman turned down the hit and said if anyone tried to hurt Mike, he would have to deal with him. Lee Chen said no. Lou Chan then hired Deng and his squad. Lee Chen told me Lou Chan paid a big price for disobeying him..."

Mike interrupted, "He was found dead this morning at the entrance to Chinatown with a note attached to his body."

Frank continued, "The note said "Our apologies." Lee Chen called me this morning and sent me a copy of another note that read, "Apologies accepted." He was elated. He was off the Iceman's hook."

"Uncle Frank, do you know who this Iceman is?"

"No. But ask your husband about him. He can tell you more than I can because I think he knows more about him."

Mike looked at Frank. Frank could see that what he had just said was very puzzling to Mike. Mike would work on it.

Mike now knew it was safe for his family to go home.

He walked out of the room to speak to Tom. "Tom, go to the

office and set up a conference call with Pierre in Paris or wherever he is. I want you on the office phone and I'll take the call here."

"What's the deal?"

"I think I have a lead on the Iceman, so get with it. Paris is a good bit ahead of us time-wise."

Tom left the Marriot and returned to their office. It was an hour and a half later when the phone rang in the suite.

"Mike, the call is set up. One minute. We are all on, Mike."

"Pierre, this is Mike. Tom is on an extension. I think I have a break in your Iceman case."

"Good."

"Pierre, have you heard what happened to me and my wife?"

"No."

"Well, Lou Chan tried to hire the Iceman to kill me, but he refused and said if I or my family were harmed, they would have to deal with him."

"That's strange, but as I told you, he is an enigma. Remember he has done this before."

"I have more information about what happened, but I will mail you the additional information. I did some brainstorming and I came to a conclusion - the Iceman knows me and my wife. He is also connected in some manner with the Giaventi Family. He definitely uses San Francisco as his base of operations."

"That's interesting. Based on what you have told me so far, I agree with your ideas. I would think he knows you better than your wife or the Giaventi Family, but I could be wrong. Send me the other information you have. Now I have some news for you.

"Our government has given us permission to arrest Carlos and Klaus," he continued. "We have already arrested Klaus. We know where Carlos is, but we have to wait for Carlos to be in a place where we can arrest and transport him to France."

"That's great, but what about Miguel, the Iceman, and Kozar."

"It seems Kozar is going to be off limits for a very long time. Miguel and the Iceman are also off limits as of now. I hope that changes."

"That's good news. I hope to have the name of the Iceman

168

sometime in the future. When I get it, I'll call you. If you come up with any additional information on him, call me."

"If we get anything, I will. I'm being paged, so I must say good-bye."

"Good-bye, Pierre."

CHAPTER 11

The mountains around Lake Tahoe were still snow capped in April, but at the lower elevations, the snow was melting fast. It was a sunny afternoon on Palm Sunday when the Johnson family decided to go for a walk at the falls near Emerald Bay.

Mr. Johnson parked his car in the parking area for the trail and his daughters, Judy and Jo, jumped out of the car and ran to the trailhead. They had hiked this trail many times and always enjoyed it.

Following close behind Judy and Jo, Mr. and Mrs. Johnson began the hike down the mountain to the bottom of the falls, from which they would continue on to the lake. It was a great day for a hike; the sun was high in the sky and the temperature in the mid sixties. They wondered how far ahead of them their children had run, but there was no reason to worry - they had hiked this trail many times before.

As they turned a bend in the trail, they found Judy and Jo staring at a partially melted snow bank. The kids glanced back toward them, then, as if they were scared and excited at the same time pointed at the snow bank. When the parents reached them and could clearly see why and what their daughters were pointing towards in the snow bank - Mrs. Johnson gasped and Mr. Johnson took a deep breath.

Jack Hall's hand was sticking out of the snow bank.

"Honey, take the children and go call the police," the husband said.

A few hours later, Mike received a call from the California State Police.

"Lt. Forester, sometime ago you requested any information we had on one Jack Hall. We found him. He has a bullet hole in his head. We estimate he was killed just before the big snowfall last year because his body was frozen and still mostly covered with snow when it was found."

"When you get finished with your investigation, please let me know everything you've found."

"We already know one interesting thing. He had eighteen one-hundred-dollar bills in his pocket. This was obviously a hit."

"Thanks for the info. I'll be waiting for your final report. Put the serial numbers of the bills in the report. I might be able to trace them."

"Sure will. Have a nice day."

After Mike hung up the telephone, he began to think. What happened to Jack? Who did it? Did Uncle Frank have anything to do with the hit? No, I don't think so. Jack was loyal to Frank and Frank was loyal to Jack, but I guess I'll have to check it out.

Maxwell Crown was with Mario Rodriguez at his crack house selling cocaine to anyone who wanted it. It was a particularly good night for business because it was the middle of June, the schools had just closed, and this was almost the first chance the college, high school, and junior high students had to party with coke. The distinctive odors of marijuana, other drugs, and alcohol filled the air.

Mario and Max heard a knock on the door to the room where they were counting money. Mario motioned to Max to see who it was while he kept counting.

"Who's there?"

"It's Denise. I want to talk to Mario?"

Max looked at Mario. "It's that uptown bitch, Denise. You know that high school cheerleader who thinks she's too good for us because her old man's rich. She wants to talk to you."

Mario thought for a moment. "Let her in."

171

Max opened the door to let Denise in. As she walked towards Mario, she saw the money on the table and kept looking at it as she walked toward Mario.

"There's over ten thousand here," Mario said. "Now, what can I do for you?"

"I need a bag of coke. I'll pay you tomorrow night. You know I'm good for it."

"I wouldn't mind giving you the bag, baby, but I need the money tonight. You see baby, I have expenses. I have to pay for more coke and pay Max and the boys. All the bag costs is $10.00."

"Mario, I don't have any more money right now. I bought over $35 of coke already tonight. You know you can trust me for it."

"I'm sorry, baby."

Max had gotten up and was eyeing Denise as he walked around her. She could feel him taking her clothes off with his eyes.

"Mario, if she would do me a favor, I think that would pay for the bag."

"What do you think I am? It'll be a cold day in hell when I'll let you get on top of me. Come on, Mario, what about that bag?"

Mario looked at Max, then to Denise. "Baby, Max has told you how you can get it. Look at it this way - you need something... and he needs something, too. If you want it that bad, all you got to do is take your clothes off and roll on the floor with Max."

"I'm no whore."

With those words, she turned and walked defiantly to the door. Mario and Max smiled at each other. They watched her reach for the doorknob, open the door, and begin to walk out of the room. She stopped, took a deep breath, and walked back to where Max and Mario were.

Max asked, "What do you want now, baby?"

"How long?"

"Long enough to please me," replied Max.

Denise began to unbutton her blouse.

After thirty minutes with Denise on the rug, Max got up, and pulled up his trousers.

"Mario, she's pretty good for a beginner. Give her two bags."

172

While dropping his trousers, Mario said, "I'll have to check out how good she is."

Twenty minutes later, Mario was finished, rose to his feet, and pulled up his pants.

"Max, I agree. For a beginner, she's good. Baby, here are three bags. Anytime you need more, you know how to get them."

Sniffling and feeling dirty, Denise dressed and walked through the door and out of the room.

Denise thought, I never thought I'd do it this way for the first time, but I needed the coke. Damn, what am I going to do? I got to do something.

She now knew she was addicted to cocaine and needed professional help.

"I bet she'll make one good whore, Max. What do you think?"

"She'll be a good one. You should get her for one of your girls."

Max was feeling good right now. He thought, I think now would be a good time to get Frank Giaventi. The Tong might even be blamed since Lou Chan was found at the entrance to Chinatown several months ago. Yes, I think now would be a good time.

"Mario, if you ever want to move uptown, we need to knock off Frank Giaventi. Let's do it now."

Mario shook his head. "Max, that would be suicide. The Giaventi Family would come down hard on us and we would have nowhere to go. The answer is no."

Max's smile turned to a frown.

Letting his feelings of the moment rule him, he thought, I'll do it anyway. I'll just have to do it without his help. Afterward, he'll thank me.

Frank called Louis into the library.

"Louis, close the door."

"What do you want, Uncle Frank?"

"Fritz has told me some disturbing news. He said Joe Andrati is skimming off us. He also said Joe is going to meet with someone shortly to make a deal on supplying him with coke. He wants to bypass us completely. He wants to take over one of the uptown areas."

"Uncle Frank, we can't let that happen. If he succeeds, then everyone else will do it. We'll have a full scale mutiny on our hands."

"I know, but Joe has been with the family for almost twenty-four years. It doesn't seem right that he should do this."

"Have you thought of talking to him?"

"Yes, but that would tell him Fritz told me and Fritz would be killed. I must reward Fritz."

"I guess you're right, but what do we do? If we can't talk to him or get to him in another way, then the only thing that can be done is to let Donna handle Joe."

"I think you're right. But let's not be too hasty. Let's sleep on this and make the decision in the morning."

The next morning, Louis went to the library to talk to Uncle Frank. Frank Giaventi was standing at the French doors looking out over the grounds as Louis walked up beside him.

"Good morning, Uncle Frank. It's a beautiful day - only a few clouds in the sky."

"Yes, it is." He turned to face Louis. "What do you think?"

"Call Donna."

"Unfortunately, I agree. Would you please get her?"

Donna was just coming up the drive in her car when she saw Louis leaving the house. He waved to her in a manner that meant that he or Uncle Frank wanted to talk to her, and she waved back.

She went to the library and closed the door behind her, with only Frank in the room with her.

"We have a problem, Donna. That envelope on my desk has $10,000 in it."

"Who is it this time?"

"It's Joe Andrati. He's been a very bad boy. He's skimmed a good deal of money from us."

"May I ask how much?"

"Our best estimate is over $200,000. He's also trying to take over one of the uptown districts."

174

"Give me some idea where he is and his daily routine."

"You'll have to find out those things for yourself. Get Mona to help you. We believe it should be done as quickly as possible. We know he's meeting someone from out of town to conclude a business deal. It'd be nice if you could get that person too."

"I'll see what I can do."

Donna left the library and went to the telephone.

Mona answered her call with a crisp, "Hello."

"Mona, this is Donna. We have a job. You live near the Pizza Hut, don't you?"

"Sure do."

"Meet me there for lunch in an hour."

"See you there."

This would be Donna's first hit without Jack and she was a little nervous. This time she would be in charge. Mona would be her assistant. She knew Mona was good, but not anywhere near as good as Jack was. She would have to go over every detail so there would be no screw up.

Donna was waiting for Mona in the corner booth of the Pizza Hut. She waved to her as she came into the restaurant.

"We have a contract," she said simply. "Joe Andrati. You're close to the Andrati bunch aren't you?"

"Yeah, but I don't think I am going to like what you're going to tell me."

"I received ten grand with the possibility of a bonus if we take out whoever he's meeting at the same time. Your share is five grand and fifty percent of any bonus. Jack worked it that way and I kind of liked it."

"That kind of money calms any feeling I had about not doing what I have to do - now what do we do and when?"

"First, find out when and where this meeting is. Then we can make our plans."

"I'll know in a few days. The only trouble is I might have to get in the sack with a jerk to get the information."

"Sorry about that, Mona. Take the next two days off."

Mona walked out of the Pizza Hut as Donna went to the counter to pay the bill.

It was a warm June day and Frank Giaventi and his wife Maria were going for their usual Sunday ride to the waterfront to get ice cream. Frank had given Donna the day off since he wasn't going anywhere dangerous and he asked Fritz to be his chauffeur for the day because his regular chauffeur, George Anderson, was on vacation and would not return until Monday. George was a big black man who was very loyal to Frank but he wanted to reward Fritz by promoting him to number two chauffeur. While Fritz wasn't as good as Donna, Mona, or George, he was acceptable. He did have a pistol in the car and he could use it effectively.

Frank walked up to the window of the ice cream stand.

"I want two cups - medium cups."

The woman behind the counter smiled. She knew Frank Giaventi and his wife as they always came to this ice cream stand in the summer. They were more than just customers - they were almost friends.

"Mr. Frank, what flavor would you and your wife like today?"

"I think I'll have some pistachio almond and my wife...."

"Will take some vanilla."

Frank grinned back at the woman. She gave Frank and his wife each a large cup of ice cream.

"The extra is on the house."

Frank replied, "Thank you very much." He handed her a ten-dollar bill. "I don't want any change. You keep it."

"Mr. Frank, you know the policy here. No tipping."

"I also know I'm a good customer, and remember one thing - the customer is always right. Now take the change."

She smiled. "Thank you, Mr. Frank."

Frank Giaventi walked back to where he left his wife sitting. She had remained on a bench near the street where some children were playing. The children's parents were watching from the open area in the small park just behind the bench. The cable car turn was just to the left of the bench.

Fritz had gone over to the ice cream stand to get some ice cream for himself and had left his pistol in the car, since there was no hint of danger and his permit to carry it was still being processed.

Frank and Maria were about half finished eating their ice cream when the roar of a motorcycle coming down the street caught Frank's attention. As he looked up, he recognized Max on the cycle. Max had an assault rifle in his right hand. Frank launched himself at Maria to throw her to the ground, but it was too late.

The assault rifle began to spit fire, bullets flying everywhere. Several of the children were hit and Frank and Maria lay bleeding on the ground, their half-eaten ice cream beside them. Max stopped the motorcycle, left it running as he walked over to the lifeless bodies of Frank and Maria. He jammed another magazine into the rifle and opened fire pointblank into their bodies. When the rifle was about half empty he looked up to see Fritz going to the car, then swung around and opened fire on Fritz, killing him and wounding several more bystanders behind him.

Carrying the assault rifle, he returned to his motorcycle and rode away without anyone chasing after him.

Five minutes later, the police radio was blaring, "Mass shooting on the waterfront. Suspect escaped on a motorcycle. Approach with caution, the suspect is armed and is considered very dangerous."

When the phone rang, Lisa was playing with the twins and Angela in the backyard while Mike was catching a nap. Mike woke up and drowsily went to the phone. Lisa was walking quickly to answer it so it would not wake Mike, but he reached it first.

"Hello."

"Mike, this is Tom. Frank Giaventi was just killed on the waterfront along with his wife. The killer sprayed the crowd, but it was a definite hit. Fritz was also killed. The total count is six dead, one critical and eight serious. We have a positive ID on the killer. It was Mad Max. We can go after him now and take him out."

"Are you sure about your facts?"

"You mean about Frank and Maria. Yes. I am also sure about Max."

"Thanks for calling. Get a warrant for Max and put out a bulletin. Also, release the information to the news media. We might

177

stop a bloodbath between the Giaventi Family and Mario's gang. I think we'll be starting a fight within the Black/Latino gang, but that's better than what'll happen if those two groups go at each other."

"I agree. Are you going to tell Lisa and Louis?"

"I guess so."

Mike hung up the telephone.

Lisa asked, "Business?"

"Yes, and unfortunately it has to do with Uncle Frank and Aunt Maria. They were both killed by Mad Max about an hour ago."

Lisa screamed and cried at the same time, "No, no, no!"

She started to sob and fell into Mike's arms.

Lisa sat down on the sofa with Mike's left arm around her. Soon he released her, reached for the telephone, and dialed Louis' number.

"Louis, this is Mike. I have some bad news. Frank is dead. Max killed him and Maria, plus some others. I don't have all the details yet, but you should get a bodyguard quick."

The telephone went silent. Finally, Louis asked, "Mike, are you sure?"

"Yes."

"Mike, thanks for calling. I have some work to do."

The first thing Louis had to do was call Donna. "Donna, Max killed Frank and Maria. Come to my house now."

He could hear the shock and grief in her voice as she said, "I'll be there within a few minutes."

"Good. Please call Mona."

"I will."

The next day, Frank Giaventi's mansion had black ribbons all over the gate and front door. Louis had contacted all the chiefs in the Family. They were told to come to Frank's house for ten in the morning. As usual, Donna and Mona were standing in the back of the room. Louis was at the head of the table.

"Gentlemen, there is no need to worry. We will continue as usual. However, anyone who wishes may step forward to ask questions. But, once a decision is made, then that is the decision."

One of the chiefs rose to say, "I vote for Louis to continue. I believe he'll be as good as Frank."

All the others said the same thing, including Joe Andrati.

However, Joe Andrati was thinking, what luck, Frank is dead. That will make it easier to take over the uptown district and maybe even more districts. I might start the Andrati Family and dispose of the Giaventi Family. Louis just can't handle the Family like Frank did. This is just great.

Louis stood up and said, "I wish to thank all of you for being so loyal to me and the Family. Now, if you will excuse me, I have to arrange for Uncle Frank and Aunt Maria's funeral."

One by one, as the chiefs were leaving the room, they passed Louis and expressed their condolences.

After they had left, Louis turned to the windows. Donna and Mona walked over to him.

"Donna, get the traitor as soon as possible. If I don't act quickly, others will join him and the Giaventi Family will have a fight on its hands."

"Louis - or should I call you Mr. Giaventi?"

"Louis will be fine."

"Louis, Mona learned Joe will be meeting his contact in Seattle Friday after next at the downtown Hilton. I had planned to be there at that time and take care of both of them."

"Good, but do not wait longer than Friday after next."

"If I can't take care of the problem then, I assure you he will be living on borrowed time. If you want it done sooner, I can do that, but I won't be able to get the contact."

"No, wait and get the contact too. That will send a clear message that I am in control and that dealing with anyone but me is dangerous." He paused, and then continued, "There's another reason for you to go to Seattle. I've learned that Max is probably there. Add another $10,000 bonus if you get him in Seattle."

The day after Frank and Maria Giaventi's death, Mike entered his office.

"Tom, come over here."

"Sure, what do you want?"

179

"Tom, the word is out on the street. Max did the hit. I don't think Mario is long for this earth. Get the boys to pick him up and maybe we can get something out of him before they get him."

At that moment, Gene Caruth walked into the room.

"Mike, I have some news for you. You have a gang war started. The Black/Latinos are breaking up. Mario has been gunned down and is dead. Some of the other gang members are also dead or in the hospital. I have alerted everyone and all police are on call. I hope this will settle down quickly."

Tom whistled softly then said, "Damn, Mike and I were just talking about that. We might be in for a long haul over this."

"Chief, I don't think it will be that long. I believe it'll be violent for a short time and then quiet down with each of the gangs having their own turf."

"I hope you're right, Mike. A lot of people could get hurt."

Louis decided visitation would be held Friday from 3:00 PM to 10:00 PM and the funeral would be held at 10:30 AM on Saturday. The Archbishop of the Roman Catholic Church for the San Francisco Archdiocese would conduct the service. It would be just as Frank would have wanted.

Both caskets were open when those paying their last respects began arriving. Lee Chen was almost the first person to arrive. He went to Maria's coffin, bowed, then to Frank's coffin. He bowed low at Frank's coffin as a sign of respect. After that, he walked over to Louis.

"My sincere condolences. It is my hope you will follow in the footsteps of Frank. I know he would want that. He was truly a good man. May I see you in the room over there - with Donna, of course."

Louis was surprised by this, but nodded yes. He rose to his feet and walked slowly over to the coffee room where he found two of Lee Chen's men sitting at a table. Donna was right behind him, and when they entered, both men left so that Lee Chen would be alone with Louis and Donna.

"Louis, your uncle and I had what I believe was a reasonably good relationship. I do not want that relationship to disappear. It is

180

because of this desire that I tell you the following - you have trouble in your Family. One of your chiefs, Joe Andrati, is recruiting other chiefs to work for him. He has not yet convinced any of them, but two are wavering. Take care of the problem quickly or you will suffer considerably."

"Lee, I know most of what you speak. The problem will be handled within a couple of weeks. I thank you for the information. I will not tell anyone you told me this."

Lee Chen and Louis bowed to each other, and then left the room.

Louis was pleased to have heard Lee Chen say what he did, but possibly, of more importance, Lee Chen's bodyguards had left the room when he and Donna entered the room - a sign of almost absolute trust.

While Louis was meeting with Lee Chen, Mike and Lisa entered the funeral home. Lisa went to see Uncle Frank and Aunt Maria for the last time. She looked at both, said a few silent prayers, stood up from kneeling, and turned to hug Mike. Instead, she almost grabbed him and pulled him away from the caskets.

"Mike, they don't look real. I hope Uncle Frank and Aunt Maria will be forgiven their sins."

Choosing not to upset her further, Mike replied, "I'm sure they will be. Honey, there's Charlie."

Charlie came over to Lisa and they embraced.

"I came as soon as I heard the news. I can't say anything except you have my condolences - you know that."

Turning to Mike, Charlie asked, "Have you caught this Max?"

"Not yet. We believe he left Frisco as soon as Mario was killed, or maybe a little before. However, we just received word he is in Seattle with some friends."

"I hope you get the SOB. Making a hit is one thing, but shooting all those other people is quite another - oh, Lisa I'm sorry! I didn't mean to hurt your feelings by what I said."

"Charlie, you just said what Mike and I have said in private many times since Uncle Frank and Aunt Maria were killed. I hope someone gets this Mad Max."

181

"I forgot to sign the register. Excuse me while I go do that. No one is there now."

Charlie left then, and Mike turned back toward the caskets. There were four people approaching the caskets now.

He whispered in Lisa's ear, "Who are they?"

"I don't know. But I seem to remember the old man from somewhere. I just can't place him."

The four people about whom Mike was curious were nicely dressed - a woman in her early forties, a man in his mid to late forties, another woman in her mid sixties, and a man in his sixties. The younger couple was obviously married or at least going together, and the older couple was related to the younger couple in some way.

They walked up to Maria's casket, bowed their heads. Then they moved over to where Frank's body lay. The younger woman looked at him and grabbed her husband.

She whispered, "That's the man. I owe him a lot."

"I know."

The older couple looked at Frank and nodded.

Both very quietly said, "Thank you."

Lisa turned to Mike. "I know who they are. I haven't seen them in almost twenty five years."

With those remarks, she got up, went over to the younger woman, and extended her hand to her. "My name is Lisa Forester. I'm Carlos Giaventi's daughter. It was nice of you to come."

With those words, both women fell into each other's arms.

"I could never repay your uncle for what he did for me that day. This is my husband, Robert Fairchild, and my parents, Edward and Ruth Lasard. I'm Rebecca."

Edward extended his hand to Lisa, but the two embraced instead.

"Let me introduce my husband, Michael Forester of the San Francisco police department."

Mike shook hands with Ed Lasard and Robert Fairchild.

Ed turned to Lisa. "I heard of your uncle's death in Edmonton. It came over the police wire."

"My God," Mike exclaimed. "You're the father of the girl

182

Frank helped almost twenty five years ago, and you must be that girl. I'm glad to finally meet you."

"Ed, Robert, you don't know Mike's job on the SFPD. He has the hardest job of all because of me. You see he's in charge of the organized crime division, but we have made our marriage work with the help of Uncle Frank and Charlie. There he is, walking over to Louis."

As Charlie approached Louis, he said, "I don't know if I should give you this, but I was signing the register and I couldn't write evenly because something was under the page. I turned the page and found this envelope addressed to you."

Louis looked closely at the envelope. He opened it, took out the note, read it, and then smiled.

"Thank you, Charlie. You've made my day."

He handed the note to Donna.

Smiling, she said, "Max better have his will in order."

She also thought, this still won't make up for Jack.

"Ask Mike to come over here. I know he'll be interested in this."

Charlie went over to Mike, told him about the envelope he had just found and that Louis wanted to talk to him. Mike excused himself and joined Louis while Charlie stayed to meet the four people with Lisa.

"Mike," Louis said, "I know my uncle talked to you about this subject when the Tong went after you, so I will share this note with you."

Mike looked at the note. It was printed by a computer using a dot matrix printer and said, "Max is on the house. Iceman."

Mike and Louis looked into each other's eyes.

Mike thought, this proves it. The Iceman knows the Giaventi Family. I wonder who it is he knows?

"You're wondering about the connection with the family. Mike, I know of no connection, and that's the absolute truth."

Knowing what he did about the Iceman, Mike believed him.

Max was getting tired of being cooped up in his safe house. He

183

also knew it was only a matter of time until the police and worse yet - the Giaventi Family would find him. He needed money to get out of Seattle. He checked out his pistol and went out into the street. It was almost a week after the Giaventi funeral, a Friday.

As he walked the streets near the underground city, he noticed a couple in their mid twenties. They were obviously on their honeymoon. He followed them towards the waterfront. As the couple walked past an alley, he caught up with them.

He shoved his pistol in the man's face and pushed the woman into the alley. There was no one and nothing in the alley except two huge boxes against one wall. He pushed the man and woman behind the boxes, which blocked any view from the street.

Max ordered the man to give him his money. The man gave him $123.00. Then he demanded the woman's money. She gave him $34 in cash and $500 in traveler's checks, and he smiled.

"That ain't enough, babe."

He reached over and grabbed her right breast. The man started to defend the woman, but Max pushed his gun in his face again. By this time, they were out from behind the boxes.

The man looked behind Max.

Smiling, he said, "There's an old man with a red beard behind you with a gun and he's pointing it at you."

Max laughed. "Good try, but that's the oldest one in the book."

The sound of a gun being fired through a silencer was heard, but not by Max. He was dead before the sound reached his ears.

A voice with a heavy German accent from behind Max said, "Sometimes you should listen to what you are told."

The couple watched Max's body crumple to the concrete and then stared at Max's body crumpled on the concrete for several seconds, then looked up and around so they could thank the man. The man with the red beard and German accent was gone.

The couple fell into each other's arms and held each other for several minutes, then looked down at Max's body. They saw the little hole on one side of his head with a large hole on the other side along with a lot of blood coming out of his head.

After several minutes, the man said, "Honey, we must report

this to the police."

"Yes. Let's go to the street and ask someone to call the police."

"Right."

The couple started to walk towards the street.

The wife said, "You know that man probably saved our lives!"

"And saved you from being raped and killed also."

"You know, honey, do you think it will be as messy as that case in New York last year where the person who was being mugged shot and killed the muggers? The police charged him with 2nd degree murder and he had a lot of legal problems to go through. He even had to defend himself against a civil wrongful death lawsuit. You know the police will ask us who did it and a lot more questions."

"Yes, and they might want to arrest him for killing that man. You know the laws are strange - he might even be convicted of murder."

"That just can't happen and I will do anything I can to prevent that from happening."

Again, she stated, "That man with the red beard probably saved our lives. And saved me from being raped!"

"You're right. But honey, I think I got a better look at the person who killed that mugger back there. It wasn't even a man, it was a woman, a black woman – a good looking woman."

The wife smiled her agreement and continued, "And she was a good looking woman with a great body that was emphasized by the black leotards she was wearing."

"She also had ... her hair was very short - just like that billboard over there," pointing to a billboard across the street.

"You are absolutely right. And she spoke with a very distinctive accent - a southern accent."

"Absolutely."

The police would receive no help in solving Max's murder from them.

Charlie rented a self-storage room, placed his gun case and disguise in it, then locked it up tight. C. C. was hungry. He went to the Needle and traveled up the elevator to the restaurant, where the

185

view was superb. The entire Seattle harbor was visible as well as some of the islands. Charlie ate very slowly and it was early afternoon when he finished. He was almost as satisfied with the day's activities as he had been when he saved Lisa.

He got in his car and drove to the locks, where he walked into the viewing area. Through the glass, he watched salmon going upstream. There were not too many fish going upriver that day. After walking around the locks and dam, he returned to his car and drove to another restaurant for supper. It was named "New Orleans Cajun Restaurant."

After he ate dinner, he decided it just didn't compare with the food in New Orleans, especially that sandwich he had eaten in Thibodaux. It was very bland and had very little or no seasoning.

He parked his car in the parking lot next to the hotel where he was staying. He was feeling good about himself for taking care of Max that morning - he had rid society of a ruthless killer, someone who had gunned down a number of innocent people as well as Frank and his wife. He got out of his car and walked back to the front entrance of the hotel. The hotel sign over the door read "The Downtown Hilton."

Two men came out of the front entrance, talking and laughing as they turned and were walking away from Charlie. Charlie saw a familiar shape get out of a van in front of the men – the exquisite shape of a woman who was wearing a ski mask and very tight clothes. C. C. recognized her as being Donna and immediately knew she was working. She was holding an assault rifle in her hands. The two men stopped in their tracks when they saw her.

Knowing what Donna's business was, Charlie instantly reacted by dropping to the ground as quickly as he could, but it was not fast enough. A burst of shots came from the rifle, one bullet tearing through one of the men and continuing on to Charlie. He felt the burning and tearing of his flesh as it entered his chest, then the pain as if a knife was implanted and twisted in his chest. He knew he had been hit and he knew the wound was serious. He could die from it.

He rolled on the ground in pain as the doorman called 911. Donna jumped back into the van and sped away with no one in pursuit.

Charlie thought, what a way to go. A victim of being in the wrong place at the wrong time, but this might be poetic justice.

His eyes closed and he became unconscious.

CHAPTER 12

Sam Pritchard was the chaplain at University Hospital. The monthly hospital chaplain's meeting at the Downtown Hilton was just breaking up. Chaplains from all the Seattle area hospitals were there. There was a lot of discussion about the living will and what it means. Sam thought there would be more discussions about this topic because, among other things, it involved the ethics of the doctors, the wishes of the patients and the patient's family, and most of all, Christian teachings. The living will concept touched the moral fiber of everyone.

As he entered the lobby of the Hilton, he heard gunfire, which sounded like a short burst from a machine gun. At first, he looked towards where the sounds came from, then realized he might be in danger and ducked behind a chair, where he stayed until the noise stopped. About 20 minutes later, when he thought it was safe, he peeked out from behind the chair, then got up and went to see what had happened.

Slightly less than twenty minutes had passed since he heard the gunfire. He approached the front door from the right. There were two EMT ambulances already there. Two of the paramedics were placing sheets over Joe Andrati and another man. Another two paramedics were working on Charlie, who was lying on the sidewalk to the right of the entrance to the hotel. Sam recognized them as one of the EMT units from university hospital.

As Sam was going over to Charlie's body, Charlie began to float over his body. He looked down at his body only to see the two

EMTs working on him. He didn't understand what was happening because he knew he was dead. He began to float away and soon he was in an area, which was black – totally black. He thought this was the blackest place he had ever been.

As he was floating away from his body, he noticed a red glow ahead of him. He was soon in the red glow. It was like a volcano with many people standing and/or kneeling around the fire that leaped out of the center of the volcano. The people who were kneeling seemed to be penitent while the ones standing seemed not to be penitent.

He saw Frank Giaventi kneeling and then he saw him. A man who had the stigmata and as he passed Frank, Frank smiled and disappeared. Charlie also saw Max and he was anything but penitent. All of a sudden, he seemed to be pushed towards the fire in the volcano and he screamed.

It was then that Charlie knew the man with the stigmata was Jesus. He had two men, one standing on each side of him with what appeared to be a pair of wings on each man. He assumed them to be angels, but as he noticed their heads, their heads were big and had eyes all around their heads.

Now he knew Jesus was talking to him, but he could not hear anything he said, but he knew he was going back to his body and he knew a good man named Sam Pritchard was praying for him.

Immediately, he was floating over his body and then he was returned to his body and he knew he would live from the moment he reentered his body.

Sam went over to where the paramedics were working. One of them was holding a bag for the IV in the air. Sam took it from him so he could do other things. The female paramedic who was kneeling next to Charlie removed her stethoscope and shook her head. She then placed a sheet over Charlie; the other paramedic took the bag back from Sam.

Sam knelled beside Charlie and began praying for him even though he did not know who he was, but he looked familiar. After waiting three or four minutes, Sam was about to get up when he saw bright red blood oozing through the white sheet. He raised the sheet

189

slightly and saw that Charlie was bleeding - not heavily, but bleeding. Pressing his hand against his neck, he felt the carotid pulse.

"Hey, you guys! I got a pulse."

The female paramedic came quickly over to him. Sam was now kneeling again on Charlie's left side, and she stepped over Charlie and around Sam to Charlie's right side and reached for his neck. She looked excited, but remained calm and professional.

She yelled at the other EMT, "I got a carotid!"

Immediately she jerked the sheet off Charlie.

She continued to yell, "Get the IV going again. Call the hospital and get them ready to receive a gunshot wound to the chest."

Charlie was taken to University Hospital, which had an excellent trauma center. Sam Pritchard went to the hospital in the ambulance with Charlie, riding up the elevator with him to the operating room. Then Sam went to the chapel and continued to pray for this stranger.

About 9:00 PM, a nurse found Sam there, still praying.

She interrupted, saying, "Sam, we've just looked through the guy's wallet and personal effects."

"The guy I came in with - the guy who was shot?"

She nodded. "His name is Charlie Cain Duncan. He lives in Sand Point, Idaho . . ."

"Sand Point!"

"Yes. Does that mean something to you?"

"I just thought it is so out of the way," he answered sheepishly. "I didn't think I would run into anyone from Sand Point here."

"Anyway, here's a number to call. You should talk to a man named Henry Teller."

Sam thought Henry Teller - another coincidence, and then he looked at the clock. It said 10:34. He thought it was late, but he had to make the call.

Sam dialed the number the nurse had given him and waited. The telephone rang four times, then on the fifth ring an answering machine cut in, "You have reached the home of C. C. Duncan. Please leave a message no longer than thirty seconds after the tone and your call will be returned by either me or Hank. Remember wait until after the tone. Be talking to you."

Sam waited for the tone, then said, "Henry, this is Sam Pritchard in Seattle. Please call me at University Hospital. Mr. Duncan has been shot and is in critical condition. It's too soon to know if he will be all right. Thank you."

Sam went to the recovery room to see Charlie. He walked over to the unconscious man.

He asked the nurse on duty, "How is he?"

"He's just been through some heavy duty surgery, but he's doing fine. The doctors think he'll make it."

"Good. I'm going home now. Ruth will wonder where I am."

THE END

THE MARRIAGE

By
SHELDON LYNNE

Book II

The Marriage

Riverhouse Publishing
St. Louis MO 63146
ISBN: 1-893892-06-4

PROLOGUE

Charlie had earned a substantial reward for discovering who killed the Mackeys. He was released from the hospital where he was sent because he had amnesia. He now became an excellent assassin working with Kozar in Switzerland. He had just killed Max in Seattle and was walking in front of the Hilton when he saw Donna with a gun. She stepped out of a vehicle and began shooting. Despite dropping to the sidewalk, he was hit and he knew it was serious. He then had an out of body experience where he went to hell where he met Jesus who forgave him his sins and returned him to his body.

A minister, Sam Pritchard, who was at a meeting in the hotel came out of the hotel and began to help the EMTs treat Charlie. The EMTs declared Charlie dead, but Sam knelled by Charlie and began to pray for him. While Sam was praying over Charlie's body, Jesus told Charlie Sam was a good man and sent him back to his body. After the emergency people discovered he was alive, they immediately brought him to the hospital where he was operated on. The surgeons said if he made it through the next day, he might make it.

Sam called the number he had been given and the phone was answered by an answer machine and he left his name and telephone number, then he went home.

CHAPTER 1

Sam walked in his house just after midnight. His wife was waiting for him."What happened?" Ruth asked...

"A man was shot just outside the Hilton and the EMTs from the hospital were treating him. I couldn't leave him. You'll never guess where he lives."

"If you don't tell me I'll never know."

"He lives in Sand Point."

"You're kidding!"

"No, I'm not. I wonder if this could be part of our dreams?"

"Honey, I don't know if it is, but I wouldn't be surprised. Another coincidence is the man who was shot, Charlie Duncan, had papers on him to call Henry in Sand Point - you know, Henry Teller, our contact there."

"This is real strange. Honey, let's sleep on it."

During the night when all the nurses were involved with their duties at the ICU desk, Charlie opened his eyes for a couple of seconds. His eyes were greeted with a soft white light that permeated the entire room.

The light had a warmth to it that he had never known before. He saw a lady garbed in a white gown much like a night gown. She smiled at Charlie.

From that moment, Charlie knew he would fully recover, but he was puzzled by the white light and the woman. He knew he saw the woman and now he felt his strength returning very quickly. He continued to think that God was returning his strength to him and he definitely would recover. Charlie drifted back to sleep as the light in the room disappeared.

At the same time, a nurse was looking into Charlie's room. She saw nothing unusual.

The following morning, the switchboard operator at University Hospital answered an incoming call. "University Hospital. How may I direct your call?"

Donna Weir replied, "I'd like to find out how a patient is doing. He was..."

"I'll connect you with patient information."

Donna was a little perturbed by the operator switching her call, but she waited for patient information to answer.

"Patient information. How may I help you?"

"I don't know this patient's name, but he was shot last night in front of the Hilton. I just want to know how he's doing."

"His name is Mr. Duncan. He must be something special. Several people have called about him already this morning. He's still listed as critical, but the surgeon has a note which says he believes he'll recover completely if he makes it through the day."

"Thanks. I'm leaving for San Francisco later today, but I just couldn't leave without knowing how he's doing."

By 8:30 AM Sam was on his third cup of coffee. "Ruth, I had my dream again. It changed a little bit and I can now recognize him. I wonder what the Lord wants me to do."

"Sam, my dream changed, too. I saw that man and I'll never forget his face. He had sort of a kind face, with a repentant look about it. I guess that's the best way to describe him."

Sam thought for a moment, and then replied, "Ruth, I want you to come to the hospital with me this morning. I want you to meet Mr. Duncan. He's probably a member of our new church. He'll need someone to visit him."

"Why didn't you say that before?"

"Remember what I told you last night. The person I had to

197

contact in Sand Point for the patient was Henry Teller. You know Henry's the chairman of the search committee for our church."

"That's a coincidence. In any case, Mr. Duncan needs someone to visit him. I can be ready in an hour."

It was a little after ten in the morning when Sam and Ruth walked into the ICU room where Charlie was. Charlie was sleeping and a nurse was taking his blood pressure.

"Nurse, how's Mr. Duncan?"

"He's doing excellent. He has been awake several times. He has even asked for you by name."

"How did he know my name? Did anyone mention me?"

"I don't believe so, but I must be mistaken. How else could he know your name?"

With those words, she left Sam and Ruth alone in the room with the patient.

They watched him briefly, and then went out to the hallway to talk. When they were alone in a small waiting area, Ruth looked at her husband and squeezed his hand tightly.

She whispered in his ear, "I know how he knew your name. He's the man in our dreams - the one I saw last night."

"That's the reason I wanted you to come with me this morning. I recognized Mr. Duncan from my dream too."

"Sam, I have a feeling we should go back in his room for just a minute."

"Honey . . . well okay. But just for a minute. I have my rounds to make."

Back inside the room, Ruth took Charlie's hand in hers. Both Sam and Ruth began to pray silently.

Charlie opened his eyes and looked up at Ruth, then towards Sam.

"Sam, we have to talk soon," he said quietly.

"Mr. Duncan, I didn't know you were awake."

"I just woke up. I'm a little weak now, but I think I am getting my strength back very quickly. I need to talk to you."

"Mr. Duncan, this is my wife Ruth."

"Good morning. I've heard all about you from Sam. I also

198

read about you in the papers."

"The nurse says you are doing just fine and I understand you might even get out of ICU today or tomorrow."

"Sam, I don't know if you are the one who will call Henry Teller in Sand Point, but I need you to tell Hank something for me. Tell him not to call Lisa. The only condition under which he may call her is if I die. Make sure you tell him that. And be emphatic. No calls to Lisa."

"I'll tell him what you said. By the way, are you a member of Henry's church?"

"Yes - sort of - at least that's the church I go to when I go to church - why do you ask?"

"I'm your new pastor."

"My God. You and I were destined to meet. We must talk soon. I must tell you, I have been to hell and back. How about early afternoon?"

Sam was intrigued by what Charlie had said. He replied, "I should be finished my morning rounds by one or one-thirty. I can come for an hour or two then."

"Fine. I'll see you then."

That afternoon as Sam was finishing his rounds for the morning, the public address system for the hospital squawked, "Reverend Sam Pritchard, please call the operator. Reverend Sam Pritchard, please call the operator."

Sam went to a telephone, dialed the operator.

"This is Sam Pritchard."

"A Mr. Teller from Sand Point is holding for you. He said he was returning your call. Do you want me to connect him to the phone you're using?"

"No, my office is just down the hall. Connect him to that phone and I'll be there within thirty seconds."

Sam rushed into his office just as the phone was beginning to ring. He snatched it up and said, "Henry? This is Sam. I suppose you are calling about my message on that answering machine."

"I sure am. How's C. C.?"

"I have good news. He's doing extremely well. I spoke to

him this morning with Ruth, my wife. He even had a message for you. He said under no conditions were you to contact Lisa, unless he died. He was very emphatic about that. Who is this Lisa?"

"Beside me, Lisa is probably the closest thing to family he has. Tell him I'll be in Seattle by midnight and I'll see him tomorrow morning."

"How about meeting me in Mr. Duncan's room about 9:30 in the morning?"

"I'd like that Sam. I'll probably beat you there and you know it'll be good to see you again. C. C. is the man I told you about - the one who saved me from a couple of crooks. I'll never forget what he did."

"He's the man! Interesting. I'm going to see him in just a little bit - right after I eat my lunch. Don't forget what Mr. Duncan said about not calling Lisa. See you tomorrow."

"I won't forget. See you then."

Sam finished eating his salad for lunch. He liked salads, especially the Caesar's Salad at the hospital cafeteria. It was probably the only thing Sam liked at the cafeteria. He threw away the paper plate on which the salad was served, left the cafeteria, and went to the elevators. He went up to ICU to see Mr. Duncan. The time was now 2:30 PM.

Arriving at Charlie's room, Sam found nurses working around him. He thought, my God, he's had a setback.

Taking a closer and more perceptive look, he saw the nurses were preparing to move their patient.

"Sam, we're moving him to a private room. He requested one. He was assigned 3423. It'll be a little while before we can get him there. We still have to disconnect him here, and then connect him to the telemetry system up there. Why don't you come back to visit with him in about two hours?"

Knowing the nurse really meant, "Don't interrupt us," Sam waved to Charlie. "I'll see you about 4:30 in your new room."

Charlie responded by weakly waving.

The head nurse at the ICU desk gestured to Sam to come over to her.

"Sam, in all my years of nursing, I have never seen a patient recover as rapidly as Mr. Duncan. He's done so well the doctor released him to a floor room in intermediate care with a monitor. I just thought you'd want to know."

"That's great. You know, the paramedics said he was dead. It's a miracle he's recovering so quickly."

"I think so, too."

Sam walked out of ICU.

At 4:15, Sam was at the nurse's desk on the third floor.

"How's Mr. Duncan?"

"Sam, if I didn't know his history, I'd want to know why he's in the hospital at all. He's doing just great."

"Good. May I see him?"

"Sure. He is in room 3423."

Sam walked down the hall and found the door partially open. He knocked on the door.

"It's Sam. Can I come in?"

"Sure can," came the response.

Sam looked at Charlie. He was sitting up in bed resting.

"I was wondering if you were coming. Have you talked to Hank?"

"Yes. That's one of the reasons I was late this afternoon. We talked for about forty-five minutes. He is one good friend. Something he said puzzled me, though. He said he and this Lisa were the closest thing to family you have. You have no relatives?"

"I don't know, Sam. You see I was in the Special Forces in Southeast Asia at the close of the war. I was wounded, but the severest wound I received was the wound that caused me to have partial amnesia. I still don't know anything about my family - if I have a family."

"That's horrible. Maybe if we pray about it, you'll recover your memory."

"Sam, I don't know if that would be good or bad right now. I answered your question. Now it's my turn to ask you a question."

Sam grinned. "Now wait a minute. Is this twenty questions?"

"No. And I promise after you answer my question, I'll burden

201

you with a story, a true story, you may not want to hear. But I believe you are the one God wants me to tell."

Sam was very puzzled by Charlie's words.

"Before the question, please call me what the people in Sand Point call me - C. C. - or call me what Lisa and Mike call me - Charlie. But cut out this Mr. Duncan stuff. I don't know him. Oh, you can call me what Hank calls me, too, but smile when you call me that. Seriously, Hank calls me either Charlie, C.C., or just plain Duncan. Pick one of the three. Okay?"

Sam thought for a moment, and then said, "Sure, C. C."

"Now for the question. I feel you had better offers than what our church in Sand Point could make. But even with better offers, you chose Sand Point. Why? What did God do, say, or tell you - to make you pick Sand Point? Did he slap you on the side of the head with a two-by-four like people do to gain the attention of mules, or what?"

"It's interesting you should ask that question. I've asked myself the same thing many times." He grinned again, lifting his hands toward the ceiling. "Why Sand Point, Lord, why San Point? But, seriously, I never question His guidance. I was about to accept an assistant pastorship in L.A. Now my wife and I had been having this dream every night for over a week, but we didn't know what it meant until the day we decided to accept this position. I should add, we were both having the same dream.

"The day I was going to write my acceptance letter to that church, Ruth came to me and told me not to accept the offer. When I asked why, she showed me the envelope from the Sand Point Christian Church. I was shocked - not by the envelope, but by the fact it came from a church in a town that was definitely tied to the dreams my wife and I had been having for over a week.

Sam hesitated, but continued, "C. C., I know the dream is somehow connected to you. I knew it was connected to Henry or someone else in Sand Point after I visited Henry's church. When Ruth and I visited there three weeks ago, we were shown the area and town by Henry. He told me to call him Hank, but I just haven't gotten the hang of that yet. We went to his old place. He

202

showed us around, his wife's grave. Both Ruth and I saw it at the same time - that point of white sand over on the far side of the lake."

"I know the place. I like to lay out in the sand over there on a sunny day."

"Well, we said we would come to Sand Point immediately. Hank also told us about you. He also told us how you saved his place and made it so he could be buried by his wife and live in the house with the red barn.

"All this really does not make sense unless you know what we were dreaming and then, what Ruth and I dreamed last night. The dream always started with sand. It developed into a real point of sand jutting out into a lake. Then the trees began to take shape. They were all pine trees except for a small grove of aspen."

"The same as on that sand beach by my lake."

"Yes, that's the vision we had in our dreams. After the trees became visible, I came out of the trees followed by Ruth. We had smiles on our faces. I lifted my arms up and a man and a woman appeared from nowhere and walked towards us. All of a sudden, two children appeared, a boy and a girl. I embraced the man and Ruth stooped over and hugged the children. When Ruth got up, she and the woman in the dream embraced."

"That's really strange. I think God was talking to you - telling you to go to Sand Point. When I tell you the rest of my story, there will be no doubt."

"I'm not finished yet. Last night, our dreams changed. Until last night, we could not identify any of the people in our dreams. The man and the woman had no faces, or if they did, they were hidden from us. Last night, the man's face became visible and we could identify him.

"When drinking coffee this morning, I thought I should ask my wife to come to the hospital to visit you as I thought you might be a member of our church. My true reason was I believed I recognized you as the man in my dream last night. When my wife saw you this morning, she confirmed it - she said she recognized you from her dream last night, too.

"I now realize God sending me to Sand Point is somehow connected to you," Sam concluded.

The public address system quietly said, "Visiting hours are over. All visitors please leave. Visitation is from 8:00 AM to 8:30 PM. It is now 8:30 PM. Please leave now so our patients and your friends and relatives can get a much-needed rest. Thank you for your cooperation."

"Where has the time gone? I guess your story will take at least the same amount of time as mine did, so let's continue this tomorrow. Incidentally, Henry - I mean Hank - will be here tomorrow. You can tell your story to both of us."

"Sam, I can't tell Hank my story. After you hear it, I know you will understand why. It will be good to see Hank though. After he leaves, come back when you have some time to spend with me. After you hear my story, I hope you will understand what I am going through and help me to live with it."

Donna's plane touched down in San Francisco at 8:27 PM. She and Mona walked out of the jet way into the terminal building. Louis was waiting for them in the concourse. He walked up and gave each of them a dozen roses.

"Donna, Mona. You did a fine job. I'll give you the bonus I promised when we get to my house."

"Louis, you know we didn't handle Max."

"Of course I know it. You saw the note from the Iceman I received at Frank's funeral, didn't you?"

Donna replied, "I remember."

Mona asked, "What did the note say?"

"The note said, "Max is on the house, Iceman. I was not surprised you didn't get to Max first."

"Mona, that's the same SOB who took Jack out."

Louis interrupted, "Donna, you must remember Jack asked for what he got."

"I know, but I still hold it against this Iceman."

Louis noted Donna was on edge.

He asked, "Donna, why are you so nervous?"

204

"Louis, there was a man right behind Joe and the contact who stopped a bullet that went through one of them. He was in critical condition this morning, but expected to make it. I have to call University Hospital to find out how he's doing. You know I don't like bystanders getting hurt if I can help it."

"I heard about him on the radio, Donna. He's been taken off the critical list and is out of ICU. The news report on TV said his recovery was almost a miracle."

"See Donna, I told you he would be fine and not to worry so much about him. Anyhow, we get the bonus."

"Mona, we did earn the bonus, but I don't like killing innocent bystanders, no matter what I'm paid."

"You're too soft-hearted."

Louis interrupted, "Donna just cares about people. That makes her different from everyone else. You might learn from her. When we get back to the house, I have another assignment for you. This time, you may not have to take care of anybody."

After returning to the house, Louis, Donna, and Mona went into the library. Louis sat behind his desk and motioned the two women to sit on the sofa.

"Donna, you will handle this for the family. You remember Uncle Frank and me talking about Cleve Ronson in Vancouver don't you?"

"Sure do."

"Well, he's agreed to ship us some supplies via a pontoon plane. He needs a lake to land the plane and he suggested one in Idaho. I had some people investigate the lake. It's near a place called Sand Point. They found it to be ideal for a seaplane.

"It was previously owned by a man named Henry Teller. Our contact in Sand Point called to tell us Mr. Teller sold it to a Mr. Duncan, but Teller still runs the place for Duncan. You might run into this Teller, but you probably won't run into Duncan. This guy travels a lot and will probably be gone.

"The only problem is, we will have to wait until Thanksgiving for the first shipment. However, this will give you time to go there and get the lay of the land. When you get there, contact Terry

205

Bracken. He's a real estate broker. Tell him you want to buy or rent the Duncan place. Money is no object."

"Is he our contact?"

"In a manner of speaking, yes. He sent me the information concerning the lake and how Mr. Duncan obtained it. I must say this Bracken is not too smart from what I know of him, but this Duncan might be. You may have to take him out to buy the place. Bracken's problem is that he is very greedy. He can be bought."

"I don't have to worry about Bracken then?"

"No, we'll just buy him. Do you have any questions?"

Mona replied, "No sir."

Donna shook her head no.

"All right then. Go home and get some sleep. You can plan your trip to Sand Point tomorrow. I want you to go there this week. I don't think you'll need to stay any longer than a couple of days. After you've returned from seeing the lake, tell me what you've seen and how you plan to accept delivery of the goods. Again, good job in Seattle."

When the orderly brought his breakfast at 7:05 AM, Charlie looked at it and decided it looked acceptable, so he poured the orange juice into the glass on the tray. As he was sipping it, Hank walked into his room.

"C. C., I hear you had a slight problem a couple of nights ago."

Charlie broke into a smile.

"Hank, it sure is good to see you. The only other friendly face I've seen is Sam Pritchard's, our new pastor."

Hank looked out the door at a nurse passing in the hallway.

"Well, I'm not including the nurses. They all have friendly faces and are nice to me."

"C. C., what happened?"

"The best I can figure out is someone wanted someone else dead. The hit man - or in this case, hit woman - shot and killed two men. I was behind one of the men. When one of the bullets went through him, it hit me as I was dropping to the ground. In

206

short, I was in a very wrong place at a very wrong time."

"You know I came through the war without being wounded," Hank said. "You know . . ."

Sam Pritchard walked into C. C.'s room just then and Hank interrupted himself to shake his hand.

"So you beat me seeing C. C. this morning. When did you get here, Hank?"

"About 7:30 this morning. That breakfast will make C. C. get well soon. I don't know how he can eat that stuff."

"Hank, you're absolutely right. I will have to get better fast and get out of here so I can get better food. It is palatable, though."

"Henry, what war were you talking about when I walked in?"

"The only war. The real war."

"Sam, he was talking about World War II. He was in the Pacific. He won't tell you this, but he was a marine. He fought on Guadalcanal through Iwo Jima. He went on R & R so he missed Saipan."

C. C. continued, "Sam, Hank will now tell you how he wasn't wounded in all those battles."

"I ducked fast when I should duck and I dug deep fox holes. I didn't volunteer for anything and kept my head down. Something C. C. didn't learn in Vietnam."

"Sam, I would take what Hank has just said with a grain of salt. I've seen his medals. He has a whole bunch of them, including the Navy Cross and the Purple Heart."

"C. C. you know I told you that Purple Heart was for breaking my ankle on Iwo."

"How did you break the ankle, Hank?"

"I stepped on a land mine."

"At least I didn't step on a landmine."

"We have talked a long time, I better be going if I'm going to make it back to the farm tonight. But before I go, why didn't you want me to call Lisa?"

"Hank, it would only have worried her and that's the last thing I want to do. By the way, what's going on at the farm? Sam, the farm is where he lives in that house with the red barn near my place by the lake."

"I suspected that."

"Well, you are the excitement in town. As soon as word about what happened got around, Terry was on the phone asking me if I had power of attorney to sell your property and could he list it. I was polite and said no, or maybe I should have told him he'd be the last person who'd get the listing. Then I told him Sam had said you were going to be okay.

"You know, that SOB wasn't happy you were going to live. I think Paul and Terry still think they have a chance to get the property."

"You mean you didn't tell them what my will states?"

"Hell no. It's fun to see them trying to get their paws on the lake."

Charlie and Hank laughed.

An orderly came into the room, picked up the tray and left.

"Charlie, what's in your will, or do you want to tell me?"

"I don't mind, but you have to promise not to tell a soul."

"I promise."

"I've left the property to the church as a youth camp, with the provision that Hank can be buried next to his wife and continue to live in the house where he now lives for as long as he wants. Another provision is that Mike and Lisa's children can go to camp there free. Also, if Mike and Lisa want to spend some time there, they can do that free - prime summer time or whenever they want. Those conditions are written in stone."

"C. C., I almost forgot. The propane dealer installed the third tank for you. He doesn't know why you need three tanks and that special valve you ordered, but you have it now. To tell the truth, I don't see why either.

"I finished fixing up the trail on the west side of the lake to the trailhead at the road near the picnic area. Beside that, nothing much happened. Damn, look at the time. I see you don't need anything, so if I'm going to get there in daylight, I have to go now. See you in about three or four weeks, huh?"

"I guess so Hank. Take care of everything for me."

"I will, friend. Take care."

Sam shook hands with Hank as he left the room.

"Sam, do you have time to listen to me for several hours?"

"Charlie, I cleared my schedule today just to talk to you."

"Please close the door."

Sam got up and closed the door. Just as he was about to sit down again, Charlie spoke.

"Sam, take this pillow and place it against the speaker/mike to the nurse's station."

Sam looked at Charlie, then walked over to the speaker and did as Charlie asked. He wondered what was so important that this amount of secrecy was needed.

"Sam, over the past few years, I have sat on Meditation Point on the lake . . ."

"Where's Meditation Point?"

"It's on the knoll above the grave. You know, where you probably saw my beach with the pine trees and the grove of aspen. I built a small shed and a bench up there. I even have a butane catalytic heater with a ten pound can to go with it. I've been up there in below-zero weather, meditating."

"You know, that is where I saw the beach. What do you meditate on?"

"Life and what I did for a living. I guess I should tell you my story. That will explain a lot of things. And remember, I said what I did for a living - past tense."

"I'm here to listen."

"I've thought about where I should start for a long time and I decided to start when I was killed."

"C. C., you were not killed. You are alive, here in this room."

"After you hear my story, tell me that again. I died on the sidewalk. Before I was shot I recognized the person who did the shooting."

"C. C., you should tell the police you know who it was!"

"Sam, I can't. The rest of my story will explain why I can't. I was already floating above my body when you came to help the paramedics. I saw you take the IV bag and hold it for them as well as seeing the female paramedic place the sheet over my body. It was then you started to pray for me. At that moment, I knew your name was Sam Pritchard. You saved me from death with your prayers, I might add.

"Anyway, in a short time, I began to float away from the scene. Incidentally, I can't tell you how long because time meant nothing to me while I was out of my body. I floated out over some land, then over water. During this time, there was reasonable light, white light. Suddenly, I was in total darkness and I mean total, black darkness. Have you ever been in a cave when they turned the lights out?"

"Yes. That's pitch black."

"Well, that darkness is bright sunlight compared to this darkness. I continued on my way. Somewhere ahead of me was a glow, a red glow, not a white light. Soon, I was floating over what looked like a volcano with fire in the center of it. There were people in the fire and on the edge of the volcano looking into the flames.

"All of a sudden, I was standing on the rim of the fire. Sam, to say the least, that fire was Hell. It was hot as Hell where I stood. I saw people I knew there. Some of the people looked cocky; others had their heads bowed as if to say they were sorry, while others were kneeling as if they were praying.

"I recognized some of them. There was Max. I sent him there."

"You sent him there?"

"Yes. The rest of my story will explain what I mean. Anyway, he was cocky, or I should say still cocky. There was another one named Jack Hall - his head was bowed - I sent him there also. Frank Giaventi was kneeling in a very repentant manner. There were others that I did not know, but there was something else. There were people there from the beginning of time around the volcano. How I knew this, I don't know, but I firmly believe that.

"The heat was unbearable and the screams coming from the

fire - I have never heard anything so horrible. Occasionally, an individual was cast into the fire by a force I couldn't see. It was then I knew I was definitely in Hell.

"Out of nowhere, I saw three men - I think they were men - walking outside the volcano. One of them was small while the other two were huge - that's the only way to describe them. The big men were on either side of the small man. They had eyes all around their heads, front and back. They had what looked like wings on each arm and were shielding the small man from the heat of the fire.

"I knew this man was Jesus, and he could, if he wanted, release me from Hell. As he passed Frank Giaventi, Frank looked up and smiled. He disappeared. I remember I hoped he was granted an exit from this hell.

"He came to me. His eyes were extremely compassionate. I don't remember saying or hearing anything but I know a conversation took place. I know it went something like this. 'Have mercy, Lord. I am truly sorry for my sins.' The Lord replied 'You have a good man praying for you.' That's when I died. 'Your sins are forgiven, return to your body, and work for me. At that time I saw a woman dressed in white and Sam, I saw that same woman in this room last night!'

"Sam, the next thing I knew, I was hovering over my body, looking at you praying for me. You saw something, checked my pulse in the neck, and called the paramedics. Then a female paramedic walked over to me and stepped over me to my right side.

"She checked the pulse in my neck. She obviously found a pulse. She did all this without lifting the sheet from my body. As she called to the other paramedics, she threw the sheet off my body. It was at this time, I returned to my body. So you see, I couldn't have known it was a woman paramedic or the other things I've described if I didn't have an out-of-body experience. After that, I remember nothing until I woke up here in the hospital.

"Then last night my room was filled with a bright light and Sam, a woman clothed in a white gown was in here smiling at me.

And Sam, she was definitely the one I saw immediately after being shot and not one of the nurses – she was too old for any of them. During that time, I could feel my strength returning to me extremely fast and I also knew I was going to make it. Sam, I was in Hell and Jesus forgave me my sins."

"C. C., what you have told me is the same as some others claim to have experienced. You could be remembering what they said and your mind may have played tricks on you."

"Sam, it was real. I know it was real because I saw the Stigmata on Jesus. Well, not the complete Stigmata, only his head, hands and feet. Incidentally, the holes were not in the palm of his hands, but in his wrists close to his hands. I knew there was a hole in his side, but I couldn't see it.

"Another reason I know what I have told you is true and you can check what I am going to say, is you were wearing a very dressy suit - a dark green suit. I want you to think about what I said happened - the woman paramedic, stepping over me to my right side, taking my pulse in the neck, and calling the other paramedics as she removed the sheet from my body."

"Your story does have some credence that other stories don't have, but I must say, it's hard to believe. You haven't told me why you were sent to Hell in the first place, though."

"I'm coming to that. He quickly related all that he knew of his life and had been able to reconstruct since the time he had been robbed of his memory. When he finished, Sam sat motionless looking at Charlie.

"You were a hit man?"

"That's right Sam. I was a hired assassin. An independent. I remembered a name given to me in New Orleans as an arms dealer. I contacted him and made him an offer. He agreed to be a broker for my services. He told me he was already helping a couple others who were in the same line of work as I was entering.

"Interpol nicknamed me Iceman. I feel Lisa's husband, Mike, is close to identifying me. That's why I can't let Lisa know I was shot here in Seattle since I sent Max to Hell just before I was shot and Lisa's husband, Mike may very well put two and two together.

Also, for the same reason Louis Giaventi would surely know if he knew about me being shot here in Seattle. Too many things would fit together if they knew. Another thing, if I told the police I knew who did the shooting, both Mike and Louis would know. So you see, I can't tell anyone and neither can you."

"You are in a mess, Charlie."

"Sam, I want you to know I have quit being the Iceman. I have developed other legal businesses over the past years - with clean money - and I intend to pursue only those businesses. After all, Jesus has forgiven me, what else matters?"

"Nothing else matters, C. C. Remember Jesus forgave Saul his sins on the road to Damascus and he became the Apostle Paul. It is a mystery why He forgave Paul his sins because Paul was the worst of the worst, but it is not for man to judge who or why God forgives anybody."

"But I must work for Him. I intend to give it my best shot. There is something else I want you to think about. I believe God ordained you to go Sand Point for a reason. I don't presume to know the full reason, but I believe I am included in his reason. Everything points to that."

"I must agree with you."

As Sam left C. C.'s room, C. C. began to think, I will have to tell Lisa I was injured here in Seattle when I see her next - what will I tell her? If I make up a story, she will know it's a story, but if I tell her the truth and say I was here on business and was in the wrong place at the wrong time, Mike might not put everything together. That's what I will do - tell her the truth.

213

CHAPTER 2

On August 7th, Charlie was discharged from University Hospital and checked into a Seattle hotel to continue his recovery for a few more days. From his hotel room, he called Lisa.

Mike answered, "Hello, this is the Forester residence."

"Mike, this is Charlie. How are you two doing?"

"Just fine, Charlie. What's with you?"

"Well, I'm in Seattle. I just got out of the hospital. It so happened I was in the wrong place at the wrong time. I was severely injured in an accident, but I'm okay now. I just have to do a little more R & R. I thought I could use some of your barbecue, Lisa's cooking..."

Mike interrupted, "Why didn't you let us know you were in the hospital. You know Lisa would have flown up there just to nurse you."

"I know that, but when I woke up, I didn't need anything extra or I would have called. Believe me, I would have called. But I want that meal you promised me, too."

"You remembered what I said. I had hoped you would forget. Just kidding. Where do you want to go?"

"To be truthful, just to relax at your house would be great."

"Fine, what time is your flight?"

"Mike, I'm driving down. It will take me an extra day, but you know I'm a frustrated truck driver. I guess I'll see you by Thursday afternoon or early Friday morning. Is that all right with you two?"

"It sure is. See you then."

Thursday came very quickly. Charlie drove up to Mike and Lisa's house, got out of his car to hear the squeals of joy from their children, who promptly jumped on Charlie. Lisa came out of the house.

"Children, I told you Uncle Charlie was hurt. Now get off him - at least until we know he's okay. Hi, Charlie!"

She went over and embraced him gently. Charlie could not hug her back as he usually did because he was still a little sore from his wound.

Lisa asked, "What happened? How were you hurt?"

"It was a freak accident. Like I said, I was in the wrong place at the wrong time. I was walking to my hotel and a stray bullet came out of nowhere and went into my chest. You remember the Andratti job. Anyway, it did a good deal of damage, but I am fine now. I just need a few more weeks to recover fully. The doctors told me I have recovered faster than anybody they've ever seen. I still hurt a little, though. Oh, I'd love to tumble around with the kids. It's one of my pleasures. Maybe we can settle for some hugs instead."

After he had embraced each of the little ones, Lisa said, "Now let's go into the house. Mike will be home shortly."

"Come on kids. I'll show you what I've brought you."

A week passed. It was a very relaxing time for Charlie. He played with the kids and went for walks in the nearby park, remembering that day when he had saved Lisa from Deng. But most of all, he did nothing and had time to think. He wondered what his visit to Hell meant and why he was forgiven - why did Jesus forgive him. He certainly didn't deserve forgiveness, but at the same time, he thanked God for His mercy and grace. It was as a weight had been lifted off his shoulders. However, a new weight appeared - the weight of guilt and remorse because of what he had

216

done over the last few years.

As he was saying his good-byes on Monday, he said, "Since I haven't shaved in a couple of weeks, I've grown attached to this stubble on my face. I think I'll grow a beard. How do you think it looks?"

Mike looked at Charlie, gestured in a way that meant - terrible, cut it off.

However, Lisa answered, "I think you look more... distinguished."

"That settles it. I'll let it stay."

Everyone smiled and then embraced. Charlie was not uncomfortable this time during the hugging. He kissed Lisa on the cheek and left to go back to Seattle.

As he drove away down the street, Mike said, "Honey, I can't believe he went to church with us yesterday. I've never seen Charlie go to church, much less want to go to church. I wonder what happened to change his attitude?"

"God speaks to everyone in mysterious ways. I hope he has gotten some religion."

Sam Pritchard had been in Sand Point for three weeks. During that time he had preached two sermons and the congregation liked Sam and his message. Hank especially liked his sermons and demonstrated his approval of Sam and Ruth by showing them and their children around the lake. When he took them to C. C.'s place, Sam became oddly quiet and intent as he looked around. He was dying to ask Hank if he knew who C. C. was, but his conversation with C. C. was confidential, so he did not ask Hank the probing questions he had in mind.

Sam and his family had invitations to eat out with the members of their congregation every night for their first twelve days in Sand Point. They got to know the congregation very well during this time.

Sam was also invited to meet with Father Brewster, the parish priest serving St. Michael's Church, and Reverend Malone, the Baptist minister at Sand Point.

217

By Labor Day, the Pritchards were accepted in Sand Point and had grown to like the people there. However, because of what he knew, Sam was uncertain as to what he would do when Charlie, better known in Sand Point as C. C., came home. He was to find out very soon.

As C. C. drove up to his house on the lake the day after Labor Day, he noticed smoke coming out of the chimney. Inside he found Hank sitting in one of the two recliners - Hank's chair.

Without turning around, the man said, "Hello, C. C."

"Hank, I'm glad to be home and I'm especially glad to walk into a warm house with a fire going. How did you know I'd be home tonight?"

"Yesterday I called Lisa to see when you left there. When I found out you had left there on Monday, I called the doctor to see when you would be discharged to come home. When I found out..."

"Okay, okay. So you investigated. Thanks. How's Sam doing?"

"He's doing great. I'd say he's as well liked as any pastor we've had. I like his sermons. They don't put me to sleep either."

"That's great. Do you think I could see him tomorrow?"

"Don't know why not. I think it would be all right except from about 11:00 in the morning to 1:30. He's meeting with the other two pastors for their weekly lunch."

"It'll be good to see Sam again."

At 2:15 PM, Sam was in his office when C. C. walked in.

"Hi, Sam. Remember me?"

"C. C. How can I forget you? Come on in and sit awhile. I've heard a lot about you since I came here. You have a good reputation."

Sam got up and closed the door behind Charlie.

"Sam, I want to tell you, this is hard for me to do - to come see you for the first time after Seattle."

"It's hard for me also. But let's pray about it and let the Lord handle our fears."

"Good idea."

218

Both men prayed for about ten minutes. During that time, not a word was spoken by either man.

Sam said, "Amen."

Charlie followed a few seconds later, "Amen."

Charlie asked, "Does Ruth know about me?"

"I haven't told her a thing, but as you know, she had you in her dreams also. I would suspect - and expect - she knows you're special in some way, but doesn't know why."

"I think it's better that way, don't you?"

"I agree," was Sam's response.

It was early in the morning on November 7th when Donna walked into Louis Giaventi's library. This was the old library of Frank Giaventi since he had moved into Frank's house. Lisa's mother was allowed to continue to live at the mansion.

Donna said, "We're ready to leave. Do you have any further instructions?"

"No, the briefcase is over there on the sofa with the money. Be sure you have the coke before you give them the money. The plane will arrive on the lake early on November 11th. Protect yourself. I have a funny feeling about this deal."

"Louis, I'm taking Mona, Kirk, Harry, Pete, and Jim. All of them are good in a fight. Nothing will go wrong. We'll stay in Spokane on November 9th and take over Mr. Duncan's camp early on the tenth. That's all there is to it."

Louis sighed, "Good luck."

Donna walked out of mansion to the van, which soon pulled out of the estate and onto the highway headed toward Seattle.

Finally, the day arrived when Joel and Sara Thompson had to leave Dawson, November 10th. They had mixed emotions. On one hand, they were happy they would soon return home and see their children after three weeks, but were not happy to leave Dawson where they had just completed their first camera hunt in that natural wonderland of untouched beauty and abundant wildlife. Joel and Sara thought their friend Ross Carruth was right

219

- it was more fun to camera hunt than to hunt with guns!

The twin-engine turbo prop plane was warming up on the all gravel runway at the small Dawson airport, which was used mostly by private planes. Leon, the pilot, had loaded Joel and Sara's gear on the airplane just before they had boarded. With everyone on board, Leon taxied the small craft to the gravel runway, and then moved the throttle to maximum. The motors responded with a roar. Joel and Sara were pushed back in their seats briefly, but the plane was soon in the air, climbing to cruising altitude, and they were able to relax in their seats. The flight was to fly south to Spokane and then turn towards Denver.

The plane wasn't airborne more than an hour when Leon started putting some little white pills under his tongue. Both Joel and Sara knew they were nitroglycerin tablets, as Sara's mother had to take them on occasion for her heart. They became worried.

Joel said, "Leon, if you're not feeling well, let's land and get you to a doctor."

Leon knew if a doctor who wouldn't hide a proper diagnosis ever diagnosed his heart condition he would be grounded forever, so he replied, "It's nothing. When I get to Denver, I'll see a doctor if my indigestion continues. Anyway, you heard what Nick said - that front is coming south like a Siberian Express train. If we delay, you might be stuck here for a long time."

Joel and Sara did not like it, but they realized what Leon said was probably true. They would have to trust that they would make it.

The morning of November 10th, Sam was drinking his juice when Ruth walked in the kitchen. They looked at each other in a strange manner.

Ruth was the first to speak, "Sam, that dream returned last night."

"I had the dream too. But it changed."

"I know, Sam. I can identify the woman in my dream now."

"So can I. I wonder what it means."

"Sam, do you think C. C. would know the woman? He was

220

still in my dream, although he now has a beard instead of being clean-shaven as he was originally. It seems the Lord has updated C. C."

"That's true, but I doubt C. C. would know the woman, even though he was still in my dream also. The Lord is the one who is causing this dream. He, and He, alone knows the outcome."

"But why is He telling us, and not others, who is coming?"

"Ruth, I never question what the Lord is doing or his motives. He hasn't told me His reasons and I'm willing to wait for Him to tell me."

"I guess you're right, but why don't you go see Charlie today. You know, for a friendly visit."

"I would except I have to be in Coeur d'Alene for most of the day talking at that conference about the problems we are encountering in trying to get a Christian Youth Conference going. I'll talk to him tomorrow morning before I do anything else."

CHAPTER 3

Sunrise had not taken place when Donna, Mona, and the others left the Ramada Inn in Spokane. It would take them almost forty-five minutes to travel to Coeur d'Alene, where they would head north to Sand Point. It was a very pleasant ride north and with the sun rising on the east side of highway 95. Mona made several comments about how lovely the route was, particularly at this time of day with the orange/red ball of the sun rising and turning into a white ball over some small mountains.

Donna drove out of Sand Point for about ten or eleven miles, and then turned onto the gravel road that led to Charlie's camp. The van came around a curve in the road where everyone in the van got their first look at the camp and the lake.

Harry exclaimed, "Nice place! I could go for this."

Jerking everyone in the van back to reality, Donna reminded them, "Remember guys, we're here on business. Jim, you take care of the briefcase. Understand?"

"Understood, Donna."

Charlie had just finished breakfast and was looking out his window at the van coming down the road and wondering who would be visiting him this early.

The van stopped in front of the camp. Donna got out, followed by Mona and the men.

Charlie recognized Donna the instant he saw her. He mumbled to himself and thought the same thing, "Shit."

He continued to think this is bad. She doesn't leave San

Francisco unless it's on business. I wonder if she knows I am a friend of Lisa's or does she even know who I am? I've grown a beard - maybe she won't recognize me. I'll play it that way. I hope I can get away quickly. She's here on business - that's not good for me or anyone else.

Donna walked up to the cabin door. Just before she knocked, Charlie opened it.

"Hi there, folks. Can I do something for you?"

Donna looked surprised that there was anyone at the camp, but recovered quickly. "Hi, I'd like to rent the camp for several days. Would three days be okay? You can name your price."

Charlie thought, she wants me out of here - and I want out of here. I'll let her have it for $100.00 per day. I can go to Hank's house, and then get my gear in the mineshaft.

Charlie said, "I guess you can have the place for..."

Mona walked up to Donna and Charlie with a drawn pistol. Charlie looked at the pistol, and then slowly put his hands up in the air.

Donna looked surprised, and then glanced back at Mona. "Mona, you stupid jack ass. He was going to rent the place to us and we wouldn't have any problems with him or the locals."

"What is this? What do you want?" Charlie asked.

Donna turned back to Charlie, looked closely at him for the first time. She thought she had seen him before, but where? "Are you Mr. Duncan?"

Charlie, feigning fear and surprise responded, "Yes."

"Have you ever been in San Francisco?"

"Once or twice."

"Where have you been in San Francisco?"

"The waterfront. The ballpark to see the Giants play and I also saw the Forty-niners play once. Nothing special."

"Kirk. Come with us as I inspect the camp. Mr. Duncan, you will come with me and show me around. Mona, unload the van. Don't disturb anything, understand?"

Mona was a little put out at being chastised by Donna, but replied crisply, "Understood."

223

Donna walked with Charlie around the camp. She even walked up to the grave overlooking the lake.

"Who's buried here?"

"A woman named Martha. She was the wife of a good friend of mine. His name is Hank."

"You mean Henry Teller?"

"That's right. Are you here to steal my place? Why are you here?"

"Mr. Duncan, that's none of your business. By the way, what do people call you?"

Charlie thought, she doesn't know who I am, but she knows she's seen me somewhere before. I can't tell her Charlie or that might trigger her memory. I'll tell her C. C.

"People call me C. C."

"Well, C. C., if you don't give us any trouble, you won't get hurt. Do as you're told." She turned to one of the men and pointing to the tool shed, said, "Kirk, take him to that shed and tie him up. Tie his feet so he can walk if we need him to talk to someone on the phone, but tie his hands real good."

Charlie smiled to himself. He was to be left in the tool shed. He knew he could escape as soon as it was dark.

Almost as soon as he was tied up and left in the tool shed, he heard a loud crash echoing down the valley, as if an automobile had crashed or there was an avalanche. It came from the north in the valley formed by the lake and the various rivers that fed the lake.

It didn't really sound like an avalanche, he decided, but more like an auto accident. Maybe a plane crash.

Outside, Kirk walked over to Donna. "What do you think that was?"

"How should I know and anyway, we don't have time to worry about it. Get everyone here. I have something to tell them."

Mona was the first to arrive, followed by Harry, Pete, and finally Jim.

"Okay. I have to go into town to see some real estate agent. Kirk will come with me. Mona, you'll be in charge while I'm gone.

224

Now don't do anything stupid. We need C. C. to answer the telephone, talk to people coming here, so don't kill him. We might have to later, but definitely not yet. Do you understand?"

Mona answered in a manner that meant she didn't like Donna's orders, "Sure."

Charlie heard the conversation and immediately decided the agent must be Terry.

Mona asked, "Where can we get in touch with you in case of an emergency?"

"Look in the telephone directory for Mr. Terry Bracken. I'll be with him or he'll know where I am."

Charlie thought, Bingo. I just knew it was that jerk. I bet they want my place for something. It has to be smuggling.

The twin-engine plane was approaching the Canadian-United States border as Leon swallowed hard. He was now in real pain!

Joel asked, "Leon, are you okay?"

The man was turning an ashen color. He switched on the automatic pilot.

"No, I'm not doing okay. I guess I should have landed back there when you suggested it. Do you know how to fly?"

Sara looked at Joel, and then answered, "No - neither of us."

Leon was grabbing his chest by now.

He said, "I'm sorry folks, but I don't think I'm going to make it. I'll do the best I can. There's a small airfield at Sand Point, Idaho. I'm going to try for there. It is the closest airfield I know. Help me guide the plane."

"What do you want me to do?"

"Look at the ground. Tell me if you see two ridges...going the same way as we are. There is a small creek between them, then a lake."

Joel answered, "There they are - over to the left."

Leon banked the plane slightly to the left, and then straightened the flight pattern to go in the middle, between the ridges.

Leon was looking and feeling worse. He said, "Joel, get in

225

the back seat with your wife. I'm going to crash land in the lake ahead. I can't make it to the airfield."

Joel climbed into the rear of the airplane with his wife.

"I don't know about trails in this area," Leon continued, "but I think there is a one on the shore leading south. I'm told it goes to a camp on the south shore. If you find it, walk to the south shore and the camp. It should only be several miles. I am going to try to crash land in the water near the shore."

The plane started to lose altitude. Leon was in severe pain by this time. His lips were blue.

Sara thought, this SOB is going to kill us because he wanted to fly when he knew he shouldn't. She turned to her husband and whispered, "I love you."

Joel had his arm around her and drew her close. "I love you, too."

They kissed and held hands. When they could see the ground racing up at them, they released their hands and bent forward with their forearms over their faces.

Leon was obviously in trouble. He could hardly fly. He yelled to the Thompsons, "Get down!"

The plane came down to the water. With the last bit of energy he could muster, Leon brought the nose up. The tail section hit the water, then the cockpit section. The plane splashed as it skimmed across the water for almost two hundred yards, then stopped and started to sink.

Joel looked at Sara and she nodded back at him, smiling. Both were shaken, but not injured. He climbed to the front of the plane to check Leon, who was unconscious or dead. As far as Joel could tell, he was dead.

The plane rested in two to three feet of water with the wing just touching dry land. As Joel opened the door, a small amount of water came in. He went through the opening and climbed out on the wing. Sara followed. Together they walked towards its tip, where Joel jumped to the shore. Sara followed him, and both sat down on a log near the tree line to rest and evaluate their situation.

Joel was the first to speak, "Even though Leon put our lives in danger, he saved us with his flying abilities and his last breath."

Sara nodded. "You're right. I was really angry with him, but he did save our lives."

"Do you think we should try to get our rifles and cameras?"

"No, the storage compartment is underwater. It would be too difficult and, anyway, we're only a few miles away from help."

"Right. Are you rested enough to start?"

"I'm ready if you are."

It was now thirty minutes after noon.

Joel and Sara walked up the side of the mountain. They had hardly gone a hundred yards when they found a good trail. It was almost six feet wide at the point where they found it. Both Sara and Joel were elated. They began to hike the trail south, the same direction their plane had been going.

They had traveled for almost three miles when they could see the south end of the lake ahead. There was a cabin there just as Leon had said. Both laughed as if everything would be fine in a short time.

Now that Sara and Joel were feeling safe, they started to look at the surrounding mountains and admire their beauty. They noticed the area had a dusting of recent snow and knew there was going to be a heavy snowfall in the next day or two, and that the temperature was going to drop dramatically.

Sara pointed to a moose eating some willows.

Joel smiled. "Yeah, I wish we had our cameras."

They were now turning into the camp area. A woman came over to meet them. It was Mona.

"What are you two doing hiking way out here?"

Joel explained their situation quickly, then said, "Can you get us some help or get us to town?"

Mona thought, I can't let these two get to town. Hell, I'll just put them in with C. C.

Mona pulled out her gun and pointed it at them. A moment later Pete and Harry showed themselves, their guns already drawn and pointed at Joel and Sara.

Sara was surprised, shocked, and scared. "What's going on?

227

All we want is a little help."

"Put your hands behind your back and shut up. Pete, tie them up real good."

At about the same time the phone in the camp started to ring.

Jim answered, "Hello."

"Where's C. C.?"

"He just stepped out for a moment. This is Jim. I'm renting his place for a couple of days. Can I give him a message or take your telephone number so he can call you back?"

"Just tell him that Sam called. I'll call him tomorrow morning early. We need to talk." Sam thought it was strange that C. C. was renting his place.

"I'll tell him."

"Thanks."

Both men hung up their telephones.

Hands tied, Joel and Sara were led towards the tool shed. As they passed the camp, they heard the telephone as it rang again.

When Jim answered it this time, a different voice said, "Where's C. C., This is Hank."

Again Jim answered, "C. C. isn't here right now. Can I give him a message?"

"Just tell him I won't be over this afternoon. Ruth wants me to do something at the church." Hank thought, who the hell is Jim and where is C. C.?

"I sure will."

Both men hung up.

Joel and Sara were placed in the tool shed with Charlie. As soon as Pete and Harry left, the new arrivals introduced themselves to Charlie.

"What the hell is going on?" the husband asked.

"I don't rightly know," Charlie told him, "but I think these guys are waiting for some sort of delivery from Canada."

"You mean they're smugglers?"

"That's what I think."

"What are they smuggling?"

"Again, I don't know, but my guess is drugs."

228

"We are in deep trouble," Sara said quietly.

Charlie replied, "I completely agree with you."

Noticing that no one was outside the door, Charlie crawled closer to Joel and Sara.

"How did you two get here?"

Sara answered by telling C. C. about the plane crash as they returned from a camera hunt in Canada.

"Pardon my manners. My name is C. C. Duncan. I own this place, but obviously, I don't run it now. Those SOBs are running it."

Charlie stopped and thought, wait a minute. These two haven't met Donna. That means they don't know about her. I wonder if I should tell them. Something tells me I shouldn't tell them about Donna yet.

Charlie then whispered, "Look, folks, we can escape. I know I can get out of these ropes, but we can't do anything until dark. Tell me what they were doing when they brought you here."

"Well, one of the men said that Mona thought they ought to put a jeep on the road to block it, so nobody can get into the camp area without them knowing it. Besides that, I can't think of anything. Can you Sara?"

"No, I can't."

Charlie thought for a minute.

"Folks, I don't believe these guys are going to let us live. So tonight, we have to escape. I want you to look at those two or three boards over there in the corner. They are loose and you can get them off with very little sound. We will have to do that at night, so look at those boards carefully. At the appropriate time, I'll free myself and then free you two. Until then, let's get some rest. We'll need it later."

Sara nodded her head accepting what Charlie said.

Joel answered, "I think you're right. They're going to kill us no matter what, so we must escape. I also think you're right about waiting for dark."

In a short time, both Joel and Sara were sleeping. Charlie was looking out the shed through a gap between two boards. He saw

229

the van with Donna and Kirk in it as it returned from town. Just as Donna and Kirk got out, Mona walked up to them.

"We had some excitement while you were gone. A couple walked into camp from that direction. They said they were in an airplane accident up the lake. Their pilot died while crash landing the plane, but they escaped without injury. We put them in the shed with Duncan."

"Damn. That's bad news. It means we can't use this lake after this delivery."

"Maybe we can, Donna. If we take care of them properly..."

"Mona, you're too quick to 'take care' of people, but you might be right. I'll think on it tonight."

"I was thinking we could use a little warning if someone was coming towards the camp. What about placing that jeep on the road to block it?"

"That's a good idea. We could use some warning if someone is coming in the camp. There's a place in the road where it's too narrow for a car - or, for that matter, anything else - to go around a jeep. Tell Pete to place the jeep there now."

In a short time, Pete drove the jeep to the narrow part of the gravel road. He parked it so it blocked the road and nobody could pass it in a vehicle, including an ATV, because of the sharp drop off at the side of the road. It took Pete less than ten minutes to return to camp.

It was now getting dark. The two mercury vapor lights went on automatically as night crept in.

Charlie set the alarm on his watch for 3:15 AM, and then let himself drift off into a light sleep.

At 3:15 the next morning, his watch began to sound its wake up alarm. He immediately shut it off, and then began to untie his legs and remove the useless rope around his wrists. He had untied the rope on his right hand hours before, but left the rope there so it would look like he was still thoroughly tied. Now he reached for the small tarp he kept in the tool shed and, spreading it out over the Thompsons, turned on a small waterproof flashlight. He then shook Joel gently.

Joel woke up, looked at Charlie and the tarp over them. It took him a moment to remember their situation. "Is it time?"

"It's time."

Joel held out his hands for Charlie to untie him. Quicker than he could imagine, Charlie cut the ropes on both his hands and feet. He handed the knife he kept in the shed to Joel to cut the ropes tying Sara's hands and feet. Three or four minutes later, Joel handed Charlie's knife back to him. The tarp was still covering them.

Sara and Joel were a little chilly, but not too cold, while Charlie was comfortable even though the temperature had dropped during the night to 19 degrees. It was now 3:30 in the morning.

Charlie said, "I want both of you to understand what I am going to say because it's very important not only for your survival, but for mine also."

While drawing a diagram in the dirt on the floor, C. C. began to explain to Joel and Sara how they could escape.

"Now this is how this valley is laid out. The lake is between two ridges. These ridges go north and eventually into Canada. The ridge to our rear is one of them. You noticed the gravel road at the base of the ridge - well, that's the road you take out of here, but you don't go the short way. It's important you understand that. On the other side of the ridge is a...well sort of a box canyon. Are you two in good condition?"

Sara answered, "Fairly good."

"That'll have to do. Now, this is what you should do. Here are a pair of pliers and the key to that ATV just outside the shed over there. Joel, you sneak over to the Chrysler, the Suburban, and the van. Begin with the one closest to the cabin. On only one tire, grab the valve and break it off. It will take some strength. Do that on each vehicle if you have time."

"Now Sara, when he is breaking the last valve or when the people in the house come out to see what the noise is, you start the ATV. If those in the cabin are still asleep, they'll wake up when the ATV is started. That's the bad news, but the good news is that the engine starts easily, almost always on the first try. Then, Joel,

231

you run for the ATV. Sara, I hope you know how to drive one of those things."

"We have three of them for our use in the mountains during summer. Ours are also four wheelers."

"Great. Drive it at top speed. I mean floor board the accelerator immediately. Those guys will be coming out of that cabin fast and that ATV can't outrun a bullet. This may sound crazy, but you turn north, that's left up at the main gravel road. The reason is the jeep they placed in the road would stop you. I doubt you noticed, but the place where the jeep is located can be seen from the cabin and if they fire their guns on automatic, they have a good chance of hitting you. Also, they may be able to catch you by cutting across the woods.

"Once on the gravel road going north, you'll be out of sight almost immediately. Turn on the headlights after you make the turn. Keep going as fast as you can. About four miles up the side of the mountain, you'll come to a sign that indicates a sharp curve in the road. Stop the vehicle. Take the sign down if you can. If you can't, dirty it up or put some bushes over it. I know - take this tarp with you and throw it over the sign. Slow down for the next half a mile."

"Why?"

"Because Joel, the curve is very sharp, almost a switch back. Anyone traveling fast will not make the curve, but will go over the cliff. It's a 300-foot drop to the first level and then another 400-foot drop down to the river that feeds the lake. Here you leave the ATV just slightly around the curve. Turn its lights off and walk to the top of the ridge on the road. The top of the ridge is less than a half mile."

Joel asked, "You think what will happen is that the people who come after us will go over the cliff, right?"

"Right. Now when you are at the top, cross the ridge. You'll find an area that looks like several roads meet there. That's exactly what happens. They're old logging roads. The main ridge continues into Canada. When you cross the ridge, you'll find two trails or logging roads. The one you'll take goes left around the small box canyon. The other one goes down the side of the mountain in switchbacks. Actually, the one you will take is maybe a quarter mile longer, but it's all down hill. If you take the other one, you'll have to climb the ridge on the other side of the canyon and meet the same trail I am telling you to take."

Sara interrupted, "We know about never giving up the high ground when hunting."

"Good. That trail is very easy to hike. I'd suggest you jog if you can. You might be able to do this for a short distance because the moon is out and it's extremely bright. The first part of the trail is also in a clear-cut area. Use your judgment, but under no conditions do anything that might get you hurt.

"The trail is almost exactly six-and-a-half miles from the trail head on top of the first ridge to Hank's house. When you are near the end of the trail, you will see a house with red trim and a red barn. That is the house where Henry Teller lives. I call him Hank. If it's daylight when you arrive, go to the barn, and call him. If it's still night, go to his back door and knock.

"When he answers your call or knock, tell him you must use his telephone to call Sam Pritchard - he's our pastor. Tell Hank this is an emergency and I asked you to do this. Then tell him what happened. He probably won't believe you, but if you insist, he'll call Sam or allow you to call him.

"Tell Sam what has happened. He may or may not believe you either, but in any case - and this is important - tell Sam for confirmation that I told you to tell him the following name - Charles A. Mackey, III. It's important you tell Sam that name. After that, I guarantee Sam will believe you. He'll convince Hank too. You'll be safe at that time, but do what Hank says. Although he looks like a country bumpkin, he's one smart cookie.

"Oh, I nearly forgot. Hank is tall, lean, and stands ramrod straight. He also has a fist full of medals for his fighting in the Pacific during World War II. He's a good man. Trust him.

"When talking to Sam, make sure you tell him to call the sheriff and to tell the sheriff to bring the cavalry and most important, not to take any chances. Any questions?"

233

Joel looked at Sara. She said, "I think you've covered everything except one thing. If we get on another trail by mistake, can we get lost?"

"Sara, if you follow my instructions, you can't get lost. There are not that many trails on that ridge. But if you do, the only problem you will have is hiking back here and keeping out of sight if the smugglers are still here."

"I have another question, C. C. What are you going to do?"

"I have a way to escape that is a little dangerous, but I have a better chance of succeeding if they are looking for you. Only one person can take the way I am taking. Also, if I don't make it, you will if you follow my directions. Yours is the safer route."

"Okay, I guess we're as ready as we'll ever be. Let's do it!"

Charlie turned out his flashlight and removed the tarp. Joel moved over to the three boards and slowly, but with some force, removed them. Sara picked up the tarp.

A few seconds later Sara and Joel slipped out of the shed.

CHAPTER 4

Once outside the shed, Joel and Sara looked around the camp and saw no one, not even a guard outside the cabin. Joel kissed Sara, and then ran to the Chrysler while Sara went to the ATV. Inserting the key in the ignition, she waited for Joel to finish his task.

Joel hid behind the Chrysler, crouching down beside the front right tire. He applied the pliers to the valve and twisted the pliers. The valve broke and air came rushing out of the stem with a loud hissing noise.

He looked nervously toward the cabin, afraid that the noise might alert someone there. No one came out of the cabin.

Everyone must be asleep, he thought.

Charlie was peering out of the tool shed between the boards, watching as Joel moved cautiously from the Chrysler to the van. Charlie went to the rear of the shed where there were some shelves with motor oil on them along with funnels and other things Charlie needed to change the oil in his vehicles. He moved the oil to the left, exposing a bolt, and then he slid the bolt to the left. Once the bolt was no longer engaged, the shelves and backboard swung forward in an arch like a door. Behind the shelving lay the darkness of the old mineshaft.

When he heard the hissing sound of another broken valve, Charlie turned to look outside at Joel and Sara one more time. Joel was running towards the Suburban now. A light appeared in a window in the cabin.

Charlie thought, they're awake now. Everything has worked so far. The only question now is if the ATV starts quickly or if it takes a little time to start. If it starts as usual, they'll have no trouble escaping. But I must leave now to avoid any problems with my escape. God go with you, Joel and Sara.

With those thoughts, Charlie moved the oil back into place so that it hid the bolt, and then went through the door into the mineshaft, closing and bolting the door from inside the old mine shaft. He was now locked in the mineshaft.

As he moved deeper into the darkness, his waterproof flashlight pierced the darkness like a beacon - a searchlight, a beam of light from a lighthouse. He started to half run, half walk.

At the sound of the second broken valve stem, Donna woke up and walked into the large room where Pete was sleeping. He was supposed to be on guard.

Donna shook him to wake him up.

"What's that hissing noise?"

Mona had come into the room by now, too.

She said, "That's a tire going flat."

Joel had reached the Suburban by now. He grabbed the valve stem and twisted it. As it hissed behind him, he dropped the pliers and ran for the ATV.

Donna said in an excited, suppressed voice, "Someone is letting the air out of the tires."

Mona went for her assault rifle while Donna went for her pistol, then both of them ran to the door. Pete grabbed his automatic pistol and beat Donna and Mona to the door by a step.

Sara twisted the ignition key in the ATV and the engine started immediately, a low, comforting rumble. She put the vehicle in gear just as Joel jumped on, and then she floored the accelerator. The ATV lunged forward and was almost out of the light from both mercury vapor lights when Pete and Donna burst out through the cabin door.

Pete saw the ATV racing towards the gravel road, recognizing Joel and Sara immediately. He raised his pistol and fired, but missed the mark by a wide margin. By now, the ATV was in the darkness beyond the light. Although they could still hear the ATV, neither Pete, Donna, nor Mona could see it.

Donna asked, "How many were on the ATV?"

Pete answered, "Two."

Donna again asked, "Could you see who they were?"

Again, Pete answered, "The guy with the beard wasn't there, so I guess it was the couple who came in after you had gone to town."

"Mona, you and Pete go after them." Then noting all three vehicles had one tire flat, Donna added, "Pete, go get the jeep and get going. Mona, meet Pete at the road where it starts up the side of the mountain."

Soon after the ATV turned left on the road, Sara switched on its headlights.

Donna, Pete, and Mona now saw the headlights dancing through the trees as the ATV climbed the mountain on the gravel road.

Donna sighed, "Mona, get them and do what's needed to prevent them from reaching the police."

"I thought you'd eventually agree with me."

With those words, she started to run towards the gravel road. Pete was already running. He was turning right towards the jeep blocking the road.

Donna and Kirk walked towards the shed. Carefully, they opened the door, turning on their flashlights. The shed was empty; C. C. was gone also.

Donna mumbled, "Damn."

They turned and left the shed without looking very well at the rear of the shed. It was now 4:15 in the morning.

The mineshaft rose almost fifteen feet over the first one hundred yards, and then became level. Within the next fifty yards, the floor started to go downhill gradually. Soon he was walking in water. Within another hundred yards, he was waist-deep in ice-cold water.

The water was extremely cold. He knew he would have to go

238

through it quickly or he would die from hypothermia. When he came to the vertical mine shaft he knew he would have to swim for about ten yards.

Charlie noted the rope on the ceiling with his flashlight. He tied the flashlight around his wrist and grabbed the rope. After several steps, his right foot stepped into the vertical shaft and he became submerged, but he managed to pull himself up enough to keep his head above the water. He released the rope and began to swim as fast as he could to the other side of the vertical mineshaft. Finally, his right foot touched the floor of the other side of the shaft. He then continued through the chest-deep water.

The water was extremely cold, below the freezing point; he kept breaking through a thin skim of ice on it. He was beginning to shake all over.

The water was now hip-deep and getting shallower quickly. C. C. pushed on, and finally he found himself in a dry section of the tunnel, with only a little stream of water flowing approximately in the middle of the floor. C. C. knew the stream, which was spring fed from the vertical mine shaft, exited the mineshaft through the other entrance. He was close to that point now. His flashlight shown ahead and soon Charlie could see the opening to a small room that had been used as a tool shed when the mine had been worked.

Charlie thought, not too soon. I'm really cold and shivering. In a short time, my body'll shut down.

As he entered the little room, his flashlight moved around the walls until he saw a small bottle of Coleman fuel and a Coleman catalytic heater. Shaking, he lifted the top off the heater, pointed the bottle at the top of it, and sprayed on the fuel. C. C. now looked for the butane cigarette lighter he kept in the room. It was right where he had left it - on the shelf by his dry clothes. He flicked the small wheel on the lighter and the wick ignited. He applied the flame to the fuel and flames jumped two to three feet high from the heater.

Charlie took off his wet clothes as quickly as possible. He stored some sweat clothes in the small room that he used as a towel. By the time he had dried himself, he had stopped shaking. He put on some hunting clothes that were very warm and had a camouflage pattern. He was now warm. The catalytic heater would keep the room warm for a number of hours.

It was almost 5:00 AM. He decided to rest until 6:00 AM before leaving the mine via the second entrance. He sat in a small chair and leaned back against the wall of the room. He did not set his watch alarm. Now warm and relatively comfortable, he let himself doze off to sleep.

Donna watched as Pete started the jeep and picked Mona up on the gravel road that intersected with the road to the camp. Immediately, with the jeep's wheels spinning in the loose gravel, they sped up the side of the ridge.

Joel and Sara had traveled quite a distance up the mountain. Pointing to a road sign that indicated a sharp curve ahead of them, Sara stopped the ATV. Joel jumped off and placed the tarp over the sign, then jumped back on.

Sara began to speed.

Joel said, "Slow down. Remember what C. C. said. The curve ahead is a real killer."

"I can handle it, but I'll slow down for you."

Just then, she entered the curve. She screamed as she turned the ATV as hard as she could to the right and slammed on the brakes. She had made it, but just barely.

Sara exclaimed, "Damn. C. C. really knew what he was talking about. That's one hell of a curve."

Joel looked pale, but answered, "Sara, we'll follow C. C.'s directions absolutely from now on."

"Absolutely - to the letter even. Let's get this ATV across the road just out of sight of the turn."

"Right."

Just after they had positioned the ATV, they saw the headlights of the jeep in the distance - coming fast up the road. Joel and Sara began to run on the gravel road towards the top of the ridge. They stopped at the top of the ridge where several

240

logging roads met. They took a few short breaths, looked back at the ATV. They could see the ATV in the bright moonlight. They also saw the jeep's headlights. From the sound of the jeep's motor, they realized it was coming too fast to make the curve. The jeep turned slightly, its headlights rested on the ATV, and the jeep veered sharply to the left to avoid hitting the other vehicle.

Seeing what was going to happen, Pete swung the jeep back towards the ATV only to snag it and bring it along with the jeep over the cliff.

Pete and Mona screamed and continued to scream as the jeep and ATV went over the cliff. There was a crash, the screams stopped abruptly, but the noise continued to echo around the ridge and then silence. Another crash followed a few moments later followed by more noise echoing around the ridge. Then abruptly, silence.

Joel looked at Sara.

Sara said, "My God. What a way to go!"

Joel responded, "That's just what C. C. thought would happen. We follow his instructions to the letter. Let's begin to walk. There's the trail we take on the left."

It was still night, but the moon was very bright and one could see the trail and the surrounding area very well using the moonlight. It was 5:45 AM and almost six and a half miles from Hank's house.

Joel and Sara began their trek to Hank's house. The first part of the trail was through a clear-cut area. It was easy to see the trail in the moonlight, so they jogged until they came to a pine forest that sprang up as if someone had drawn a line - on one side of the line was the clear cut area and on the other a forest.

Sara said, "Joel, it's too dark to jog. We'll have to walk. Remember, we can't get hurt."

"That's what C. C. said. I guess you're right. I can't see the trail very well, but I feel good."

"I know, that little jogging made me warm inside and I feel good also - like I could jog for the entire distance."

"Same here."

Both Sara and Joel began walking at a fast pace. They were about halfway to Hank's house when they noticed that the sky was turning gray. Dawn was breaking over Sand Point, Idaho.

A short time later, they could see the trail easily in the gray light of dawn.

Joel pointed ahead of them to a red barn with a house on the other side of it.

Sara smiled, "That must be Hank's house and barn."

It was now 7:55 AM. Joel and Sara walked up to the barn.

Joel called, "Hank. C. C. sent us. We must talk to you."

Sara smiled and pointed to a man dressed in coveralls who walked out of the barn. He was just as C. C. had described him - a tall man who walked and stood ramrod straight. He was wiping his hands with a towel as they approached.

Hank asked, "What can I do for you folks?"

Donna spoke to Kirk, "Go outside and hide so you can look for that Duncan. He has to be out in the woods somewhere. If he shows himself, take care of him."

"Will do."

Just then, they heard what sounded like a crash, then another crash.

Donna said, "Kirk, if I was a betting person, I would bet Pete and Mona crashed the jeep and probably killed themselves."

"Maybe."

Donna walked back into the house. Harry and Jim were now up and dressed. Harry had put some wood on the fire, which burned brightly as it heated the room. There was a warmth about the room that the propane heater just couldn't supply.

Donna sat in the chair in front of the fire, in what was normally Hank's chair. She sank into deep thought. Mr. Duncan did not go with that couple. He did not seem stupid. He would know we would be looking for him outside. Where is he and how did he escape?

She kept asking herself the same question - How did he escape and where was he?

242

Dawn was breaking over the East Ridge. Donna got up from her chair and walked over to the door.

"Kirk, let's go have a little closer look at that shed."

Kirk sighed, but anyway got up from the chair where he was sitting. "I don't think we'll find anything, but if you insist, let's go."

When they reached the building, Kirk opened the door and flashed his flashlight into the darkness of the shed.

This time Donna walked into the shed and continued back to where C. C. and the Thompsons had been tied. She examined the ground, finding the dirt etched as if in a quarter circle.

She exclaimed, "Damn."

She went immediately to the shelves at the rear of the shed. Sweeping the bottles of oil off the shelf, she saw the bolt and slid it back, then grabbed the shelving and pulled. The door moved toward her and Donna and Kirk could now see the old mineshaft.

Both drew their guns as their flashlights pierced the darkness. Donna walked into the mine and Kirk followed her. They continued until they saw the water.

"Kirk, that water is going to get deep. There has to be another entrance. We find the entrance, we find Duncan."

"I think you're right."

With those words, both Kirk and Donna all but ran out of the old mine.

Once outside again, they noticed that although the sun had not risen over the ridge, there was ample light to turn off the mercury vapor lights in the camp area.

Donna began to think; the shaft rose for a little while, and then dropped. My guess the other opening is about on a level with the gravel road.

Kirk and Donna went to the gravel road. Turned to the right and began walking along the road, looking around for slag from a mine or an opening in the side of the ridge.

The catalytic heater had warmed the little room in the mineshaft until it was toasty warm when the room became aglow

243

with white light.

The figure of a woman in her late fifties stood in the middle of the light near the door to the room and spoke softly, "C. C., it's time to wake up."

C. C. opened his eyes to see the woman, then as soon as he saw the woman in the light; the woman and light disappeared. C. C. wondered about what he had just seen because it was the same woman as he had seen when he was shot and in the hospital with the same white light; then he looked at his watch that jolted him back to the reality of the moment.

He thought, damn. It's almost seven o'clock. I gotta get going. Okay bones, move.

He put on his camouflage jacket, opened his gun case, put silencers on his M-16 and Ruger pistol, loaded the guns, then cautiously left the room and walked to the entrance of the mine.

He thought, there's enough light to aim my rifle. That's good. I don't like to shoot if I can't see where I am aiming or what I am going to kill.

He started up the side of the ridge. After he had gone almost 300 yards, he heard voices coming from the road. He immediately hid behind a bush.

Kirk and Donna were not talking very loudly, but their voices and the sound of them walking in the gravel carried for some distance.

Charlie saw them as they passed the entrance to the mineshaft.

They continued on the road for another 100 yards when Donna said, "Kirk, if the other entrance to that old mine is any further, then he might make it. He could make it only if he had some dry clothes but I don't think he had any. I don't think he will make it because that water was cold - real cold."

"I don't know, Donna. Duncan seemed to be a tough SOB."

"I agree he looked like a tough bastard, but cold water will take care of anybody."

"I guess so. Look at that little stream back there. It's coming from under the road. I wonder how far under the road the spring is?"

Donna looked at the stream. She looked up the side of the ridge. There was no spring there. There was only a small bridge over the road. There was a little slag in front of the bridge.

"Kirk, you've just found the other entrance."

Both Donna and Kirk half jumped down to the stream bed and looked into the other entrance to the mineshaft. Both became very cautious, pointing their guns into the old mine.

Donna went into the shaft first, Kirk followed.

Charlie thought, well they found it. I had better get to the ridge overlooking the camp.

The beam of Donna's flashlight landed on an opening on the right of the mine and she motioned to Kirk. They both noted that the mine was warmer by the opening or doorway.

Kirk saw a red glow coming from a little room. He pointed his flashlight into the room, briefly letting it illuminate the burning catalytic heater and Charlie's wet clothes lying on the floor.

Donna said, "He's got dry clothes and he's flown the coop. That means the police will be here sooner than we'd like. Let's go."

As Donna was about to walk out of the room, she noticed an open gun case sitting on a box and went over to it. The impressions of two silencers, an M-16, and a pistol were in the foam cushion in the box. She closed the lid. She had seen this box before - in the motel where Jack was killed. It was still beautiful, but she now knew a secret known only to Sam Pritchard and Charlie. Charlie, Duncan, or C. C. Duncan was the Iceman.

Her thoughts and words were the same, "Son of a bitch. Duncan's the Iceman. Oh, shit! He could take us out without half trying if he wanted, but he won't call the police. We have a chance to get the shipment."

Kirk asked, "What are you saying?"

"Kirk, Duncan isn't as innocent as he might seem. I know of him. He's good, very good. We have to get back to the camp as quick as possible."

Donna and Kirk left the mine. As soon as they were outside

the mine, they heard an airplane in the distance and began to run toward the camp.

Joel responded to Hank's question, "Mr. Teller, C. C. said to tell you we have to talk to Sam Pritchard, the pastor of your church. We must tell him what happened. C. C. also said you would ask what we are going to tell Sam and he said you probably wouldn't believe us. That's why we must talk to Sam."

"Well, what are you going to tell Sam?"

Sara began, "Joel and I were returning from a camera hunt in Canada when our pilot had a heart attack and died just as he crash landed the plane in the lake."

Joel continued, "We were unhurt and walked to the camp. A woman came up to us along with a couple of men with guns. They put us in a tool shed with Mr. Duncan. He had worked his hands free and told us how to escape over the ridge."

It was Sara's turn now.

"Everything he said came true. We need to call and talk to Sam. Will you please permit us to use your phone?"

Hank's mind was racing with thoughts, C. C. knew about the old mineshaft. Why did he send these two over the ridge? The spring - these two could have easily frozen to death. He might have frozen to death too. I don't know. I guess I'll dial Sam's number and let them talk to him. However, I think I'll keep a close watch on these two just in case.

"Come into the house."

Joel and Sara followed Hank into his house through the back door. Both Joel and Sara were grateful because the kitchen was warm and they were now a little chilly. Hank motioned for them to sit in the chairs by the kitchen table and pointed to a pot of hot coffee on the stove as if to say - "Have some." He walked over to the telephone, dialed a number.

Joel and Sara heard Hank's side of the conversation.

"Sam, there's a couple here who says they were in a plane which crashed in the lake. They also have a wild story about last night - about C. C. being held prisoner, smugglers and so on. They said C. C. said they must talk to you because you would believe them."

A pause.

During the pause, Sam thought, some gunmen getting the drop on C. C. - impossible, but I guess I should talk to them.

"Okay. Here's the man. His name is Joel."

"Sam. My name is Joel Thompson. We were in a plane crash, and then we were captured by some gunmen. There were at least four of them, maybe more we didn't see. Mr. Duncan said you should call the sheriff and get the cavalry moving. He also said they were probably smugglers bringing drugs into the country. These guys are probably very good with their guns and Sam, the sheriff, should not take any chances."

"Incidentally, our name again is Thompson and my wife's name is Sara. You can check a plane's failure to arrive in Denver yesterday."

Sam asked, "Is that all C. C. said?"

"No, he said you would probably be skeptical, but if I mentioned a certain name, you would know I was telling the truth."

"Well, what's the name?"

"Sara, what was the name?"

Sara came to the telephone.

"Sam, this is Sara Thompson. The name Mr. Duncan told us was Charles A. Mackey, III. Do you believe us now?"

Sam was very surprised that Sara mentioned the Mackey name. He now knew Joel and Sara were telling the truth and responded, "Definitely. Please put Hank on the phone."

"Hank, these two are telling the truth. That name - only C. C. and I know it. Help them any way you can."

Hank's response was, "Yep."

Hank hung up the telephone, went into the bedroom. He returned with three rifles. Two of them had scopes on them.

He asked, "Do you know how to shoot one of these?"

"Yes sir," came the response from Sara. "We were and still are to great extent avid hunters. We're also good shots."

247

"We're going to that bridge over there and we're going to prevent any of those people from escaping. Have you ever killed a man before? It's an awful feeling."

Joel shook his head. "No, we haven't."

"Well, you just might have to kill someone today. Here's a 30.06 for you and a 270 for you, young lady. Here's the ammunition."

Pointing to the third rifle Hank was holding, Joel asked, "Is that an M-1 rifle?"

"Yes it is. I sort of kept it when I was discharged. Not quite legal, but I did it. This rifle and me have been through a lot together. Now let's go."

Hank, Joel, and Sara left the house and walked to the bridge. Hank motioned for them to follow him down a trail by the river. Soon he stopped and pointed towards the gravel road across the river.

"You two take up your positions here. If you see any cars coming down that road, you shoot at them. You can miss intentionally, hit the radiator, or shoot to kill the driver, but you shoot. I'm going to be over there by the bridge. If they get by you, I'll shoot to kill and I generally kill what I shoot at. I am taking that position because when the sheriff comes, I should be the one to greet him. Understand?"

Joel and Sara nodded their heads yes. Hank walked back to the bridge as Joel and Sara took up firing positions.

After taking up their firing positions, Sara said, "Joel, I'm going to shoot to kill. How about you?"

"I am too."

Sam hung up the telephone and immediately dialed the sheriff's number.

The phone was answered, "Sheriff's office."

"This is Sam Pritchard. Please put Sheriff Coomey on the phone. This is an emergency."

A short time later, a voice came over the telephone.

"This is Coomey. What do you have, Sam?"

248

"Sheriff, C. C. is in trouble. Don't ask me how I know, but I know he is in trouble. He thinks some smugglers have taken over his camp and have taken him prisoner. He escaped along with two people. The two people walked to Hank's house and called me. Their names are Joel and Sara Thompson. They claim they were in a plane accident, but were uninjured and captured by the smugglers. They said their plane was supposed to land in Denver yesterday. You could probably check that, but C. C. said bring the cavalry and don't take chances. These guys are dangerous."

"I'll check with Denver and if what you say is true about the overdue plane, I'll come with the cavalry."

"Call me back after you've confirmed the overdue plane."

"I'll call you."

The sheriff did not call right away because he had been invited to breakfast by Terry Bracken and Paul Croket. It wasn't every day that the sheriff was invited to eat breakfast with the president of the bank and the biggest real estate agent in Sand Point, especially with the sheriff's election about a year from then. He wondered what the occasion was since they did not support him in the last election.

All that was discussed was the upcoming election and their support for him in his reelection bid. While he was cordial, the sheriff still wondered why he had been invited to breakfast.

After they had finished breakfast, the sheriff returned to his office. It was almost 11:00 AM when he called Denver. He talked to the FAA representative in Denver. The sheriff was very surprised to hear that there was in fact an overdue plane and that the overdue airplane had two passengers named Joel and Sara Thompson. He immediately called Sam to tell him what he found out. Next, he called in all four of his deputies. They left in two cars with their sirens screaming they were coming.

CHAPTER 5

Charlie was now in a position overlooking his camp and the boat dock in front of his cabin. There were two men walking around the cabin, one carrying a briefcase, the other an assault rifle. He heard an airplane coming from the north. By the sound of the airplane, it was obviously in the valley between the two ridges and over the lake.

It didn't take the plane long to fly over the cabin. It was a pontoon type seaplane with a single engine and room for at least four passengers. After going over the cabin, it passed over the small ridge behind the camp, banked, and turned to the west. Charlie watched the plane as it continued its turn until it was going north again, then faded out of sight.

Charlie turned his attention back to the road. Donna and Kirk were running back to the camp. He assumed they were responding to the plane's arrival.

The sound coming from over the lake had changed to that of a plane landing on the water. That confirmed it. This was why Donna and the others were there. Whatever they were waiting for was on that plane.

The plane taxied in toward shore, then cut its engine and

floated to the dock. A man jumped out of the passenger seat onto the dock, where a man with an assault weapon caught his hand and helped him ashore. The men shook hands. With a rope the passenger had taken from the plane, the man who had just arrived lassoed the left pontoon.

After the plane's two pontoons cleared the dock, the passenger and the other man pulled the rope and the plane turned in the water so that it pointed north. It was now lined up for a quick takeoff. The men secured it to the dock by two ropes with the left pontoon gently touching the dock.

The pilot climbed out of the plane and Charlie could see there had only been two men in it. He wondered about that. Donna and Kirk were now walking up to the two mew arrivals.

The passenger extended his hand to her. "You must be Donna. I'm Andrew Briggs. Everybody calls me Andy, though."

Shaking his hand, Donna replied, "Yes, I'm Donna. This is Kirk and that is Harry. Jim is in the house."

The pilot climbed out of the airplane and walked towards Donna and Andy. "My name's Gene Browne. We have some snow for you."

"I hope the snow you've brought us is different from the snow that's forecast to fall here this afternoon and tonight."

Donna and all the men laughed.

Donna continued, "We must act quickly. We have had complications yesterday and today. Where's the coke?"

Andy motioned for Donna to come over to the plane. He opened the door to where the rear seats were supposed to be, but there were several boxes instead. He started to open one of them, but Donna stopped him with her hand. She now reached up and opened a different box instead, pulling out a Ziploc bag with some white powder in it. She looked at it, opened another box, and retrieved another Ziploc bag with more white powder in it. She handed both bags to Harry.

She watched Harry go over to the cabin. Andy walked behind him into the cabin.

Donna ordered, "Kirk, let's start moving the rest of the coke to
252

the van.

Gene added, "Let me help you. By the way, what happened here?"

"We were forced to take three people prisoners and we put them in the shed over there. They escaped last night. My thought is we have a very short time before the police arrive."

Harry came out of the cabin carrying the two test bags. He threw them into the van, shook his head. "It's the real stuff," he told her. "Jim and Andy are counting the money. I'll go back inside and watch them."

"Fine."

Gene, Kirk, and Donna carried the unopened cases to the van. Kirk was arranging them so he could get the last box in the van. Donna was holding it while he arranged the other boxes. Gene had gone over to the plane and seemed a little too nervous for Donna. Donna opened the box she was holding. She reached in, opened one of the Ziploc bags, and inserted her finger to touch the white powder. Then she withdrew her finger.

Donna whispered to Kirk, "This is sugar. Continue as you are while I go get my rifle. When you see I have it, go for that SOB."

Kirk nodded he understood.

Donna left the van and started to walk over to where she had put her rifle. She was cursing herself under her breath because she had taken her pistol off when she had gotten back from looking for C. C.

Gene had retrieved his assault rifle from the plane. He saw Donna reach into the box, then begin to walk away. He thought, she knows. It's either her or us.

Gene switched his rifle to full automatic and fired at Kirk, killing him with a blaze of bullets. Kirk fell to the ground as Gene continued to fire. One of the bullets hit and ignited the gas tank of the van, which burst into flames.

Then Gene turned to look at Donna, who was now running toward her rifle as fast as she could. He still had a number of rounds left in the magazine and he unleashed them on Donna. She had almost reached her rifle when two bullets hit her. She fell to the ground face down.

Harry and Jim ran to the window when the shooting started. Andy, however, stayed where he was. He reached under his coat, retrieved his automatic pistol, and opened fire on them while they were still trying to figure out what had happened. Both men fell to the floor, dead.

Andy opened the door and shouted, "You okay, Gene?"

When Charlie saw Gene shoot Kirk, he realized he must now act. He lifted up his M-16 and began to fire. Charlie decided to put holes in the pontoons of the plane as Gene was completely hidden from view by his suburban. His bullets hit each of the pontoons on the plane many times almost like a machine gun was firing.

Andy shouted to Gene, "What's happening over by the plane? It sounds like bullets are hitting the water around the pontoons."

Gene shouted back, "Whoever is shooting at the plane can't hit the side of a barn. He's hitting the water around the pontoons. Do you see anyone?"

"Nar, I don't see anyone."

Gene crouched as he ran to where Donna was lying. Although the Chrysler was between them and Charlie, Charlie could see Gene's head and Donna lying on the ground.

Gene looked at Donna, put his foot under her left shoulder, and rolled her over. Her left arm crossed her body and landed on the ground slightly away from her. She was smiling. Through her smile, a trickle of blood oozed out of her mouth.

In a weak voice she said, "He's using a silencer, you stupid jackass."

She coughed up some blood.

As Gene looked at Donna, he said, "I was told you were good. You were easy, bitch. I think you deserve to have a few more holes in your body, especially your pretty face."

Donna replied, "If you knew who was shooting, you wouldn't be so comfortable. You poor son of a bitch. You'd better have your will made out because you are as good as dead, if he wants you dead. He hits exactly where he wants. He's putting holes in the pontoons so you can't take off."

He changed magazines, pointed his rifle towards Donna. "It's a shame to waste a body like yours, but you're there and I'm here."

"I bet you get to hell before I do. See you there, Gene"

With a snicker, Gene said, "Goodbye, Donna." He started to lift his rifle up to his shoulder, but before he could fire, a little hole appeared in his left temple. The right side of Gene's head disappeared with his brains exploding out of his head. Gene was dead before he could raise the rifle to his shoulder and before his body hit the ground.

Donna thought this evens us up for Jack. Thanks, Iceman.

She coughed up some more blood, and then closed her eyes. She was still breathing, but she knew her wounds were very serious.

Andy saw Gene drop. He looked towards the ridge where Charlie was. Another little hole appeared, but this time in Andy's forehead. The rear of his head disappeared, showering the front of the camp and the post by the steps with blood and Andy's brains.

Charlie laid his guns down on the ridge and came running down to the area. He knew there were no more people alive in the camp or the cabin who could hurt him.

He went to the area where the van was burning. Its contents had now been consumed by the fire and Kirk's body was burned beyond all recognition. He went over to where Donna was. She was still breathing, but Charlie could tell by her wounds that she would die soon.

He knelled beside her. "Dear Lord," he prayed, "Just as you preserved my life to do your work here on earth, please save this woman. I know what she is and some of what she's done. She doesn't deserve to be saved, but neither did I. I ask you to save her life so she can do your work. I also know she was the one who shot me. I still ask you to help her and save her from herself. I forgive her."

Charlie heard Donna's last breath, but he continued to pray silently. After a couple of minutes, Charlie felt her neck for the carotid pulse. There was none. Still, he continued to pray silently.

It had been five minutes since he began to pray. He again felt for a carotid pulse. This time, however, he found it, pulsing weakly, and he quickly turned her over to examine her wounds. From his pocket, he pulled his Swiss Army knife, and used it to cut the clothes off her back. He immediately put one of his handkerchiefs in one wound and another over the second wound.

Charlie thought, It's happening just like it happened to me. Sam's dream was a man and a woman. I'll bet Donna is the woman. I'm going to call Sam and ask him to come over now. I guess I can leave Donna. The Lord has given her life again and if He wants her to live, she will live regardless of what I do or don't do.

Charlie left Donna's side and went into the cabin to his phone. While he was dialing a telephone number, he heard some sirens coming in his direction. The sound soon stopped, though.

Charlie thought, the sheriff must be talking to Hank now.

The telephone answered, "Hello."

"Sam, this is Charlie. Can you identify the woman in your dreams if you see her in the flesh and blood?"

"Yes, I think we can."

"Good. Bring Ruth with you and come to my place. I think the woman is going through or I should say has gone through what I went through in Seattle. I - no, we need you."

Not knowing if it was safe to go to the camp, Sam asked, "Charlie, is everything okay for us to come there?"

"Yes, it is. See if you can get a copter to take Donna to Spokane for treatment. She'll need heavy-duty treatment."

"I'll do what I can. In the meantime, Ruth and I will leave immediately. You know I'll have to tell Ruth a little about you."

"I know she will be on your case to tell her everything. How about telling her only that I was in Hell and that you saved me? Leave out the part as to why I was sent to Hell."

"I'll see if I can. See you soon."

Charlie went out to be with Donna.

As he passed Andy's body in the front of the cabin, he thought of the briefcase. He took it, returned to the cabin, and went to the closet where he placed the briefcase in with his suitcases. Although he didn't absolutely know that there was a good deal of money in it, he thought it probably contained the pay off money.

He was back outside, kneeling down beside Donna, when two sheriff's cars came down the gravel road. They had turned off their sirens.

Hank was in the lead car. When it arrived, he jumped out and ran to Charlie as he looked around the place at the dead men lying around the area. He saw that Donna was alive and that Charlie was tending to her wounds.

"You okay, Duncan?"

"Yes, I am. Thanks for bringing the cavalry. Donna needs heavy-duty treatment. Get the sheriff to call for an air ambulance to take her to Spokane. I'll pay all her medical bills."

"C. C., what happened?"

"Hank, I don't rightly know. All I know is these people - there's another woman and a man who went after Joel and Sara. I don't know where they are. The woman pulled a gun on me and put me in the tool shed. Then this woman was loading the van over there and all hell broke loose."

"The two who went after the Thompsons are probably dead. The Thompsons' said they didn't make the curve going up the side of the ridge. The Thompsons said you told them about the curve."

"Did they tell you any more?"

"No, but they did their share. There they are, walking on the road."

Charlie saw the Thompsons coming toward the camp road. The sheriff was now kneeling over Donna.

"C. C., is she alive?"

"She's alive, Sheriff, but she'll need plenty of medical help. I'll pay for any treatment she needs. Can you get an air ambulance to fly her to Spokane?"

"Let me call for one. Then you and I have to talk."

While the sheriff was calling for an air ambulance, the deputies were checking out the area and the dead bodies. Sam and Ruth passed Joel and Sara on the road and drove up to where

Charlie was standing.

"C. C., is that her?"

"Yes, it is, Sam."

Ruth went over to look at Donna. She put her hand over her mouth, took a deep breath, and then returned to C. C.

Sam stood quietly over Donna, staring down at her, and then joined them.

"C. C.," Ruth said, "Sam has told me of your visit to Hell and why he believes you really went there. He told me he told you about our dreams. I must tell you and Sam - that is the woman in my dream."

Sam nodded his head in agreement. He said, "She's the woman in my dreams, too. I don't know what it means, but I'd bet it means you two are going to get married."

Ruth continued, "That's a good possibility."

By this time, Joel and Sara had walked up to the group.

"Sam, Ruth, I'd like to introduce Joel and Sara Thompson."

"You must be the people who called me this morning. How are you folks doing?"

Sara answered, "To tell you the truth, I don't know. We're very tired and we need to call our home in Fort Collins."

C. C. said, "Use my phone. It's right inside."

Joel thanked him and went in the cabin with Sara to make their phone call.

"Sam, could you and Ruth take care of Joel and Sara for a while. I have to think about what happened."

Ruth replied, "Sure. Go get yourself together."

Charlie went up to where Martha was. He sat on the bench by her grave, looking over the lake - the bench Hank sat on when he talked to Martha.

He began to think. I must tell the sheriff the truth, but I can't tell him everything. I must return the money to Louis. God, what do I tell the sheriff? And how do I get Donna and myself out of here? Mike and Lisa will know who I am and what I've done. So will Louis. God, how do I handle this? And I'll bet the woman that woke me up in the room was you, Martha - wasn't it?

The sheriff walked up to C. C. "Now C. C., we have to talk. What happened?"

"I don't know where to start, and I don't know everything. I guess it started when that woman who is wounded drove into the camp and asked to rent my camp to her for a few days. There was this other woman, I think her name was Mona, she drew a pistol, and I was put in the tool shed. She and the wounded woman had words like she didn't approve of Mona's actions, but she couldn't do anything about it."

"Did Mona seem like she had a hold over the wounded woman?"

"I don't know - she could have, but I really couldn't say. She had a gun though. Then the wounded woman went into town to talk with Terry and someone else, I believe. She only mentioned Terry by name. She left the camp.

"I heard a crash and a couple of hours later, Joel and Sara were put in the shed by Mona. I was loose, but I was waiting for night to escape. Joel and Sara complicated things. I told them how to escape and go to Hank's house the back way and to call Sam and tell Sam to call you."

C. C. looked over at the plane. The pontoons were now resting on the bottom of the lake in four feet of water. The plane would have to be lifted out of the water and the pontoons drained and fixed before the plane would be able to take off. C. C. smiled.

The sheriff looked at the plane. He asked, "How did the plane sink?"

"I guess someone shot some holes in the pontoons during the shootout. To continue, Joel and Sara escaped over the ridge and I escaped through the old mine shaft. I didn't think they could take the cold water in the old mine, so I didn't take them with me. I watched the shootout from the ridge. When it was over, I came down and saw that everyone was dead except the woman.

"Oh - he continued, as if it were an afterthought - "I think I saw her once at the wedding of my friend Lisa in San Francisco. Her husband is Mike Forester. Mike is with the SFPD. That's about all I know, Sheriff. If you have any more questions, I'll be

259

happy to answer them."

"C. C., there are some holes in your story, but the two questions I have are - first, what were these people doing here, and second, what was the relationship of the wounded woman to this Mona?"

"I don't know the answer to either question, but my guess is the people were waiting for the plane to unload something, maybe drugs, but I don't really know. I saw a couple of them loading the van over there. Whatever was loaded in the van was destroyed by the fire. The relationship between the two women, I just don't know."

The sheriff looked over at the van. He noticed the fire had consumed the entire van and all that was in it. He also noticed the body of a man lying beside the burned van, burned beyond recognition. It would be impossible to determine what had been loaded in the van, but the people from the state police would try anyway.

C. C. was staring at the burned body. He thought, if I had a woman and a man's body burned beyond recognition, the sheriff might...

One of the deputies walked up to the sheriff, interrupting Charlie's thoughts.

"Sheriff, there is a cocaine testing kit in the house, but no coke - nothing. The kit looks like it was used, but we can't be sure."

The sheriff asked, "Have you found any money?"

"No, sir. There's no briefcase or suitcase in the cabin, or anything that could be used to carry money - at least we couldn't find any."

C. C. thought, they probably looked right at it, but thought it was mine and never bothered to open any of the suitcases.

The sheriff responded in a quiet voice as if he were talking to himself. "Damn, this is funny. A drug deal going down and no money or evidence of drugs. But one thing is for sure, Terry and Paul wanted me to be at breakfast with them so I wouldn't be out this way this morning to see that plane land. They must know something. I'll get to them when I get back to town."

The deputy continued, "Sheriff, we found a purse that belonged to a Donna Weir. The photo on her driver's license matches the woman who is wounded. We also found a permit to carry a concealed weapon, issued in California."

"This gets more confusing as I get more information. C. C., where does your friend fit into this?"

"Let me think. I guess Donna was a bodyguard for Frank Giaventi. He was the Godfather in San Francisco until he was killed a few months ago. Lisa, my friend, was his niece, but I'm sure she had nothing to do with the family. She's married to the head of the organized crime unit of the SFPD. I can see how this is getting deep.

"Sheriff, I have some more thoughts for you. If you can't find any drugs and you can't find any money, then you must assume that this was just a shootout between two rival gangs. I didn't see Donna fire any gun. She was shot in the back also. I'd check her hands to see if she fired any guns in the last day or so. If she didn't, then you can't hold her because she hasn't committed any crime that is provable. I'd say you have an interesting situation here."

Charlie thought, I know Donna hadn't fired a gun in the past day and she will pass the test. That will place the sheriff in a position where he will have to let her go in two days because he doesn't have any evidence. He could hold her as a material witness, but that would be very flimsy. Now how do I set it up that everybody thinks we are dead?

The sheriff thought for a moment, and then replied, "C. C., that's a good idea you have. I'll have the police in Spokane check her out."

The deep wop-wop-wop noise of a helicopter sounded nearby, getting louder. Everybody at the camp looked towards the sky. The helicopter came over the small ridge behind the camp, turned to the east, and came down to land between the lake and where Donna was laying.

Two paramedics jumped out of the air ambulance and ran

261

over to the unconscious woman. They started an IV immediately. One of them radioed to Spokane to tell them of the patient's condition.

He said, "I don't think she'll make it to the hospital, but if she does, she'll need blood and a quick operation to remove at least two bullets. I'll let you know of her progress after we're in the air and close to Spokane."

The radio answered, "We'll wait for your in-flight report."

With those words, the men around Donna lifted her onto a stretcher, carried her to the helicopter, and placed her inside. It was a long way to Spokane. A few moments later, the helicopter was on its way to Spokane.

C. C. thought Donna will make it because God wants her to live. Go with God, Donna.

The sheriff spoke to C. C., "I'll want to talk to you some more, so stick close to town."

"Sheriff, I have to take a short trip over the next several days to Canada and Seattle. My trip may even last five or six days, but I hope no longer. It's business. Would that be all right?"

"Knowing you, I guess it's all right, but tell me when you leave and when you expect to return."

"Sure will."

"Good."

With those words, the sheriff got in his vehicle and left for town.

Charlie went into his cabin, dialed a number in San Francisco. The voice on the telephone answered, "Bank of America. How may I direct your call?"

"This is C. C. Duncan. Please connect me with the department that wires money. I want to wire some money to a hospital in Spokane."

After he had arranged for Donna's bill to be paid, he called Mike.

"Mike, this is Charlie. I don't know what the complete story is, but I think you should know about it. Also, I think you should tell Louis what I'm about to tell you."

"What have you got?"

"Well, yesterday some men and two women took over my camp. A plane landed in my lake this morning and a shootout followed. The only person left alive is Donna, and she's on her way to a hospital in Spokane in very critical condition. Now here is the kicker. As of now, the police have no motive for the shootout, no drugs, and no money to pay for the delivery of any drugs. I think you should call Louis and tell him about Donna."

"Who's doing the investigation?"

"The sheriff here in Sand Point. He's a fairly sharp character. He just left to go back to town. You could call him in about two hours, I guess."

"Thanks for the info, Charlie. I'll call Louis and tell him. That is a strange situation. Take care of yourself now."

"Sure will try, Mike. Take care."

Charlie walked outside the cabin to change the tire on his suburban. Hank was standing by Joel, Sara, Sam, and Ruth.

Sam walked over to C. C. "What are your plans now?"

"First, I'm going to Canada on some business. Then I'm going into Coeur d'Alene and talk to that attorney there. I'm going to give this property to the church with basically the same caveats as in my will. After that, I have to go to Seattle and conclude some business there, and then return to Spokane to see how Donna is. After that, I don't know. I may even try to combine my trips to Canada and Seattle. I don't really know if I'll go to those places in that order, but I do have to go there on business."

Sam shook his head thinking Charlie hasn't told me everything. I wonder what he is really going to do and what's the business he must complete?

"C. C., we have to go now. We'll take Joel and Sara to our house and let them stay there for a while."

Hank said, "That'll be fine, Ruth. When the search and rescue guys arrive, I'll have to go look for the downed airplane and those two who went over the cliff. Sam, will you tell the sheriff I'll be waiting at my house for the search parties?"

"Sure Hank."

With those words, Hank took his guns back from the Thompsons and started to walk to his house. Sam and Ruth escorted Joel and Sara to their car and waved to Hank and C. C. as they pulled away.

Charlie continued to change the tire on the suburban. As soon as the tire was changed, he drove the truck up to the curve. Just as he suspected, the tarp was covering the curve sign. He stopped the truck and removed it.

Charlie then walked over to the edge of the cliff and looked where he thought the bodies would be. They were there, all right, but so were two bears. The animals already had made a mess of both corpses.

He would have to get down there in a hurry if he was to recover any part of the bodies at all. C. C. drove up to the top of the ridge, turned his truck around. The suburban was now headed down the ridge as fast as Charlie thought was safe. Once at his camp, he recovered his guns on the side of the ridge. Then he returned to the little room in the mine, gathered up all of his things, and took them to his cabin and hid most of them there for possible future use.

He grabbed his hunting rifle, a 7mm Mag, and drove back to where the bears were holding their feast. He fired two quick shots and killed them both.

The search party knocked on the door at Hank's house.

"Be there in a minute. You guys got any guns?"

"We don't need any for this, Hank."

"We might, so I'll take my rifle."

Hank got in their vehicles and they drove to the camp. They found C. C. there changing the tire on the Chrysler.

"Hank, I went up on the ridge to look for those two. I don't think you'll find much of them. Two bears had already gotten to work on them and I killed them. I only saw parts of the bodies. I guess you'll have to cut the bears open to get the rest of the bodies."

Hank turned to the others.

264

"And you thought you wouldn't need a rifle. Come on, let's go. Now you drive a little into the lake over there close to shore and we'll get what parts are left."

After several hours, Hank and the recovery team returned to the camp. They had the body of the pilot of the Thompson's plane and some of the body parts of Mona and Pete.

Hank got out of the truck and waved to the recovery team as they drove off.

He walked over to Charlie. "It was a mess. I guess you were right. There were wolf tracks also. I don't know if we will ever recover all the body parts. I gutted one of the bears and sure enough, some clothing from one of them was in the stomach. Damn, I'm sure glad they were dead when the bears found them."

"It sure wouldn't have been pleasant otherwise."

Hank replied, "Nope!"

Chapter 6

Sheriff Coomey was thinking about the events of the morning -how, out of nowhere, Terry and Paul had called him about his bid for reelection. He hadn't even thought about it before. Too early, he thought. Also, those two had opposed him last time, because he wouldn't do Hank dirt and take the camp away from him. Also, why did the wounded woman...Donna...meet with him and someone else? It had to be Paul. They know something, he thought; and I am going to get them.

Sheriff Coomey turned to the deputy driving the car.

"Nick, after you drop me off at the office, I want you to invite Paul and Terry over to my office for a chat. And Nick, insist they come now. Understand?"

Smiling, he replied, "Yes, sir."

Nick let Sheriff Coomey off at his office, then drove to the bank.

"Hi, Missy," he told the petite, pretty girl inside, "I have to see Paul."

"Mr. Croket is busy, but you can come back in an hour. He'll be able to see you then."

"Missy, the sheriff wants to see him now. I w-i-l-l see Mr.

Croket now. You call him and tell him."

Missy was surprised by what Nick said and especially the tone of his voice. She reached for the telephone and dialed a number. The phone rang in Paul Croket's office.

He answered, "Missy, what is it? You know I am in the middle of the Callahan deal and I told you I wasn't to be disturbed."

"Mr. Croket, Nick is here and he says he has to see you immediately."

"You mean Deputy Nick?"

"Yes sir."

"Tell him he will have to wait."

"Mr. Croket, I don't think that would be a good idea. He says the sheriff wants to see you now and he is very emphatic about seeing you now and you going to see the sheriff."

"Okay, tell him I'll be there in a minute."

It was five minutes later when Deputy Nick got up from his chair and walked towards the office where Paul Croket was conducting his business. He knocked on the office door.

As soon as he saw the deputy knocked on the door to his office, Paul Croket came out of his office.

"Nick, now what is so important?"

"Mr. Croket, Sheriff Coomey told me to insist you come to his office immediately and not take later for an answer. I'll give you five minutes. Do you wish to drive your own car or ride in the squad car?"

Paul Croket's face changed to a concerned look.

"I'll drive myself. It'll take me about ten minutes to get there."

"That'll be fine, Mr. Croket."

Paul Croket went into another office and dialed a number.

Terry Bracken answered the telephone, "Real estate, Terry speaking."

"Terry, Nick just came here and said Sheriff Coomey demanded that I go to his office now. What's up?"

"I don't know, Paul. Say, Nick just drove up. I guess I'll be

268

there, too. See you in a few minutes. Remember, don't say anything."

"Right."

Deputy Nick walked into Terry's office.

"What can I do for you, Nick?"

"Mr. Bracken, Sheriff Coomey wants you to come to his office now. Do you want to drive your car or do you want to ride in my squad car?"

"Heck, I'll drive my car. Tell Coomey I will be there in less than fifteen minutes. Should I bring an attorney?"

"I don't know. I was just told to get you."

"Well, I don't guess I'll need one. See you in fifteen minutes."

The sheriff's office was next to the building that housed City Hall and the Fire Department. The jail was also in the same building as the sheriff's office. It was a typical small town municipal set of buildings.

Paul Croket was the first to arrive. He walked into the building, turned to his left, and entered the sheriff's office.

"Where's the sheriff?"

"He's in his office. Please have a seat Mr. Croket. He shouldn't be too long."

"He damn well better not be too long. I have some important business to conclude back at the bank."

Terry Bracken walked in as Paul Croket ended his comment.

The secretary said, "Hello, Terry. The sheriff will be with you in a short time. Please have a seat."

Taking his cue from Paul, Terry said, "You buzz Coomey and tell him I am here and I have to leave to attend to an act of sale."

He really didn't have any business, but that line always worked for him in the past.

The secretary looked him straight in the eyes and replied, "Have a seat over there with Mr. Croket. I would appreciate it very much if you would direct your comments to the sheriff and not to me."

Terry sensed he had better keep quiet, as he had never been treated this way before.

269

A few minutes later, Sheriff Coomey walked into the room.

"Paul, Terry, please come in and have a seat." He turned to his secretary, "I'm not to be disturbed for anything short of a life and death problem. Understand?"

"Yes, sir!"

Terry Bracken sat in the chair to the left of the sheriff's desk and Paul Croket sat in front of the desk.

Sheriff Coomey started, "First, I want you both to know you are suspects as accessories before and after the fact of the shootout at Hank's old camp. If you wish to have your lawyer present during this conversation, please call him. If he can't come now, you'll be placed in a jail cell until he arrives. If you wish me to proceed with this conversation without your lawyer, then please sign this paper and we will proceed."

Sheriff Coomey knew the attorneys for both Paul and Terry would not come any time soon and his threat of keeping them in jail would get them to sign the paper so he could proceed without an attorney present.

Terry looked at Paul and Paul looked back at him; then both men signed their names.

"Now, Terry, Paul, I want to know the real reason why you treated me to breakfast this morning and tried to keep me at the table past 10:30. You answer first, Terry."

"Sheriff, I don't know what you're thinking, but I only wanted to tell you that I would support you in the next election."

"Same here, Sheriff.

"Terry, I know Donna Weir met with you yesterday morning. There were other people there, and I know who they were. But for the record, please name all those who were present."

Terry looked pale, but replied, "Paul Croket and a man named Kirk. He came with Donna. What happened out at the camp?"

"I'll answer that question soon. Now what was the topic of conversation? You answer the question, Paul."

"I wanted to obtain title to the camp for myself. I've always wanted the property. I made a deal that if I got the property, then I would rent the property to Donna ever so often for a weekend.

270

That's all, I swear it."

"Is that all? Is that the full gist of the conversation, Terry?"

"That's about all, Sheriff."

"Terry, let's return to the question I posed to both of you when we started this talk. Why did you really take me to breakfast and keep me there as long as you did? I know you wanted to keep me longer, but I left anyway."

"Sheriff, I think I'd better not answer any more questions."

"Paul, will you answer?"

"I think Terry has the right idea. No more answers."

"Okay. Now you two listen to me. Some people were bringing drugs into this country at the camp. They were delivering it to Donna who was there to receive it for the Giaventi family. You two had to know something illegal was going down and that makes you as guilty as them. I warn you now, as soon as I get all my ducks lined up, you two will become guests of the State of Idaho for at least a couple of years.

"Right now, I don't have enough evidence, but I hope to have more than enough when Donna wakes up. She's severely wounded and in a hospital in Spokane undergoing surgery right now. Hopefully, she will recover and tell me what happened.

"Now what happened at the camp was a real shootout. There are at least five people dead and two more thought to be dead. This does not include the pilot of the crashed plane that carried a couple named Thompsons. You may or may not know that C. C. and the Thompsons were held prisoners against their will. That amounts to kidnapping.

"I don't want either of you to leave Sand Point for any reason until I say you can leave. Do you understand me?"

Terry shook his head yes.

Paul looked worried, but mumbled, "Yes."

"Good. That about ends this little talk. Oh Paul, this means you do not leave to go to Coeur d'Alene for your high school class reunion, either."

Paul Croket and Terry Bracken left the sheriff's office looking very worried.

The sheriff watched them leave through his window, smiled, thinking they're guilty as sin – I know it and I have those two scared stiff. I hope they'll break under the pressure and talk. That would make things a lot easier for me. I wonder if they really knew what they were getting themselves into?

Terry hung his head and walked to his car. Paul's face wore a look of deep concern. It was obvious both men were deeply concerned about the day's events.

It was now snowing very hard. It would be the first blizzard of the year.

The phone rang in Louis Giaventi's house. A male voice answered, "This is Louis Giaventi."

"Louis, this is Mike. Charlie just phoned me from Idaho. I haven't even told Lisa yet, but Donna and a few of your boys took over Charlie's place."

"Charlie's place. I told them to rent a camp in Idaho, not take it over." As an afterthought, he said, "I wanted to have a quiet vacation there."

"Right now, it doesn't matter. Someone landed a pontoon plane in Charlie's lake and a gunfight erupted. Charlie said the only survivor is Donna and she's in a Spokane hospital, critically wounded. The sheriff wants to talk to Donna and might have her in protective custody by now.

"Also, Charlie says he's guaranteed all medical bills for Donna. I think he'll see her shortly. I don't know exactly when, but I suspect he has gone sweet on her."

The telephone fell silent.

Louis replied, "Mike, I can't leave to go there for a couple of days, but I'll go see Donna as soon as I can. Thanks for calling."

"Louis, because this has to do with Charlie, this is off the record. I hope you understand that."

"Yes, I do. Now I must go. Thanks again, Mike."

The next morning the snow had stopped. C. C. looked out the window at the lake. That was a heavy snowfall, but if the sun comes out, it would all melt soon, except in the shaded places. The lake wouldn't freeze over just yet, but maybe soon.

His thoughts turned to Donna what do I do to get Donna out of the hospital? Let's see...go to

Canada, buy a truck, an ATV, and...oh, a trailer for the ATV. Place the truck in position on the trail. Get the propane tank ready. Gee I almost forgot. Clean out my account in Switzerland. How do I get the money. I need to get the rest of my money out of the Bank of America, too. I want to leave Lisa some money - three million should be enough.

It seemed as if he had ten million things to do - Get the bank to wire the money to Spokane, no, to a bank in Seattle. Then get cash, fly to Mexico, wait to transfer the money to the Oregon State Bank where Donna and I would live - if she would agree to marry him. Getting married to Donna seemed the best way to take care of Donna. While in Seattle, he had to return the briefcase to Louis. After all that was done, he could finally see Donna. He'd have to ask Sam to look in on her every day, and to do him a big favor if he wasn't there when she woke up.

C. C. finished his chores around the camp, and then called Hank. "I have to leave for several days," he told him, "if the sheriff will let me. Look after the place for me. Oh, within the next few days I am going to deed the camp to the church with the conditions I promised. I thought you'd be interested. See you in a few days."

"Have a good trip."

Something's funny here, Hank thought. C. C. knows more than he is telling people. I wonder what it is. I don't guess I really care. He's done a lot for me and I owe him. He's a good man.

C. C. went outside into the snow and got in his suburban. He started the engine, placed it in four-wheel drive, let the motor warm up, and started up the slope towards the gravel road. He crossed the bridge and onto the black top road towards town. It was a short ride to town. He pulled to a stop in front of the sheriff's office, got out, and walked inside.

Nick was sitting behind one of the desks.

"Hi, Nick. Sheriff in?"

273

"He sure is, and I think he wants to talk to you. Go right in."

"Hi, Sheriff. I didn't leave last night because of the blizzard, but I really have to get going unless you need me to stick around here for a while. In either case, can I help you with anything?"

Sheriff Coomey replied, "I want to know more about what happened - specifically what happened when you bought the camp."

"Well, Terry brought me over to the property and I struck a deal with Hank. We went to the bank and Paul was upset. Both Hank and I saw Paul was not being cooperative and probably wanted to get the camp cheap. You know, cheat Hank out of everything he had. We went to Coeur d'Alene, found an attorney, and he processed the sale. A few days later, Paul and Terry came out to the camp and demanded we leave, saying it was the bank's property. I told them where to get off. That's about all of it I guess."

"Interesting, but that fits with what Paul and Terry said. I still wonder what that woman was doing up there at your camp? Any more ideas?"

"Not really, but if I come up with any, I'll let you know. By the way, how did those tests come out on her? Had she fired a gun recently?"

"All negative."

"That's strange with all that shooting. But that means she wasn't part of the shootout. All you can hold her for is being a witness, huh?"

"Yes, I plan on holding her as a material witness. That way, I can keep hold of her a little longer. She knows things I want to know."

"Well, Sheriff, I'd like to leave now. I plan to go to Spokane and see Donna, then go to Seattle and Vancouver on business. After that, I will come home and check in with you. If you want me to call you from any of those places, just let me know and I will. I guess it'll take me four or five days to complete my business. Is that okay with you?"

"C. C., I trust you, but check back with me at least every two days."

"Will do, Sheriff. One more thing. If you have Donna under house arrest, so to speak, I'd appreciate it if you would call the hospital and let them know that I plan to visit her. Tell them it's all right for me to visit. I know Sam wants to see her also."

The sheriff replied, "Okay. Actually, C. C., anyone can visit her because I haven't placed her in protective custody yet, or had her arrested as a material witness. However, the Washington State Police does have a man there to see who visits her. Have a pleasant trip."

C. C. walked out of the office and to his Suburban.

The sheriff watched him walk to the truck, thinking, he knows more than he is telling me, but I don't know...

As C. C. drove towards Coeur d'Alene on Highway 95, he was hoping Coomey wouldn't discover that he was going to take a quick trip to Mexico. It was risky, but he would just have to take that risk.

At the intersection with I-90, the suburban turned right onto a long entry ramp that went down a hill and then merged onto the interstate. The traffic was traveling faster than the speed limit so Charlie eased his suburban up to a little over 70 MPH.

The twenty-seven miles to the exit in Spokane, where he must go to the hospital went by rapidly and he soon spotted the blue sign that read "Hospital Next Right." C. C. slowed down, exited the interstate, made a few turns, passed through a traffic light, and drove into the hospital parking lot.

Inside the hospital, he walked to the information desk.

"I'm here to see Donna Weir. She's in ICU. Can you direct me?"

The woman looked up at Charlie and gave him a Flirting smile. "ICU is on the second floor. When you get off the elevators, turn to the right and you'll see the ICU doors. She is in ICU room 4. You must ask the nurse for permission to see her, though. It's not ICU visiting hours."

"Will do."

When the elevator reached the second floor, he followed the

woman's directions and passed through the ICU doors.

He found a nurse and said, "May I see Donna Weir. I believe Sheriff Coomey called and said it would be all right for me to visit her."

The nurse looked at Charlie, then at the police officer sitting by the door to room number 4. The officer got up and came over to Charlie.

"What's your name?"

"My name is C. C. Duncan. Didn't Sheriff Coomey call?"

"He sure did. Do you have any I.D.?

"Will my driver's license do?"

"Sure will."

The officer scrutinized Charlie's driver's license, nodded his head, and pointed to Donna's room.

The nurse tugged at Charlie's shirt.

"She's resting now. Try not to excite her or do anything that would cause her to become excited. We think she's just come out of a coma, but she isn't awake yet. Please be brief."

"I sure will, nurse. If she doesn't wake up, I can leave her a note, can't I?"

"Yes, you can."

Charlie entered Donna's room and found her lying on the bed with IV's in both arms and an ECG hooked up to her. The little lines on her monitor were going to the right on the recorder above her bed.

He knew she was alive. He also felt - no, knew - she would make it and probably would become his wife.

Standing beside her bed, he took her hand, bowed his head, and started to pray. After a couple of minutes, Donna's hand weakly squeezed his. He stopped praying and looked at her. Donna's eyes were open and she had a faint smile on her face.

"Thanks, Charlie," she said softly.

Charlie's face lit up with a big smile.

"You're awake. I must talk fast. Do not talk to anyone else about the shootout except Sam Pritchard and me. He's a minister in Sand Point. I'll return in four or five days and fill you in then.

Okay?"

"Anything you say is fine with me. Charlie, I know you are the Iceman."

"I thought you might know, but that is in my past. You probably saved my life. Donna, I have forgiven you for Seattle. But we'll talk about all that when I see you next. Remember, don't talk to anyone except Sam."

"I won't. Thanks again for saving me from Hell."

"Donna, before I leave, I want to ask you something. Will you be my wife? Will you marry me?"

Donna smiled, nodded her head yes. She didn't know why she said yes, but she was certain it was the right answer.

Charlie kissed her forehead.

Donna settled her head back into her pillow, closed her eyes, and went back to sleep.

Charlie smiled and thought she definitely had the same experience I had. She was a changed person - he knew it. He got up, walked out of the room, and found the nurse.

"Nurse, Donna woke up for a few moments. She'll be fine. I'll return in four or five days to visit her again."

"She woke up?"

"Yes, but she went right back to sleep."

"Thanks for telling me." The woman was grinning.

The nurse immediately went to Donna's room. As she entered, Donna's eyes opened and then closed again as Donna drifted into a deep sleep.

Knowing that Donna would recover, Charlie left the hospital. He returned to I-90, and drove west. He would cross the Columbia River. As he drove into Seattle, he saw a shopping mall off to the right of the highway and pulled into the mall parking lot there.

As luck would have it, he saw a "Box It and Mail It" store. He walked into the store.

"I need to send this UPS. Do you send UPS?"

"Sure do. The driver should be here in about fifteen minutes."

"Good. I need a box to hold this briefcase."

"We have special boxes for briefcases. Let me get you one."

Charlie placed the briefcase into the box, and then placed the label he had prepared in Sand Point on the box. He handed the box back to the attendant.

Charlie said, "I'm sending this for someone else. That's her address in San Francisco."

"That's fine. That will be $16.78."

Charlie handed him a twenty-dollar bill. The attendant handed Charlie his change. He put the change in his pocket and walked out the door.

He thought I wonder what that guy would do if he knew that box contained more money than he's ever seen.

Charlie smiled and continued to think; now I must get my truck, ATV, and trailer, and go to Mexico. Got a lot to do.

Charlie left the mall and returned to the interstate. He turned south towards Sea Tac. He would use one of his false passports to enter Mexico.

He checked in at the Airport Hilton, then went to a pay telephone and dialed a number in Vancouver. It was a Ford Truck dealership.

"Vancouver Ford," a voice answered.

"My name is Gordon Phillips. I'll be in Vancouver two, three, or four days from now. When I arrive, I'd like to have a one ton, king cab, four by four truck with a winch ready for me to pick up. If you cannot get a one-ton pick up, then a three-quarter-ton truck will do, but it must be a king cab, four-by-four with a winch. I would like it to be licensed, also.

"In addition, I want to buy a four wheel ATV with a small trailer that I can use to carry the ATV. Two more items. I want two ramps so I can place the ATV in the truck bed. The second item I need is a triangular towing bar to tow the truck behind my suburban when I pick it up. Make sure I'll have all the needed safety lights and gear for towing a truck. How much money do you want?"

The salesman replied, "Just a minute. I'll let you talk to the sales manager."

Soon a voice came over the telephone. "This is Bryan. How

278

may I help you?"

"I suppose the salesman told you what I wanted, but he didn't know how much money I would have to send for you to accomplish what I want. I don't really care about the color of the truck, ATV, or the trailer. How much do you want me to wire you?

The sales manager thought for a moment, and then said, "Mr. Phillips, we'd need $50,000.00 American to accomplish what you want. There would be some excess and we'll refund whatever isn't needed after we have the exact amount. Is that satisfactory?"

Charlie replied, "I can send $40,000.00 and we will debit and credit the balance when I get there."

Without hesitation, the man replied, "That'll be satisfactory. When will the money arrive?"

"Probably within the hour."

Charlie hung up and dialed the Bank of America in San Francisco.

With all of that arranged, Charlie now checked his tickets for Mexico.

On the third day after the shootout at the camp, Sam Pritchard and his wife decided to drive to Spokane to see Donna. It was cold that day, the heavy snowfall from a couple of days before was just beginning to melt. The side of the road was still covered with snow, but the road was clear.

After Sam and Ruth arrived at the hospital, they went up to the second floor and into the ICU area. Sam, being a pastor, was admitted without question.

Donna was awake. Looking at Sam and Ruth, she asked, "Who are you?"

"My name is Sam Pritchard and this is my wife, Ruth. I am the pastor of C. C. Duncan's church in Sand Point. C. C. has told me some things about you, but first I must tell you about some dreams Ruth and I have had over the past year or so."

Donna nodded to indicate that she was listening.

Ruth said, "Donna, we were deciding where to relocate and

279

had just about decided to go somewhere else when we had these dreams. They were always the same. A man and a woman walking towards us on what looked like a river or lake, with a point of sand sticking out into the water."

Sam continued, "We decided to move to Sand Point. That evening, C. C. was shot in front of a hotel in Seattle. It was an accident because the killer wanted to kill two other men."

Donna interrupted, "What were the names of the two men the killer wanted to kill?"

"I remember only one name - Andrati."

Donna gasped because she now realized why Charlie had told her he had forgiven her for Seattle. It was Charlie she shot by accident – the same person who was the Iceman and now her fiancé.

Sam seemed surprised at Donna's reaction, but he continued, "Just before I saw C. C. for the first time, my dream cleared up and I was able to recognize the man in it. When I saw C. C., I knew he was the man I had seen in my dreams. When Ruth visited the hospital, she immediately recognized him too.

"About three days ago, our dreams cleared up a little more. We could recognize the woman now. When we saw you lying on the ground, we recognized you as that woman."

Ruth interrupted, "There's more. We have also seen two children about the same age with you and C. C. We cannot recognize them as yet. We think it means you and he will marry and have children, but we don't know for sure. Only the Lord knows."

"Sam - may I call you Sam?"

"Sure."

"Sam, Charlie, that's what I call C. C., came to see me yesterday - I think it was yesterday - and told me I could talk to you. Do you know who shot Charlie in Seattle?"

"Yes. C. C. told me."

Donna sighed, then continued, "Sam, I don't know if this makes any sense, but I know I was relegated to Hell, but my sins were forgiven and I was told to return to this life by a beautiful

280

woman dressed in white . . . that there were things - good things for God - I was to accomplish here before I am to die."

Sam and Ruth looked at each other, then back to Donna who continued, "At first, I was floating over my body. Then I went into a dark place. I have never seen anything so black before. After floating and going into this dark place, I saw a red light or glow at the end of the darkness. All of a sudden, I was over a lake no, it was more like an ocean of fire. Flames were leaping out of the ocean hundreds of feet into the air. People were standing around on the shoreline. Everyone was screaming. Some actually were in the fire. Their screams were the worst. I even recognized one man - Gene. He was killed in the shootout, I think.

"Then three men came walking by me. The one walking in the middle was Jesus - I know it, but I don't know how. The two on each side were shielding him from the heat of the fire with something - like a mother bird would protect her young.

"The Lord looked at me and said, 'There is a good man praying for your recovery. You have repented. Your sins are forgiven. Return to your body and work for me.'

"With those words, I came back to where my body lay. Flying overhead, it was then I realized it was Charlie praying over me. Immediately, I was back in my body and I don't remember anything after that until Charlie was here yesterday. Does that sound crazy or what?"

"Donna, that is much the same story that C. C. told me. I believe you and C. C. are truly fortunate and both of you have been forgiven by the Lord."

The nurse came into the room and interrupted. "Folks, you've been with Donna for over an hour. I think she must get some rest now if she's to continue to recover as well as she has."

Sam responded, "You're right. Donna, we'll keep you in our prayers. We hope you will be able to get in a room of your own soon. By the way, C. C. has paid all your medical bills. He's quite wealthy, you know."

"I would think so," came the reply.

Three days later after Charlie had been in Mexico, his plane returning from Mexico was circling over Seattle to begin its final approach to Sea Tac. He could see the water and the floating bridges over the water as the plane approached the runway. It was mid morning. He would check in at the Hilton, pay for a night's stay, but leave before dark if the weather didn't close in on him.

In his room, he dialed a number in Sand Point. The telephone answered, "Sand Point Sheriff's office"

"This is C. C. Is the sheriff in?"

"Just a minute, C. C."

"C. C., Sheriff Coomey. Where are you?"

"I'm at the airport Hilton now, but I plan to go north to Vancouver later today. I just finished my business in Seattle. Thought I'd check in before I left for Vancouver."

"Thanks for calling. I don't see why you can't go to Vancouver. Did you see Donna?"

"Yes. I saw her a couple of days ago. She actually woke up while I was there. Any news about her or anything else?"

"I guess it's all good news from her point of view. She's improving like crazy. She should be moved to a regular room in one or two days. I got a call from two people in San Francisco. One was Mike Forester and the other was Louis Giaventi. They both want to see her tomorrow. Didn't you say you knew them?"

"I know Mike well. He's the husband of my adopted relative, Lisa. Louis is Lisa's cousin, but I don't know him so well - just enough to recognize him when I see him, that's all."

"What do you think of them visiting Donna?"

"I don't think it can do any harm, but you must decide."

Sheriff Coomey thought for a minute, and then said, "I think I'll let them see her."

"Sheriff, I'd like to get some sleep. I'm tuckered out right now. I'd like to leave before dark to go to Vancouver. Can we continue this conversation when I return to Sand Point?"

"Sure, but we need to talk when you get back. See you then."

282

CHAPTER 7

The UPS truck drove up to the gate of the Giaventi mansion. The deliveryman got out and rang the bell. Within a minute, a voice came over the speaker.

"Please state your name and your business."

"UPS. I'm delivering a package to Mr. Louis Giaventi. He must sign for it."

"Just a minute."

Four minutes later, the voice returned. "Who's the package from?"

"The return address is someone named Mrs. Lisa Forester in town. It was sent from Seattle though."

After a short time, the voice said, "Come up to the house. We will accept delivery."

As Louis watched the UPS truck coming up the driveway, he began to think, Lisa didn't send the package. She hasn't been in Seattle in a long time. Maybe Mike...no, he'd put his name on the package, not hers. I wonder if it's a bomb? Well, I'll see and if I don't like it, I just won't open it until I have it checked out.

The UPS driver rang the doorbell and Louis came to the door.

"I'm Louis Giaventi. Let me see the package."

The UPS man gave the package to Louis, and then held out

284

his logbook. "Please sign the receipt, sir."

Louis waited until the UPS truck had almost reached the gate before turning to go back inside. He carried the package gingerly, carefully inspecting it as he walked. Finally, deciding that it didn't look so threatening, he gave it a tentative, gentle shake. He heard a small rattle that made him think of a handle on a briefcase. Walking through the French doors to the patio, he placed the package on a table, took out his pocketknife, and cut the package to open it.

With one side of the package open, he could see that there was, indeed, a briefcase inside. He was elated, but still cautious - it looked like the briefcase he had sent with Donna - the one that had held his money.

He pulled it from the package and confirmed it was the same briefcase. An envelope fell to the floor. Louis reached for it, and then tore it open.

The note inside the envelope read, "I believe this is yours. I am returning it to you as it is not mine." The note was signed C. C. Duncan.

Louis opened the briefcase. Inside he found the money he had sent with Donna. He stopped, sat down, and just looked at the money for several minutes.

He thought, who in the hell is C. C. Duncan and why did he return the money to me? Wait a minute - that's the name Lisa's friend took because he couldn't remember his name. It was his place where the shootout occurred. Why would he...? He was good with a rifle, martial arts...he has the abilities a great hit man would need. Uncle Frank even offered him the job, but he turned it down. I'll bet he's the Iceman. But why did he return the money? Why is he helping Donna? I'll have to visit Donna and talk to her. I wonder when Mike is going to Spokane? I'll have to fly to Spokane before Mike and talk to Donna.

Mike was sitting at his desk in police headquarters when the phone on his desk rang.

"Lt. Michael Forester."

"Mike, this is Pierre Richard in Paris. I think we know who the Iceman is."

"We may be getting close to him also, Pierre. Who do you think?"

"We think he's your friend, Charles Cain Duncan."

"I doubt that, but I learned a long time ago that anything's possible. Tell me what you have."

"Every time we know the Iceman has been active, we found out that Mr. Duncan was out of the USA too and probably near where the Iceman was active. We obtained his records at the hospital and found he has the abilities the Iceman would need to have. In short, he looks like our man."

"I never thought of Charlie, but you could be right. I know he is good with a rifle from the tests run at Pendleton. You might be right. Let me look into it this week. He was somehow involved in a shootout on his place in Idaho a few days ago. It ties in with a lot of other things. There was one survivor - Donna Weir."

"Mike, is that the Donna who was the bodyguard for Frank Giaventi?"

"Yes, it is. But there's something strange about the entire shootout. Donna didn't fire a gun. Believe me, Pierre, she's quick and deadly with a gun. No money was found on the property, even though the sheriff thinks a drug deal was going down, but turned bad. This would fit the pattern of a drug deal that went sour except there was no evidence of a drug deal – that is except the testing kit."

"I was going to fly to Spokane next week to talk to Donna, but I think I'll fly there tomorrow instead. I'll call you with any information I get from Donna."

"That will be good, Mike. I'll wait for your call."

"Pierre, I have to ask the question. What will you do if we agree Charlie is the Iceman?"

"We'll wait until the government says it is acceptable to arrest him and then ask you to arrest and extradite him to France."

"Playing the devil's advocate, Pierre, do you have any concrete evidence that the Iceman even exists, or that he did all the things you say he did? Also, if you have such evidence, is there

286

enough to prove that Charlie is the Iceman? Before you answer, let me say that personally I'm convinced he exists and did the things you say he did, but you must have enough proof for any extradition."

"You have a point, Mike. We don't have enough proof at this time, but we're working on it."

"An additional question, Pierre. What will you do if we agree he is the Iceman and you can't get enough evidence for extradition or a conviction?"

"Mike, it would be out of my hands at that time. I don't know what the politicians would do."

"Thanks for being candid with me, Pierre. I must go now. I have some other things to do before I fly to Spokane tomorrow."

"I will wait for your call, Mike."

It was 4:00 PM when Charlie checked out of the Hilton. He nosed his suburban onto Interstate 5 and increased his speed to accommodate the traffic. By 5:30 PM he was north of Seattle and out of the five o'clock traffic traveling toward Vancouver. He passed a sign that said "Ferry Next Right, Then Turn Left". There was a Burger King at that exit, so he turned right to eat supper and relax.

After a burger, some fries, and a drink, he left the restaurant and continued towards Vancouver. Soon he was approaching the border between the United States and Canada.

As he was waiting to pass through customs, he began to think about everything that had happened over the past year - how he had been shot in Seattle, gone to Hell, gotten in the middle of a drug smuggling operation that went bad, prayed for Donna - the driver in the car behind him sounded his horn.

Charlie immediately came out of his thoughts and pulled forward toward the small house where the Canadian Custom's agent was.

"Where are you going sir?" the Custom Agent asked.

"Vancouver."

"How long are you going to stay there?"

"I'm not sure. It depends on how my business goes, but I guess about two days or less."

"Have you any firearms?"

"No, sir."

"Have a good trip, sir."

Charlie depressed the accelerator of the truck and proceeded towards Vancouver. He started to wonder if he could find the north end of the trail on the west side of the lake. He had only seen it once when he had been hiking. As the lights of Vancouver came into view, he saw a Holiday Inn.

He decided to stay there for the night and pick up the truck and the ATV tomorrow. It's been a long day. Morning in Mexico and now in Vancouver. What a day!

He checked in at the local hotel.

As he climbed into bed, he began to make his final plans for their escape. I'll have to devise a plan that Donna can literally live with. Let's see. Burn the suburban after I place the bones in it, take the ATV to the truck...yes, I guess it will work, but I must do a little preparation and set up camp on the trail.

Charlie drifted off to sleep. It was past midnight.

The alarm woke him at 6:00 AM. He rolled out of bed, shaved, tended to his beard, brushed his teeth, then got dressed to go to the coffee shop, where he ordered two eggs, hot cakes and bacon for breakfast and two ham biscuits to go. Then, while checking out, he asked for directions to the Vancouver Ford Truck dealership.

The desk clerk responded that it was close to the motel. All he would have to do was go to the second traffic light, turn right for about a kilometer, and he'd find it on the left side of the road.

Charlie drove towards Vancouver. He turned right at the second traffic light and found the dealership very easily. Parking his suburban in the parking lot, he went into the show room.

Charlie spoke to the secretary, "My name is Gordon Phillips. I'd like to speak with Bryan?"

"Just a minute."

She reached for the telephone, which doubled as the PA

288

system microphone, and dialed a number.

"Mr. Cooper, a Mr. Phillips is here and wants to speak to you. Can you...?"

Bryan Cooper interrupted, "I'll be there within a minute."

She looked at Charlie, pointed to a man in his late thirties coming out of his office towards them. "That's Mr. Cooper now."

Charlie walked over to meet him.

"Hi, I am Gordon Phillips. I trust you received your money after our conversation."

Extending his hand to shake hands with Charlie, he answered, "We sure did. We couldn't find a one ton-truck, but I got a three-quarter ton for you. I made a couple of decisions about your ATV and the trailer you wanted. I hope they meet with your approval. The tow bar was no problem."

"Good. I'd like to settle with you and leave as soon as possible. Let's go see the truck."

The men walked out of the showroom into the lot where the new trucks were parked. They walked over to a solid brown truck.

"Here's the truck, with the king cab you wanted. We installed the winch on the front; it's got 30 meters of cable. Is that enough?"

"That's plenty. Now where is the ATV? You said you had to make a few decisions about it and the trailer."

"We kept the trailer in the service area for safety. Right this way."

The men walked into the service area. The ATV was red, had a trailer hitch and four wheels. The trailer was large enough to carry the ATV, and he estimated that the truck bed was large enough to carry both the ATV and the trailer with a little room left over. This was what he wanted.

Charlie asked, "I haven't seen the loading ramps. Where are they?"

"In the bed of the truck. Didn't you see them?"

"No, I didn't. Everything else is fine. I'd appreciate it very much if you could fill both the truck and the ATV with gas as soon as possible. Also, please load the ATV, trailer, and ramps into the back of the truck. After that, install the tow bar and connect the truck to my suburban. While your mechanics are doing all that, we can settle up."

"That'll take only about an hour. Why don't you come into my office and we will have some hot chocolate. I don't particularly like coffee, but if you want some, we also have a pot brewed."

"Hot chocolate will be fine."

Both men walked into Bryan's office.

Bryan said, "Look these papers over. The total cost is $38,765.23 American. We owe you some money. There is one thing we could not do, however. We could not get a license plate for you without a place where the truck will be garaged. Do you have an address?"

"Right now, no. How long is a temporary plate good?"

"We can make it good for 90 days as long as the license fee is paid for the 90 days."

Charlie thought for a moment, then replied, "That'll be fine."

Eventually a mechanic came into Bryan's office.

"The truck's all hooked up, Mr. Cooper."

"Good, now we can draw a check for your money. Do you want it in Canadian dollars or American?"

Charlie thought, that check can be traced if I accept it. I think I'll give it to all the employees as a gift.

"Bryan, your firm really did a first rate job. Divide it among all your employees as my thanks for their work in getting my truck ready."

"Do you mean that?"

"Yes I do. Tell them to continue doing a good job. Now I must get going if I'm to get where I need to be by nightfall."

Charlie and Bryan shook hands. Charlie walked out to his suburban, checked the fuel gauge in the Ford and the ATV, checked the safety hook up, then the tow bar hook up, nodded his head, got in the suburban, and turned on the engine.

It was 9:30 AM by the time he left the Ford Truck Dealership. He looked for his road signs. Just a block from the dealership, he saw the Highway 1 sign. He was on the right route, a sort of chamber of commerce type highway, excellent roadbed, and beautiful scenery. He eased the Suburban up to slightly over 55 MPH.

Charlie was admiring the scenery including the occasional lake and almost missed the road sign that said "Hope 10 K". That is where he was to switch over to Highway 3. It was now almost 1 PM.

Charlie decided to take a short break. He saw a small roadside picnic area, so he pulled off the road there.

He sat on the bench, took out his lunch. After eating, he walked around the rest area, enjoying the fresh air. It was like his place in Sand Point. After forty-five minutes, he returned to the Suburban, started its engine, and continued his drive East on Highway 3. He arrived on the outskirts of Creston well after dark. As he approached Creston, he noticed a motel named Mountain Vue. It looked nice and had a vacancy.

He checked in for the night. The next day would be hectic.

The first flight to Seattle that would connect with a flight to Spokane left San Francisco at 9:32 AM. Louis was always early for flights, as was Mike. Louis arrived first and was sitting with his wife and Lisa's mother in the waiting area when Mike walked in.

Mike went over to Lisa's mother and said, "Hi mom."

Louis turned to see him. "Mike, you here to catch a plane?"

"Yes. I'm going to Spokane to talk to Donna. Is that where you're going?"

Louis was not happy with what Mike had said, but replied without showing it, "Yes. She and I are very close. I want to see that everything is being done to take care of her."

"I just called up there. The doctor's told me she's doing remarkably well for her injury. They expect her to make a full recovery."

"That's good news. But I want to see for myself. You know how that is."

"Yes, I know..."

291

Mike was interrupted by the PA system. The announcer said, "Alaska Flight 479 to Seattle will be boarding in a few minutes. All passengers with small children or passengers who are in need of assistance may board now. Others will board according to seat number in a few minutes. First class passengers may board at any time."

Louis got up, kissed his wife and Lisa's mother, then walked to the gate; he was riding in first class. Mike was not. He was traveling coach.

After all the passengers were on board, the big jet took off for Seattle.

In Seattle, Mike and Louis had just a forty-five minute layover before boarding another plane for Spokane. Their plane would touch down at 2:30 in the afternoon.

Louis and Mike checked in at the airport Ramada Inn. Louis called the hospital, asked to talk to

Donna, but was put on hold.

Finally, Donna answered, "Hello."

"Donna, this is Louis. How are you?" Not letting her answer, he continued, "I heard you were hurt in a gun fight. I also heard that Charlie has paid your hospital bill. I came out here just to see how you're doing and there are so many other things I'd like to know, but they can wait until tomorrow when I see you."

"Louis, you could never guess in a million years what happened. I will tell you what happened and how it has affected me. It's saved my life - literally."

"Well, I just wanted you to know I'm in town and I will be seeing you tomorrow. Oh, I almost forgot, Mike is in town and will probably want to ask you some questions. I hope you'll answer truthfully, but with only as much information as is needed."

"Louis, I would like to see you first, alone, then both you and Mike at the same time, then Mike alone. Could you arrange that for me?"

Louis was not sure what Donna wanted to do, but replied, "Sure, anything for you."

"Thanks, Louis. I see the nurses coming now. I have to go.

See you in the morning."

"See you then, and don't forget what I told you."

Donna knew what Louis meant - don't answer too many questions. She remembered Charlie had said not to answer any questions until after he had talked to her. She would follow Charlie's advice to a point.

Charlie had set the alarm for five AM, as he would have to get going very early. Although he did not check out of the motel, he left at 5:35 AM. He took highway 21 south for several miles, driving at only thirty-five miles per hour. He was looking for a turn off to the trailhead. As he approached the Canadian-U.S. boarder, he saw a sign - "West Lake Trail" - with an arrow pointing to the west. He followed the arrow onto a rugged road.

Almost 17 Kilometers passed by before he saw another sign. This one read, "West Lake Trail Trailhead next left." Less than a kilometer farther, Charlie got out of the suburban, unhitched the Ford truck, and started the truck's engine for the first time.

Day was just breaking. Charlie was glad because he had a long way to go. He put the truck in four-wheel drive and started south on a trail that would have been good for hiking, but didn't offer much for trucks. There were trees in the way that he had to drive around, once on a relatively severe slant.

Finally, he arrived at a sign, which read "United States-Canada," which meant he knew he still had a long way to go.

Bright daylight had arrived. The sun was high in the sky with sunlight filtering through the trees. This was ideal weather, he thought. He came to a place on the trail that was wide enough for him to turn the truck around and face it north. He knew the lake was almost visible from here, which meant this area was closer than twenty-five miles to the camp. Charlie turned the truck around so it faced toward Canada, placed the ramps on the back of the truck, and after connecting the trailer with the ATV on it to the wench, slowly winched the trailer down the ramps. Once it was on the ground, he backed the ATV off the trailer and then he could move the trailer by himself. He attached it to the ATV, made some preparations in the king cab of the truck, and locked the truck.

Charlie now set up camp. He erected a tent and placed air mattresses and a catalytic heater inside. After all this was completed, he looked around the area, and then left in the ATV pulling the trailer. It would not take as long to return to his suburban as it took to get there.

The ATV traveled much faster than the tuck since it was small enough to pass easily along the trail, which was maintained by the Canadian Government north of the border and the U. S. Forest Service south of the boarder for the backpackers who frequented it from May through early October. Generally speaking, no hikers use the trail from November 1st on through the winter months. There was one area where he had to go around a tree that had fallen, but he thought it would pose no problem. The snow that covered the trail had almost melted. There was snow up the side of the mountain, however.

Charlie saw his suburban about noon. He smiled. The first part of his plan had gone well. Now he parked the ATV, unhitched the trailer, and hitched the trailer up to the Suburban.

C. C. mumbled to himself, "Damn, I forgot to keep the ramps with me. Now how do I get the ATV on the trailer?"

As luck would have it, there were two large planks of wood nearby. He placed them on the trailer as if they were ramps, then hooked the ATV up to his winch by running the cable over the cab. This would scratch the suburban, but he would have to accept that. The winch pulled the ATV onto the trailer.

Now Charlie tied the ATV to the trailer and took a deep breath; he was ready to travel. After he returned to the motel, he made additional arrangements with the clerk.

"I'd like to rent the room I have for two more weeks, although I probably won't need it for several days. I like the room. It has an outside entrance to the parking lot and I'll be getting in very late when I return. I don't want to wake anybody up. Is that possible?"

The clerk replied, "Sure thing. Just tell me how long you want it and I'll reserve it for you, sir."

"I'll take it until December 10th. Here is $500.00 American for the rent. When I return, I'll pay any difference. Will that be enough money?"

Charlie was glad he had registered under one of his aliases.

The clerk smiled at Charlie, nodding. "Yes, sir. Do you have any idea when you'll return, Mr. Phillips?"

"All I know is it will probably be within a week."

After a quick shower, he left the motel. It was now 3:15 PM. This was about right for his purpose, he thought. He would arrive at his camp after dark tonight.

He returned to Highway 21, driving south and passing through customs at the border without incident. Even though Sand Point is a short distance from the border and would be on the easiest route to his place, he did not go through town; instead, he followed a back road that eventually took him to the black top road to his place.

As he passed Hank's house, he noted there were no lights on. He thought Hank would be sleeping by this time. As he turned from the gravel road into his camp, he let out a big sigh of relief. Tomorrow morning he would prepare for their trip to the truck. He did not think Donna could make the trip to Canada in one night, but that probably she could make it to the truck in one night, although he was not too certain. He would just have to wait and see.

He turned on the TV to see what the weather was going to be for the next few days. The report was acceptable. Light snow tomorrow after midnight, temperatures in the teens, then a warming trend for two days. It was expected to warm up to thirty-eight degrees three nights from now, then to snow heavily again. He would have to move before then, or it might be too late. It was now past midnight and Charlie was tired, very tired.

He thought, I'll sleep until 8:30 or 9:00 in the morning and then call the sheriff. Make an appointment to see him tomorrow afternoon, complete the camp setup, set things up with Sam, then go to Spokane and get Donna. He was happy he had set up an intermediate camp so Donna would not have to travel all night.

295

Louis walked into Donna's room at 8:30 AM. He carried a bouquet of spring flowers over to her, put them on her table, then bent over and kissed her on the cheek.

"Well, Donna, what happened?"

"I don't know much, but what I do know is that Mona messed up real bad. She forced me to take Mr. Duncan prisoner and she was on the way to forcing us to kill C. C. Duncan. As it turned out, she couldn't have come close to killing Mr. Duncan or as I call him, Charlie. I think she was killed when she went after a couple who stumbled into the camp. You know about the plane accident?"

He nodded.

"The people in Vancouver sent mostly sugar - that's all. I don't know if it was planned that way, or if the pilot and the contact did it on their own. Louis, that's all I know, because I was shot after I found out about the sugar. I don't know anything else."

She paused, and then continued, "Well, maybe I do know a little more. Your contacts, Terry Bracken and Paul Croket - don't trust them as far as you can jump. They're small, little men with no character at all."

"Donna, do you know that briefcase, with its contents, was returned to me?"

"No, I didn't, but I'll bet it was returned by Charlie."

"You're right. Do you know anything else about him?"

"I think I know that he is a good man."

"Donna, you're not answering me straightforwardly. I think he is the Iceman. Am I correct?"

"As of now, I believe I can say the Iceman does not exist anymore."

"Quit the BS Donna. Is he or isn't he the..."

Louis was interrupted as the door to Donna's room opened and Mike walked in.

"Louis, we agreed you'd be alone with Donna for forty-five minutes. Your time's up. Now we are in the room together to hear what Donna has to say."

296

Donna looked at Mike, smiled. "Long time no see, Mike. How are things in the Forester household?"

"Fine, Donna. But you know this visit is more business than a hospital visit with a friend. Let's get the business over with so we can get on to the pleasant stuff."

Just then, Sam Pritchard entered through the door.

Donna smiled; she was expecting Sam. She said, "Sam, this is my friend and employer, Louis Giaventi, and this is my friend Michael Forester of the San Francisco Police Department. Guys, this is Charlie's pastor, Sam Pritchard."

"Gentlemen."

Mike looked at Louis, then to Sam. He nodded his head and shook Sam's hand. Louis did the same.

Donna began, "It looks like we are all here. I can begin my story. The only person I know who will believe my story is Sam because of what he has already told me. But you two will just have to believe on faith and faith alone.

"For starters, sometime ago, a hit was carried out in Seattle. It was just after Max was taken out. In fact, it was that very night. Charlie was walking near the hit and was shot accidentally. He had an out of body experience that Sam can tell you about.

"Now, guys, when I was shot, I went to Hell. I won't bore you with all the details, but I had an out of body experience. I saw Hell - a burning fire that is all consuming. Jesus walked by me and said 'Your sins are forgiven, return to your body.' The next thing I knew, I was hovering over my body, then back in my body. After that, I knew nothing until I woke up in this hospital.

"While I was hovering over my body, I saw Charlie praying for me. Jesus also said a good man was praying for me. Louis, I can't work for you any more, but be assured I will not violate any confidence you have placed in me.

"Incidentally, Sam knows this already. He also knows more, but he cannot say anything because it was told in confidence. Also, he's had some dreams that add credence to the story I've just told.

"Well, that's it, guys. Mike, would you mind if we talk later today or tomorrow. I'm very tired."

297

Mike thought for a while, and then replied, "I guess it would be all right. I'll see you later today or possibly tomorrow."

Sam remained in the room when Mike and Louis left. They just walked into the hallway outside the room. It wasn't three minutes later when Sam walked out.

Sam said, "I've wanted to meet both of you for some time and I must tell you, what she related to you was a true experience. You should believe her. I'll tell you this. I know Charlie had a similar experience when he was shot in Seattle. I was the one who prayed for him then."

Mike looked at Sam and thought, that was the freak accident Charlie had before he came to Frisco to recover. It fits.

Sam walked away, leaving the two men together.

Louis looked at the police officer. "Mike, this is so far off the record, I want your promise never to think about telling anyone else what I am going to say."

"Louis, you have my word.

"Mike, I think Charlie is the Iceman. Everything fits too snug. I hope that will not upset Lisa when she finds out. But you know, the strangest thing is, I have the feeling he retired from being the Iceman."

"Louis, people in Interpol have the same idea about Charlie and the Iceman. I must say, I've been coming to the same conclusion. The way Lisa was saved that day. If it wasn't the family, then who? Charlie came into town right before that incident. Coincidence? Too many of those, but there's no proof."

"You never heard me say this before, Mike, but Donna has me almost convinced that Jesus is still out there, and He's running the show. I think I'll go to church with my wife next Sunday."

"Louis, what Donna said does have a ring of truth to it, especially after what Sam told us. I think I'll have to go visit this sheriff in Sand Point before I see Donna again. I think I'll get a better picture of what happened. You wouldn't know what happened, would you?"

"Now, Mike, anything I've heard is second hand, and you know that can't be used as evidence."

298

"Yeah, that means you won't tell me anything."

Louis smiled. "That's because I can't tell you anything you don't know or suspect already. I have to catch the 3:00 plane back to San Francisco. I guess you'll be staying over another day, huh?"

"Yes, I will. See you in church Sunday."

"You sure will. See you then."

With those words, the two men parted, neither one completely believing the other. Louis went to the airport and Mike returned to his rented car.

Charlie was up early. His adrenal glands were working overtime, pumping adrenaline into his system. He got onto his ATV with the trailer behind it. The trailer contained the Iceman's gear and other supplies.

He began his drive north on the West Lake trail. About seven miles from his camp, he passed the wreckage of the crashed airplane the Thompsons were in. Finally he reached the campsite he had set up the day before. He nodded to himself, being pleased with the campsite; this was indeed a good place for a camp. It had good cover and could not readily be seen from the air or the ground. He started the catalytic heater in the tent, knowing its ten-pound can of propane would last through the next day. He left the food and other supplies in the king cab so the animals could not get to them, and then looked around the camp for the last time. Finally, he got on the ATV.

Returning to his place in Sand Point, he surveyed the camp area where he had three large propane tanks. The exposed gas lines to the cabin were just as he wanted them.

He thought, everything is ready. Now if Sam and Hank can do it tonight, it'll be tonight.

Charlie went inside his camp. He walked to the telephone, dialed a number.

A woman's voice answered, "This is the Pritchard residence."

"Ruth, this is Charlie. May I speak to Sam?"

"Just a minute, C. C."

"This is Sam. How can I help you, Charlie?"

299

"Sam, I need you to stay awake tonight until I see you. I am going to see if Hank will keep you company. It's very important to me."

"I guess Ruth and I can stay up if you want us to. Check back with me and tell me if Hank is going to be here."

"I'll call you back if he isn't. See you tonight."

Charlie dialed another number.

"Yep."

"Hank, I have to ask a big favor of you. I'm going to see Sam late tonight. I would personally appreciate it if you'd be present. Can you make it?"

Hank thought for a minute, and then responded, "I'll be there from 7:00 PM until you come."

"Thanks, you're a real friend."

Charlie had to make one more phone call, to Sheriff Coomey.

"Sheriff speaking."

"Sheriff, this is C. C. When do you want to have that little talk with me?"

"Glad you called, C. C. How about tomorrow morning about 9:00 AM? I have to meet some hotshot policeman from San Francisco this afternoon."

Charlie thought, this is my day. We will be long gone by that time. He said, "That'll be just fine, Sheriff. See you then."

With that meeting arranged, Charlie started his Suburban and began the drive to Spokane. He thought he would arrive about five or six PM. Unknown to him, he would also pass Mike, who was on his way to see Sheriff Coomey in Sand Point.

Charlie thought it was going to be an interesting night for everyone involved, but tomorrow would even be more interesting for me...and Donna.

CHAPTER 8

Clouds were gathering above Sand Point when Charlie began his drive to Spokane. A bright sun was peeking through them. As the sunrays came from around the clouds, it seemed like there was indeed a silver lining in the heavens. The road was dry without snow but there was a chance of black ice on the highway now and after dark. Traffic was a little heavier than usual, but nothing really noteworthy.

As Charlie looked at the sky, he thought it looks like we are in for some snow just when the weatherman said we would get it. I hope it will only be a flurry or two and not a blizzard like we had a couple of days ago.

By now, he was turning onto Interstate 90 towards Spokane. He arrived at the hospital just after 6:00 PM. The sun was going down over the horizon as he walked into the hospital. Donna had been moved to a private room since he had visited her last and he went to the information desk to find out where she was. Even though he was wearing a very warm jacket, he had on a big overcoat that concealed his clothes. A large cowboy hat rested on his head and a rather large package was tucked under one arm.

"Hello, I would like to visit Donna Weir. What room is she in?"

The information clerk answered, "Room 457. The elevators are over there on the left."

"Thank you."

Charlie walked to the elevators and pressed the call button.

When the doors opened, he boarded the elevator and pushed the button for the fourth floor. As luck would have it, the elevator went directly to the fourth floor without stopping. Charlie stepped out into the hallway, noted that room numbers under 450 were to the right and those above 450 to the left. Turning left, he soon found 457.

He knocked on the door. "Donna, may I come in?"

Recognizing the voice, Donna became both happy and excited. "Come in Charlie."

"You remembered my name," he said, smiling as he entered. That's a good sign." He placed a kiss on her forehead. "How are you feeling?"

She reached up and pulled him down so he would kiss her on her lips, too.

"I am feeling a million times better, and another million times better now that you're here. Now we can talk."

Charlie responded, "First, have you eaten supper?"

"Yes, it was lousy hospital food. Healthy, but hospital food."

"That's good. Now listen carefully. You must leave the hospital tonight. If you don't, you'll be arrested on some charge and kept here. Then you'll be returned to Idaho when you're able to travel - which, by the way, you feel, probably won't be too long.

"Right now, you can leave the hospital and they can't stop you. It would be better if nobody knew you had left, though. I've brought you some clothes so you can disguise yourself. It'll be best if we have as much time as possible to travel before they discover you're missing because we need to disappear completely."

"Charlie, I have to ask. Why do you want to marry me?"

"Donna, I believe we were meant to be together. I also have feelings for you I didn't know I had. When I got them, I don't know, but I have them. Also, if we're married, we can't be forced testify against each other. I think we'll have a perfect marriage."

"That's all I wanted to hear. But I want to talk to you about my experience."

"Donna, let's talk on the way to Sand Point. I've arranged for Sam to be up, and he will marry us. You must sign this marriage

302

license though. Here's a pen. Sign on that line."

Donna smiled. "You take a lot for granted, don't you?"

She signed the license.

They kissed lightly.

"Now where are the clothes you brought me?"

"First, you must call the nurse and tell her I'm using the potty. Tell her that you're getting tired and want to go to sleep as soon as I leave. You must convince her to take your blood pressure and temperature now, and let you sleep until the change of shift at eleven. That will give us a couple hours head start."

"Good idea."

After the nurse took Donna's blood pressure and temperature, she left the room. Charlie had come out of the bathroom by this time with the clothes he had brought for her. He gave her the hat and overcoat he had worn, blue jeans, shirt, bra, and a pair of panties. He had brought everything she would need.

He walked over to her, kissed her, and gently removed the IV's from her arm. Donna moved slowly, but she got out of bed under her own power. While Charlie watched for the nurse through the almost closed door, Donna took off her hospital gown and put on the clothes Charlie brought for her. The last part of the disguise was to hide her hair and even though it was reasonably short, she would have to wear a hat to completely hide her hair. The large hat Charlie brought would completely hide her hair and last she put on Charlie's overcoat.

Charlie said, "You must write a note to the nurses thanking them for the care you received, but tell them you just wanted to leave the hospital. Then sign your name. Don't mention me. Understand?"

"Yes, I understand. If your name is mentioned, they may connect me to you and figure out where we're going."

"Right. Look, I'll meet you downstairs by the elevators. You must get there by yourself. That will also delay them knowing you are leaving and leaving with me. Okay."

"Fine. Meet you there."

Charlie left the room, walked to the elevator, pressed the

303

down button to call the elevator. It took a very long time to come.

When Donna thought enough time had passed, she left her room, closed the door behind her, and walked towards the elevators, her disguise fully in place. No one paid any attention to her.

The nurses were occupied by their duties. Donna found Charlie still waiting for the elevator to arrive. He acted as if he didn't know her. Finally, the elevator arrived and the door opened. There were three people inside when they entered.

Charlie stood close to Donna so she could lean on him a little. She was very appreciative of his actions. At the ground floor, they exited together. Charlie was now holding her to support her.

They walked out of the hospital to the suburban. Charlie opened the door and almost lifted her into the passenger seat, then leaned the seat back into the rest position. Now he all but ran around to the other side of the truck, jumped in and started the engine.

Charlie thought, the first part of my plan worked. Now if the rest works as well, we'll be on the trail before daybreak and in Canada tomorrow night.

As the lights of Spokane disappeared behind the suburban, Donna grew more relaxed. She looked at Charlie in admiration, maybe even love...she did not know which.

She thought I don't know a thing about this guy except that he is, or was, the best hit man in the world. He also prayed for me when I was wounded and Jesus said he was a good man. I must know more about him.

"Charlie, tell me a little about yourself. I'd like to know more about the man I intend to marry tonight."

"Well, Donna, I don't know exactly how it started, but from what I was told it all started about the end of the Vietnam War..."

During the long drive, he told her all that he knew about himself. "Incidentally," he said when he got to the part about the reward money he had earned, "I invested the money with the Bank of America in San Francisco and that money has more than doubled in value. I have slightly over twenty three million dollars

304

from the original ten million. I have more money from my 'business' though, a little over thirty million. That money has been given to the Salvation Army. I'll keep the twenty three million because I earned it legally. Well, I'll keep about twenty million. The rest will go to Lisa."

When he finished his story, they were both quiet for awhile.

Lights could now be seen in the distance. Donna pointed to them.

Charlie said, "That's Coeur d'Alene. It's a peaceful small town with a lake. A beautiful place."

"I seem to remember seeing it as I passed through it on the way to Sand Point. A small town with mountains around it, I think. Yes, really pretty."

He paused, then went on, "Telling you my story has brought back some of my feelings about not knowing who I am. I thought I had lost them or most of them over the years, but I guess I haven't. I guess my desire to learn about my life will always be with me, until I know everything about my past...before Vietnam. Just like Dr. Wells said, I have to get on with my life even though I don't know much about myself."

Donna looked at Charlie, "Charlie, I can't imagine how you feel, but I believe Dr. Wells is right - you must get on with your life. I think if your memory does come back, it will be a blessing. Something you said leads me to believe you do know a little bit about yourself. Am I reading you right?"

"Yes. I've had a few flashbacks over the past three years, and they've increased since my out-of-body experience. I now know my name is indeed Charles A. Mackey III, but not the Charles Allen Mackey III who lived in Thibodaux. My name is Charles Abner Mackey III who lived in snow country - New England – I believe Vermont. The flashbacks I've been having had snow in them. Right now, I don't know if those random memories are a blessing or not.

"But who I was doesn't much matter. After tonight, Mr. and Mrs. Duncan will be dead. I can never return to whom I was or to whom I am now. Even if I do remember everything about myself,

I can't go back to learn more about my past because if I do, I'll be opening not only myself, but everyone around me, to the danger of being killed."

"I guess you're right, but why do you say that?"

"I'll get to that a little later."

As the suburban turned onto the highway to Sand Point, the conversation came to a halt. Donna leaned back on the reclined bucket seat to rest.

Fifteen minutes later, Charlie looked at her. He thought she was asleep, but as he watched her, she opened her eyes.

"So why are we in danger?" she asked. "You said you'd tell me later."

"There are, or I should say were, three others who were as good as me at my profession – Klaus, Carlos and Miguel. According to the news, Klaus and Carlos have been arrested and put in jail. Miguel is alive and well. My guess is he'll be given the contract on me. And I could almost bet that Israel will be paying the bill. They may want Miguel dead after he kills me because he knows too much, too. Don't know that as fact, but I strongly suspect it."

"Why would Israel want you dead?"

"Remember the politician who was killed in New York City two - no, three years ago?"

"There was a big flap about the hit as I remember. He was a big supporter of Israel, also."

"That's right, but he was changing his views to support a negotiated peace. The leadership in Israel didn't like it and were afraid he would sway many of Israel's supporters in America, so they gave me the contract.

"They also gave me the contract for the Arab League's spokesman in Los Angeles. They would be hard pressed at the peace table right now if everyone knew those facts. Also, Israel might lose a good deal of American support because both of them were American citizens - born in America."

"I can see why they would want you out of the way."

"I didn't mean to shoot you," Donna said abruptly, as though it was something she'd been meaning to tell him. I did check up on you until I knew you would live, but I didn't know who you were. I'm really sorry for that."

"I forgave you for shooting me immediately after waking up after surgery. I also want to thank you for shooting me. You see, I went to Hell, saw the fire. It was horrible. Then Jesus walked to me, saw I was repentant, forgave me my sins, and returned me to my body. I don't know how I know it was Jesus, but I just know. You see if you hadn't shot me, I never would have had the chance to be forgiven and saved. I'd have gone to hell when I died. Now I have an opportunity to be saved. I hope you understand what I've just said."

"I do, dear . . ."

"That's the first time you called me 'dear.' I kind of like it, honey."

Donna took a deep breath and looked at him. At that moment, she knew she loved Charlie.

"That's the first time you said 'honey,' and I like it, too. But let me continue. When I was shot, I too saw the fires of Hell..."

"I suspected that, Donna."

"I believe Jesus was the person who forgave me my sins. He said a good man was praying for me. When I returned to my body, I briefly saw you and recognized you. I really needed and appreciated your prayers."

The clouds were becoming thick, so neither Charlie nor Donna could see any stars in the sky. These were snow clouds. Charlie wondered if they would make it before the snow began to fall.

Charlie thought the weatherman was right again. I hope it won't get too cold tonight.

Charlie turned the suburban onto the main street in Sand Point and traveled to the northern part of town before turning first right, then left. He saw his church on the hill and Sam's house right beside the church. There was a light on in Sam's house.

From a window in the house, Hank watched the suburban turn into the driveway and come up to the house.

"Charlie's here and it looks like he has someone with him."

Sam and Ruth looked at each other.

They both said, "Donna!"

"What did you and Ruth say, Sam?"

"We said 'Donna.'"

Hank thought for a moment, "Wouldn't surprise me."

Charlie got out of the truck, walked around to the passenger side to help Donna out. He discovered he did not need to help her a great deal; she was gaining strength rapidly.

Sam, Ruth, and Hank came outside to greet them.

Sam said, "Come on in and get warm. There's supposed to be some snow tonight, but not like several nights ago."

Inside Charlie introduced Donna to Hank, whom she had not met before.

Ruth pulled Sam away from the other three. "Sam, there is something different about C. C. and Donna. They both have a glow - a loving glow about them. I've seen that glow in new brides and in special pastors who are dedicated to the Lord. Do you see it?"

"I see it, but if you think about our dreams, it isn't surprising, is it?"

"When you put it that way, I guess it isn't."

"Sam, we need your help," Charlie said, turning toward the pastor and his wife. "Donna and I want to get married right now, and then I want to take her to her new home."

Without hesitation Sam replied, "Sure, let's go into the church."

"Hank, the reason I wanted you to be here is I want you to be my best man. Will you?"

"I would be honored. I'd have been hurt if you wouldn't have asked me."

The two men embraced each other.

Donna turned to Ruth. "Will you be my matron of honor?"

"Sure."

Ruth kissed Donna on the check.

Donna now turned to Charlie. Her eyes said "ask him now."

"Sam, Donna doesn't know if she was ever baptized. Would you please baptize her before the wedding and baptize me again."

"Let me set everything up. It will only take a minute."

"Please hurry, Sam. Donna is still very weak."

Hank broke into the conversation, "I'll help Sam. Excuse me."

Donna sat in the first pew with Ruth and Charlie while Hank and Sam made the necessary preparations.

Sam came with some water to baptize Donna and Charlie.

"I don't think the Lord would mind if I baptized you sitting in the pew."

Donna replied, "But I would. Charlie, help me kneel."

With those words, Charlie helped Donna kneel in the front of the pew, and then kneeled beside her.

Sam realized he would have to baptize them quickly. He anointed Donna first. He said, "I baptize you in the name of the Father, Son, and Holy Spirit. Amen."

He turned to Charlie, anointed him, and said, "I baptize you in the name of the Father, Son and Holy Spirit, Amen.

Charlie helped Donna sit back in the pew and then settled down beside her.

Sam could see Donna was getting weaker by the minute, so he eliminated all but the most important parts of the wedding service. At last, he asked, "Will you, Donna, take Charles to be your lawfully wedded husband?"

"Yes, oh yes."

"Charles, will you take Donna to be your wife?"

"I do with all my heart."

"Then under the laws of Idaho, I pronounce you husband and wife."

After the ceremony, Ruth said, "How about some hot chocolate?"

"Ruth, it's late and we have to get home. Thank you anyway and thanks to all of you for being here when we needed you."

Charlie helped Donna to the suburban. This time she needed a little assistance getting into the truck. The two ceremonies had left her fatigued after the long ride.

Donna leaned back in her seat and looked at Charlie in a most loving manner. "Charlie, I never thought I'd say this to any man, especially you, because you took care of Jack, but...I love you."

Charlie responded by reaching over to touch Donna's thigh with his right hand.

"Donna, I love you too. But now I must tell you what we have to do tonight. First, you must get as much rest as possible while we are driving to my camp. We must reach the camp and leave it tonight, and never look back."

Donna began to smile.

"Why are you smiling?"

"I just thought of something. Most marriages are said to have been made in Heaven, but ours was made in Hell!"

Charlie thought for a second, then replied, "That's true, but remember, God brought us together, which makes all the difference."

"You're right, but Charlie, I still don't know if I can travel tonight."

"It will be harder than you imagine, but you have to make it or you will be arrested and I will probably be dead, because I'll be the subject of a contract. When we get to camp, the camp will be warm. You must go into the camp - I'll help you - and get dressed for the rest of our trip."

"Why don't we just drive away in this truck?"

"It would be too easy to follow. We must make everyone believe we're dead, at least for a short time. I doubt that Hank or Sam will be taken in, nor do I think Mike will believe it. I am almost positive that a man named Pierre Richard will not believe it either. He is the person who investigates terrorism and assassins at Interpol. He's one smart cop and he's the one who supplies most of the governments with their information. I don't care about any of them except Israel."

"What do I do?"

"First, you go into the house. I have some thermal underwear hanging in the closet just to the right and inside the small hallway.

Keep your undies on, but put the thermals on too. Right next to the thermals is a blizzard suit. Put it on over your blue jeans. You'll need it tonight when we go camping."

"Come on, camping on a night like this!"

"Yes, it's our only possible escape route that will not be covered tonight. I doubt it will even be checked for a few days. While you're putting the clothes on, I'll be getting things ready. This truck has to burn with our bodies in it. After the truck is ready and I've prepared the ATV and the trailer, I'll start the fire as we drive away. I hope the truck will not explode, but just burn. If it does explode, I hope we'll have had at least a little head start."

"Wait a minute; you said our bodies will be in the truck. Whose bodies are you using?"

Charlie frowned, then answered, "When I first hatched this idea, I was going after the two people who were going after the Thompsons; I believe Mona and - I don't know the man's name. I had to make sure those two were dead.

"When I found them, their bodies were dismembered by a couple of bears and possibly by some wolves. I killed the two bears and took most of the bones left by the bears. Their bones are the ones I'll use to hopefully persuade the sheriff that we're dead. They should also delay Pierre and Mike from looking for us for at least a couple of days. At least it should delay them from looking in the right place for a while."

Feeling sorry for Mona, Donna said, "Poor Mona. She wasn't all that bad."

The suburban turned onto the gravel road by Hank's house. It would not be too long now until they would be at the camp.

"Then, we go on the West Lake trail to Canada. Tonight we'll go only as far as where the other truck is waiting. I have a camp set up there. Tomorrow morning we go into Canada, assume new names, and get lost. I'll tell you what we'll do after that when we're in Canada. Okay?"

"Charlie, I trust you with my life."

"I hope your trust is well founded."

Charlie helped Donna out of the suburban and into the house.

311

He then went outside to prepare the ATV, trailer, propane gas lines - everything necessary for their "deaths" and their trip to Canada.

It was 1:30 in the morning when Mike returned to the airport Ramada Inn. He was deep in thought as he entered his room. After talking to Sheriff Coomey, he thought, I'm sure Charlie is the Iceman. The sheriff would really have a fit if he knew who Charlie is. I wonder if I should call Pierre or not. I guess I should, but I really don't want to. After all, he saved Lisa and the kids from the Tong's killers. Damn, what do I do? I know I'll have to tell Pierre, but I hope he doesn't have and cannot get any evidence to support the existence of the Iceman. If he can prove the existence of the Iceman, I sure hope he can't prove the Iceman is Charlie. Well here's my room. I'll call him now.

Mike dialed the overseas operator, gave him the San Francisco Police Department's number for the charge, and then gave him the number in Paris for Pierre.

He thought, I'll never get used to the operator being a man. Maybe in time, but not now.

The telephone answered and the operator asked for Pierre Richard.

Soon, Pierre answered in English, "How are you, Mike?"

"I'm fine. Listen, it hurts to tell you this, but I think you are right. Charlie is the Iceman, but I firmly believe he is retired. Right now, I believe he's at his camp in Idaho. If you want to come here, make reservations to fly into Spokane. I don't like the idea of arresting him either. Remember, he saved my wife and kids."

"Mike, remember what I said - he is an enigma. He does not fit the usual profile of an assassin. I will fly into Spokane as soon as I can get a flight. I will let you know when I will arrive."

"It'll be good to see you, but I hope you will elect to do nothing. I'm staying at the airport Ramada Inn in Spokane. Call me there when you get your flight reservations."

"I will call you. Good-bye."

"Bye."

Mike went over to the bed and flopped down on it, thinking he had just sentenced his friend, the person who saved his wife and family, to death. At the moment, he couldn't face talking to Lisa.

Charlie returned to the camp to find Donna dressed, as he wanted and sitting in Hank's easy chair, sleeping. He thought she must have been asleep for about thirty minutes. He went into the closet and retrieved his blizzard suit.

He looked at Donna for maybe five minutes, then thought, enough, we must go now.

He gently shook her. She opened her eyes, smiled.

"I love you Charlie."

"That's all well and good, honey, but we have to move now."

"Okay."

Donna got up out of the chair without any help from Charlie and walked to the door. Charlie turned the thermostat down to where he usually kept it and they went outside together.

"Donna, when we leave you can lie down on the trailer or you can ride on the back of the seat, holding me."

"I'll try to sit and hold you for a little while."

"Good. Now let's get on the ATV."

Charlie got on the ATV with Donna behind him on the seat. As he started the engine, Donna noticed there was a little fire underneath the suburban. Charlie yanked on a long piece of cord, which came loose from a valve on the propane tanks after turning the valve. He reeled the cord in and placed it beside himself on the vehicle. All of a sudden, flames shot up from the ground under the suburban.

Charlie depressed the accelerator and they were off. It was a short distance from the camp to the West Lake trail so it was a short ride until he turned onto the trail with the headlights of the ATV piercing the darkness ahead of them.

They had traveled almost thirty minutes when they heard an explosion.

Charlie said, "The gas tank in the suburban."

Nothing more was said during the remainder of the ride. The

313

snow was coming down rather heavily now, but Charlie could see some stars in the sky ahead of them. That meant the snow would end soon. That would be good for Donna. Also, because the snow was falling as heavily as it was, it would cover the ATV's, as well as the trailer's tracks - that was also good for them.

The headlights reflected off a brown Ford truck parked on the trail ahead of them.

Charlie thought we made it. The first part of my plan worked. Now if only the rest of the plan works too . . .

Charlie got off the ATV and entered the tent. It was warm as he knew it would be. He had to help Donna into the tent, where he had the floor covered with air mattresses - thick ones with insulating material on them. In addition there were down-filled sleeping bags which he had zipped together.

He helped Donna out of her clothes, but left her thermals on. The blizzard suit was placed in the tent next to her. Next, he took off his blizzard suit and laid it next to him.

Leaning over Donna, he whispered in her ear, "We made it through the first part of my plan. Tomorrow, I probably won't be here when you wake up."

Donna looked surprised. "Where will you be?"

"I'll be just outside the tent, getting the truck ready to move and cooking breakfast. Now get some rest, darling. You'll need it for tomorrow. After that, we can rest up for a couple of days. Good night."

Charlie reached over, kissed her, and placed his arm around her.

He thought, Donna's a good woman and she is going to make me a good wife. Jesus forgave us our sins and I think we love each other and that's all that counts. My arm, it's in the same position that Mackey's arm was in when he and his wife were killed! They must have been in love - even after forty-plus years of marriage. I hope we can do as well.

Charlie drifted off to sleep.

CHAPTER 9

The explosion woke Henry Teller from a deep sleep. He jumped out of bed and went to a window only to see a red glow in the sky reflected down from the low clouds. From the direction of the glow, he knew it was coming from the camp. He put on his coveralls, boots, and winter parka as quickly as he could, and then called Sam.

"Sam, this is Hank. There's been an explosion over at the camp. I'm on my way there now. I think you should come. Call the volunteer fire truck and call the sheriff, too. I just got a hunch."

"So do I, Hank. I'll call them while you get over there to see what happened."

"Right. See you in a short while."

Hank ran out of his house to his jeep. He drove as fast as road conditions and the snowfall would permit to the camp. As he came around the last curve in the gravel road, he could see the suburban burning. It was already consumed by the fire and the fire was near the propane tanks.

As Hank arrived, he saw that the fire was being fed by propane gas from a broken pipe under the truck. It looked as if the Suburban had rolled over an exposed propane pipe which fed the

316

house. Hank knew he had to shut off the propane supply tank before the propane tanks exploded.

Hank saw the main valve was turned on, as it should be. He had to get to it to turn it off; that would stop the gas from feeding the fire.

He looked for the long garden hose that was usually around the back of the cabin. He found it where it was supposed to be, but was afraid the water would be frozen inside. Nevertheless, he connected it to a freeze-protected faucet outside the cabin.

The water came gushing out of the hose. Now he put on the thick winter gloves he carried in his parka, pulled the parka hood over his head, and extended the hose to its full length so that it would pull easily. It was long enough that he could pull it all the way to the valve.

Pointing the hose in the air and over his head, but slightly towards the fire, he moved as fast as he could towards the valve. The heat was searing him as he reached it. His gloved hand touched the valve and immediately the glove began to melt, but the insulation in the glove was enough so that he was able to grasp the valve and turn it. The gas stopped.

Immediately, the fire reduced in intensity. Hank moved away from the propane tanks and the fire as quickly as he could. He turned the hose on himself, drenching his gloved hands that were very close to being burned. He peeled the gloves off as quickly as he could. He thought he was fortunate that the fire was not that big.

Now, he turned his attention to the suburban, which was still burning. Hank knew this was Charlie's favorite vehicle. He was puzzled by the fire and explosion, but he didn't quite know what it was that was bothering him.

Sam's car came around the curve in the road with its headlights cutting through the darkness. As the headlights hit the burning suburban, Hank suddenly realized what was wrong - the timing of the fire. Charlie and Donna had left the church minutes ahead of him. He had time to go home, undress, get into bed, and fall asleep. If the fire was caused by the truck rolling over the gas lines and breaking them, why did the fire take so long to develop?

Sam ran up to Hank.

"The sheriff and the volunteers are on their way. Were Charlie and Donna in the truck?"

"I don't see them anywhere around, but I doubt it. It looks like the truck rolled over that pipe under the suburban, broke it, and somehow the gas caught fire. Then the truck caught fire. I guess that's what happened, but I'm not too sure."

The fire truck with its red light flashing came down from the gravel road towards the camp, closely followed by the sheriff. The volunteers quickly put the fire out. The sheriff walked over to what was left of the suburban.

"This was one hot fire. It's a good thing the tanks didn't go up. Let's have a look in the truck."

"Sheriff, I turned the main valve off when I arrived. The gas from that pipe under the suburban was leaking like a sieve."

"That explains why some of the metal is melted."

Sheriff Coomey looked into what was left of the front seats of the suburban. "Damn, there are charred bones in here. Looks like two hipbones, a couple of arms or legs and even a part of one skull. There isn't any flesh left on the bones."

Sam looked into the truck, turned to the sheriff, took a deep breath, "Sheriff, you must know that I married Charlie and Donna just before the fire. They left the church riding in this truck."

Sheriff Coomey looked at Sam in a way he had never looked at him before.

"Sam, Donna wasn't supposed to leave the hospital until next week. How did she...I'll have to call the police who were supposed to be guarding her and check with them. This really screws up my investigation."

He turned and walked towards his car. Sheriff Coomey radioed for the coroner to come to the camp.

Soon, a vehicle marked "Coroner" came down the road, its red light on top of the car rotating but its siren silent.

After a brief examination of the bones, the coroner turned to Sheriff Coomey.

318

"Sheriff, these are the bones of a man and a woman. The hipbones don't lie about that kind of thing. I don't think I'll be able to tell you any more about them because they are really burned beyond recognition."

"Thanks."

Sam looked at Hank. "Well, what do you think?"

"I can't believe that's C. C. and Donna in the there. C. C. is too smart to let himself burn to death. Suicide, that's a slim possibility, but again, I don't think C. C. is the type. I think he staged this for the sheriff's benefit and maybe someone else's. What do you think?"

"What you said makes sense, especially if you take into consideration what C. C. did for a living not too long ago."

"What did he do, Sam?"

"I shouldn't have said what I did, but if you promise not to tell anyone, I'll tell you because you're his best friend."

"I won't tell anyone except Martha."

Sam knew Hank "talked to Martha" when he sat by her grave, just to satisfy his feelings.

"Okay, C. C. or Charlie was called the Iceman. He was the premier hit man or assassin in the world. His story is long, but this shootout could trigger the authorities finding out who he was. He changed several months ago and retired from his profession. I know that, but the police probably don't. Now you see why what you think happened might be or not be the truth."

"I thought something was funny about him, but he was - or is my friend. He was a good man. I'd bet you him being shot in Seattle wasn't an accident the way he told everyone it was."

"Hank, part of what he said was true. It was an accident that he was shot, but he was shot. To add to the puzzle, Donna was the person who shot him."

"Damn, Sam, you're going to have to come to my house for coffee and tell me the rest of the story."

"Hank, it also involves dreams that Ruth and I had. It gets **reaaal** complicated. I think a good cup of hot coffee would be fine."

A clear blue sky greeted Charlie as he emerged from the tent. It was cold and crisp and he did not need his blizzard suit. He lit two catalytic heaters; they blazed two feet high, and then subsided to a glow. He placed one in the cab and the other under the motor of the truck. He knew it would be early afternoon before they would be ready to travel again, since it was now almost 11:00 AM. The motor should be warm so it wouldn't blow a piston and the cab needed to be warm for Donna.

After placing the heaters, he walked to the rear of the truck and hitched the trailer up to the truck. He pulled ramps out of the truck bed, attached them to the trailer, started the ATV, and drove it onto the trailer. He was just tying it down when he saw Donna coming out of the tent.

He jumped down and went to meet her. "How do you feel this morning?"

"I feel just great. It's wonderful to be alive...and with you."

She hugged and kissed him, and he responded enthusiastically.

She broke off the hug. "Charlie, I guess I go behind a tree or something, huh?"

"That's about right, but we have to get busy because if Hank or the Sheriff come up this trail, we're in deep do-do."

"Well, let's get with it."

Donna walked away from Charlie. He would wait until after they ate to strike the tent.

The two-burner stove was lit. When the water came to a boil, Charlie added some grits to it. In three minutes, the grits was ready. He mixed some butter in and served their breakfast sprinkled with sugar in two plastic bowls. Donna was watching him as he did all this.

"Charlie, what is that?"

"That's grits. I learned to like it when I was in New Orleans. It's real good."

Donna took a small, tentative bite, then nodded and grinned at him to indicate that she liked it, too.

320

"This is real good, Charlie. I have never tasted grits like this before. The sugar and the butter add so much to the taste."

Donna and Charlie had a morning cup of hot chocolate; then while Donna watched, Charlie struck the tent and packed everything into the back of the truck. With some difficulty, Donna carried the heater to him from the cab so he could place it with the other things, and he reached under the truck and retrieved the second heater.

Now, he placed a tarp over the entire truck bed and tied it down.

Donna got into the cab of the truck by herself, surprised to find it toasty warm from the heater Charlie had placed there. She started the engine and by the time she scooted out of the way to let Charlie into the driver's seat, the engine was fully warmed up and ready to go. Charlie put the truck into four-wheel drive and it began to move slowly north toward Canada.

"Donna, this will be a slow drive out. It may be a little rough, but I'm certain we can make it. There is only one area where we might tip over when we have to leave the trail. That will come about halfway to the trailhead from here."

"You've done everything great so far. I have confidence you will get us out of here."

They came to the area where they had to go around the big tree lying across the trail. Charlie maneuvered the vehicle around the tree easily enough, but it had weight in the rear and it felt like it might tip over. Still, he made it back onto the trail without a catastrophe.

"Charlie, where do we go from here?"

"Well, honey, first we go to a motel I have booked for several nights. We'll stay there only today or, at most, a couple of days. That is so you can get some badly needed rest. After we leave the motel, we'll travel to Vancouver or Jasper. I'll sell the truck and we'll only go by public transportation for a few days. Ultimately, we will wind up in a small town in Oregon.

"I bought a piece of property there several years ago and established myself as a millionaire. We'll just disappear with no

321

one knowing where we are. My property is near Crater Lake. You'll just love it."

"What if someone finds out who we are?"

"Then we'll move to plan B. In other words, we'll look into real estate in another area, possibly Brazil, Mexico, or Switzerland. We might even go to Alaska or New Orleans. I don't think anyone will find us, though."

"That would be fun. We're going to have a good life together away from our past."

"Donna, I don't guess I've told you this, but ever since I returned to my body, I've been full of remorse for the things I did. I think of my past sins constantly. I think of the sorrow I put innocent people through. I'm going through a living hell!"

Donna was thoughtful, and then responded, "I've felt that way, too. I thought you had overcome that, and because you had, I would eventually overcome my guilt, too. I don't know if I can take it."

"Donna, we have to do the best we can while we are in these bodies."

Donna took a deep breath. "You're right, but that doesn't mean I like it or that I will get used to it."

A few minutes passed. Donna looked at Charlie.

"Charlie, I had a dream last night which seemed so real. A woman came to me and said some strange things."

"I bet I had the same dream, and I think I know who the woman was, because in my dream she was standing on the spot where Martha is buried."

"At your place."

"Right. In my dream, she said that we are good and compassionate, but we have certain talents that God may want us to use in the future. She also said we should use these talents only when and in the way that God directs, and to trust our instincts about when and how we are to use them."

"That's what she said in my dream also. That scares me because I think the talents she was referring to are our skills as...killers."

322

"I believe you're right. But remember, the Lord forgave us our sins."

"One more thing she said was - our sins have been forgiven and no one, not even us, has the right to question God's will, His orders, or His mercy. We are truly forgiven."

"Yes, we are truly forgiven, but I still have two questions. What does God want us to do and how do we escape?"

Charlie smiled and responded, "I don't have an answer to the first question, but I have chosen a route through Canada for our escape."

THE END

Book III

THE ESCAPE

By
SHELDON LYNNE

The Escape

Riverhouse Publishing
St. Louis MO 63146
ISBN: 978-1-893892-07-1
© 2013 Sheldon Lynne

PREFACE

Charlie and Donna had out-of-body experiences where Jesus saved them from Hell, returned them to their bodies, as well as forgiving them their sins. After being married by Sam, Charlie faked their deaths. Then they started their escape to Canada on the West Lake Trail, but Mike, Hank, and Sam did not believe they died in the fire that burned Charlie's suburban.

Charlie and Donna, who was having significant pain, knew they must affect an escape so they could completely disappear. But first, Donna must completely regain her strength and then they could go to their new home in Oregon.

They were now going to the Mountain Vue Motel in Canada just north of the Canadian – United States boarder.

CHAPTER 1

The sky was an orange red as the sun was just setting in the west when the brown Ford pickup truck pulled into the parking place at the Mountain Vue Motel marked 128. There were several bushes on either side of the short walkway to room 128, which were just in front of where Charlie parked his truck. Charlie looked over at Donna, smiled as she was sleeping and was about to get out of the truck when Donna opened her eyes.

"Charlie, are we at the motel?"

"Yes. I have to go open the door and check the room. While I'm doing that, I will leave the motor running so you will stay warm."

"Thanks honey. I'll be just fine until you come back for me."

With those words, Charlie left the truck and went to the room right in front of the parking place. It was room 128. Charlie liked these rooms at the motel because each room on the ground floor had a door to the outside with shrubbery lining both sides of the sidewalk up to the outside door and another door to an inside hallway. He thought this room was perfect for their needs.

He inserted the room key in the lock, unlocked the door, and entered the room. There was still enough light from the sun to see in the room, but he still would have to turn on the lights. He walked to the door to the hallway and turned on the light switch. The lights on the table and the ceiling light immediately cast a bright light over the entire room.

Charlie checked the bathroom while he was near the bathroom

door and then he walked towards the door to the parking lot. He noted on his left there were two mirrors on the wall and there were two paintings of mountains hanging on the wall to his right over the two double beds. One bed was closer to the door to the hallway and the other bed was near the door to the parking lot. Charlie thought that Donna would want to get in bed immediately so he pulled down the powder blue bedspread, the wool blanket, and the sheets on the bed closer to the parking lot.

After he looked around the room for a last time, he went outside to the truck. He opened the door on the driver's side to the truck and turned the motor off. Next he went around to the passenger side of the truck and opened the door.

Without a word, Donna slowly swung her feet to her right where they came to rest on a running board.

Charlie said, "Donna, put your arms around me and I will help you down."

Donna smiled and did as Charlie suggested.

As she stepped down to the ground, she winced as she had some pain, but even with the pain she began to walk slowly towards the room with Charlie helping her up the curb and into the room.

Donna went straight to the bed that was turned down and she lay in the bed immediately as Charlie closed the door behind them.

Charlie had some clothes for Donna in the dresser and the closet. He hadn't bought a lot of clothes, just a dress, some pajamas, a couple of pairs of blue jeans, and a light, but warm coat because it was the Tuesday before Thanksgiving and it would get cold very soon.

After he had finished getting everything settled, he turned to Donna and said, "Honey, now you must remember what I'm going to tell you. We may have to change names frequently over the next few days as we move from motel to motel. The name I am using here is Phillips. Here is your California driver's license saying you are Mrs. Donna Phillips. Now I must go to the clerk, tell him my wife has just joined me and because you have just had a serious injury in an automobile accident, you cannot be disturbed. And in general, set things up so we can stay here for a couple of days and not be

329

disturbed.

"Please don't leave the room or open the door for anyone – except for me of course. I won't be too long - just rest and I'll bring you your supper. How about that - supper in bed on our second night together."

Donna smiled and replied, "I hope this won't be the last time you serve me in bed."

With those words, Charlie smiled and walked out of the room, being careful to take his key and lock the door.

After a brief walk down the corridor, he went up to the registration desk in the lobby.

"Sir, my name is Phillips and I am in room 128. My wife has just joined me, but because she has just had a serious injury she cannot be disturbed. Please mark your records that we do not want our room cleaned unless I say differently. Now, can I bring her some food from the coffee shop?"

"Glad to have you back with us, Mr. Phillips. As for bringing your wife some food, I'm sure the coffee shop will help you as much as they can. By the way, we have an excellent house doctor if you need one and I can assure you no one will clean your room unless you want your room cleaned. I hope your wife will recover soon."

"I hope she won't need a doctor, but if she does, I will certainly keep your offer in mind."

The coffee shop was neat and well decorated with pictures of mountain scenes along the walls. Charlie found the people in the coffee shop to be nice and very helpful. He ordered dinner for Donna and himself. They gave him the food on a tray and let him use a little pushcart to carry the food to the room.

As he pushed the cart down the hall to their room as fast as he thought he could go without spilling the food he thought these nice people will probably remember me and Donna being injured. I must see if we can alter their perception. He reached the door rather quickly. He unlocked the door, went in, and closed the door. He noticed Donna was sleeping or at least had her eyes closed, so he just pushed the cart between the beds, placed her supper on her side of the cart and his meal on the other side.

Next he went over to Donna and whispered in her ear, "Honey, din-din."

She opened her eyes and looked at Charlie and smiled. She slowly sat up on the side of the bed. "Hummmm, soup and it's chicken noodle, too. My favorite."

"I'm glad. Let's eat so I can return the cart."

As Charlie picked up his knife and fork, Donna said, "Charlie, shouldn't we give thanks to God for everything that's happened to us the past week?"

Charlie put down his fork, looked at Donna, then said, "Donna, you're right, we should give thanks to God before every meal. I think I remember something Sam says every time he eats."

"If it's good enough for Sam, it should be good enough for us."

"Okay. Let's see. May the God of grace and mercy bless this food to our nourishment and us to His service. In the name of Jesus, who is the Christ. Amen."

"That's a good prayer, Charlie."

Charlie and Donna ate slowly. Donna ate all of her soup and all of the noodles, but she did not eat any of the meat although she tried a couple of chunks of chicken. Charlie ate everything, wiped his face with his napkin, drank some water and rearranged the dishes so he could push the cart easily. He left the room and returned the cart to the coffee shop.

While Charlie returned the cart to the coffee shop, Donna slowly removed the clothes she was wearing and before she put on her pajama top, she looked in a hand held mirror so she could look in the mirror on the wall which made it possible to look where she had been shot. But instead of where the small bullet holes should have been, she found only the larger incisions from the operation. She noted the many sutures that closed the incisions. Having seen the wounds, she proceeded to put on her pajama top.

As she put on her pajamas, she thought, I need a first aid kit. I'll ask Charlie to get me one.

Charlie walked back into the room from returning the cart and saw Donna for the first time in her pajamas. He thought, damn, she is really beautiful. I'm a lucky man to have her for my wife.

331

She was sitting up in her bed looking at Charlie as he closed the door.

She said, "Charlie, I think it's about time I told you a little about myself just so you know what you've gotten yourself into. And after I finish, I hope you will tell me a little more about yourself."

"I guess it's time to talk to each other so I'm all ears."

Donna sighed and then started, "The first thing is I'm an orphan. I don't know anything about my parents. I was raised in an orphanage near Columbus, Ohio. Enough said about that part of my life.

"I guess you should know I have been with only four men in my life. The first three raped me when I was only seventeen and about to graduate from high school. That was a shock to say the least, but it was my introduction to sex. The only other person I've had sex with was Jack and I wanted to go to bed with him.

"You must know, he was the first person who showed me any affection at all. We met right after I moved to California in a karate class. I joined the class because I was determined not to let any more SOBs rape me. Jack was in the class and he started to show some legitimate interest in me. After a while, we started to date and we struck it off after a while and I moved in with him. He taught me how to shoot and told me what his job was with Frank Giaventi. He talked Frank into hiring me as his assistant, which was my first good paying job.

"You know after you killed him, I swore I would kill you for that, but this has all changed now. I would protect you with my life now. Frank talked me out of looking for you and I decided only to kill you if you did something else to me or to Frank. Frank convinced me Jack deserved what he got. Of course nobody knew who you were at that time so I could only kill you if I found out who you were.

"I still wanted to get you, but I sort of softened when you took out Max. And when you killed Gene and saved me from death, I completely forgave you. I guess that came in handy because the Lord forgave me my sins and I remember in the Lord's prayer, it says "Forgive me my trespasses as I forgive those who trespass against

332

me". I think you know the rest of my story."

In almost a comic voice, Charlie replied, "I know a little, but honey, you almost did what you swore you would do in Seattle - you know you almost took me out there..."

In a soft voice, Donna interrupted, "At that time, if I would have known it was you, I would have made sure you were dead. But I wouldn't even think about it now - I love you and I hope you don't hold it against me."

In a now loving and serious voice, "I forgave you almost as soon as I woke up in the hospital. And you can be assured I will protect you with my life and will kill anyone who would do you harm. I would gladly give my life to save you. To tell you the truth, I would like to get my hands on those three jerks who raped you and do something to them that I'm sure Jesus would frown upon, but now to my story. Before I tell you my story, this might relieve you of any guilt you might have about shooting me. I doubt you or anybody else could have killed me because I was dead and Jesus returned me to my body and if He says I will not die, nobody can veto His command. You know, I just had a funny thought – our marriage was made in hell by Jesus. That's just a funny thought.

"And now to begin - as I have told you, I am getting and I have had flashbacks over the last couple of years. The only thing I can really remember about my youth is I come from, I think, Vermont, and my name is in fact Charles A. Mackey, III. My mother and father were linguists and my father taught me how to shoot – at least that is what I think. I don't know what happened to them except they are dead. I have seen their graves in several of my flashbacks. Beside that, I know nothing about what happened before I woke up the hospital in Pearl Harbor with amnesia.

"Incidentally, the name on our marriage license is Charles A. Mackey III. I used a little deception to get our name on it, but when we arrive at our home, we will be Mr. and Mrs. Mackey."

"That's good. I was wondering what my real name is. It would get old changing our name every so often."

"It sure would. Now I will tell you, I have transferred almost twenty million dollars to our bank account in the town where we will

333

live. And honey, I mean **our** bank account. It is in Oregon and I thought we could start a restaurant or something like that. What do you think?"

Donna replied, "I think that will be just great. Let's plan on that. Now, I have to tell you something. I really want to sleep with you, but...honey we can't. I just hurt too much, but when I don't hurt too much, I definitely will want you and I hope I will please you."

"Honey, I'm confident we will please each other and yes, I understand about the pain you have. I love you."

Just as Charlie was leaning over to kiss Donna, Donna said, "Honey, I'm going to need a good First Aid kit. Could you get one for me?"

"Honey, I already have one although I might have to get additional supplies along the way."

With those words, they kissed and went to sleep in separate beds. Tomorrow will be another day.

It was Wednesday, the day before Thanksgiving. Charlie was looking out the window in their room looking at the parking lot not thinking about anything in particular. He heard a sound from his rear and turned to see Donna walking back to bed from just doing her morning things.

"Charlie, I'm getting stronger by the day, but I still hurt quite a bit. I wonder how long it's going to take for me to fully recover?"

"Probably a month or so, but we have to plan our next move. You may have a problem getting up and talking, but it will be up to you to convince the clerk that we are going to Vancouver and then to Victoria on Vancouver Island."

Breathing deeply, she responded, "That's okay, but I'll have to know a little about Victoria. What's there?"

"Well, the salmon run should be about over, but we can see the last of it and there is Buchert Gardens. I don't know a lot about Victoria, but we must convince him that's where we are headed because I feel certain Mike, Pierre or someone else will be looking for us and that will give us some extra time to really get lost."

"I understand. Give me another day before I talk to him."

"Okay, but we should leave here no later than Friday morning."

Donna took another deep breath because she knew she would have to be feeling much better by Friday so she could travel and even before then so she could convince the clerk they were headed to Victoria.

It was the day before Thanksgiving when the phone rang at the home of Michael Forester in San Francisco.

A cherry voice answered, "Hello."

"Honey, this is Mike."

"Mike, when are you coming home? We thought you would be home by now. What's happened?"

"First, I must wait for Pierre Richard. You remember him - he's from Interpol. He will arrive here the day after Thanksgiving. I will miss you and the family, but this just can't be helped.

"Second, I don't know how to tell you, but the coroner has signed Charlie's death certificate."

"Oh no. He can't be dead!"

"Well honey, I don't think he is really dead, but the evidence points to his death. He married Donna..."

"What!!!"

"He married Donna just before he died. On the surface, it looks like they ran over a pipe from a propane tank and both Charlie and Donna burned to death. I think Charlie staged their deaths. It's a long story, so the full details will have to wait until I get home. I will also tell you what I believe he has been doing over the last few years. It may shock you, but I can't say anything about that over the telephone and to be quite truthful, I can't prove any of what I believe."

"Mike, how sure are you that Charlie is dead?"

"About 25% sure. You know the minister Charlie always talks about?"

"Yes, I believe his name is Sam something or other."

"His name is Sam Pritchard. I will be eating with him and his wife, Ruth, on Turkey Day. Henry Teller will be eating with us also. They're really nice people."

"When do you think you will get home?"

335

"I don't really know, but a good guess would be Sunday or Monday."

"Well, have a good meal. We'll be thinking of you. Love you!"

"I love you too. Tell the children hello for me."

"I will. Bye."

Mike felt like he had been dealt a crushing blow. This was the first Thanksgiving he would be without Lisa since they were married.

CHAPTER 2

Mike was anxiously waiting for Northwest flight 1587 to land because Pierre was on this flight and he thought the quicker the plane lands, the quicker we can do our investigation and I can get back to Lisa and the children.

He continued to think, I will take him to Sand Point, let him look around, talk to him and maybe, and just maybe I can leave tomorrow to go home.

He looked at the big jet as it slowly came forward towards the terminal where a ground crew member was signaling the plane to move forward. The plane stopped and cut its engines when the ground crew member crossed his signal lights. Soon the jet way was filled with passengers walking off the plane.

Since the plane held over two hundred people, the concourse immediately became filled with people getting off the plane. After about half of the passengers had walked down the jet way and into the airport, Pierre walked out of the jet way.

Mike called, "Pierre, good to see you again."

"Mike, you are looking well. How is your family?"

"Lisa and the kids are just great. But they missed me over Thanksgiving, but that couldn't be helped."

"I am sorry, but this was the first and only flight on which I could get reservations. You Americans fly a lot on Thanksgiving Day. Now, where are we staying?"

"At the airport Ramada Inn. I have a room reserved for you

there."

By this time, the two men had walked to the baggage area. They were waiting for Pierre's luggage to slide from the conveyor belt onto the circular luggage recovery unit. As the many pieces of luggage were sliding down the ramp to the recovery unit, Pierre spotted his luggage and grabbed his two pieces.

"Nothing seems damaged. Almost a first for me. Now where is your car?"

"It's right outside. I obtained some police courtesy. They let me park in their parking area."

After checking into the motel, Pierre invited Mike to come to his room for a little talk.

"Mike, tell me what has happened and where can I interview your friend, Charlie?"

"A lot has happened since we last talked. First, Charlie somehow got Donna out of the hospital in a manner that the hospital staff did not know so she was gone for over two hours. Next the police there didn't think it was that important to notify Sheriff Coomey immediately, so they waited until morning."

Pierre in a matter of fact voice said, "By then it was too late. Charlie had made good his escape. Am I correct, Mike?"

"Not quite, Pierre. Charlie married Donna just after he got her out of the hospital. They went to Charlie's house by the lake where the shoot out occurred. Their vehicle apparently rolled over an exposed propane gas line, breaking it."

Pierre responded: "Let me guess. Two bodies were found in the vehicle that could not be identified, so the medical examiner ruled Charlie and Donna are dead."

"That's just about what happened. The vehicle was burned to the point where some of the metal melted. But there were two partial sets of bones found where they would have been sitting. One was a woman's hip, some long bones and possibly a lower jaw. The other set of bones was a man's hip, some other bones, and part of a skull. The coroner said it would be impossible to positively identify the bones as those of Charlie and Donna. They were just too badly burned, but since they were the probable victims, he declared them

338

both dead and signed the death certificates saying accidental death caused by fire."

"This will complicate matters. When did you strongly suspect Charlie was the Iceman?"

"In San Francisco, but after I talked to the sheriff, I had no more doubts. He is or was the Iceman."

"How sure are you that he is dead?"

"Not too sure - maybe 25%"

"You mean you do not believe either he or Donna is dead?"

"That's right. For one thing, the timing doesn't fit. Charlie's friend, Henry Teller was at the wedding. He left the same time they did, but he had time to go home, get undressed, and sleep for several hours before the explosion. Yet the evidence points to the break in the pipeline as soon as the vehicle rolled over the exposed pipe, which would have occurred as soon as they arrived at the camp.

"Of course, they could have driven around for a while and then went to the camp, but I doubt that because of Donna's condition. Or they could have rested there for a while and then got back in the truck so they could escape from the law and that is when the pipe broke. I don't believe they did that. I believe they are still alive."

"Good thinking, Mike."

"Another thing. If he is as good as you say he is, he wouldn't be that careless."

"I totally concur."

"The things which point to them being the victims are of course the hips which were recovered and it would be awfully hard for Donna to get out of the area in her condition. She was still regarded as in serious condition. And the last piece of evidence is there weren't any tracks in the snow leading from the camp and it had just snowed."

"You have done, what you say, your homework."

"Pierre, I had wanted to go to Sand Point tonight, but it's too late for that now. I made a phone call just before coming to your room and arranged for you to eat with Sam Pritchard, his wife Ruth, Henry Teller and me tomorrow. We might be able to go to the camp where everything took place and look around for a while before we eat."

"I would like that. One thing, where did Charlie have his bank account?"

"In San Francisco at the Bank of America. I have someone getting the needed subpoena to examine his account. They should have it by Monday. This means we can look at it either Monday or Tuesday."

"Good. Now let me buy you dinner. Then we can get a good night's rest and go to Sand Point early tomorrow morning."

Pierre and Mike were up and moving by 5:30 AM. The coffee shop had just opened, so they ate an early breakfast. After eating, they left the motel to begin the drive to Sand Point.

The weather was beautiful. It was a crisp, cloudless day with the wind coming out of the north at twelve miles per hour. Pierre was looking at the scenery and not talking very much. Soon, Mike turned north towards Sand Point.

Pierre said, "That was a beautiful town. What's its name?"

"Coeur d'Alene. It is beautiful, isn't it?"

"Yes, it is."

"Pierre, the couple we will eat with, along with Mr. Teller, are probably the best friends Charlie had besides Lisa. They knew him better than anyone else did. Sheriff Coomey is a pretty sharp guy, but he doesn't know anything about Charlie's past. He thinks Charlie knew more than he told him about the shoot out, but he accepts Charlie and Donna's death because there are no bones missing from any cemeteries and no missing persons for a great distance from Sand Point. I must say he does have a point, but I didn't think it wise to tell him everything."

"I agree."

"I have arranged for us to meet him at the camp this afternoon. I forgot to tell you something else. Sam Pritchard, who was Charlie's pastor, believes if they are alive and if Charlie is who we think he is and even though Donna was the enforcer for the Giaventi family, they will never return to their previous professions. They both reformed because both of them had out-of-body experiences and met Jesus in Hell.

340

"There, Jesus supposedly forgave them their sins and told them to work for God. Both Charlie and Donna told him of their experience in Hell. He will add, even if they were or might have been professional killers, they are not now because of their out-of-body experiences. He also will tell you it is strange how everyone here who knew Charlie will try to protect his reputation."

"Mike I told you once and I will tell you again, the Iceman is good and he is also an enigma. This out of body experience could be true, but I do not completely believe those things happen."

"Sam absolutely believes Charlie and Donna's story because of some dreams he and his wife had and what they told him their observations were while out-of-their bodies. I must tell you after Sam tells you his story, it may change your mind about the possibility that each of them had an out-of-body experience."

Mike and Pierre's car was now entering the outskirts of Sand Point. Their sedan crossed a bridge over a lake, then turned left towards the west. It wasn't long until Mike turned the car onto a gravel road. They crossed the bridge near Hank's house, then turned left.

Mike pointed to the house on the right of the car and said, "That's where Hank lives."

The car went around several curves until they saw the camp and the blue waters of the lake.

After Mike parked the car in front of the camp, they got out, walked passed patches of snow to the burned out remains of the suburban. Pierre looked at the burned vehicle for several minutes. After looking at the burned suburban, he walked over to where the pontoon plane was next to the small dock. Pierre noted the pontoons of the plane were resting on the floor of the lake. He looked down into the crystal clear water noting he could see the bottom of the lake even though he thought the lake was six to seven feet deep at that point because of the size and how the plane was resting on the bottom. He saw a coke can on the bottom, frowned, thought trash in such a beautiful lake, then he looked to the west.

"Mike, is there a trail over there?"

"Yes there is. It's called the West Lake Trail. It ends in

341

Canada."

"If they are not dead, that is the trail they used to escape."

"It could be, but remember what I told you, there were no tracks in the snow leading from the cabin area to the trail. Anyhow, I requested the help of the RCMP, but I haven't heard anything yet."

Pierre and Mike left the camp and found Sam's house just before noon. Sam opened the door and greeted the two men.

"Hi Mike. This must be Pierre Richard. Glad to have you eat with us."

"Sam, may I use your telephone. I need to call Coomey and tell him we won't need to talk to him today. Pierre and I agree on everything."

Sam looked at Mike and shook his head.

After Pierre and Mike ate lunch, they climbed back into Mike's rented car and began their ride back to Spokane. The ride back to Spokane was quiet for the first twenty miles.

Pierre broke the silence and said, "Mike, I must tell you Interpol found out that a large amount of money - almost thirty -one million dollars, American - was withdrawn from a Swiss bank account. Do to a mistake by one of our men, we lost track of it almost immediately, but later, we found out a like amount of money was given to the Salvation Army. We think that was the bank account of the Iceman. Strange, isn't it?"

"I didn't know he had that much money. I know he had ten million dollars in the Bank of America several years ago. I also know he invested the money in a profitable manner and last month he told Lisa his investments had paid off and he had much more than the original amount – maybe two to three times the ten million.

"He earned that money in sort of a strange manner. He and a Dr. Wells solved a murder for a police chief in Louisiana. The murderer was the one who actually put up the reward to cover herself because she hired the killers. That's a long story in itself, but the money was legally his."

"It would be interesting to know if the money is still there."

"Let's get the first flight we can to San Francisco so we can be there when the bank opens on Monday."

342

Since the Sunday after Thanksgiving is the most traveled day of the year for the airlines, Mike knew it would be hard to obtain tickets. He thought he would have to pull some strings to get tickets to fly to San Francisco Sunday.

But, as luck would have it, Northwest Airline had several seats available to San Francisco from Spokane via Seattle. Mike and Pierre took two of them.

Friday morning Donna accompanied Charlie to the coffee shop just before eight AM. Donna was feeling better, but still very weak. She was hoping she could talk to the clerk in such a manner as to convince him they were going west.

Just as their breakfast was being served, the clerk walked up to them and said, "Hi folks. And how are you feeling today, Mrs. Phillips? And will you be checking out today, Mr. Phillips?"

Donna replied, "Yes we are. We thought about seeing Vancouver and Victoria. We heard they were nice places to visit. Do you know anything about them?"

"Yes, and I have some pamphlets about them. I'll get them for you."

The clerk left and returned almost immediately to the table where Charlie and Donna were.

"Here are the pamphlets. I have to return to the desk – some people are checking out."

Charlie asked the clerk, "I want to sell the four wheel ATV and the trailer it's sitting on in the bed of the truck. Do you know anybody who wants to buy an ATV?"

The clerk responded, "I sure do. How much do you want for it?"

Charlie thought he could get $1,000.00 for the ATV, but this is a golden opportunity to unload it quickly. "I'll take $200.00 American."

The clerk looked at Charlie, smiled, and while appreciating his good luck replied, "Sold. Just give me thirty minutes to get the money."

Twenty-five minutes later, Charlie unloaded the ATV and the

trailer from the truck and handed the clerk the title to the ATV.

After the ATV was sold, Donna said, "Charlie, that was quick and easy convincing him we are going west. Thank God. I don't think I could have lasted talking to him at the desk."

Charlie added, "All but giving him the ATV didn't hurt any, either."

By the time Donna and Charlie were able to get into the truck and leave the Mountain Vue motel, it was almost ten. Charlie first turned west from the parking lot to give the illusion they were going west towards Vancouver, then he made a couple of turns on some back roads. When he returned to the main highway, he was driving towards Calgary. When they reached a northbound highway, he turned north.

Donna asked, "Where are we going?"

"We're going to Jasper. I understand it's a nice tourist type town. That means we won't have to answer a lot of questions and the railroad goes through the town. Also, Jasper has bus service to the south and also north to Edmonton. I think we can really get lost there. It would be very hard for the law to trace us after we leave there."

"I certainly hope so."

Charlie looked at Donna and thought, I'll wait until later to tell her we have to separate in Jasper and go different ways to Mt. Hood. I don't think she would take it too well if I told her now.

344

CHAPTER 3

Pierre stayed in the downtown Hilton, the same hotel where he stayed when he was in San Francisco for his briefing. Mike was happy to go home and see Lisa and his family on Sunday. Lisa and the children were happy to have Mike home to say the least. Sunday would be a happy time for everyone. Monday morning would come and Pierre and Mike would be at the bank with the subpoena.

On Monday, Mike arrived at the Hilton at 7:45 AM so he could eat breakfast with Pierre. Before they were finished eating, Tom Buckley walked into the restaurant bringing the subpoena with him. Since they were in walking distance of the bank, they could and would now walk to the Bank of America and present the subpoena to the bank. The bank was only two blocks away.

Mike, Pierre, and Tom walked up to the entrance to the bank just before 9:30 AM. The bank was already open for business when the three men arrived. After entering the bank through the revolving glass doors, Mike walked up to one of the secretaries seated behind a desk. The sign on her desk read Mrs. Jessica Wilder.

"Excuse me." Showing her his identification he continued, "I am a police officer and I have a subpoena to see the account of one Mr. C. C. Duncan."

The secretary looked at Mike's credentials, then replied, "I will have to let you talk to Mr. Bruning, he is vice president in charge of accounts. He will take care of you. Have a seat over there. It will only take a minute."

She rose to her feet and walked away from her desk.

In a short time, a slim, neatly dressed man who was in his late thirties, but was almost totally bald, walked over to where the three men were sitting. He extended his hand to the three men.

"Hi, I'm Paul Bruning, vice president of the bank."

Mike, Tom, and Pierre stood up. Mike took Paul Bruning's hand first.

"My name is Michael Forester, this is Sgt. Tom Buckley, and this is Pierre Richard from Interpol. We would like to see..."

"Yes I know. Mrs. Wilder says you are police officers and you have a subpoena to see one of our accounts. Please follow me. While we are walking, may I see the subpoena?"

Sgt. Buckley handed Mr. Burning the subpoena.

"Thank you, Sgt. Buckley. I see by the subpoena you wish to see Mr. C. C. Duncan's account, is that correct?"

"Yes, it is," replied Mike.

The four men entered Paul Bruning's office. Mr. Bruning then escorted them into a conference room adjacent to his office. Mr. Bruning motioned for them to sit around the conference table.

Mr. Bruning looked at the three men, but looked at Mike in a strange manner and very hard.

"You said your name is Michael Forester, didn't you?"

"Yes, Lieutenant Michael Forester. What's that got to do with seeing Mr. Duncan's account?"

"Are you related to one Mrs. Lisa Giaventi Forester?"

Getting a little agitated, "Yes, but what has that got to do with us seeing Mr. Duncan's account?"

"Nothing, but everything. Let me explain. Last Friday, the bank received a letter from an attorney in Coeur d'Alene named Kirk Jasper. He informed us that Mr. Duncan had died. He enclosed a copy of his death certificate as evidence of his death. The bank of course immediately froze his account.

"Mr. Jasper also informed us that besides leaving his property to his church with several provisions which apply to a Mr. Teller, Mr. and Mrs. Michael Forester's family, and a few small bequests, the sole heir to Mr. Duncan's estate is one Mrs. Lisa Giaventi

Forester, wife of Michael Forester. That must be you, Lt. Forester."

Mike was stunned. He leaned back in his chair and wondered why did Charlie do this and at the same time, how much money is involved.

Tom looked at Mike. "You son of a bitch. Now you can retire with a million bucks in the bank. You owe me and the wife a good meal - and you owe me a stiff drink."

Pierre said, "I don't know whether to congratulate you or what."

Mr. Bruning said, "I think congratulations are in order, if having your wife become a millionaire is the criteria. Mr. Duncan left Mrs. Forester a little over three million dollars. After taxes, Mrs. Forester will receive a little over two million dollars or that is what Mr. Jasper thinks. Our bank attorneys believe that is about correct."

The three men sat motionless in their chairs. Mike was stunned. Pierre and Tom were staring at Mike.

Pierre broke the silence, "Mr. Bruning, were there any recent withdrawals from his account, and if so, how much were the withdrawals?"

"Let me see. He withdrew almost thirty million dollars over a period of several weeks with the last seven million a little less than a week ago. He had us wire that money to a bank in Mexico. Some of the money he took over a period of time was taken in cash. Where he took that money, I don't know."

"Mike, this fits the pattern."

Mike recovered from the shock.

Mike said, "Mr. Bruning, will you please forward a copy of his account to my office at the SFPD?"

"Sure Lieutenant. Will you convey the information to your wife about her being a beneficiary and tell her to contact me as soon as she can?"

"I sure will."

The three men left the bank.

When they were on the street, Mike said to Tom, "Tom, go back to the office and ask for the department to investigate this. I am uncomfortable with that news even though I know Lisa and I did nothing wrong or anything to promote her receiving such an amount

347

of money. I want the department to know that too. Pierre and I are going to his hotel now to discuss what Mr. Bruning told us."

"Right. Are you sure you want internal affairs to investigate this?"

"Yes."

"Okay, I will set the investigation in motion. See you later this afternoon."

"Tom, is Mike needed this afternoon?"

"Not really."

"Mike, if I can get a flight out today, will you take me to the airport?"

"Sure, Tom I'll see you tomorrow morning."

"Okay, but don't spend all that money before you pay me that dinner and stiff drink...maybe you should throw a party for the division...with dancing girls and...."

Mike interrupted, "Tom, go back to the office. I will take your suggestion under advisement."

All three men laughed as Tom got into his squad car.

When Pierre returned to his room, he immediately called the airline. There was one ticket left from San Francisco to New York. He did not have any problems getting a ticket from New York to Paris. He would have to be at the airport by 5:00 PM though. It was now 11:45 AM. He could make it.

Mike said, "Pierre, it seems that the withdrawals here seem to prove your ideas except for one fact - why did he leave three million dollars in the account when he could have withdrawn all of it?"

"I don't know the answer to that question. It could be he wanted to leave Lisa some money and he doesn't plan to - how would you say - come back to life – so he took the rest of the money for himself."

Pierre paused for a short time, then interrupted his packing and sat down on the bed next to the chair where Mike was sitting.

"Mike, I want to tell you a story again - you know like the story I told you some time ago. I want you to know I am telling you this story because I believe you have earnestly tried to do a good job and not hide anything from me.

348

"After you and I talked a couple of weeks ago, I knew it was time for me to speak to Kozar. I went to Switzerland to talk with him. I had heard that he had received an extra large sum of money. He kept about $500,000.00 dollars American of the money he received. He distributed another million dollars to someone else. We believe it to be Miguel - the remaining assassin out of Klaus, Carlos, and the Iceman.

"At first when we talked he said he did not know anything. I then used an American movie tactic. I reached over and grabbed him.

"By the way, he is an absolute coward. He told me a lot after that, off the record of course. But he still wouldn't tell me that he paid Miguel, nor would he tell me whom Miguel would have to kill for his fee. I was frustrated, but I had one more idea.

"I told him I knew some people in America who had the number of a man who could take care of things. This man had a number in San Francisco. It was 555-0187. His eyes spoke for him. I told him there is a new number and my friend has it. If he didn't tell me everything, I will have my friend call that number.

"He gave in completely. He showed me a copy of a report I made less than three weeks before. It stated that I thought the Iceman was C. C. Duncan. The contract was on C. C. Duncan and the assassin was Miguel. The contract was from Israel."

"That is definitely an interesting story, Pierre."

"I just had to tell you before I left for Paris. There is something else you should know. Miguel is very persistent. He will not give up even if it takes him several years to accomplish the task, especially for that kind of money."

"If what you have told me about the Iceman is accurate and if we are correct with what we believe, then it will probably be a long time before Charlie and Donna surface or as you might say, come back to life. But I will remember the story you have told me and if anyone asks, I will say what story. I believe that is what you want."

"It is Mike. But now I must pack and then, we must be off to the airport so I can catch my plane."

CHAPTER 4

It was a beautiful Monday afternoon in Jasper as Charlie looked at Donna lying on the bed in their motel room. She had on the set of light pink pajamas he had bought for her in Spokane. Again, he thought she will make a wonderful wife and an equally good mother. I wonder why God chose her - and me. We must get her some decent and warm clothes if she is to make it back to the states.

About this time, Donna woke up and looked at Charlie looking at her.

"Charlie, I am so sorry, but I am just not ready to have you by my side, but soon. I am feeling stronger by the day."

"I know honey and I can and will wait, even if it kills me. Now what we have to do is go out and buy you some clothes in order for you to look decent as you travel back to the states. Also, it won't be too long until Mike and maybe Pierre or the RCMP will figure out how we escaped and will be looking for us. I wouldn't doubt that the Mounties are looking right now.

"With this in mind, tomorrow morning - maybe Wednesday morning - we must separate and return back to the states separately."

"I don't like that, Charlie!"

"I don't like it either, but the police will be or are looking for a man and a woman with reddish hair, not just a man or just a woman. Understand?"

A little dejected, she answered, "When you put it that way, I guess so."

"Okay. Now I will tell you where we are to meet and when. There is a lodge at Mount Hood in Oregon called Timberline Lodge. People can ski all year round there - even in August. That's something, but to continue, meet me there two days after Christmas. I have made reservations there for that time. Do not arrive earlier because they won't have any rooms. It's a very popular lodge, especially at that time of the year.

"You can stay at a hotel in Portland where you can see Mt. Hood and if you get a room facing east - you probably would be able see the mountain from your room. You can also get some more clothes while there - you know some pretty woman - I mean lady things. You know what I mean. Have any suggestions as to what we should do or do you like what I have planned?"

"I like what you've planned so far." She got up out of the bed in a manner that indicated she was indeed recovering her strength rapidly. Walked over to Charlie and kissed him, then said, "You know, I think I truly love you."

"I know I love you Donna."

"I do have a few questions, through. How are you going to get back to the states and how do you think would be the best way for me to get there?"

"I think it best we don't tell each other how we will get there because if either of us is caught, the other one will still be free to help out. By the way, here is a little over $25,000.00 for your trip." He handed her a rather large fanny pack that contained the money.

Donna unzipped the fanny pack, looked inside, but did not count the money. She zipped the pack closed.

"Charlie, will you have some money too?"

"Yes. I'll have about the same amount - maybe a little more. And I forgot - the room in Timberline Lodge will be in our real name - Mr. and Mrs. Charles A. Mackey. They have been told you may arrive there before I do. I think it will be better if we leave Jasper Wednesday, but separate tomorrow. I will get a room at the southern end of town - you can stay here and pay the bill."

Smiling, Donna replied as she took the $25,000.00 in the fanny pack and waived it at Charlie, "You mean you are not going to pay my bills?"

Playfully Charlie grabbed her and said, "You little gold digger."

But before he could kiss her, she exclaimed in some pain, "Charlie stop!"

"Oh, I'm sorry. I didn't mean to hurt you."

"I know. Let me get dressed, then we can go shopping and eat our last meal together until after Christmas."

Charlie gently kissed her, then said, "I almost forgot. Dye your hair some color - I think you would look real good with your hair colored coal black. What do you think?"

Donna thought for a moment and replied, "I think I would like that. We can get some hair dye when we're out shopping and I'll color my hair before I leave Jasper. It'll be good for at least two weeks."

They left the motel, got in the truck, and drove downtown by the railroad station where Charlie parked the truck. Both Charlie and Donna got out of the truck and walked to several shops in the area. Charlie took Donna to a shoe store first where Charlie insisted she buy a good pair of lightweight, insulated hiking boots. They also purchased some very warm socks to wear with the boots.

Next they went to a small shop which had winter clothing. She bought some stylish, but warm trousers and a heavy parka. After they had finished shopping, they were passing by the railroad station and saw a train pulling into the station that had an observation bubble on two cars.

"Look Charlie, I've never been in one of those cars."

"Neither have I. I think that's the train that goes from Vancouver to Toronto. I've heard it's a beautiful ride."

"Charlie, see if you can get me a ticket on that train going east as far as Winnipeg. Frank once told me you could easily slip into the states from there."

"Frank? Oh, you mean Frank Giaventi, but why do you want me to get you the ticket?"

"If you get me the ticket and the ticket agent remembers you, then the police will be looking for a man, not a woman."

"You're beginning to think like I do - good idea."

353

Donna was waiting outside the station when Charlie came out. He went over to where she was sitting on a bench near a large totem pole.

"I got your ticket. You have a compartment all to yourself and your name is D. Brown. I told the ticket agent my name was D. Brown so you could use your real first name."

"That'll be good. Thanks."

Back at the motel, Charlie said, "Honey, I think it's time to remove the sutures from your surgery. What do you think?"

"I was thinking the same thing. Do you have some scissors?"

"I not only have some scissors, but I have some tweezers in the first aid kit I bought for you."

"You think of everything!"

"I hope I haven't forgotten anything. Now, if you would take off your blouse and bra so I can get at the sutures."

With those words, Donna removed her blouse and her bra. She lay on her stomach so Charlie could see the sutures.

He pulled on the sutures one at a time, then cut each of the sutures and removed them one at a time.

"Honey, the wounds, and the surgery look as if they have healed quite well."

Leaving her bra on the bed and as Donna was putting on her pajama top, she said, "I certainly hope so."

Charlie left Donna early the next morning before the day shift of the motel came on duty. Now Donna was alone, but she knew if she needed Charlie, she could get in touch with him. She knew the motel where he was now staying. He had said he would wait for her to leave on the train to Winnipeg on Wednesday. The train was to leave around 1:00 PM, then he could prepare to leave Jasper and maybe he could leave the next day.

On Wednesday as Donna was boarding the train, she instinctively turned and saw Charlie sitting on the bench by the totem pole. Neither waved to each other, as they did not want anyone to notice they knew each other, though her heart said she wanted everyone to know.

With an "All Aboard" and a couple of whistles, the porters

placed the small steps onto the train and the train began to move towards Edmonton.

Mike was talking to Tom in his office on the Wednesday afternoon after Thanksgiving when Gene walked in.

"Here you are, you millionaire. When are you going to give us a party?"

"Damn, is that all you two think about is having a party?"

Tom smiled and responded, "Especially if someone else is paying for it. Right, Gene?"

"Absolutely. Now to business. Mike, you know that idea you had about looking into Louis Giaventi's income taxes?"

"Yes, how did it pan out?"

"The feds have him cold on tax evasion. They are going to prosecute him and they might be able to put him away for three to five. Good work!"

Gene walked over to Mike and shook his hand. Tom grinned and shook his hand also.

Mike was torn between two emotions - one of pride they got Louis and the other one was sad for having got the idea that would send Lisa's cousin to jail.

Just as Mike was about to leave the room because of the conflicting emotions, the telephone rang.

He answered the phone just to break the conversation, "Lt. Forester."

"Ah Mike. You are the one I wish to talk to. This is Edward Lasard from Edmonton."

This surprised Mike, but he wondered if the RCMP had found Charlie. "Who is this?"

"Edward Lasard - I met you at Frank Giaventi's funeral."

"Of course. How are you and your family doing? I hope everyone is in good health."

"I'm fine and everyone in the family is doing fine. A little less than two weeks ago, you sent a request for us to attempt to find one Charles Cain Duncan and his wife, Donna. When it came across my desk, I remembered your name and since it was your request, I

355

ordered our people to immediately investigate it. After some further checking, I discovered this Duncan was your friend Charlie who I also met at the funeral.

"I was really puzzled by the request, but we did start our investigation. We discovered that a man and a woman registered in a motel named Mountain Vue, just north of Sand Point under the name of Phillips. The woman could not leave their room at any time because of an injury and the man brought food to her for almost every meal. Before they left, the woman made a point to tell the clerk they would be going to Victoria on Vancouver Island so she could see the end of the salmon run. They left soon after and we are still trying to trace them. We have gone as far west as Victoria and as far east as Calgary with no luck. We are now going to check north to Lake Louise, Jasper, and Edmonton.

"Now the question which popped into my mind - I get the feeling this is a similar case as to what happened to my family with regards to Frank. If it is, do you really want us to find him? I know if I would have had the opportunity to arrest Frank, I don't know if I could have done it."

"Your perceptions are accurate, but yes I want you to find them."

"That's what I thought. Can you tell me any more?"

"Maybe someday, but not right now."

"Well, we will be able to check here in Edmonton immediately, but we won't be able to get down to Jasper until maybe Sunday. Is that okay?"

"That'll be fine, Edward. Call me back when you get some information."

"Will do. And now a word of wisdom. Leave the San Francisco Police Department if you can because this situation will tear you apart. You cannot go after a good friend and arrest him without it taking a toll on you and your wife – mentally and in other ways. Take care now."

"Thanks for the advice. Take care."

Mike started to think, if Lisa does get a couple of million dollars, it might be a good idea to leave the force and move to Idaho near where Charlie lived and be close to Sam because I feel he knows more than he has told us. I also feel that Charlie will contact him sometime in the future. Yes, that is what we will do if Lisa agrees with me.

CHAPTER 5

As Donna was lead to her compartment by the steward for her coach, she noticed several things. First his nametag identified him as Arthur and the passageway to her compartment was very narrow - maybe two and a half feet wide with the compartments on one side of the passageway and windows with a handrail on the other side. She also noted that two people might not be able to pass in the passageway or if they could pass, it would be close and with some difficulty.

She was pleased to learn that her compartment, "D", was in the middle of the coach. She thought this might make for a smoother ride. There were Pullman bunks with curtains at both ends of the coach. She noticed a man at the end of the passageway had moved to a corner where the passageway turned. A few moments later, a woman passed him with relative ease. She thought if someone had to pass me, that's the best place for me to be where that man was standing.

Arthur had opened her compartment door and placed her one piece of luggage - a duffel bag type that could be used as a backpack on the lower bunk in the compartment. Her first look at the compartment was that of surprise at the small size. It might have been six feet by eight feet. The upper and lower bunks were on the left side of the compartment with a small basin for washing hands, etc., on the right side of the compartment. There was a small vanity with a mirror on the right side also.

Arthur said, "Mam, the toilet is over here in this corner behind

359

this door. Please call me when you want your bed pulled down. Generally, I pull the bunks down when you go to eat dinner.

"The diner is the next car forward and the Park Car is three cars behind us. My room is the last one on this car towards the Park Car and I am always there or checking on the passengers in this car. You will see my name above the curtains for my room.

"At the front of the car is the shower. Now if I can answer any questions."

"Not really. I think you have...I just thought, what is the Park Car?"

"That's the car with the dome on top where you can sit and see the surrounding landscape easily from the train. They serve free snacks there from time to time and before every meal in the car."

"That's great. When is lunch served?"

"It will be served as soon as we are under way." Feeling the train lurch to one side and the motion of the train, he continued, "Lunch should be served shortly."

"Thanks. Can I see the shower?"

"Sure. This way."

Arthur opened the door to the shower to show Donna the shower room. Donna thought small, but nice. It even had a small, but nice dressing room in addition to the shower room.

Arthur continued, "For water in the shower you press this lever and it slowly returns to its original position, shutting off the water. Unless someone has just used the shower, the water will be cold, but press it a couple of times and the water will become hot. There's plenty of hot water."

Now the train was moving much faster with the coach swaying to the right and then to the left. Donna had to catch herself on the handrail or she would have fallen. Holding on to the rail, she walked slowly back to her compartment.

She thought I'll rest for a while and then go to lunch. After that, I'll go to the Park Car.

By 1:30, she felt strong enough to walk to the dinning car. She opened the door and noticed the key hole in her compartment door – at that moment, she realized she had no key or any way to lock her compartment from outside the compartment. She stopped and went back into the compartment.

She took most of money Charlie had given her and looked for a place to hide it. She found a small place with a door on it. She placed the money in the storage area, then put some socks, panties and a bra in front of the money and closed the door. Now, with almost $5,000.00 in her fanny pack and $127.00 in her wallet for use on the train, she walked out of her compartment towards the diner.

Arriving at the diner, she noticed the diner was relatively full of people eating their lunch.

The man who was obviously in charge of the diner asked, "Would you mind sitting with someone else?"

"No." She noticed his nametag read Roger.

He walked her over to a table for four. There were two people sitting there - a man who was in his mid to late sixties and a woman who was obviously his wife and who was in her sixties.

Donna said, "Hi. Mind if I sit here."

The man answered, "Of course not. We enjoy people, especially Americans. My name is Philip and my wife's name is Yvette."

"Mine is Donna. How far are you going?" she asked as she sat down at the table.

Yvette answered, "We are going home to Winnipeg - actually we live a little to the north of the city. We went to Victoria to visit our son and his family."

"That's nice. Do you have grandchildren?"

Philip replied with some pride as he reached for his wallet, "We sure do. Here are some pictures of them - all three. We are expecting a fourth from our daughter in February, too."

"They look like they are teenagers."

"They are, replied Yvette.

Donna ordered soup and a sandwich.

A short time later, the waiter served her a cup of soup and a sandwich with some hot tea.

Yvette nudged Philip to get up so they could go back to their compartment.

Yvette said, "Philip we must let Donna eat in peace. Let us return to our compartment." Turning to Donna, she continued, "We have compartment "E" in car 122." Please visit us if you can."

"That's next to mine - I have compartment "D"."

"Good, later this afternoon we will expect you."

When Philip and Yvette stood up, she could see Philip was at least six feet one or two inches, muscular, had a large mustache, stood erect, and was quite agile for his age. Yvette was just a little more than petite, but she too showed she too was agile for her age and had some muscles also. Both had graying hair, but they were well groomed and extremely well mannered.

After Yvette and Philip were in their compartment, Yvette said, "Donna is a nice girl, but I suspect she was in some pain by the way she moved."

"I noticed that also, but we cannot pry - it's none of our business."

"You're right, but maybe we could help her."

"Maybe, but let's go to the Park Car for a while."

"Yes."

Just as Philip and Yvette were leaving their compartment, they looked down the passageway towards the diner and saw Donna standing in the corner waiting for three men to pass her.

The three men had just passed Philip and Yvette's compartment as they stood in the doorway to their compartment. All three men were cleanly dressed, but not too neat. Two of the men had their hair slicked back and in pony tails while the third man who one of the other men called Harry, had bushy hair about four inches long. He was the only one who did not look as if he had a haircut in a few weeks.

As the three men passed Donna, they pushed her to the wall and in addition to using their hands; they each rubbed himself against her.

Donna thought I am not going to let these bastards grope me and definitely not rape me - no I am not going to be raped again and she began to push them back, but they just shoved her back hard. Because she was still weak, she could not fight back the way she

362

wanted, so she just dropped to the floor in some pain and started to cry.

Seeing what was happening, Philip started to walk towards the men and yelled in a commanding voice, "Leave her alone."

With that, the three men walked away smiling and laughing.

Philip walked over and helped Donna to her feet. He held on to her arm with his left hand and put his right arm around her back. He held on to Donna a little longer than needed to help her up, but he released her as Yvette walked up to them.

Yvette asked, "Please don't think all Canadians are like those three. We just don't do things like that. Philip will tell the conductor and he will straighten them out."

Donna thought, I can't let them do that or it might let the police find me especially if I have to file charges.

"Oh please, it was nothing. Let it be. I'll just go to my room and rest for a while, but thanks for the help."

"Philip asked, "Are you sure?"

Donna answered, "Quite sure," as she entered her compartment.

Philip took Yvette's arm and began to lead her away. As soon as they were in the next coach and Philip was sure they could not be heard, he turned to Yvette and said, "That woman has enough muscle to be strong as an ox, but she is weak for some reason. She has well developed muscles. I believe she deliberately did not fight or she is too weak from an illness."

Yvette replied, "I hope she did not notice you held onto her a little extra, but did you see her eyes?

"I saw them. They were not of a woman who was afraid, but eyes of hate, eyes of steel..."

"They were the eyes of a killer - cold steel. We have seen such eyes in the past."

"Yes, my love. Her eyes were like yours in the Resistance - I am afraid we should know more about this young American. We must be on our guard also."

"I agree, Philip, but I think she is good and I like her. I wonder if she will ever give us her correct name."

"I don't know, pet, but I agree with you – I like her and I think

363

she is a good person in trouble."

Just after Donna closed the door, she thought Philip held on to me a little too long, but he was feeling my muscles and not groping me. I guess that was okay, but I will just have to watch myself on this train. Now, to get some rest. She noted the time was 2:15. Just before she sat in one of the two chairs, she reached for a pillow and placed it behind her head. Then she put her feet up on the second chair. She looked at the window, reached up and pulled the shade down, then closed her eyes.

As soon as Donna was asleep, the room was suddenly filled with a bright, yet soft, white light. The light had a warmth that encircled Donna as she rested with her eyes closed. For reasons she did not know, she felt, even with her eyes closed and half asleep, a warmth unlike anything else she had ever felt.

When she opened her eyes, she noticed the clock read 2:22, just seven minutes after she had closed her eyes. She also felt much better - in fact, she felt like all her strength had returned as well as her agility had completely returned. She thought this was strange, but as she moved around the compartment, she realized she was now completely healed and her strength had indeed returned to her.

I wonder...

Just then the room was engulfed with another bright light that consumed the entire room and a woman in a white gown appeared before her. The woman smiled at Donna and said, "Your strength has been returned to you as you will need it. There are four of them. Be careful."

Then the woman smiled again and disappeared.

Donna remembered her dream or previous vision and this was the same woman. She now knew her strength had been returned to her by God because she must be ready to use her skills. I wonder what she meant by "There are four of them." She sat down and took a few deep breaths, then got up and walked towards the Park Car. This time her legs were not weak and wobbly, but strong and she did not loose her balance easily although the train was still swaying as it moved along the tracks.

She now walked back three cars to the park car and then walked

364

up the steps to the dome and saw Philip and Yvette sitting in the rear seat by the steps. She sat across the aisle from them.

She said, "I feel much better now. I feel like I can lick the world."

Philip replied, "That's good. I have some good amaretto and wine in our compartment. Would you like some?"

Donna thought if I go to their compartment, I will get to know them better, then I will know if I can rely upon them.

She replied, "Sure. How about in a half hour?"

Yvette answered as she was getting out of her seat, "That will be fine Donna. We'll expect you by 3:15."

Philip and Yvette walked down the stairs with Donna thinking they are good people and I think I could rely on them, but I cannot tell them anything about me.

After Donna was safely on the train, Charlie drove towards the local Ford dealership. He went up to the used car division and spoke to a man dressed in a heavy, plaid shirt - much like a lumberjack.

"Sir, I wish to sell my truck. How much will you give me for this truck?"

The salesman immediately looked at Charlie and then looked at the truck. He thought this is a new truck. I bet it's stolen or something is wrong with it. He further thought, I better be careful.

"Have you got the title and papers?"

"Yes sir. And to answer your question why I am selling the truck, I just don't like it as much as I thought I would. I bought it in Vancouver several weeks ago. I don't know of anything wrong with it, but I just want to sell it."

The salesman looked at the title and shook his head. He said, "Mr...er ...Phillips, how much do you want for the truck?"

Charlie looked at the salesman, shrugged his shoulders and replied, "I don't want too much - $25,000.00 American."

The salesman looked at him knowing a great deal when he saw it, but trying to get Charlie's price down replied, "As soon as I have the title checked, I'll have your check drawn, but I don't think I can pay any more than $20,000.00 American...."

Charlie thought that SOB is starting to dicker - I can't wait for this and interrupted the salesman, "If you give me the money in cash, I'll take the $20,000.00, but no lower. I don't trust banks and also I want you to make payment in American."

Again, Charlie's request caused the salesman to raise his suspicions, but he had gotten an even better price than he thought he could get, so he replied, "Sure. You can pick up the money tomorrow morning anytime after 8:00 AM."

Charlie now said, "That'll be fine, but I need the truck until then. If you want to keep the truck, I'll need a loaner vehicle until tomorrow."

"You keep the truck while I check the title. See you tomorrow morning."

"Fine."

With that out of the way, Charlie got in the truck and began to drive back to his motel. While driving back to the motel, he began to think about his guns and gun case. If I get caught with a pistol in Canada, the authorities will certainly arrest me, but I have grown attached to my guns and the gun case – they're one of a kind - now how can I get it and my guns past the police and any inquisitive people?

I know, I will build a box for the case, take the guns out of the case and put them in some foam rubber that will surround the case in the box. Then encase the gun case in the box with more foam rubber so it won't be scratched and I'll just take the box with me on the bus. It'll be risky, but I want to keep my guns and gun case even though it reminds me of my past. Now to build the box....

It was a little after 3:15 when Donna knocked on the door of Philip and Yvette's compartment. It was Philip who opened the door.

"Come in, my dear."

"Thanks. It was real nice of you two to invite me to your compartment."

"Donna, first things first. Our names are Philip and Yvette Boudreaux. But please call us Philip and Yvette."

Donna smiled and replied, "My name is Donna Brown. Please

366

call me Donna." As an after thought, she continued, "You know if you wouldn't have introduced yourself, I guess I wouldn't ever have known your last names."

"What would you like to drink?"

"I think I would like a glass of red wine if you have some."

Yvette looked at Philip, smiled while saying, "I told you she had class and would want some wine."

"Yes pet, you did say she would want some wine." Turning to Donna, Philip continued, "You see Yvette is from France and I am from Canada. She likes her wine, especially wine from Bordeaux."

Philip poured Donna glass of red wine and another glass for Yvette. He then poured himself a glass of chilled amaretto.

Donna sipped her wine and said, "This is one good wine."

"It is my favorite. We take some where ever we go."

"It was her idea to do that because it is rare we can get the wine she likes when we travel."

"I hope you don't mind me asking, but how did you meet." Looking at Philip, she continued, "You said Yvette was from France and you were from Canada and I am just curious how you met."

Philip took a sip of his drink, looked at a smiling Yvette, then replied, "It all started when I was in the Canadian army during the war..."

"The Korean War?"

"She wasn't born yet my dear. Philip means the war - World War II. You must remember we think everyone knows when we say the war, we mean the big war."

"To continue, since I spoke French fluently, I could be smuggled into France and help the Resistance. Our story would not be complete without mentioning my friend John Singleton. We grew up together in Winnipeg. We are still best friends."

Yvette interrupted, "We live on a wheat farm north of Winnipeg and John and Marie own a small motel on highway 75 near a small town called Morris. Highway 75 goes to the United States from Winnipeg. We visit each other often, but we visit them a little more than they visit us because they cannot get people to watch their business for long periods of time."

"But to continue, my dear. John and I were selected to parachute into France to help train a certain Resistance group. So one night in late 1943, we landed in France. To our amazement, the first voice we heard was a German ordering us to lay on the ground with our hands above our heads. What else were we to do in the glare of truck headlights? I was pretty dejected because we were captured before we had a chance to start, much less complete our mission. As soon as we had lain down, the next sound we heard was the staccato of machine guns. We kept our heads down and when silence returned we raised our heads carefully..."

"I might add, very carefully and slowly."

"Now Yvette, if you want to tell the story, I'll let you continue."

Giggling, Yvette added, "You know, I just like to add a few things now and then."

"Well to continue, after we raised our heads we saw the most beautiful sight - two women along with four other Frenchmen, all with submachine guns looking at us. The first person I saw was Yvette and the first person John saw was Marie.

"Marie said and these two are going to teach us how to kill Germans?Yvette answered well they are supposed to teach us something. Then all the people laughed. What I learned later was they had set a trap for the Germans and we were the bait. After learning that, I could have killed every one of them, but eventually everything turned out fine.

"Over the next nine months, we worked closely and we learned from each other and in June 1944 when the invasion took place, we did our part by blowing up bridges to slow any reinforcements going to Normandy."

Yvette interrupted, "In late September, our village was liberated - and by the Americans. They were so nice - they gave us food and medical help all the time.

Philip interrupted Yvette, "John and I reported to the American unit which liberated us and they began to make arrangements for us to report to a combat unit.

"We had grown close to Yvette and Marie. Almost three months later after we had won the Battle of the Bulge, our orders finally arrived..."

Yvette interrupted, "Marie and I grabbed them and took them to our priest who married us. That was a glorious night, wasn't it?"

"A glorious night, pet!"

"Anyway, the next day they left vowing to return. Marie and I thought we would never see them again, but three weeks after the Germans surrendered, they showed up in our village. They took us back to Canada with them. By the way, I was pregnant with our first child from that night. I was so happy and still am."

"Yvette hasn't told you everything about her Resistance group. She was the leader and she killed more Germans and saved more people in her village than anyone else. I am very proud of her actions during the war. Now, we have told you about us, tell us a little about you."

Donna had sat with her eyes wide open listening to Philip and Yvette telling their tale as to how they met. She thought now it was her turn, but where to start. I can't tell them the whole truth - I guess I'll start with the shoot out.

"I guess my life started when I was accidentally shot and my husband prayed over my body for my recovery. I went to Hell, but was returned to my body - you know, an out-of-body experience. After that, my husband and I took a trip to Jasper. Then, he received some information and he had to leave me and I am taking the train to Winnipeg. I am taking this trip to recover from my wounds. That's about all there is from dullsville."

"How long ago were you shot, Donna?"

"Just before Thanksgiving, Yvette."

"Love, let's pick up Donna when we go for dinner and we can eat together and talk again."

Donna rose from her seat and said, "I'd like that. I'll be in my room when you're ready."

Donna left the compartment and returned to her room.

After Donna had left their compartment, Yvette said, "Philip, she doesn't want us to know her past, and I feel we should not press her for information. Did you see her eyes?"

"Yes pet. They were your eyes of forty years ago - loving, yet

when they had to be, cold steel, the eyes of a killer – a resistance
fighter."

"I agree, love."

As the train sped through the countryside on its way to
Winnipeg, Donna was looking out her window at the sunset and
noting the mercury vapor lights were turning on automatically at
many of the farms the train passed. She thought I can even see into
the farmhouses and what they are doing - eating, reading or talking.
This gets very personal. I wonder if they realize they can be seen
and so easily. And if I can see them, I wonder if they can see me in
the train. I doubt it – the train's moving too fast for them to see
anything. So much for privacy.

CHAPTER 6

Donna was listening to the clackity-clack of the train's wheels over the railroad tracks as it sped along the tracks and at the same time, noting the swaying of the coach as the train's speed picked up and slowed down. The swaying motion was much like being in a small boat on water with medium wave action, but not quite as bad. She wondered if the steward had any seasickness pills for the passengers who got motion sickness. He could dispense or even sell, but...

A knock at her door interrupted her thoughts. She got up and went to the door. "Who is it?"

The happy voice of Yvette replied, "It is I, Yvette."

Donna opened the door and looked into the sparkling eyes of Yvette. Yvette saw something in Donna's eyes, but could not recognize what she saw.

"Give me less than a minute."

As Donna turned to go to the chair where she had her purse, Yvette stepped into the room as another person was passing in the passageway. Donna turned abruptly and with some agility to face Yvette which startled Yvette.

"I was just getting out of the way for those people to pass."

"I'm sorry, but when you stepped into my room, you startled me and I guess I just reacted."

"That's all right. You know, years ago I would have reacted as you did, but I guess I am getting a little older. Let's go to the diner where Philip is."

As they were walking towards the diner, Yvette thought Donna had recovered awfully fast for her weakened condition that she demonstrated when she was cornered by those three men. Continuing her thoughts - I don't think it would be wise for those men to attempt to push this woman around again or they will be very surprised.

Philip was sitting at a table when Yvette and Donna walked into the diner. It was strange, but Donna sat by the window and instead of Yvette sitting next to Philip, she sat next to Donna. Donna noted this, as did Philip.

Donna shrugged her shoulders and Philip just looked at Yvette knowing full well that she must have a good reason. He would find out later he thought.

The train moved through a short tunnel with Philip saying, "A tunnel, pet."

Yvette replied, "Yes, love."

They all ordered the same thing - vegetable soup and roast turkey, sweet potatoes and beans. For desert they would have ice cream.

Just as the waiter was returning from the kitchen with their order, the three men who groped Donna came into the diner. The man, who seemed to be the leader looked at Donna, spoke to the other two men and all three laughed. It was quite obvious that they were laughing at Donna and what they did earlier in the day.

Donna was doing a fast boil. She began to get up, but Yvette reached over and caught her arm just above the wrist with some strength. She now felt Donna's muscles for the first time and even though Yvette was in her sixties, Donna could feel she was strong for her age.

"Dear, they are not worth it. You will only get yourself in trouble and you might even get put off the train. And anyway, it has been my experience that people like that always seem to place themselves in harm's way sometime in the future."

Donna, realizing Yvette's advice was good, began to sit down while saying, "I certainly hope so!" and thought I hope I am the harm's way.

Now Philip turned to look at the men, frowned at them as much as to say leave us alone and if you don't, it won't be as easy as it was earlier.

Donna looked at Yvette and thought she's right for reasons she doesn't even know. I can't get involved with the police, but if those bastards even think about doing that to me again, I'll destroy their manhood and make them "its"...gee I hope they try it ...that would be fun.

Again, Yvette and Philip saw Donna's eyes. It was Yvette who spoke, "Donna, dear, forgive me and Philip but we have noticed your eyes. They are loving one minute and cold steel the next. We suspect you can take care of yourself extremely well, but I suspect it has something to do with your "out-of-body" experience, yes?"

What Yvette said surprised Donna, but answered, "You two are very perceptive. I am trying not to get my blood pressure up and you saved me from myself just a minute ago. And yes, your suspicions are correct."

Yvette smiled, "We had to be perceptive while in the Resistance."

Just as Yvette had finished talking, the waiter walked up with their soup. They began to eat, but Donna and Yvette watched the three men. Donna noted Yvette's eyes had somehow changed to...for want of a better description, to those of a Resistance fighter about to do battle with the Germans. She noted Philip's attitude had changed also.

Arthur stopped by the table where the three men were sitting and began to talk to them. Neither Donna, Yvette, nor Philip could hear what they were talking about.

As if a light was turned on in Donna, she thought that's what Martha meant. There are four of those jerks, not just three. Is the fourth man Arthur? Also, what in the hell are they doing on this train?"

Arthur left their table and walked over to another table to talk. Donna watched Arthur as he walked to another table and began to talk to them. She decided Arthur was just being sociable with the passengers who were in the diner. If Arthur isn't the fourth man, who is?

After eating their dinner, Donna, Yvette, and Philip got up and were walking by the three men on their way to their compartments. The man, who was their leader and while reading a list of names, deliberately stuck his foot out to trip Donna, but received a different response than before.

With some agility, Donna sidestepped his foot and stepped on his foot with her left foot with some force. Pulling his foot back, the man screamed in pain.

Donna immediately became solicitous of the man.

"O dear, please excuse me. I didn't mean to step on your foot. Are you hurt? Let me look at it. I know a little first aid. You should get some ice and put on it."

Philip and Yvette stepped between Donna and the other two men effectively preventing them from getting up and coming to the aid of the man whose foot Donna had stepped on.

The man looked up at Donna, and said, "That's okay. I think it's just a bruise."

"I'm so glad," Donna said, but really thought damn only a bruise - I had hoped to really hurt him. I'm slipping. All this while she was smiling at him.

Donna, Yvette, and Philip now walked back to their rooms. As Donna left the Boudreaux's compartment, Yvette smiled at Donna and asked, "Are you happy now?"

Donna smiled while replying, "I feel a little better."

After Philip and Yvette had closed the door to their room, Philip said, "You know, I believe we saved those three men from being beat to a pulp."

"Yvette replied, "I think so too. As you have noticed, she is very strong."

Donna was now in her room when she began to think what were those men doing with that list - I think it was the passenger list and where the passenger's sleeping quarters are - why do they have that and who gave it to them. There must be a fourth man.

After the incident, the three men began to talk to one another.

Harry spoke to David, the leader, "When are we going to do it? I'd like to get that old couple, you know the Boudreaux's for standing in my way preventing me from getting another chance at that gal - you know Donna."

"Tomorrow morning, before breakfast and I am going to screw that bitch before I get off this train and then I'm going to...maybe take her with me so I can screw her again and again..."

He began to laugh as did Harry and Sid.

"Maybe I'll let the two of you have her after I'm finished."

Harry and Sid nodded their heads like they would like that.

Sid replied for both himself and Harry, "That would be just delectable."

Harry added, "I just want to beat that old man up and maybe hit the woman a little." He giggled. Harry was the youngest of the three and obviously trying to impress David and Sid by his remarks because he wanted to be "in" with them. However, he was not succeeding at impressing them.

David now started to speak, "This is how we do it. Tomorrow morning when the diner opens for breakfast, we wait until a number of people are in here eating, then we start at the Park Car and work our way forward to the diner going into their rooms. We take what they have left in their compartments and take anything of value. After we've finished getting what they left in their rooms, we'll come here and take what they have on them. That will put the train about where we need to get off. After that, we go for the kid.

Sid asked, "How sure are you that he's on board?"

"Sid, trust me. Walker's grandson is on board along with Walker himself. Roger gave us the passenger list didn't he and Walker and the kid's name are on the list, aren't they?"

"But will this Walker pay the ransom?"

"Walker is a billionaire and it's his only grandson. He'll pay. Remember, he can't have any more blood line grandchildren. He'll pay and pay a great deal of money! Also remember this, Roger won't get involved unless we have trouble. We'll take the key Roger gave us to unlock the doors of the locked compartments.

"Now, again all three of us will start from the rear of the train,

375

making sure no one can use any radio to contact the engine as we work our way forward. And remember - this is important - we must make it look like this is just a train robbery at least until we grab the kid. Any questions?"

Harry answered quickly, "We've got it down pat."

"I hope so kid."

Mike had just walked in his house as Lisa was walking from the kitchen to the living room.

"Hi honey. Today was a day to end all days. Gene came into my office and started on me about your inheritance. Then Tom started. Soon everyone in the office had his say."

"You knew that was going to happen. I had some good news from our lawyer. He said as long as there is a death certificate stating that Charlie is dead and his will says what we have been told, there is nothing anyone can do. We are rich darling!"

"Even if Charlie faked his death and is alive?"

"The lawyer didn't go into that possibility very much, but he reiterated if there is a death certificate..."

"I guess that's all he can say. The more I think about it, the more certain I am that Charlie and Donna are still alive...somewhere in Canada. I wish I knew where they were heading."

"Now quit worrying. Where would you like to take us to celebrate?"

"I don't know, but I want to talk to you before we go anywhere. I received a call from Ed Lasard today?"

"Ed Lasard? Who's that - Oh I remember. He's the father of the girl Uncle Frank rescued."

"That's right. I had asked the RCMP to look for Charlie and Donna. The request came across his desk and he called me to tell me what results they have obtained so far. He said a couple that fits the description of Charlie and Donna stayed in a motel near the Canadian border for a couple of days, then left to go possibly to Victoria, but they couldn't find them there. So they are looking northward towards Edmonton and he will let me know what they find after they complete their search.

"He also gave me some advice. Retire from the department before it really gets to me."

"Why would it get to you after the number of years you have put in?

"I haven't told you yet, but Gene came in to tell us the IRS has Louis for tax evasion and will put him in jail for at least 3 to 5 years. They investigated him because I suggested they do. Great, huh - putting your cousin in jail!"

Sensing Mike was getting depressed over his job, Lisa responded in an unconvincing tone of voice to support her husband, "You're only doing your job, honey."

"Yeah, but putting our cousin in jail. That is just not my cup of tea. And second, Charlie. You know he was the one who saved you from Deng. Now I have to go after him because everything points to him being the Iceman. Police work just isn't fun anymore."

Suddenly realizing that Mike might have to arrest Charlie and Donna if he succeeds in finding Charlie and then Charlie might be executed for being the Iceman, Lisa now came to appreciate Mike's thoughts.

"I was thinking, honey. If we could use some of that inheritance, I could retire from the department and we could move to Idaho. We could buy a tree farm - you know grow blue spruce and Christmas trees or do something else. You could get a part time job nursing in Spokane or in a small clinic.

"I understand if we farm about a hundred acres, that will support us and I won't have to work as hard. The only catch is the first crop won't be for four years.

"That also means I won't have to go after Charlie or make any more suggestions as to how to get Louis and I wouldn't have the pressure on me to get convictions - I would unload all, well most of my stress. What do you think?"

"What you have said sounds pretty good to me. Let's take our vacation next month and look into it. We do have some friends in Idaho plus two people who I think will help us all they can because of Charlie – you know, Sam and Hank. But what are you going to do about Louis? Are you going to tell him or what?"

"I thought I wouldn't tell him, but he is a relative. I plan to call him tonight right after supper.

The telephone rang in Louis Giaventi's house. Louis answered the phone himself, "Hello."

"Louis, this is Mike and I have some bad news. It seems the IRS has uncovered sufficient evidence to charge you with filing fraudulent tax returns over the past three or four years. I just wanted..."

Louis interrupted Mike, "That's great, Mike. I'm going to tell you something nobody else knows. I want out of the family. This might give me the one chance I have to get out. The only problem is Tony Andratti will probably take over. He acts too quickly and I think he would start a gang war - a bad one - but if I can get out and that is the only way out, then I'll do it. I think...I have some planning to do Mike. If the IRS comes tomorrow, I'll have to have everything in order. Thanks for the information. Bye."

While hanging up the telephone, Mike turned to Lisa, "Honey, Louis wasn't mad at all, in fact he seemed happy the IRS was going to arrest him. He also said he was thinking of getting out of the family, but he is sad that Tony Andratti would take over. Now that's a switch."

Charlie had just finished making the box to hide his gun case and his guns. It wasn't anything special - just a box with foam rubber in all the right places. He found out it was a little heavy, but he would have to carry it - there was no other way.

Charlie now went to the bus station to find out when the bus left. The ticket agent told him the bus left at 11:00 AM. That meant he would have to be there for 10:30 to load the box onto the bus. The bus would take until 10:00 PM to get to Calgary because the bus would stop at a good many small towns and Calgary was on Mountain Time and not Pacific Time. He would lose one hour because of the time difference. Also, he could not risk making a reservation on an airline or train because they would require his name. After he was in Calgary, he would stop for a short time and make plans as to how he would enter the States.

378

He looked at the clock. It said 10:30 PM. He thought he would have to get some sleep because he had a big day the following day, sell the truck then get on the bus to Calgary. Only after he was on the bus could he relax and that was only for the seven or so hours it would take to get to Calgary.

CHAPTER 7

It was 6:00 AM when Harry, Sid, and David woke up and got dressed for the day. They carefully hid their pistols under their coats. By the time they had dressed and were ready to go to the Park Car, it was almost 7:00 AM. They had to wait until 7:20 AM to begin their walk towards the diner to rob the passengers and to kidnap the young Walker. Harry and Sid began to eat the rolls that had been made for the passengers in the Park Car. David just sat in a comfortable chair not eating anything, eyeing everybody who was in the lounge part of the car.

Donna woke up early because she wanted to take a bath on the train before she got off at Winnipeg. She would have to decide what she was going to do at that time. She was glad she had bought a robe to wear, but she now realized she had no slippers.

She thought what can I wear - I know, I'll wear the boots, tie the shoelaces loosely and not put any socks on. She had not taken a bath in two days and except to put on her pajamas, she had not changed her clothes in that time. She reached in her duffel, got some clean underclothes and wrapped them in the towel that was furnished in the compartment. She then looked around the compartment. She was sure she was leaving something behind. She had it - her blue jeans and shirt.

As she was going to get the blue jeans and shirt, the ladder to the upper bunk got in her way.

She said in a quiet whisper, "Damn. I'll take care of that ladder."

381

With those words, she removed the ladder from the clamp that held it firmly attached to the upper bunk and placed the ladder on the top bunk. Immediately after placing the ladder on the top bunk, she picked up her towel and left the compartment for the shower forgetting her blue jeans and her shirt.

As she was walking to the shower, a sense of concern came over her. She put it out of her mind as she entered the shower. She locked the door, and took her robe off and became upset with herself as she now realized she had indeed forgotten her clothing back in her compartment.

Again, she whispered, "Damn" and thought I'll just dress in the room instead of here in the shower.

She completely undressed and got into the shower, turned the temperature control almost to hot and pressed the lever to get water.

What she got was anything but hot - in fact it was cold. She jumped back out of the shower stall and thought that was really cold. Why? Arthur said they had hot water. I remember - he said it takes time for the hot water to get here - at least I hope that's the reason. The lever had returned to its original position and the water stopped.

Standing outside of the shower, Donna pressed the lever again. Again, cold water came out of the showerhead, but just as the water was stopping, the water became warm. She thought the next water would be hot or at least warm. She got in the shower stall and pressed the lever. True to what she had thought, the water was indeed hot. She made an adjustment on the temperature control and now the water was the right temperature for her to take her shower. She soaped herself and took her shower. Donna had to press the lever two more times to complete her shower and rinse the soap off her body.

She got out of the shower stall, dried herself, and put on her clean panties and bra. She then put on clean socks and her boots and through habit, laced them tightly. Next she put on her robe and opened the door and walked to her compartment.

By this time, David, Harry, and Sid had begun to rob the passengers and had worked their way to car 122, Donna's car. David was getting anxious because of what he thought he was going to do to Donna. Harry was getting nervous as he had never done anything like this before, but he said he would beat up Philip so he would have to do that to make believers out of David and Sid.

There was barely enough room between the bunks and the wall for Donna to move, but there was a little room. She could turn around without touching the bunk or the wall and do some things in front of the mirror. She removed her robe and had just placed her right foot on the lower bunk to untie the laces on her boot so she could put on her blue jeans. Donna was about to cuss because she had tied them so tight when the door burst open.

Donna looked up and saw David with a pistol.

Her thoughts and her words were the same, "Shit."

When David saw her, he did not realize Donna was extremely good in defending herself using karate and most important, she had regained all of her strength. She was not the weak, frail woman who dropped to the floor and cried when he fondled her, but she was what some people would say the best enforcer ever.

He said, "Damn, you knew I was coming for you so you started to get ready for me." And now in an authoritative tone of voice he ordered, "Take your panties and bra off for me. I like my women naked when..."

Just then the train lurched and threw him slightly off balance so the pistol was pointed away from Donna for a split second. He spread his legs apart to stabilize himself.

In that moment of time, Donna's right foot came quickly down and hit the floor with a thud and at the same time, she drove her left leg high in a karate kick which hit David's hand that held the gun.

David let out a sort of a quiet yell because his hand was somewhat hurt when the boot on her left foot hit his hand catapulting the pistol up to the ceiling. The pistol hit the ceiling with a loud thud, then dropped on the top bunk. Somehow, it missed the ladder that Donna had placed on the top bunk.

With this turn of events all David's thoughts were not good as he looked at Donna who was grinning from ear to ear. He realized what was coming next and said, "Crap". His eyes told the story – he knew what was coming next as his legs were wide apart to stable himself and he was afraid of what was coming.

He did not have long to wait for Donna's reaction and her Taekwondo-Karate moves.

He was now looking at Donna's face with a sly grin on it as the pistol was falling onto the upper bunk, Donna's left foot came down to the floor where Donna would have leverage for her next kick. Donna executed the same move except with different feet and a different target. Her right foot came up with as much force as she could muster. The foot struck exactly where she intended it to strike - between his legs - in his groin striking his gonads.

David's eyes all but popped out of their sockets as he uttered an almost inaudible groan because of the pain he now experienced. He just crumpled to the floor in a kneeling position, holding his gonads. Donna now struck him in the face with several karate blows and with the last blow from her fists, she hit him in the front part of his neck. This made him gasp for air as he could not breathe easily now. He released his grasp on his male organs and grasped his throat.

Next, in a deliberate manner and while still hearing his choking sounds because of the blow to his neck and his moans from the beating she had administered to him, she deliberately laced her fingers together behind his head. Now she pulled his head down towards the floor with as much force as she could and at the same time brought her right knee up to meet his face, again with as much force as she could muster. When her knee met his face it became a mass of blood as his nose was immediately broken along with several other facial bones.

Normally David wouldn't be happy to receive such a blow, but much to David's delight with this blow he was rendered unconscious and thus he was out of pain - at least for a little while.

David was now lying on the floor on his stomach with Donna standing over him. As she was just about to come crashing down on his spine with the heel of her boot which would have broken his back possibly killing him, she thought why do that, give him a little slack. Let the police have him.

She reached up to where she had the first aid kit and removed the adhesive tape from the kit. Next she wrapped his hands together and then his feet. Next she taped his mouth so he could not scream. She now grabbed, lifted, shoved, and even dragged him onto the lower bunk. He was sure heavy, she thought.

Donna took a deep breath and thought I need help. I sure hope Yvette and Philip will help...maybe they're in trouble. With those thoughts, she quickly slipped on her blue jeans and reached for a blouse, but stopped when she thought I might have to hide the pistol.

She now looked through her clothes and selected a blouse that was as loosely fitting as she had with her. Now she reached for the pistol. It was an old colt 45 automatic. It felt good in her hand - like an old friend.

Donna looked out the door to the left, then to the right to see if any other people were in the passageway. She heard a voice, Philip's voice, "Son, don't do this. You're too young to get so involved and go to jail."

"Look you old son-of-a-bitch, you're going to get what you deserve right now."

Donna had just quietly walked in behind Harry as he said those words.

Yvette was looking behind Harry and saw Donna coming into her compartment with a pistol in her hand, "I think you are the one who is going to be surprised and get what you deserve, young man."

Harry turned to look at Yvette and said, "After I beat your husband up, I'll get to you..."

Before he could finish the sentence, Donna grabbed his bushy hair and with a great deal of force, pulled his head back until the pistol was jammed into the bottom part of his head at the top part of the back of his neck.

In a commanding, yet quiet voice, Donna said, "Give Philip the gun or I will blow your head away at the count of three and your face will go all over Yvette."

Harry was now scared. He had not expected this turn of events. He was in danger of being killed.

"One!"

Yvette smiled, "You poor fool. She will kill you when she counts three - don't you know that."

He looked at Yvette and became even more frightened. "Two!"

With the count reaching two, he released his grip on the pistol and Philip grabbed the gun.

Yvette interrupted and spoke to Philip, "Just like the old days, my love."

"Yes, but I still don't like it."

Donna handed the rest of the adhesive tape to Yvette. She showed her abilities and agility by wrapping Harry's hands very quickly, then without ceremony, pushed him down on the bunk.

His head hit the top bunk and he yelled, "That hurt."

Philip replied, "Be glad that is the only thing she did to hurt you. She has killed many people in the war and punks like you aren't nearly as good as some of the Germans she took care of."

Yvette wrapped his legs with almost the rest of the tape, saving a little strip for Harry's mouth.

Philip now turned his attention to Donna. "Thank you. What's going on?"

"Well, I know there are four of them..."

"How do you know?"

"You wouldn't believe me if I told you, but believe me, there are four of them. I don't know who the fourth one is, so we must be careful. If David wakes up, he will moan and groan even though he is all tied up in my compartment. Let's go to the diner and see if we can't get them to radio ahead to the police."

"Good idea," came the response from Yvette.

Philip had Harry's gun. It was a 9mm that had maybe a fifteen shot capacity. He was holding it as if he knew how to use it. He went first, followed by Yvette and then by Donna.

The three of them moved towards the turn in the passageway and just as Philip turned the corner, the train lurched to one side. At the same time, Sid who had just entered the coach from the other end of the coach, fired his pistol in the passageway, but his bullets missed their mark and went through one of the windows in the side of the coach.

Donna having her pistol in her hand when she left the

compartment whirled around and went into a crouched position and holding the gun with two hands, fired two shots.

The first shot hit Sid in the right shoulder throwing him back against the wall of the coach and causing him to drop his pistol. The second shot slammed into his right leg just below the knee causing him to fall to the floor screaming in pain.

Philip and Yvette turned around just a split second after Donna had fired her first shot and before she fired the second shot. Yvette and Philip saw the results of Donna's shooting.

Philip said, "I think your fourth man will show himself now because he knows these men will talk and he will be discovered."

"I think you are right, dear."

"I agree. Let's go to the diner for help."

As Philip started to move towards the diner, he saw Roger who had just entered the coach pulling a little boy with him with the door slamming closed behind them. Roger saw Philip and immediately pulled the boy in front of him and placed his gun to the head of the boy.

Philip deliberately took aim at Roger's head and said, "That doesn't work with me."

Roger sensing Philip was going to shoot, pushed the boy towards Philip to knock Philip off balance and fired his pistol, just nicking Philip's left arm. Philip fired, hitting Roger in the right chest, slamming him back towards the door.

All four of the would be kidnappers were now helpless.

This gave Donna time to think. She turned to Yvette and said, "Yvette. Please don't ask any questions, but I can't get involved with the police and I must return to the states. Will you help me?"

Yvette looked at Donna's pleading eyes, shook her head, and responded, "Hand me your pistol."

Donna sensing Yvette was going to help her, gave her the pistol.

Immediately Yvette fired three shots through two more windows.

"Everyone will believe a Resistance fighter when she says she shot the man back there, especially when the paraffin test proves she fired a gun. You are an excellent shot, my dear."

"I was just lucky."

Yvette smiled and responded, "Luck? Your bullets hit exactly where you were aiming. Don't try to kid an old woman who has seen a good many shots being fired. But now, I must help that poor man you shot. Please help Philip. He doesn't have a serious wound."

"Sure...and thanks!"

CHAPTER 8

Donna went to where Philip was standing to look at his arm. She immediately saw Yvette was right. It was only a flesh wound - a scratch. He was now standing over Roger who had a very serious wound. Donna stooped down to look at Roger.

"You have a bad one, Roger. Maybe you shouldn't have started this thing."

She took a deep breath, reached in her pocket, and produced a handkerchief. Next she reached for his shirt and tore it off him as gently as possible, exposing his wound. It was not bleeding very much, but she knew there must be internal bleeding. She lowered her head a little bit and prayed for his recovery.

Before she had finished her prayer, another man came from the diner. He was one of the waiters.

"I've contacted the conductor up front. He's coming now."

The waiter looked at Philip and saw he was wounded, but he was also holding a gun.

Philip smiled and said, "Don't be afraid, I won't hurt you." Slightly waiving the pistol he continued, "I took this from another man who tried to rob Yvette and me. He is tied up in our compartment. Do not let him loose. There is another one in the compartment next to mine."

Philip had diverted his attention from Donna. The waiter did not recognize her because she was on her knees with her back to him tending to Roger.

The waiter returned to the diner with the boy.

Donna got up and went to see if she could help Yvette, but she met Yvette coming towards her who pulled her into Donna's compartment.

Yvette called to Philip, "Sweet, leave him there and come here. We have to talk."

From the tone of her voice, Philip knew Yvette meant now, so he got up from kneeling beside Roger and walked back not to their compartment, but to Donna's compartment where Yvette and Donna were.

"What do you want, my pet?"

"We must help Donna. She cannot get involved with the police and she must return to the states."

Philip thought for a moment, then replied, "The second part will be easy. We are coming to Portage la Prairie. Donna, you will get off with me when the train stops there. I will call John and Marie and they will take care of you from there. I will then call the local police to report what has happened and wait for them to arrive." "Then," nodding to Yvette, "I will rejoin you on the train.

"It is the first part which will be difficult. Let's see, Donna must have gotten off the train before the kidnapping and robbery attempt. Let's say she got off the train at Saskatoon - yes without anyone knowing she got off."

Yvette continued, "And the reason we know she got off the train was I couldn't sleep last night and I was walking the passageway in my night gown and robe when she left the train. That takes care of everything except who did this to this poor excuse for a man over on Donna's lower bunk and who put the gun to the head of our man in our compartment?"

Philip answered, "My dear, would it be too much to ask you to wake this person up and inform him Donna was kind to him when she did not...let me say emasculate him by cutting everything off he has between his legs. If he does not agree that I did this to him, I will finish what has been started and he might wish he would have died at Donna's hands."

"I think a better way would be for me just to take care of the

390

loose ends now and not worry about him talking."

Donna now entered the conversation, "Please don't kill him. I shouldn't have hurt him that much," but smiling, she continued, "but as you said, people like that usually place themselves in harms way. There has to be another way."

Yvette answered, "I will take care of him. Philip, you will think of something to tell that young man in our room. The other two wounded won't say anything because they couldn't have recognized Donna."

A balding man who appeared to be in his late sixties walked up to the door.

"My name is Walker. I want you to know I appreciate what you did very much - rescuing my grandson. How can I repay you for saving my grandson?"

Yvette and Philip knowing who Walker was just looked at each other and smiled.

It was Philip who spoke. "Mr. Walker, we have a slight problem. I was responsible for Roger down the hall, but Donna here is the true heroine because she captured or I should say rendered three of them unable to continue their kidnapping attempt, but she has a problem.

"She cannot meet with the police for her own reasons and since she helped us and we believe she is a good person, we have decided to help her in her endeavors. To that end, we have, no we are developing a story which might solve her problem. I'm sure she would appreciate any help you can give in this regard if you would back..."

Walker replied, "I will do more than that. I will secure the passenger list and have her name deleted."

"No, but it would be better if she had bought a ticket only to Saskatoon."

"So be it. From where?"

Yvette answered, "Jasper to Saskatoon."

"Done. As soon as I can use the phone."

"Yvette, Philip, even with Mr. Walker's help it won't wash. Any cop worth being called a cop would see through that story in a moment."

Now Mr. Walker spoke, "My dear, I didn't get to be exceedingly wealthy because I did not use my influence where I wanted and was gentle with those who opposed me. Now dear, I do not mind using the influence I have acquired over the years to return the most - no the greatest favor ever done for me. I will see to it that you have nothing to fear from the police. I guess you would call them the Mounties."

Donna looking at a smiling Walker was reassured, but she realized they might be able to give her maybe only a couple of hours or at best a couple of days head start.

She began to pack her clothes in her duffel bag that could be used as a backpack. Philip and Mr. Walker left the room leaving Yvette alone with Donna.

Yvette saw Donna pull the $20,000.00 from its hiding place and put it in her fanny pack. She also saw the money she had in the fanny pack before she placed additional money there.

"Dear, is the reason you do not want the police to find you connected to that money?"

"No. This was given to me by my husband. Please..."

"Dear, I must know more about you. Why are you running away from the police?"

Feeling that she must tell her something, Donna replied, "I can only tell you this. I was once an employee for the mob - you know, the Mafia in San Francisco. After being shot and dying, my journey into Hell changed all that and my husband faked our deaths. There are some police who do not believe we are dead and they are still looking for us. We cannot be found. And Yvette, my husband is not on this train. Please don't ask any more questions."

Yvette smiled and replied, "You have told me enough. Your eyes have told me you speak the truth. They also told me you were very good at what you did."

The train was slowing down for Portage la Prairie. Philip now returned to the compartment.

"My dear, it is time we get ready to depart from this train."

Donna walked to the door of her coach and stood in the

392

doorway. Philip motioned her to step back so he could open the floor and expose the steps.

"Now my dear, you must listen very carefully to what I am going to tell you. Find the north - south road and travel it south until you come to an east - west road at Jordan - that's highway 23. Turn east or left and continue to walk until you reach highway 75. That's the highway to the United States. You may see John and Marie's motel signs along the highway, but you will see their motel at the intersection of Highways 75 and 23. The name of their motel is "The Canadian". It is a nice motel - no going's on there. They will help you.

"If someone asks if you are Donna Brown while you are walking, reply truthfully and if there are two people in the vehicle, ask them if they are the Singletons or if only one person is driving, ask that one if he or she is John or Marie. If they reply yes, then you are safe with our friends."

The train had just come to a complete stop. Yvette appeared in the doorway.

"Go with God, my dear." Yvette embraced Donna and kissed her on the check.

Donna returned the embrace and kiss. She then embraced Philip and kissed him on the lips.

Yvette spoke, "That's enough. He's my pet, you know." Then laughed. Philip and Donna laughed with Yvette.

"I will miss you - both of you. If I get the chance, I will look you up later. Thanks for all you have done for me." As an after thought, Donna said, "As you might have guessed, Brown is not my real name, but if I am able to see you later, I will tell you my real name and more about my situation."

Yvette answered, "That would be nice to know your correct name, but we look at the person and not just one's name."

With those words, Yvette and Donna embraced one more time, and then Donna went to the stairs.

By this time Philip had gone down the stairs and had turned back towards the coach to help Donna down the steps that were high off the ground. Donna climbed down the steps and was thankful for

Philip's help as he took her duffel. Philip motioned to the left where he saw a telephone just outside the station near an entrance to the station. They walked over to the telephone booth. Philip placed two coins in the telephone and dialed a number. Donna listened to his side of the conversation.

Philip said, "Marie, I do not have much time. Yvette and I want you to take care of a very deserving young woman. She must be returned to the United States without the authorities noting her arrival there or departure from here.

"Do you understand? Yes, just like the Resistance. Her name is Donna Brown. She has no distinguishing features except she is very distinguished.

"Yes, very good looking. I have told her. She will be walking on the north - south highway. Thank you. You will see what I mean. Either Yvette or I will explain later when it is possible. Watch the news tonight. Good bye and thank you again."

Philip hung up the telephone and turned to Donna. "I know Yvette and I have said good bye, but...go with God, my dear. He will never let you down."

He placed a kiss on Donna's forehead.

Donna turned and just walked away from the train and into the small town. Philip watched her for a few seconds, then turned and walked into the station and over to the small RCMP office in the station.

Donna thought she was safe - at least for the present. She easily found the north - south highway and started to walk south on the highway. She also began to wonder why she felt better by not killing the two men on the train. She knew she had not lost any of her talents because of what she did on the train. She was still wondering as she began her walk south on the north-south highway where she hoped she would meet Philip and Yvette's friends.

As Philip walked up to the office, he thought the train will have more police and medical help on the train than what is actually needed in a short time - as soon as he tells his story.

He walked up to the open counter and started to speak to a red coated, uniformed officer. "Sir, there has been a shooting on the train..."

Charlie went to the car dealership to deliver his truck and get paid for it. The salesman was eagerly waiting for Charlie because he wanted to buy the truck for his own use. When he saw Charlie drive up with the truck, he waived to him.

Charlie stepped out of the cab into a waiting handshake from an excited salesman.

"Let's go into the office and get your money. I want you to know it took a lot of effort, but I got your money just as we agreed."

"Good, I have one more request. Drop me off at the totem pole by the train station. I have someone picking me up there."

Not thinking about whether Charlie was telling the truth or not, replied, "Sure. Now let's get this deal closed."

After Charlie had the money and had placed it in his fanny pack, the salesman drove the truck and Charlie to the train station where the totem pole was. Charlie got out and pulled the wood box out of the truck's bed.

"Thanks for the ride."

"Have a safe trip, my friend."

Charlie thought he doesn't give a damn about me. He just knows he made a killing on the deal. The jerk.

Now Charlie picked up the box and walked over to the bus station that was in or people might say, next to the train station.

He walked up to the ticket agent. "I want to check this box. It's sort of heavy."

"The box is a little big. What's in it?"

"I have my gun case in it. It's very special and I have it encased in foam rubber. I'm quite proud of it. Want to see it?"

The ticket agent looked at Charlie and replied, "I've got a little time. Sure."

Charlie took the hammer he used to make the box and pried the top boards open. He lifted the top foam rubber from the case to expose the gun case. He reached into the box and retrieved the case. The foam rubber beneath the case hid his guns from the ticket agent.

The ticket agent whistled. "That's the best looking gun case I

395

have ever seen. I can see why you wanted to protect it. Would you mind if someone else saw it?"

"No."

"I'll be back in a minute."

With those words, the ticket agent left Charlie and went in the room back of the ticket counter.

After several people had looked at the gun case and admired it, Charlie replaced the case in the foam rubber and nailed the boards securely.

Charlie smiled with pride and with the knowledge he had passed the first test to get his gun case and guns back to the states with him.

He got in line to board the bus and watched the ticket agent carrying the box to the bus with his name on the box and ticket so he could get the box when he arrived in Calgary. The bus driver started to let passengers on the bus while he took the tickets.

When Charlie walked up to give him his ticket, he asked, "Are you the guy with the gun case?"

Charlie replied, "Yes, did you see it?"

"No, but several people said it was beautiful," while pointing to the ticket agent.

Charlie breathed a sigh of relief and boarded the bus. The bus was eleven minutes late and just before he sat in the driver's seat and started the engine, the driver said, "Folks, we are a little late leaving here, but I think I can make up the time on the highway. Thanks for choosing to ride the bus with us."

Charlie had planned to sleep during the trip, but even though he had seen these mountains before, the mountains were so beautiful; all he could do was look out the window and marvel at them. He saw elk, deer, and even a moose. The bus stopped at several places during the trip where he could get a couple of sandwiches and get back on the bus. Soon the bus was at Lake Louise, then he was passing through Banff and on the way to Calgary.

He arrived at Calgary slightly after 9:30 PM. It was dark by this time. He retrieved his box and walked out of the station into the cold night. Across the street he saw a nice looking motel named The

Stampede with a coffee shop. He thought he would stay there a couple of days until he decided his next move.

He walked across the street and registered as Mr. Charles W. Brown. As he was walking to his room on the ground floor, he thought Charlie Brown! Nobody in his right mind would fake a name like that. That dog in the comic strip is an excellent cover. No one will suspect a thing.

He opened the door to his room, pulled the box inside, and closed the door. His thoughts were now of Donna I wonder how she is doing - is she well?

Almost as soon as he had thoughts about Donna's well being, a bright, yet warm light engulfed the room. A woman clothed in white appeared.

She smiled and said, "Donna is fine. A minister and his family need help. Be careful after you enter Montana. You will be needed there also."

As quickly as she appeared, she disappeared along with the bright light.

Charlie knew Donna was safe now, but wondered what awaited him in Montana and who was this minister?

CHAPTER 9

Donna had been walking for several hours since leaving Philip at the railroad station. Finding the north – south highway was easy, but walking south along the highway for so long she found hard. There was snow on both sides of highway 13 and also some black ice on the highway. There were not too many trees on either side of the highway nor was there much of any vegetation, but the snow had begun to accumulate on the ground.

She had passed one intersection where the sign said Winnipeg, but she just kept on walking south. Even though she was carrying her duffel as a backpack so she could carry it easier – it weighed almost forty pounds – she found she was getting tired!

The black curtain of night had fallen, but the road was well lighted, as the moon was almost full. Donna had no trouble seeing the road not only because of the amount of light coming from the moon but also because of the amount of light being reflected off the fallen snow. The land was flat for the most part, only little rises in the terrain on either side of the highway.

She began to wonder if she had the right road as less than a dozen cars had passed her and no car had passed her in over an hour, but she somehow knew this was the road Philip told her to take. She also noted nobody had stopped to offer help. The temperature was dropping fast and now she began to wonder if even her warm parka would be enough to keep her warm. Her boots and wool socks were still keeping her feet warm. She was glad Charlie made her buy the boots and the heavy socks.

Several lights, which appeared to be streetlights, began to be visible ahead of her indicating another intersection. She estimated that the distance to the lights was about a mile and she hoped that would be the intersection where she was to turn to the east. As she came closer to the lights, she could make out a vehicle on the side of the road with its parking lights on. Soon Donna began to notice other things as she approached the vehicle.

It was a pickup truck with a small second seat and it had its motor running because there was smoke coming from the exhaust pipe. Also there was someone in the truck. When she got within thirty yards of the truck, a man stepped out of the vehicle. He had on a big parka with his head being covered by what appeared to be a very large, warm hood. He began to walk towards Donna.

Instinctively, Donna started to cross the highway to avoid any problems. As she did this, the man pulled the hood off his head to reveal a tall clean-shaven man who Donna guessed was in his late sixties.

The man asked in what could only be described as a booming voice, "Are you Donna Brown?"

Donna looked at the man and replied, "Yes! Are you John Singleton?"

"Yes."

"Thank God, it's you!"

Donna walked towards the man as he walked towards her.

As they got closer, John in almost a commanding voice said, "Let me carry your backpack. Go get in the truck. It's warm there."

Donna looked at him and answered as she slipped the duffel turned backpack off her shoulders, "That would be a big relief. Thanks!"

Donna let John carry her duffel, but she walked beside John to the vehicle in silence.

And in a terse manner John Singleton said, "I've been looking for you for over three hours."

"I'm sorry you have been looking that long, but I am truly grateful you didn't give up on me."

He commented, "Your duffel is quite heavy."

"Yes it is!"

He thought she must be a strong little lady and in very good condition to have carried her duffel as far as she had.

As Donna reached the truck, John opened the door for Donna and she got into the vehicle on the passenger side. She appreciated the heated cab of the truck as she loosened her parka. John now placed the backpack in the rear of the truck then walked around to the driver's side and got in.

John put the truck in gear, began to drive, and turned left at the intersection. Donna noted he was very quiet and assumed he was either a quiet person or not very happy about the situation.

As the pickup continued on the highway, Donna saw some lights up ahead and as they got closer she saw a sign which said The Canadian and an arrow pointing towards the motel. John passed the entrance and pulled into a carport on the side of the motel.

Donna and John stepped out of the vehicle with John retrieving the duffel and carrying the duffel to the door. With his free left hand, he opened the door for Donna to enter the building. Walking to the door was a woman in her sixties who was smiling.

"So you are Donna - the expert marksman."

John asked, "Did they call?"

"Yvette called from Winnipeg and told me everything that happened."

Donna remained silent, but listened to what Marie told John and to John's responses.

Marie turned to Donna, "Sweetheart, Yvette wanted me to tell you that you have no worries. She said Mr. Walker took care of almost everything and what he didn't take care of, Philip and she took care of. She said don't worry about a thing.

"I have prepared some hot soup for you. Now eat your soup and then you can go to your room and get a good night's sleep. We can talk in the morning and you can rest up all day. On Saturday, we'll take you to Grand Forks.

After Donna had finished her soup, Marie motioned for her to follow her down a hallway.

Donna lifted her duffel onto her shoulder with one hand and

401

began to follow Marie down a short hallway to a room that was for personal guests and not part of the motel.

After Marie left her, Donna started to look around the room. She noted a picture on the wall and immediately felt comfortable in her room. It was a picture of four people - two men and two women. Two of the people were a young Philip and Yvette and the other two were young John and Marie. She felt completely safe after recognizing the people in the picture.

The next morning, Donna was up at 7:20. By the time she had put on her clothes and walked out of her room into the kitchen it was 8:15. She wasn't surprised to see Marie and John already up and sitting at the kitchen table.

"Good morning, Donna. I hope you had a good night's rest," John said in a happy tone of voice.

"I sure did. How are you two feeling?"

Marie answered, "Just fine. How about some eggs and bacon. We have some coffee, too."

"That's sounds great, but first I want to thank John for picking me up on the highway last night. He was a God send."

"My dear, last night when I picked you up, I didn't know you saved Philip and Yvette's life or at least saved them from a great deal of injury. If I had known that, I would have been more sociable and possibly more aggressive looking for you. Marie told me what Yvette told her and I want to thank you for what you did for our friends."

Marie interrupted, "Now, you might want to know a little about us and...or did John and Yvette tell you all about us too."

"Well, they did tell me some things about how you met and about some of your exploits during the war – the real war, World War II." As she was saying this, she smiled.

Marie responded, "Philip and Yvette have certainly convinced you as to what was the only war!"

All three laughed.

"I like to tell our story. May I," asked John.

"Of course."

"Since you said they told you how we met, I guess Philip told

402

you how we landed in France and how Marie and Yvette rescued us, but I bet he didn't tell you Yvette and Marie saved 46 airmen from capture and returned them to England! That was a job, but they did it. I must add that it was both Yvette and Marie who smuggled them out of France. Philip and I just went along for the ride. We became quite experienced in smuggling people during that time.

"By the way, we shouldn't have any problems in getting you into the States. In France, the Germans required papers, identification and much more. The border here is quite open. We will just drive up to the border with you sitting in the back seat of our truck. We will answer a few questions and then drive to Grand Forks. It will be as simple as that."

"What John has told you is true. There will be no trouble unless they have a description of you. Do they?"

"I don't think so. If they did, I would think Yvette or Philip would have told you about that, but didn't Yvette say not to worry?"

Nodding her head, Marie answered, "You're right. Yvette would have told me. Now finish your breakfast and I will show you around."

After Donna had finished her breakfast and returned to her room to wash her face, John turned to Marie, "Marie, she is just what Philip said, nothing outstanding, but everything outstanding. She is one nice looking woman."

"That she is and a lady, too, but I suspect she could turn into a Resistance fighter very quickly from what Yvette said," replied Marie.

John replied, "I concur."

Charlie woke up just before 5:30 which was a little unusual for him as he was now in the habit of getting up about 7:00 in the morning. He looked at the information pamphlet in his room that would tell the guest what is available in the motel. He noticed there was a small fitness center and a hot tub. He would use these two facilities.

Charlie walked to the fitness center room with the weight machines and worked out for almost an hour. After the work out, he

403

went to the hot tub thinking about what Martha had told him. Who was he to help and when was he to meet them he thought while he just sat in the tub as the water whirled around him and gave him a much-needed massage.

After he was finished with the tub, he went back to his room. He was now well rested and relaxed. He began to look at several maps of the western United States. He noted one route to Oregon was through Spokane and Seattle. There were other routes, but the route through Spokane was the most direct, but he knew he could not travel this route because he might be recognized. He then walked over to the mirror and started to finger his beard. He thought the beard has to go, at least for a while. People might recognize him with the beard because in the past several years very few people had seen him without the beard.

After shaving his beard, he again looked in the mirror. He shook his head as much as to say I look different, but I still hope I won't run into anyone who knew me in Idaho.

He turned on the TV to catch the morning news and weather. He wanted to know the weather for the next few days. Once again, he returned to look at the maps. Waterton Park is just north of Glacier Park and there are probably many trails to Glacier from Waterton. Even though it's winter and not knowing the boarder is an open boarder thought, that's where I will cross into the States.

With his plans made, he went to the coffee shop for breakfast. He sat down at a table where he could see most of the lobby. Sitting at a table in the far corner of the coffee shop was a woman who was just sitting there either sobbing or trying to hold back the tears. Feeling compassion for the woman, Charlie got up and walked over to her table.

"Excuse me, but is there anything I can do for you?"

"No - there's nothing anyone can do except maybe God."

Smiling, Charlie replied, "Well, he might have sent me to help you. Do you want to tell me about your problem? By the way, my name is Charlie Brown and no, I am not any relation to the comic strip Charlie Brown and yes my name is Charlie Brown."

This brought a smile to her face through the sobs, yet Charlie could tell she was still crying. For some reason, she now felt at ease with Charlie.

She began, "My name is Darlene Peterson and we arrived here yesterday about 7:00 PM. We are going to Denver where my husband has just been offered a pulpit in a small church..."

Charlie thought this must be the minister and his family Martha told me about.

"You see my daughter, Kristi, is very sick. Just before we left our mission in Alaska for Denver, a doctor diagnosed Kristi as having Hodgkin's Disease. This disease is a form of cancer or so I am told. But we had hope - until yesterday when she started to throw up all over the car. We brought her to the emergency room last night and they gave her some medicine to help prevent her from throwing up."

A man in his mid thirties walked up to the table. He was clean-shaven, was about five feet ten or so and stood erect, but was a little over weight.

"Charlie, I'd like to introduce my husband, Al Peterson. I'll let you tell him your last name."

Charlie got up and shook his hand, then as Al sat down, Charlie sat also.

 Al looked at Charlie and said, "I bet your last name is Brown."

"How did you guess?"

"Simple. That's the only name that I wouldn't suspect."

All three laughed.

"Honey, Kristi wants to see you. She's feeling somewhat better. I've left Vicki with her."

"I must go and thanks Charlie for lending me your ear."

"That's quite all right. I hope to see you again."

After Darlene had left, Al looked at Charlie and asked, "Did Darlene tell you of our problems?"

"She told me of one big problem, yes."

"I might as well fill you in on the rest of our story. It will be good to get it off my chest. I was a chaplain in Vietnam with the 24th division during the early days of Vietnam. After I was discharged, I came home and got married. While in Vietnam, I met a doctor named Dr. William Olsen.

"After Darlene and I were married, we wanted, no I wanted to become a missionary somewhere in Alaska. The mission board sent me to just where I wanted - Alaska. Late last year, Darlene told me she would like to return to the States so the girls could meet some boys.

"So, I submitted my name to become a pastor at a church in the lower 48. Then out of the blue, Bill - that's the doctor I became friends with in Nam - called me and as the representative of a small Presbyterian church in a Denver suburb, offered me the pulpit.

"We had just been told about Kristi having Hodgkin's Disease and so I asked him about it. He said the disease is now curable in a great number of cases and he would see to it that she would get the very best treatment in Denver.

"Well, as you can guess, I immediately accepted the pulpit at Bill's church. We started to pack our bags that very night, put what little we had in the trailer over the next three days, and began the drive south on the Alcan Highway. We got as far as Lake Louise when she started to throw up constantly, but God was with us.

"He sent us a catholic priest, Father Calloway. He got us a room at the hotel on the lake. We couldn't afford it, but the manager told us he had just been to confession and Father Calloway blackmailed him into giving us the room for the night. Later, Father Calloway told us as we were leaving that the manager has a very big heart and is a big liar. He would have to pay a lot of penitence for the lie he told me about him being blackmailed when he sees him next in the confessional.

"As you realize, both men were joking and not telling the truth, but it was a good experience as we are almost down to our last dollar. Well that's our story."

"I can truthfully say, you have some problems. I guess the reason you don't fly Kristi to Denver is money."

"Yes."

"When do you plan to leave Calgary?"

"We hope to leave today or tomorrow because every day we delay getting to Denver and Kristi's treatment is delayed becomes extremely important as early treatment was stressed by Bill. Treatment cannot be delayed much longer and have Kristi survive."

Charlie thought for a moment, then replied, "Now don't get your hopes up, but I know a few people and I might be able to pull a few strings. Give me two hours to look into what I can do."

Al was totally surprised by what Charlie had just said, looked at Charlie, and said, "If you could do anything for us, we would greatly appreciate it."

Charlie got up and shook his hand. "I'll call you in your room when I find out something."

He walked away from Al towards the woman at the cash register.

"You see that man sitting at the table. Serve him breakfast - serve his entire family breakfast and all other meals. Put it on my bill as well as their room bill."

The clerk looked at Charlie in an approving manner and said, "I'll be happy to do that for you, sir."

Charlie walked out of the coffee shop and back to his room. He picked up in the telephone directory he found in a dresser draw; then he looked for a travel agency. He dialed a number.

"Calgary Travel. How may I help you?"

"I'm staying at the Stampede Motel and I need to know if there are any Medical Flights from Calgary to Denver and how much they cost."

"That's a little out of our line, but call this number. It's for Charter Flights of Canada out of Calgary."

"Thanks." Charlie dialed the number.

"Charter Flights of Canada, Mark speaking."

"Mark, I would like to charter a flight to Denver for a very sick girl. Do you have any medical charter flights?"

"Yes sir," came the reply.

"First, how much would such a flight cost - American? Second, would you accept cash as that is all I have? And also, could you carry four people?

"The answer to your first question is $2,700.00, American. If you will hold the phone, I will ask how you can pay for the flight as paying in cash is a little unusual."

Several minutes later, Mark returned to the phone and said, "We would appreciate it if you would deposit the money direct in our bank – The Bank of Canada. There is a branch close to the Stampede. However, we cannot take four people on the plane we have here. We can only take the sick person and one other person. Will that be acceptable?"

Charlie thought for a minute and answered, "Yes that'll be fine."

"We'll have the plane ready by three o'clock this afternoon if you can get to our bank, pay the bill, and be at the airport by 2:00 PM."

"Thanks. My name is Charlie Brown and you can confirm my name by calling The Stampede Motel."

"I'll have to wait for the bank to get in touch with me, but you still have to be here by 2:00PM."

"We'll be there. The name of the passengers are Kristi Peterson and Mrs. Darlene Peterson."

"Fine. We'll be waiting."

With the charter flight now set up, Charlie went back to the lobby to discover Al and Darlene and their two daughters sitting down on one of the chairs and the sofa.

As Charlie walked in, Al got up. "We want to thank you for breakfast and paying our bill here at the motel, but we must leave now. You know we must conserve the little time we have."

"Remember I told you to let me look into your problem. Well, I have chartered a flight to Denver for Kristi and one other passenger. I told the charter people it would be you, Darlene.

In a serious tone of voice, yet smiling, "Now I want something in return. Since you are going to the States from here and will pass through Montana, you must give me a ride to Billings."

Al and Darlene were speechless.

Al asked, "How can we repay you for this?"

"I told you. Give me a ride to Billings. And Al, I am what you would call a rich American and I won't miss the money."Darlene, thinking only of her daughter, spoke, "God must have sent you.

That's the only explanation. Thank you very much."

Charlie thought you don't know how true your words are, then said, "Folks it's now almost 11:00 AM. I have to pay for the plane at the bank and we must be at the airport by 2:00 PM to catch the plane.

Al said, "Can I give you a ride to the bank?"

"Sure," came the reply.

Soon after Charlie had paid for the charter and they had eaten lunch at the coffee shop, Al, Darlene, Kristi and Vicki with Charlie sitting in the back seat of their van, drove to the airport. Charlie went into the administration building and easily found the Charter Flights of Canada office. A young woman in her early twenties who was sitting behind a relatively large desk greeted Charlie.

"What can I do for you, sir?"

"My name is Charlie Brown and I was told I am to give you the receipt for the money I paid the bank."

A smile creased her lips and she replied, "Of course, Mr. Brown. May I have the receipt? The bank called about ten minutes ago and confirmed the payment."

"Sure." Charlie handed the woman the receipt.

"The plane is on the tarmac over by the hanger just east of the terminal the airlines use."

Charlie led the Petersons to the plane. The charter included a nurse to travel with Kristi who actually doubled as the copilot. She helped Kristi into the plane and to her seat. Darlene first kissed Charlie on the check, then Vicki and last Al. As she was climbing on board the plane, Charlie rushed up to her.

"Darlene, I have an envelope for you. Use it for a few creature comforts. I feel Kristi will be fine. Now go with God."

With those comments, Charlie left Darlene and the door to the jet closed. Charlie, Vicki and Al watched as the plane took off for Denver.

Charlie thought the plane would be in Denver tonight and Kristi would be in the hospital before midnight. Dr. Olsen would see to that.

Darlene looked at the envelope Charlie had given her. She opened it and was shocked - the envelope contained $2,500.00. She looked out of the window towards the hanger where they boarded the plane and seeing the three people standing there said in a low voice, "Thank you from the bottom of my heart Charlie Brown and thank you God for sending him to us."

CHAPTER 10

The ride back to the motel from the airport was very quiet, but electricity, jubilance was in the air. Hope for Kristi was now a reality.

Al was the first to speak, "Vicki, we'll leave immediately for Denver and we..."

Charlie butted in, "Al, remember you have to take me to Billings and I can't leave until tomorrow morning."

"In the excitement, I completely forgot about your price for the charter - taking you to Billings will be a very small price to pay for what you have done and by your comment, you weren't kidding, were you?"

"No, I wasn't. I have a large box and I hope you can put it in your trailer. I really need to take this box with me and it would help me a great deal by you taking me to Billings."

Charlie was thinking it would be easier to ride into Montana than to hike from Waterton Parks to Glacier Park and riding with a minister would avoid the attention of the custom's agent.

"Daddy, we could leave tomorrow and that wouldn't delay us too much."

"Well, a debt is a debt. Considering what you did, we'll be happy to leave tomorrow morning. Anyway, it'll give us some time to rest. We might need it when we get to Denver. How about eight o'clock in the morning?"

"That would be fine. We can pack tonight and eat a quick

411

breakfast in the morning."

At dinner, Charlie asked, "Didn't you say you were a chaplain for the 24th in Nam? I served in Nam with the Special Forces near the end of the war - I was probably one of the last Americans to get out of Southeast Asia."

Al looked at Charlie and started to study him for the first time. He noted everything about him, then thought he looks like a Special Forces type - possibly even a soldier of fortune. But he helped us when we needed help. I guess he is a good man who was just caught up in a nasty situation.

Vicki asked, "Mr. Brown, what did you do in Vietnam?"

"Vicki, I'm sorry, but I can't tell you. It was classified at the time and I don't know if what I did has been reclassified."

Again Al thought he knows what he did - he killed people. Why doesn't he tell Vicki? I wonder if he is as good a person as he seems."

Donna was up and ready to go to Grand Forks by 6:30 on Saturday morning. She walked in the kitchen and was a little surprised to see John and Marie already sitting at the table drinking coffee.

"Pull up a chair and have a cup of coffee while Marie fixes you a couple of poached eggs on a muffin."

"Thanks, John. But all I really want is the cup of coffee. Thanks for the offer, though."

After several minutes, all three had finished their coffee and were waiting for a man named Andrew to arrive so they could leave. He was going to take care of the motel for John and Marie while they drove Donna to Grand Forks.

Immediately on hearing a knock on the side door, John got up and opened the door.

"Hi Andrew. You know where we keep everything. While we are in Grand Forks, we'll stop and see our friend for a few hours. We'll be back late today. Is that all right?"

"Sure. No problem. Have a nice trip."

"Forgive our manners, Andrew. This is the friend we told you

412

we were taking to Grand Forks. This is Donna and Donna, this is Andrew."

Andrew walked over to Donna and extended his hand as he said, "Pleased to meet you"

"I really appreciate you doing this for John and Marie. They are so kind in taking me to Grand Forks."

"Well we should start our trip. I have to fill up the gas tank before we go," interrupted John.

Marie, John, and Donna went outside into the cold air and got in the truck. There were a few white clouds in the sky, but blue sky dominated. There was no wind, but the weather report was that the weather would change dramatically just before midnight. A blizzard was coming.

John stopped at a BP service station and began to pump the gas. Donna got out of the truck and went in the station to the cashier. As soon as John was finished pumping the gas, she paid for the gas and as she left the building, John was coming in to pay for the gas.

"John, I've paid for the gas. It's the least I can do for you."

John smiled, "Thank you, but you know you didn't have to do that."

"I know, but I wanted to."

The truck moved out onto Highway 75 and traveled south towards the United States. After almost thirty miles, they saw the border. John drove up to the little building that housed the U. S. Custom Service agent.

"Well hi there, John." Looking at Marie, he continued, "Nice seeing you two again. How have you two been?"

"We're doing really fine. And to answer your question, we are bringing our friend Donna to Grand Forks and we will be returning late today."

"You two have been through here so often, you know my questions before I ask them. Have a nice trip."

He waived them through and into the United States. Donna sighed deeply. She was back in the States.

John and Marie let Donna off in front of the bus station and after saying goodbye and thanking them for their help, Donna walked into the bus station.

After John turned the truck around and headed for their friend's house to visit for the rest of the day, he said, "Marie, I think she is a very good person just like Yvette said."

"I agree, but she did have the air of a good resistance fighter about her - her character could change in a moment, I suspect."

"I agree."

Donna was looking at the bus schedules to determine how she was going to Portland. She noticed she could catch a bus to Minneapolis and she knew Minneapolis had a fairly large airport. She thought she could then catch a plane to Portland. That would put me in Portland before December 16th. I could do a little shopping with the money Charlie gave me, then go to Mt. Hood. I don't think my real name would mean anything to anyone at the airline - yes, that's the name I will use and how I will go to Portland. I kinda like using Donna Mackey. It has a certain ring to it.

Charlie was up just as dawn was breaking over the horizon and down in the lobby by 7:00 AM. Al and Vicki were only a couple of minutes behind him. They were still excited. They ate their breakfast, checked out of the motel and piled into the van.

They drove out of Calgary on Highway 2. It was only 180 miles to the United States border. As the van approached the border, Charlie became tense and alert, especially when they stopped at the small custom's building.

The custom's agent asked, "Where're you going and how long are you going to stay in the U. S.?"

Al answered, "I am a minister from Alaska, and I am taking a pulpit in Denver. This is my daughter Vicki and this is my friend, Charlie."

The custom agent looked at everyone and asked, "Did you buy anything of value in Canada?"

Al answered, "No, not that I know of."

"Welcome to the lower forty eight."

With those words, Charlie breathed a sigh of relief. He was back in the States. Now he must get to Oregon, he thought.

414

Almost as soon as they crossed into the United States, the van started to cough, chug, and miss.

After a few minutes of the motor missing, Al said, "Now what?"

As if to answer her father's question, Vicki said, "It's probably the gas we got at the last station. You know water in the gas or dirt - something like that."

Charlie looked at Al. "I doubt that, but it's possible. Look at that billboard. We're only a few miles from a Sinclair station. They should be able to help us."

Breathing deeply, Al nodded in agreement. Soon they chugged down a hill and saw over to the west some mountains and a sign that read, "Going to the Sun road closed for the winter". They were close to the east entrance to Glacier Park and the Sinclair gas station.

They chugged into the station and up to a closed garage door. A man who was dressed as a mechanic with grease on his coveralls walked out of the door to the station office and over to the van. Al was getting out of the van to greet the man.

The gas station attendant asked, "What can I do for you folks?"

"Hi! My van has been missing for the last forty or so miles. Could you look at it and tell me if you can fix it or what can be done?"

"Sure. Why don't you folks step out and go into the station office. We have some hot coffee in there or you can have some hot chocolate."

"Thanks."

Charlie and Vicki climbed out of the van and with Al, went into the office. It was warm inside, but there were three young men in the office with their heads shaved. Charlie recognized one of them as a skin head from the Sand Point area. He remembered his name was Eddie and he also remembered Sheriff Coomey telling him that Eddie was no good and he thought Eddie should be locked up before he hurts someone.

Charlie raised his hand to cover his face and turned away from Eddie so the skinhead wouldn't recognize him. Charlie thought Eddie had only seen him with a beard and only on one occasion, so

415

even if he sees me, he may not recognize me without the beard. I hope so.

Al and Vicki walked over to where the coffee and hot chocolate were and began to pour themselves some hot chocolate. Charlie was right next to them with his back towards the three young men.

One of the young men walked up to Vicki, "Hi there. My name is Ronald, Ronnie for short and that guy over there is Riche and that one's name is Eddie. We're just in here to see Gus over there. He runs the place. How about coming over to the counter so we can get to know each other better."

Vicki sensed this wouldn't be a good idea. "I'm sorry, but I must stay with my father and Mr. Brown."

Al turned to look at Ronnie and instantly knew Vicki was right. "Vicki, you stay close to me."

Charlie did not speak, but when he turned to look at the skinheads, his eyes betrayed him. Al saw what he had seen so many times in Vietnam - eyes of cold steel with a resolution to do whatever is necessary to complete the mission or to protect himself. Al felt a chill go up his spine, but he thought that Charlie's eyes said he would protect him and Vicki as well. This was good but now he realized Charlie was definitely a Special Forces type person who could and would kill in a moment.

Eddie came over to where the four of them were standing near where the coffee pot was and said, "Hey all we wanted to do was talk to the little lady. Do you think she is too good for us?"

Al looked Eddie straight in the eyes and said, "My daughter does not talk to strangers especially when she is approached in the manner she was. I concur with what she said and as of now, she does not have any choice - she will stay with me."

Trying to start a fight, Eddie replied, "So you really think she's too good for us?"

Charlie now started to speak, but with a heavy German accent, "I read about people like you a few weeks ago. Nobody wants to associate with your kind. Even the Germans remembered the Nazis, the Holocaust, but even then when the Germans were polite, they called your kind Neo-Nazis. At other times, what your type were

416

called is not said in polite company. We do not want any trouble, please leave us alone."

Eddie looked at Gus coming into the office, shrugged his shoulders, and walked over to where the other two men were standing.

Gus walked over to Al. "Those skin heads causing you any trouble?"

Al responded, "I hope not, but they were making a pass at my daughter and I didn't appreciate it."

"I'll have a talk with them. They usually listen to me. But you have a problem. One of the spark plug wires is bad; another one is going bad along with three bad plugs. It's easy to fix if I had the wire harness for the van, but I don't have one here in the station. I'll call another station up the road and see if they have what I need and if they can get it to me today; I can fix your van today."

Charlie spoke again with the German accent, "Money is no object. We need to be on the road as quickly as possible. Could you call now? I will pay extra for the part to get here and placed today."

Al looked at Charlie again in a puzzled manner. He would have to ask him about his sudden German accent and why is he offering to pay for the repairs?

Gus walked over to a telephone and dialed a number.

"Hi! This is Gus. You got a wire harness for a van. Good. How soon can you get it to me? One hour. I'll be waiting. Thanks."

"Well you heard. I'll have you fixed up in about two hours. It'll be dark by then, so if you want to stay over night, I can recommend a B and B to you. My sister in law runs the place. She supplements my brother's income with income from her B & B operation. Not much, but it keeps the wolf away from the door. She calls her B and B the Glacier B and B. Incidentally, my brother works for the park service and he was called to work for a few days to fix something or other in the park, so he won't be there tonight."

Al looked at Charlie. "What do you think? I doubt we can get much further tonight. We might as well stay there."

Charlie looked towards the three skinheads who looked like they were leaving.

Still speaking with a German accent replied, "I guess it would be all right."

"Good. Would you mind telling me where her place is and how much it will cost?"

Gus responded, "It's down the main highway about two miles and east of the highway only a half mile. You can go over to the cafe and get something to eat while you wait for me to fix your van."

"I am a little hungry, daddy."

Charlie spoke, still with an accent, "Then let's eat. And it's on me."

Al again looked at Charlie and still looked at him with a puzzled look wondering about the German accent.

Once outside, Al pulled Charlie away from Vicki and asked, "Why the German accent and why are you wanting to pay for everything?"

Now speaking without an accent, Charlie replied, "I thought you would ask those questions. But to answer them, I thought if I spoke with a German accent, it would add some credence to what I said about the neo-Nazis or as they are called here, skin heads. I read about the neo-Nazis in U. S. News and World Report a few weeks ago and what they are doing in Germany is reminding many people of the Nazis and they are in fact beginning to have trouble with those kind of people. I don't know if my accent worked or not, but it was worth a try.

"As for as offering to pay for the repairs and food, I told you, I'm a millionaire and I know you are having money problems. That's just my way of saying thanks for the ride."

After hearing Charlie's answer, Al just shook his head as if he believed him.

As they walked across the road from the service station to the cafe, Al was thinking he wanted to believe Charlie, but yet he had a feeling about Charlie and he was hesitant in believing him. Charlie did appear to be a good man though.

CHAPTER 11

Al Peterson, Vicki, and Charlie walked into the Park Cafe and were greeted by a woman who appeared to be in her mid thirties. She was wearing blue jeans with a plaid shirt and a grayish apron. Looking at the café and the woman, Charlie and Al knew the dress code was very informal.

She said, "Hi folks. Just take a seat anywhere and I'll be with you in a minute."

Al walked over to a booth on one side of the room, but Charlie said, "Al, let's take this table over there in that corner. We can see the entire café from that table."

Al looked at Charlie with a look that said "Why?"

Almost as soon as he asked himself the question why that table, he answered the question himself - if we have trouble with those skinheads, our back will be protected. Charlie is definitely someone to be reckoned with - I wonder what his story is?

Al sat down in one of the chairs with his back to one of the walls, and Vicki sat in the other chair with her back to the other wall. Charlie sat in a third chair with his back unprotected, but he could get out of the chair quickly if the need arose. Moreover, he could see the door and most of the room from the chair.

The woman came over to their table and said, "Hi, my name is Peggy. I understand you have trouble with your van and you are waiting for Gus to fix it. He's a good mechanic and an honest one too. I also heard you had a run in with the skin heads."

419

Al responded, "The information mill is certainly good in this town."

"There's not much I don't know and I get the word quickly. Anyhow, what would you like? We have steak with fries and if I do say so myself, Asa cooks up a mean steak. He came from New York where he was a cook, but moved out here to escape the problems of the big apple."

Charlie responded, "That's sounds like a winner. I'll take that."

Al shook his head in an approving manner and returned the menu to Peggy saying, "My daughter and myself will have the same."

"How do you want your steaks?"

Charlie replied, "Medium well."

Vicki answered, "Medium."

Al responded last, "Medium."

"What do you want to drink?"

Al and Vicki responded, "Ice tea."

Charlie thought for a minute, then answered, "Hot tea and do you have Barq's root beer?"

"We don't carry root beer. Sorry."

"I didn't think you would, but I always try."

Vicki looked at Charlie and asked, "Why did you speak with an accent in the service station?"

"It's a long story, but I thought it would impress those jerks and they would leave us alone. I don't think it worked, but it was worth a try. I think they left us alone because Gus came back into the room at the same time."

"I wonder if they will come back after us - or even attack me. I've heard of things like that happening here in the lower 48."

"It happens everywhere sweetie, even in Alaska where we were."

"Your father is right, but hopefully, those jerks won't bother us anymore."

Peggy brought their salads to the table and placed them in front of the three people.

Al said, "You know, I didn't know I was that hungry, but the

420

sight of the salad made me realize I am starved" as he reached for the crackers.

Charlie asked, "Peggy, are those skin heads local or did they just come into town?"

"Strange you should ask that question. The one they call Eddie came to town about three, no four months ago with several of them and they have been nothing but trouble since. They leave Gus alone though. He was in the Marines in Korea and he doesn't put up with their garbage.

"Most of those who came with Eddie left and went back to Idaho or whatever rock they crawled out from under, but three of them stayed here with Eddie.

"Eddie converted two locals to their way of thinking. The one named Ronnie has been in trouble with the law several times, but Riche was a good kid until Eddie came to town. Now he has turned out to be no good. His father has gotten him out of trouble several times, but I think his patience is wearing thin.

"He's the local law. He was in Korea just like Gus and he also remembers his father telling him about what happened in Germany - you know the Holocaust. His father was one of the soldiers who liberated one of the concentration camps.

"But you know, I wonder when he's going to put a stop to Eddie and his skin heads? I hope soon."

Charlie replied, "He probably can't because they haven't broken any law, but wants to put a stop to him more than you realize."

Then he sank into deep thought, could this be what Martha meant?

"You okay mister?"

"Yeah, sure. I just started to daydream. I hope his father puts a stop to those skinheads. They are nothing but trouble - big trouble."

Al added, "I completely concur."

As they finished their salad, Charlie noticed the three skinheads, Eddie, Ronnie and Riche were walking towards the cafe. He bent his head to the table as much as to say God, please don't let them do anything - please Lord.

421

Riche opened the door to the cafe to let Ronnie and Eddie enter the cafe, then followed the two men over to the serving counter.

"Hey, Peg, we want some service."

"Just a minute, Ronnie. Just have a seat."

"Now that's no way to treat a real man. You should know we're better than your cook is and we're repeat customers, not like those over there. Hey guys, look who is over there. Our girl friend and her daddy along with that wanna be German."

Al tensed up as Vicki recoiled with a little fear and concern. Charlie just continued to look at the table and wish he wouldn't have the feeling he had in the pit of his stomach - the knot that said there was going to be trouble and he would be called upon to defend the people in the cafe.

Eddie leaned over and whispered to Riche, "Get behind that guy over there and take care of him if he interferes."

Riche nodded his head to say will do. He moved to the end of the counter just out of eyesight of Charlie.

As Riche was moving towards the end of the counter, Asa came out of the kitchen to bring the steaks to the table where Al, Charlie, and Vicki were sitting. Ronnie went over to where Asa would have to pass to get to the table, but he did not move fast enough and Asa had passed the intercept point.

Charlie sighed with relief at this.

Asa placed the steaks on the table as ordered. The three started to cut their steaks and eat them while Asa returned to the kitchen.

Eddie turned to Peggy, "You know that Jew will poison everybody here in town, don't you?"

"You guys are really off the wall! Now get out of here or I'll call the sheriff."

"Hey Riche, Peggy says she'll call your old man if we don't leave. What do you think?"

Feeling his father might side with Peggy, Riche answered, "Maybe we should leave for a little while. It'll give Peg a chance to rethink everything."

Ronnie, who didn't want any trouble with the sheriff agreed, "Yeah, that's a good idea."

422

Al breathed a sigh of relief as he was getting concerned about how things were going. Charlie just continued to look at the table while eating.

The three skinheads left the cafe which made everyone much happier.

Charlie was still not convinced. It was getting dark as they finished their steaks.

Peggy walked over to their table, "Now didn't I tell you Asa could really cook steaks."

Charlie answered for the three of them, "You sure told us the truth."

Just then the door opened to the cafe and three skinheads walked in only Eddie wasn't with them. He was waiting outside the door as if he was a look out.

The new skinhead walked up to Peggy.

"Hi. My name is Kenneth, Ken for short. Now we here in this community don't want any Jews around us. First they come into the area, then they get all the money and take over all the businesses. In short, they take over all businesses from good Christians. Hitler had the right idea when he wanted to exterminate the scum. I'm just sorry he didn't succeed.

"Now what I'm telling you is get rid of that no good cook you have so he won't poison everybody and we won't bother you again. And for a little money each month, we will keep the area clean from Jews. Do you understand what we are saying, Peggy?"

While Kenneth was talking to Peggy in such a voice that everyone in the cafe could hear him, Al was doing a slow burn. He got up and walked over to where Kenneth, Ronnie, and Peggy were.

"You listen to me you jerks. Asa is as good a cook as I have ever had the pleasure to taste his food and what you are saying is just pure garbage so I'd suggest a call to the sheriff is in order. Now go to the phone Peggy."

Before Peggy could get to the phone, Ronnie moved over to where the phone was and ripped the phone out from the wall and giggled while doing it.

Kenneth looked at Al, "Look mister, this doesn't concern you.

Go back to your table."

"Let me tell you something. I am a Presbyterian minister and what you are doing and saying has no roots in Christianity - in fact it could be considered the work of the anti-Christ or the devil."

"You poor slob. Don't you know that the Jews killed Jesus? What more evidence do you want?"

"You are defaming the Bible when you use it in that way. Jesus was even a Jew."

Pointing his finger in Al's face, Ken replied, "You don't get it. You are the one who is not following the bible and" now looking at Vicki said, "I know you would like for us to get to know your daughter better, so when we are finished here, I'll introduce myself to her."

Al started to move towards Kenneth in a threatening way.

Immediately Ronnie grabbed Al from behind and Kenneth hit Al several times causing Al to bend over from the pain.

Vicki screamed and started to go to her father, but Charlie reached over to her and caught her arm. "Sit down. I'll take care of this."

Just as Charlie began to get up out of his chair, Riche grabbed Charlie around his neck and placed a knife at his throat.

"Now what are you going to do? Be a dead hero?"

"No, but if you have any sense, you will put that knife down and leave before you get hurt."

Ronnie and Kenneth laughed. "Now how are you going to hurt Riche when he's holding the knife?"

Charlie had slipped his hand to an advantageous position unnoticed by Riche and the other two skinheads. When Riche began to laugh, he let his guard down for a second, which was enough time for Charlie.

He reached up, grabbed Riche's arm and twisted it violently away from his throat. The knife dropped to the floor and the snap everyone heard in Riche's elbow told everyone his elbow was broken. In an instant, Charlie was standing with his foot behind Riche. He pushed Riche over his leg and he fell to the floor and immediately Charlie stomped on his left leg. Again the snap everyone heard told everyone his leg was broken.

Ronnie came running towards Charlie with disastrous results as Charlie did a karate kick that hit his lower jaw. Blood spurted everywhere from his face and Ronnie fell to the floor unconscious.

As Kenneth saw what had happened to Riche and Ronnie, he began to run towards the door only to see Eddie running from the cafe towards the car.

Kenneth said, "Shit," and turned to face Charlie.

A few karate kicks and punches and Kenneth had several broken bones as well as lying unconscious on the floor.

Peggy went to the door and yelled at Gus who was coming over to the cafe to tell Al his truck was ready, "Gus, call the sheriff. We need him ASAP."

Gus could tell something was wrong by Peggy's voice and the way Eddie had run from the cafe, so he immediately ran back to his shop and dialed the sheriff. He then ran back across the street to the cafe. He saw Vicki and Charlie tending to Al. As soon as Charlie saw that Al was okay, he got up and went over to Riche.

"Now where does it hurt, son?"

In a voice which meant, "My daddy will get you for this" he answered, "You broke my elbow and my leg, you son-of-a-bitch."

"I hope you'll learn before it's too late for you, but I suspect you are going to jail for some time because of what you did here."

Just as Charlie was putting a splint on Riche's leg, a big, well-built man in a sheriff's uniform walked into the cafe. It was Sheriff Rodney Jenkins.

Sheriff Jenkins looked over the room seeing and noting the three skinheads on the floor as well as noting that one of the skinheads was his son. Charlie looked at the sheriff and continued to render first aid to Riche.

When Riche saw his father, he smiled and said to Charlie, "Now you are going to get it. That's my dad and he knows how to take care of people like you."

"I suspect you will be surprised this time."

Gus had walked into the cafe and stood at the side of his friend Rod Jenkins.

Peggy walked up to the sheriff.

"Peggy, what happened here? It looks like someone took care of those skinheads. Before you tell me, let me call for the air medics and some back up."

After he had called his office, he again turned to Peggy and asked, "Now what the hell happened?"

"Well, those two over there came in here with Riche. The one called Ken started telling me to fire Asa because he is a Jew. That guy sitting over there came up to that skin head, told him he was a minister and told him off. When the skinhead said he would have to get to know his daughter better, the minister made a move towards Ken, but Ronnie grabbed him and Ken beat him up.

"Now as this was happening, the guy kneeling over Riche started to get up and Riche grabbed him and put a knife to his throat. The guy didn't move for a short time, but when he moved, he moved as fast as I have ever seen a person move and broke some of Riche's bones, then did what you see to Ronnie and Ken. Eddie looked inside and ran. He's nothing but a yellow belly coward. And Rod, that guy leaning over Riche seems to know what he is doing as far as first aid and he certainly knows how to defend himself."

Asa said, "That's the way it happened, sheriff."

Gus added, "I can't say what happened inside here Rod, but I saw Eddie running away from here as I was walking over here to tell those folks their van was ready."

Sheriff Jenkins was shaking his head when he heard his son call.

"Daddy, help me. This guy took advantage of me and really hurt me."

Charlie was a little nervous as he looked up towards the sheriff walking towards them. When the sheriff arrived where his son was lying, Charlie stood up.

Sheriff Jenkins kneeled beside his son. "Son, don't say anything until you see a lawyer. I have medical help on the way. It looks like this guy knows what he did. He really gave you some good first aid."

"Daddy, you're not going to believe Peggy and not me are

426

you?"

"Son, there are two eyewitnesses and Gus, all saying the same thing. Don't make it worse than what it is."

"You mean you're going to take the word of a Jew over me?"

Rod Jenkins looked at his son in a manner Riche had never seen before.

"Son, I was in the army and so was your grandfather. My father told me about the Holocaust and it was not pretty. If you ever..."

Sheriff could not finish what he was going to tell his son, but got up and walked away from him and over to the counter where he put his head down on the counter. Peggy and Gus walked over to him and put their arms around him, trying to console him as Rod now realized what his son had become. Al, with Vicki at his side, walked over to the sheriff and placed his hand on his shoulder also.

Charlie bent over Riche and said, "Riche, I think you have hurt your father more than you could imagine. If I were you, I would just ask him to forgive you and ask Asa for forgiveness also. And don't forget God. In any case, I think you are going to jail. I don't see how you can get out of what you did this time."

Riche looking at his father realized what Charlie was saying was true and turned his head away from the people in the room as much as to say, "Daddy's not going to protect me - what's going to happen to me?"

CHAPTER 12

The thumping of the wop-wop-wop of a helicopter coming signaled to everyone that the medical helicopter was approaching the cafe. It turned on its bright light under the body of the helicopter so the pilot could see to land. It landed near the cafe in a cleared area. Two medics climbed out of the helicopter and walked very fast towards the cafe where Rod Jenkins was waiting for them. After greeting the sheriff, they walked into the cafe.

"Rod, what do we have here?"

"All three of them have broken bones. The one over there bleeding from the face has his face broken pretty bad. I think he's the only serious one."

One of the paramedics looked at Riche and asked, "Isn't that Riche?"

"Yes it is and I'll take him to Doc's and then to jail. He was as guilty as the other skin heads."

Riche's eyes began to water.

Charlie kneeled next to him and said, "Look son, you can change. Listen to your father and not to jerks like Eddie and Ken. I hope you won't have a long stay in jail. Remember what I told you. Apologize to everyone and ask their forgiveness – especially God's forgiveness."

Charlie got up only to see Rod standing over the two of them.

"Listen to what he says, Riche. I won't and actually I can't help you out of this."

Riche started to cry.

The medics had carried the other two skinheads to the helicopter and came back to tell Rod they were leaving.

"See you guys. Tell my office I'll bring in Riche."

"Sure thing Rod," and they left.

The helicopter's blades began to turn faster and faster until it took off and with the familiar wop-wop-wop and flew away towards the hospital.

Charlie helped put Riche in the police car and watched as the car pulled away.

Charlie, Al, and Vicki walked over to the Sinclair station to see Gus who had returned to the station.

"Well, we're back. How much is it?"

Gus replied, "$125.00 - and that includes the special shipping."

"Here's the cash. Could you tell us again how to get to your sister in law's house again?"

"Sure. Go south on the main highway for almost two miles. You'll see a sign on the right side of the road that says Glacier B and B. That sign will tell you where to turn. You turn left and go for about a half mile. The house is on the left side of the road and down in sort of a cup between several hills...almost at the bottom of one of the hills. You can see the mountains from the house and it's a beautiful sight."

Al now responded, "Thank you for all you have done for us, but could you do one more thing?"

"Sure."

"Call your sister in law and tell her we are coming."

"I'll call her as soon as you leave. How many rooms do you want?"

Al looked at Charlie and then replied, "I think two will be sufficient."

"Good. I don't think you will be disappointed with her B & B."

Al, Charlie, and Vicki got into the van and it moved out onto the highway without missing. Al gave a sigh of relief as he thought the van was now fixed. As the van turned south, Charlie, Al and Vicki saw a full moon was just coming into view at the horizon. It was a huge orange ball that changed over a short time to a smaller white ball, but it gave off a great deal of light. The moonlight hit the snow-covered mountains and the land between the highway and the mountains giving off an eerie, yet bright light reflected from the fallen snow.

Vicki was looking out the side window at the mountains and said, "Daddy, look at the mountains with the moonlight on them. It's so beautiful!"

Al turned to look at the mountains and replied, "It certainly is a fabulous sight..."

About that time the van hit some ice on the road and skidded.

Vicki screamed, "Daddy!"

Charlie added, "Vicki, I think your father needs to watch the road. You know it's already dark and there may very possibly be ice on the road."

"I think Charlie is right, but what I saw of the mountains just reinforces my belief in God and Jesus."

Charlie pointed to a sign ahead on the right that said, "Glacier B & B - Next left turn".

Al turned left onto a dirt road.

Charlie noted the land was rolling hills with little valleys between the hills. Small brushes abounded all over the terrain, but especially in the small areas between the hills. The moonlight still lit up the entire area almost as well as sunlight.

Soon Vicki pointed to a house on the left of the road with a sign on it saying, "Glacier B & B".

Al pulled into the drive, crunching some snow and ice with the tires on the van. The temperature was below freezing and getting colder. A small rather pert looking woman wearing a dark green sweater with her hands folded over each other came out of the house.

"Hi! I'm Frances, but everybody calls me Fran. Gus called and told me to expect you folks."

Al and Vicki were now out of the van and going over to Fran.

"My name is Al and this is Vicki. The man over there getting some things out of the trailer is Charlie. Don't make fun of his last name - it's Brown."

"Well I'll be, I have the real Charlie Brown staying with me."

431

She laughed as well as Al and Vicki.

Charlie turned around and asked, "What's so funny?"

Al replied, "Charlie Brown."

"Oh that again. Okay, have your laugh."

Charlie had removed his gun case with his rifle and pistol in it along with his clothes. As he was walking towards the house, he wondered why he brought the case with him. He wouldn't need it and it would only clutter his room, but he was walking into the house by this time and he put the thought out of his mind.

Fran spoke to all three, "Gus told me you folks had some trouble with those skin heads. I'm sure sorry about that and I hope you won't judge the people in this area by those few jerks. Anyway, I don't think you'll have any more trouble with them since Rod took his son to jail. What Rod did will get around quickly and I think those jerks will think twice before they cross him. He's one tough cop."

Charlie added, "You may be right about the sheriff, but what Eddie did will have a definite effect on the skin heads in this area also."

"What did he do?"

Vicki smiled, then answered, "As soon as he saw his friends getting clobbered, he took off - he ran!"

"He did!"

"He's a coward."

"He likes to say he is very brave, but he's just a coward! That sure will get around. People don't like cowards around here. Anyway, your rooms are ready anytime you want to go to bed."

Al and Vicki went to their room. The room was on the second floor and was a nice, clean room, two beds and with a view of the mountains from the window as it was on the front of the house. The bathroom was one door away from the bedroom, which made it very nice also.

There was what could be called a night table where some flowers were. Vicki noted they were silk flowers, but very pretty.

Al was admiring the mountains in Glacier National Park from the window as Vicki walked up to him.

"Daddy, those mountains look almost as pretty as the ones in Alaska."

"They look just as beautiful, Vicki. All God's work is beautiful. We just have to see the beauty, but I must admit the snow capped mountains bathed in the moonlight are a little special."

"You're right. I'm going to take my bath and say a few prayers for mom and Kristi."

"I was just thinking of them myself. I wonder how they are doing. I hope the doctors can do something for Kristi."

Al turned around to look at Vicki, but she was gone. A few minutes later he heard the shower running in the bathroom and just nodded his head. He would take his shower after Vicki and then go to bed.

Charlie had a room on the ground floor and as luck would have it, he had a bathroom all to himself and a Queen sized bed. He was looking out of the window and all he saw was a small hill behind the house. The moonlight was so bright he could have read a book in his room without turning on any lights.

Outside the house, the moonlight was almost like daylight. It made the patches of snow look extremely white and beautiful. While the snow was in patches, there were so many patches of snow it almost looked like a solid mass of snow on the ground.

Charlie was tired so he took his shower and returned to the room. He was tired - very tired - yet he walked over to the window and looked skyward.

"Lord, help that Riche turn out better and help him in every way you can. Thank you for the Peterson's. They are a nice family. Help their daughter and Mrs. Peterson in Denver. And finally, be with my wife, Donna, wherever she is and bring us together as soon as possible. Amen."

With those words and thoughts, Charlie pulled the shade down, shutting out the moonlight from the room, but the room still glowed in bright light. Charlie turned around to see the same woman he saw in Calgary, Martha, standing in a corner of the room.

He took a deep breath as he thought whatever news she brought wouldn't be good news.

She smiled at him, then said, "You did well this afternoon. Your skills will be needed before morning."

The light and the woman disappeared and the room became dark.

Charlie got into bed and began to think about what she had said. "Your skills will be needed..." She must have meant my skills with my guns. Yes, that must have been what she meant. I'll have to get up before dawn and leave the house. I'll lock the door and climb out of the window so nobody will know I'm gone, then walk up that hill where I can see the front of the house.

The clock read 5:00 AM when Charlie opened his eyes. Nobody was in the room except him. He got out of bed and locked the door. Next he went into the bathroom to do the morning things. When he came out of the bathroom, he put on the warmest clothes he had as it was in the mid teens outside. He was fortunate to have a warm parka.

Next, he opened his gun case and took out the M-16 with silencer and the Ruger pistol with its silencer. He loaded both guns and walked to the window. He raised the window and climbed outside. Next he closed the window. He looked around the ground to see if he was going to have to walk on snow. He noted there was enough space between the patches of snow so he probably wouldn't have to leave any footprints.

He began to walk to the right of the window. As he reached the side of the house, he looked up the hill. He saw a good-sized group of bushes and decided that was where he would wait. He continued to walk so he wouldn't leave any footprints and walked up the small hill and hid himself so he would be hidden from the house by the bushes. He could see the entire front of the house from this vantage point and it would be hard for anyone to see him. Add to that, he was only about three hundred fifty yards from the front of the house. Charlie could see the road they used to come to the house for only a short distance before the turn off into the drive of the B & B.

It was now 6:30 and the sun was just peeking up over the horizon in the east and the gray light of dawn was giving way to an orange glow of what promised to be a bright sunny day for a short time. It was supposed to snow heavily later in the day.

Charlie was warm because of the heavy parka he was wearing except, that is, for his face. His face was cold because of the freezing temperatures and not being covered.

He began to wonder why am I here. Just because he thought some apparition said he would have to use his skills in the morning. This is ridiculous. Nothing's going to happen and if it did, I could handle it in the house just as good as I could handle it outside. This is...

Charlie looked towards the house and saw a car pulling in the drive. He saw three figures in the car. They were all skinheads. The car stopped on the other side of the van from him and backed in so the car could pull away quickly without turning around.

Charlie thought damn; this must be why Martha said what she said. Those skinheads are up to no good. That's Eddie and I don't know the other two.

Eddie got out of the car and followed the other two skinheads into the house. Soon, he heard Fran scream and then Vicki. Within five minutes one of the skinheads came out of the house and ran to their car. He opened the trunk and got a gasoline can and carried it inside.

As he was carrying the can onto the porch, Eddie and the other man who had rifles pushed Fran, Vicki and Al outside. None of them had on anything except their nightclothes and a robe.

They began to huddle together and Eddie along with the other skinhead pointed at them and laughed. The third skinhead came out of the house pouring some liquid on the porch as he came towards the people standing by the van who were shaking from the cold.

Eddie now said in a voice loud enough for Charlie to hear, "Now I want all of you to thank me as I am going to give you a fire to get warm." The three skin heads laughed.

Another one said, "Eddie, the other guy's door is locked. Shouldn't we at least wake him up and get his ass out here too?"

"Let him get warm in his room. He can get out his window if he has to, now folks, to show you I am all heart, I'm going to light a match and throw it...damn, I left the matches in the car. Wait a minute while I get them."

While Eddie was walking over to the car, Charlie had heard enough as he raised his rifle and fired two quick shots from his rifle that had a silencer.

The first skinhead screamed in pain and the second screamed a second later.

Eddie heard them scream and looked over at them on the ground. One of them called, "Eddie, we've been shot. Help us!"

Eddie seeing both men squirming and crying out in pain on the ground looked towards the hill where Charlie was and ducked behind the van. He quickly made up his mind - get in the car and get away from here. That shooter could shoot him.

The car's wheels spun as he gunned the car and drove away. Charlie could not get another shot away because the car was behind the van and after the car began to move, several large trees got in the way until the car was out of sight.

Al looked at the two men on the ground and started towards them. One of them said, "Stay away or I'll kill you and the others."

Fran and Vicki just looked at the two men on the ground.

Al replied, "Look, neither of you are going anywhere with wounds like that. Each of you has had one of your knees blown away. I've seen wounds like that in Vietnam and they are painful. Let me help you."

"Not on your life."

"Consider your position. You kill us. How are you going to escape and what about the sharpshooter who shot you? Do you think he will let you live if you kill us? Lay down your guns and let me help you. You saw how brave your friend is. He ran because he knew he would be next in line to be shot."

One of the men threw his gun down and said, "Help me, please!"

The second skinhead wasn't far behind in asking for help.

After seeing the two men asking for help, Charlie left his firing position and crouching; running behind several bushes and making sure he did not leave any footprints in the snow, returned to the house. Charlie was now in his room and placed his guns back in

their case. He opened the door and walked towards the front door.
The odor of gasoline was heavy in the house.

As he walked out of the door, he asked, "What happened?"

Al looked over at Charlie and briefly explained what had
happened.

Fran had started to walk back towards the house and Charlie
called to her. "Open all the windows, then get all the fans you have,
place them outside the house so they will blow the air from inside the
house outside and turn them on. Don't turn them on in the house.
An electrical spark from one of the fans could ignite the gas and start
a fire. The gas will be gone in a short time, but under no
circumstances, light a match and hope the gas fumes don't get ignited
from the stove or somewhere else."

Fran turned towards them and said, "That's what I was going to
do. I'm also going to turn the heater for the house off." She hurried
into the house and soon the windows were being opened.

Charlie now bent over one of the wounded men.

"That's a very bad wound. You could lose your knee."

Al, who was kneeling over the other man, echoed Charlie's
words. "You really have a bad wound."

The man on the ground by Al looked at him and said, "I like to
look at the bright side. The guy who shot us was just lucky. He
missed killing us and got lucky and hit our legs."

Al looked over at Charlie who smiled at what the man said as
Al replied to the man, "I don't think he missed what he was shooting
at - I think he hit exactly where he was aiming."

"You must be kidding. He would have had to be at least 200 or
300 yards away."

Al answered, "So!"

Curiously, Charlie felt comfortable with the thought he didn't
kill the two men lying on the ground.

Just then, the sound of a siren was heard coming fast in the
distant. Fran and Vicki had gone inside, got dressed, called the
sheriff, and had returned outside.

"Daddy, go inside and get dressed. You'll get sick if you stay
out here like that."

437

"You're right. Charlie, could you come with me?"
"Sure."

CHAPTER 13

Al and Charlie walked up the front steps of the house and went inside. As soon as they were alone Al said, "The gas odor would make me sick if I had to smell it for too long."

"It would certainly make me sick," replied Charlie.

"Charlie, since you are dressed, come upstairs with me. I have to ask you some questions."

"Sure. I was wondering when you were going to ask the questions which have been bugging you."

Once in Al's room, Charlie looked out of the window and saw a police car coming fast on the dirt road with its blue lights pulsating on the top of the car. It would be here in less than two minutes, Charlie thought.

Al had put on his warm clothes and now was looking at Charlie.

"Charlie, how I know I don't know, but I know you were the sharpshooter who shot those two skin heads downstairs. Why didn't you kill them?"

"I don't kill people any more - at least I hope I will not kill any more people. Let me ask you something. If I say this conversation is confidential as in a confessional, would you ever tell what I tell you to anyone else?"

"Absolutely not!"

"Okay. Well to begin with, yes I shot those two men. My story begins in Vietnam, but not quite like you suspect. I think I was destroying one of our last bases in Laos when I was knocked out.

439

The blow caused me to have and I still have to some extent, amnesia.

"I don't think I killed anyone while in the service, but after Nam, I know I killed some people and committed many sins because almost a year ago when I was in Seattle, I was accidentally shot and died. I was just in the wrong place at the wrong time.

"But to continue, I had an out of body experience. I was sent to Hell where I met Jesus. He forgave me my sins and returned me to my body.

"Later, after I married a member of the mafia or I should say an ex member of the mafia, an angel appeared to us and basically told us we were to use our skills in God's service. This scared us because the skills the angel was talking about were my special service skills and her killer skills. We really don't want to hurt anyone anymore.

"You must know something else. I am a millionaire and my angel told me before I met you and your family to help a minister and his family. I hope I would have helped you without being told, but what I have told you is the truth. I hope you believe me, but in no event, tell anyone what I have just told you. It might be disastrous for me and for you. I cannot tell you anymore, but please believe me."

Al was sitting on the bed listening to what Charlie was saying.

He was very quiet, then began to speak, "What you have told me is an interesting story, but how sure are you that you had an out of body experience?"

"Extremely sure. I have what could be said is absolute corroborating evidence. I can't tell you the evidence."

"I don't know why, but I believe you and I believe you met Jesus in Hell."

After saying that, Al became quiet.

"There's something else. I can't become known to the police. There are people looking for me who are very influential and would like, I believe, to kill me. I would appreciate it if you would help me in avoiding the police."

Al looking at Charlie very closely saw something in his eyes that confirmed he was telling the truth. He decided to help Charlie if for no other reason than he had helped his daughter receive medical help and he had prevented serious harm to himself and his other daughter, Vicki.

Al and Charlie walked downstairs and out into the front yard of the B & B. Sheriff Jenkins was talking to Fran and another man who had just driven up in a park service car he didn't know. Vicki was there also.

Vicki said, "Here they come now."

"Well we meet again. Now what is it with you folks that you have these run-ins with these jerks?"

Charlie answered, "I think you might ask your son that question, but I don't know what their fascination is with us. Do you know Al?"

Al looked at the ground and then up to meet the eyes of the sheriff.

"I think it has to do with two things. First, my daughter. Second, Charlie here beat them up pretty bad and this Eddie had to get revenge or he would lose face because when the going got tough, he ran and that brands him a coward."

Rod Jenkins thought for a moment, then spoke, "That seems logical. I want you folks to know I have given orders to clamp down on these skinheads - hard. And I have a bulletin out for Eddie. I hope I can get my hands on him."

Looking at Charlie, "What you did to those men in the cafe is nothing like what I would do to Eddie if I ever get him."

"Sheriff, remember you are the law and...."

"I remember, but that is why I want to teach him a lesson he will never forget. Now what happened here?"

Al answered, "Well we were being hustled outside in our night clothes by those two and Eddie when those two were shot. That's about all there was to it."

"Who did the shooting? Did you shoot them Charlie?"

Al quickly answered, "Sheriff, one of the men asked if they should wake Charlie up and make him unlock his door or light the fire. Eddie replied light the fire so he would be warm when he woke up or something like that."

Fran holding on to the other man said, "That's the truth Rod.

441

Unless Charlie had got out his window and walked up that hill over there, he was still in his room. Oh people; let me introduce my husband, Steve. He came home as soon as he heard about what was going on here. It came over the park service radio."

Charlie reached out his hand to shake his hand with Al shaking his hand right after Charlie.

Charlie and Al were talking to Steve while Sheriff Jenkins walked around the back of the house to Charlie's window. He looked at the window very closely. He noted the window was locked, but some of the snow was brushed away from the windowsill. He looked on the ground at the patches of snow - he didn't see any tracks. He shook his head and returned to the front of the house.

"Well I don't think you got out of your room through your window because there just wasn't enough snow which was disturbed and there were no footprints in the patches of snow.

Charlie breathed a sigh of relief. He had once more eluded discovery. Everything had worked fine even to the point that nobody lied about what had happened, but now he had to get out of here so he could get to Oregon and Donna.

It was after Al gave his word he would call the sheriff when he arrived in Denver and give him a number where he could contact him as a witness. The sheriff gave Al the okay to continue his trip to Billings and take Charlie with him. He decided he would not need Charlie as a witness, so he let Charlie go with Al.

Fran fixed Charlie, Al, and Vicki a couple of eggs and sausage. Steve, her husband also ate breakfast with them. It was a quiet breakfast because of the events of the morning.

After looking at the map, Charlie said, "It looks like it's a little over 300 miles to Billings from here. Al, do you think we can make it by tonight?"

"Unless the car breaks down again, we will make it."

"That'll be good. I need to catch a plane there and the next day, you can be in Denver. I understand the interstate is completed all the way to Denver from Billings, but that's just hearsay. There may be a short stretch of highway not yet complete."

"I know what you mean - even if you call the highway

442

department, sometimes they don't even know if a highway is opened or not."

Charlie looked in the back seat and saw Vicki had lain down and was sleeping.

With Vicki sleeping, Charlie said very softly, "Al, I want to thank you for not giving me away back there. And you didn't lie either!"

Al breathed deeply, then replied, "I wouldn't have lied for you, but I could say what Eddie and the other skin head had said. If the sheriff got the wrong idea, then that was his problem. I thought you were a goner when Fran said you could have gotten out of the window. The fact that you didn't disturb the snow saved you."

"I agree, but thanks again. Because I want to help you, please accept this."

Charlie gave Al another envelope containing some money. Later, Al would find $2,000.00 in the envelope.

Charlie pointed at a sign on the side of the road that read Squadron A, No. 3.

There's a nuclear tipped missile somewhere around. "There it is over there."

"You mean that concrete slab?"

"Right. If the missile is to be fired, the slab moves back and away it goes. Scary huh - riding this close to a missile with a nuclear warhead."

"It brings me back to the present. I wonder when we won't need to have nukes."

"I don't know, but I sure hope it's soon."

The van continued its drive south towards Billings through Great Falls, then on to Billings. It was getting dark and Al had turned on his headlights so he could see the highway. Soon they saw the lights of Billings in the sky ahead of them. Charlie pointed out that the airport was on a flat piece of ground just before the highway went down a steep grade.

"Al, would you mind dropping me off at the airport?"

"Not at all."

Al pulled into the airport and Charlie got out. He took his gun case with him and thought now to get to Portland, then to Crater Lake, Mt. Hood to pick Donna up and then back to our home. And I still have my gun case and guns.

Charlie poked his head in the window and said, "I hope Kristi gets better. I have a feeling God wouldn't have set it up as he did if he intended Kristi not to make it. In any case, go with God, Al."

"The same with you Charlie, go with God!"

Charlie watched Al drive down the hill, and then he rented a cab to go to a hotel downtown. After checking into the hotel, he relaxed and was soon asleep.

The bus to Minneapolis was making good time. Donna thought she would be there just about dark unless something happened. Everything was going quite well at this time - she was in the U.S., she was almost to Minneapolis and a plane ride to Portland where she could shop until she dropped. She smiled at this and she had met no one who could recognize her. Even if someone knew her, her new coal black hair would make it hard for anyone to recognize her.

Donna looked out the window of the bus and wondered at the beauty of the flat land. It was arid even though the Red River was running along side the highway. It was like an oasis in an arid land. Everything was beautiful.

The bus was now just a few miles outside Minneapolis when she awoke from a short nap. She could see the Minneapolis' skyline with the tall buildings. The bus entered the bus station and Donna got off the bus, went to the women's rest room.

After she got out of the rest room, she found a cab.

"Is there any hotel at the airport?"

"Sure is. There are several nice ones. Which one do you want to go to?"

"Just drive me to the airport and I'll tell you when we arrive."

"We're on our way."

The drive to the airport was a relatively short drive and Donna signaled the driver to stop at a Best Western Motel. She paid the driver and registered to stay the night.

Once in her room, she called Northwest Airline to find out the schedule to Portland the next day. She made a reservation for the 9:35 AM flight to Portland. She would be in Portland before noon, she thought.

CHAPTER 14

The sun didn't come up the morning after Charlie arrived in Billings. When he woke up, he looked out his window only to see a snowstorm raging outside. He walked down to the street and went to the only drugstore open within walking distance from his hotel. Charlie looked over what they had in the way of make up, selected what he needed and bought the needed items. He would disguise himself and use his real name - Charles A. Mackey. It would be nice to use his real name for a change, he thought.

After he returned to the hotel, he arranged to have a late check out, then paid for the room, and returned to his room to disguise himself. Looking at himself in the mirror and being satisfied with his disguise, he left the hotel and caught a cab to the airport.

It was 9:45 when he arrived at the airport. Charlie walked up to the Delta Airline ticket counter.

"Hi! When is your next flight to Portland?"

The ticket agent replied, "It leaves at 3:35 today and it has three intermediate stops and arrives in Portland at 7:55 tonight."

"Can I get a ticket on that flight?"

"Sure can. What's your name?"

"Charles A. Mackey, III," came the reply.

Charlie thought he would board the plane and arrive in Portland that night - sometime after 8:00 PM because the flight was making several intermediate stops before it arrived in Portland and he just thought the plane could not possibly be on time with three stops.

Charlie now walked over to a pay telephone because wanted to

447

call his bank in Eugene. He thought he could make arrangements to buy a truck, maybe another suburban or some kind of sports utility vehicle from a dealership there. Once he had bought the vehicle, he would go to Mt. Hood and pick Donna up. After making all those arrangements, he would just sit in the airport until flight time.

Donna was walking down the concourse at the Minneapolis Airport at 7:50 AM towards the gate where she would board her plane at 9:50 AM. She stopped to get a little breakfast, then continued on to the gate. She was extremely happy at this time.

Near one of the gates she passed, three men were talking.

One of the men, Vincent was speaking, "Runt, it was good to see you again. Tell everyone in Frisco hello for us."

Todd now spoke, "And tell Tony congratulations on becoming the boss out there. What happened to Louis?"

Runt was a runner for the Giaventi family and now the Andratti family. He was dressed in a nice suit, was clean-shaven, and looked like any other businessman. He had just brought over two hundred thousand dollars to Minneapolis for a payoff to a politician. This money would protect the Minneapolis family and help solidify Tony Andretti's position in the "Big Family".

"Vincent,I don't really know what happened except Louis called a big meeting two days ago and gave the family to Tony. Rumor has it, Louis is going to jail, and he made some sort of deal with Tony that involves telling the feds about some family business, but not the important stuff. That just doesn't sound like Louis, but that's the rumor. That's all I know."

Todd was looking around the airport when he saw a good-looking woman walking down the concourse. She was only about nine yards from the men when Todd saw her. She passed the three men and went towards another gate.

"Now that is what I call a good looking woman!"

The other two men turned to look at the woman walking in the concourse. She had black hair, was wearing nice fitting blue jeans, but not the tight kind, a pair of hiking boots, a colorful blouse and a parka.

Vincent agreed, "She sure is a good looker. I'd like to get her in the sack."

Runt smiled, then added, "Only if she wanted to get in the sack with you. I think I know her from somewhere - she really looks familiar."

The PA system interrupted the conversation; "The flight to San Francisco is boarding. The plane will be boarding by row numbers..."

Vincent and Todd turned to Runt and Vincent said, "Well, that's your plane. See you next time."

Runt replied, "Hope so. See you guys."

Runt boarded the plane and as the plane was climbing to cruising altitude for San Francisco, he thought damn, that woman sure looked good, I wonder where...I know who that was...it was Donna and she's alive like Tony thought. I bet Tony will be glad to know she's alive - I might even get a bonus for seeing her. She is still really a good-looking woman.

Donna was looking around the concourse when she saw Runt. She thought hey, there's Runt. I never knew his real name. I wonder what it is and what he's up to in Minneapolis. Must be Louis sent him here...Oh my God, I hope he doesn't recognize me. I've only seen him a couple of times, but if he recognized me, that may mean trouble. I'll just have to hope the color of my hair threw him off and he doesn't remember me.

Donna walked to her gate and sat down with her back to where Runt was boarding his plane. She now looked at the newspaper she had bought to read while waiting for her plane. The bold print on the second page at the top left corner caught her eye. It read, "Louis Giaventi arrested". She began to read the first paragraph, "Louis Giaventi, reputed mob boss in San Francisco, was arrested yesterday on tax evasion charges. An anonymous source says he will plead guilty in court next Friday and after that, the source says he will cooperate for a reduced sentence. It is also rumored that Anthony Andratti will become the boss in San Francisco. This source also said...."

Damn, that means if Runt recognized me, Tony will be looking

449

for me. I'll have to tell Charlie about this turn of events.

The PA system interrupted her thoughts as it announced Donna's flight was now boarding passengers.

Tony Andretti was waiting in the airport waiting area for the flight from Minneapolis with three of his men. He was nervous because he found out that Runt had skimmed some money from him. It was his first crisis since taking over from Louis. As the plane docked and the passengers were walking off the plane, Tony started to look for Runt. The three men were also looking for him.

Tony was a man with average build, but muscular. He was also hot headed and had a quick temper. Otto was robust and six foot two inches with a barrel chest and strong as an ox. Rex was an ordinary looking man, but very handy with a gun and a knife and last; Clive was a black man who was extremely muscular and very strong. He too was very good with a gun as was Tony and Otto.

Runt came off the plane to see Tony and his three men. He became nervous because this was definitely unusual for Tony to meet him with his three enforcers.

"Hi Runt. Have a nice trip?"

"Yeah. A great trip. Vincent and Todd send their best wishes to you on being selected boss out here. And you'll never guess who I saw in Minneapolis."

"Later, Runt. We have to talk."

The five men had walked down to the parking area where Tony had his car parked. All five men got in the car and the car drove away. The car drove to a secluded area near the waterfront and into an empty warehouse. Runt became even more nervous if that's possible because he knew when Tony or his enforcers drove to this particular warehouse someone always died.

After they got out of the car, Tony said, "Runt, you have been a bad boy. You skimmed almost $1,000.00 from collections before you left for Minneapolis. Do you have it or have you spent it?"

"Tony, I didn't skim anything. I promise you - I didn't skim anything. And you'll be surprised at who I saw in Minneapolis."

"Runt, Runt. You know I'll have to make an example of you

because if you get away with skimming that money, everybody else will start to skim money off me. Now I am going to let Otto teach you a real lesson, but first, who did you see?"

Runt now knew only this information would save him.

"I saw Donna. She had died her hair black, but I'd recognize that body anywhere."

Tony perked up when he said Donna. He wanted more than anything else to kill Donna for killing his uncle, Joe Andratti.

"Where did you see her?"

"In the airport where I caught the plane. Vincent and Todd were there and they saw her, too, but they didn't know who she was, but they admired her body. They even commented about her."

"Are you sure it was Donna?"

"Yes sir, Tony."

Tony frowned and went into deep thought.

After a short time, Tony spoke, "Keep him here while I call Minneapolis."

He left the four men and went to a phone in a room off to the left of where they were. Tony returned about fifteen minutes later.

"Runt, you have earned a painless death with that information. Kill him quickly."

With those words, Clive reached in his coat and had his pistol in his hand before anyone else and fired. Runt's head jerked back with a small hole in the front right of his temple and the rear of his head had a big hole. Runt was dead before his body hit the concrete.

Otto and Rex picked Runt up and put him in a wheelbarrow. With Rex walking beside Otto, Otto pushed the wheelbarrow outside to a wrecked car. Both Rex and Otto put the body in the trunk of the car. A wrecker picked the car up and placed it on a truck. Later in the day, the car would be dropped into a smasher and reduced to a very small cube of metal. Runt had paid the price for skimming off of Tony.

Tony turned to Clive as Otto was pushing the wheelbarrow with Rex walking beside him, "Clive, Vincent said they did see a good looking woman with black hair in the airport. Check where all the planes were going that morning and get back to me. Maybe we'll get

451

lucky and find the bitch."

"I'll check the airline schedules as soon as I can Mr. Andratti," Clive replied.

"Good!"

Donna arrived in Portland at twenty minutes to noon. She got off the plane, carried her only luggage to a cabstand, and got in the cab.

"Where to, miss?"

"Take me to a nice hotel with a view of Mt. Hood."

"Yes mam."

The cab finally turned into a street near a river and soon turned into a covered drive at what appeared to be a first class hotel.

Donna got out of the cab, handed the driver thirty dollars and said, "Keep the change."

"Thank you mam."

Donna walked into the hotel and up to the desk.

"I'd like a room that has a view of Mt. Hood and a queen size bed, please."

The desk clerk couldn't help but admire Donna's beauty even though she wore a large parka and was dressed in a very casual, but not a very sexy manner.

"We have just such a room. The room is $200.00 per night."

Donna softly exclaimed, "$200.00 a night?"

The desk clerk responded, "Yes mam, but you can reduce the rent substantially if you want."

Donna thought "and I thought this was a respectable place".

Donna sighed, then responded, "I'll pay the $200.00 per night. I'll be staying at least a week."

Surprised, the clerk placed a registration card in front of Donna to sign.

After she completed the card, she returned it to the clerk.

"What credit card will you be using, Mrs. Mackey?"

Donna reached into her purse and withdrew $1,000.00 in cash, eight one hundred bills with four fifty dollar bills and gave them to the clerk.

"I hope that will be enough for the present. I'll pay the rest of my bill when I check out."

The clerk looked at the money in a surprised, yet in a manner which accepted the fact she paid her bill, then answered just after he looked at her registration form, "That'll be fine, Mrs. Mackey."

The clerk signaled for a bellboy to take her luggage and show Donna to her room.

"Take Mrs. Mackey to her room."

Once in her room, Donna looked out her window and true to her request, she could see Mt. Hood in the distance. It was snow covered, at least at the top of the mountain, but the sun was shinning in such a manner as to give the mountain a pink glow. The pink glow surrounded the entire mountain and to Donna it was a beautiful sight.

Donna looked at Mt. Hood for ten or twelve minutes, then decided to take a bath. Before taking her bath, she placed all her clothes in the dresser and closet as she was going to be there for several days. After her bath, she dressed in her only dress that Charlie had bought her. She looked in the mirror over the dresser to see how she looked. She decided Charlie had good taste and much to her surprise, the dress fit her extremely well. She would wear it tonight when she ate dinner. Donna noted the time was 4:07 by the clock radio. She thought she would go find a good department store so she could begin her shopping spree tomorrow morning.

The elevator she got on was not crowded - it only had two other persons on it. She got off the elevator and went to the bell captain's desk.

"Could you tell me where a good department store is?"

"Yes mam. We have a Nordstrom store about three blocks from the hotel. Just walk out the front door and turn to the left one block, then left again for one or two blocks and you're there."

"Thank you."

As Donna began to walk out the front door, she saw the clerk and another man who appeared to be the manager looking at her in a manner that indicated they were taking her clothes off with their eyes.

As Donna walked to Nordstrom's, she thought those guys are going to give me trouble. What can I do to stop the hassle? I think I know. I'll get some camcorders and set them up in my room as soon as possible. Then if they come after me, I'll have a record of what they were up to and I hope that will solve the problem. There's the store.

Donna went in the store and started to look around. She saw many things she wanted - stylish things for women.

She thought how am I going to pick what is right for me?

She asked a lady at the information desk, "Do you have someone who can help guide me as to what would look good on me?"

The lady looked at Donna and thought, anything would look good on her, then replied, "Yes we have a personal shopper service. Can I make an appointment for you?"

"Yes, for tomorrow morning at ten o'clock."

"Fine, you'll meet her on the second floor. Her name is Nadine. Now is there anything else I can do for you?"

"Yes, where can I buy a small camcorder - you know one I can hide."

"We have some on the third floor, but if you are looking for a really small one, I suggest you talk to the Surveillance Store. It's down by the river in that little shopping center."

"Thanks."

Donna walked out of Nordstrom's and down to the river. She walked in front of a small strip mall and near the end of the mall, she found the Surveillance Store and made arrangements for what she needed and returned to the hotel. Soon after, the man who rented her the equipment, their service and his serviceman walked into the hotel with a large suitcase and went immediately to the elevators. He went up to the twelfth floor and got off. He looked for room number 1214. After finding the room, he knocked on the door. Donna looked through the peephole and recognizing the men, opened the door.

It took the men only 45 minutes to install the cameras and other equipment; then they left the hotel.

454

The digital read out on the clock radio read 6:50. Donna thought it was time to eat dinner and then to bed. She would have a big day tomorrow.

Charlie's plane landed in Portland the same day as Donna's, but at 8:14 at night. Charlie walked outside to the National Car Rental and rented a car. It was a small car, but all he wanted was transportation to Eugene. He thought he would stay in the Holiday Inn in Eugene that night and buy his vehicle the next day, go to the bank, then go look at his property near Crater Lake. He just wanted to look at it one more time before he brought Donna there. He estimated the business he needed to do in Eugene and at his property would take another week which would mean he would be finished his business the day before Christmas - just in time to meet Donna at Timberline Lodge at Mt. Hood.

CHAPTER 15

The alarm sounded in Donna's room at 7:15 AM. She reached over to the alarm clock and shut it off. Donna got up and went to the bathroom, turned on the light and turned another switch to the off position, which the man from the Surveillance Store had installed. She took off her nightclothes and put on her street clothes. She elected to put on the dress she had on the day before - it made her feel more feminine.

She dressed in the bathroom and just before she left the bathroom, she turned the switch back to the on position and turned the light out in the bathroom. When she was in her room proper, she opened the curtains to see Mt. Hood, but only saw snow coming down. While it wasn't a blizzard, it was heavy snowfall. She could not see the river or anything else she saw the day before because of the snowfall.

Donna shrugged her shoulders, got her parka, and left the room to go to the third floor where the coffee shop was. Donna entered the coffee shop just as the minute hand on the clock on the wall jumped to the six. It was 8:30 AM.

She saw one of the men who she thought was taking her clothes off with his eyes having breakfast a few tables from her. He smiled at her and Donna smiled back just as the waitress brought her some water.

"Hi, my name is Ellen and I'll be your waitress. We have a buffet or you can order from the menu. I recommend the buffet. I think it's better and it's a lot cheaper."

457

"Thanks, that's what I'll have."

"Can I get you some coffee and some juice? Both the coffee and the juice are bottomless."

"Please. I'd like some grapefruit juice and a cup of decaf."

"I'll bring you the coffee and juice while you go to the buffet. Enjoy your breakfast."

Donna thought she had to know more about the man in the suit who was sitting a few tables from her.

When Ellen came to the buffet table to service the table, Donna asked without looking at the man asked, "Ellen, who is that man in the dark gray suit sitting at the table on the right?"

Ellen looked towards where Donna had described and with somewhat of a sigh replied, "That's Lance Hunter. He's the assistant manager."

"The way you answered, you don't think much of him, do you?"

Ellen looked at Donna, then answered, "If I were you, I'd keep my distance from him. I was demoted from the greeter here in the coffee shop because I wouldn't go to a room with him." Immediately realizing if Lance Hunter learned what she said, she would lose her job, she added, "I shouldn't have said that - please don't tell anyone what I said."

"I won't tell a soul and Ellen, that's the impression I got from just being around him a short time yesterday when I checked in. Does he have a family?"

"Yes, but his wife is so in love with the bum, she doesn't believe and won't believe anything bad about him. He's also very careful about who he goes after because if his wife ever finds out about him, she will divorce him and she's got the money. He doesn't want to lose her money or her inheritance."

"So that's what he's like. Ellen, could you meet me for lunch today and tell me a little more about him - you know where he lives, etc."

"I can't meet you for lunch, but I can meet you around 2:30 - that's after lunch is served and we have set up the coffee shop for dinner."

"Fine. I'll stop by later this afternoon and we can meet at that

458

nice little coffee shop in the strip mall on the river. And Ellen, let's keep this between us."

"I have to."

Ellen thought, "What have I gotten myself into – She does look decent and I might not get into trouble."

After breakfast, Donna charged her breakfast to her room and left to go to Nordstrom's Department Store.

She went up to the second floor on the escalator, turned to the left and saw a sign which read "Personal Shopper".

Donna walked up to the desk under the sign and asked, "I have an appointment with Nadine. Is she here?"

"You must be Mrs. Mackey. She'll be right out."

A few moments later, a strikingly beautiful woman in her mid twenties walked up to Donna.

"Hi! I'm Nadine. Now what would you like?"

Donna took a deep breath, then answered, "I want the latest styles in clothing, ski togs, blue jeans, blouses, dresses, etc. I have a budget of $10,000.00. Now what can you do for me or I should say, what do you think I should get?"

Although Nadine's eyes were looking Donna over, they were not taking her clothes off as did Lance's eyes.

Nadine began, "I think red is one of your colors. It would compliment your black hair. And before we go to the ski department, I must say your black hair compliments your complexion and your figure. Now let's go first to the ski department."

Dawn broke over Eugene's Holiday Inn on Interstate 5. Charlie had not drawn his curtains that overlooked the Holidome and the swimming pool. As the alarm clock in Charlie's room went off, he turned over and reached for the snooze bar and pressed it. The alarm stopped sounding and Charlie knew he had another ten minutes to sleep, then he should get up. The ten minutes went by very fast as the alarm again went off at 8:10.

This time Charlie got up and dressed. He shaved and went to the Coffee Shop for breakfast. After eating breakfast, he called his banker at the Oregon State Bank. After talking with him for a few minutes, he went to the Dodge dealership. He looked over the pick up trucks and decided to buy a 3/4 ton Ram truck.

The inside was nice and the truck had a good reputation as to its ability to haul material. Charlie thought he would need that ability until his house and restaurant were built. He then asked the car salesman where the closest National Car Rental place was.

"You follow this street to the next light, then turn right and it's on the right side of the road. Why do you ask?"

"I have to return the vehicle I rented in Portland because I don't need it anymore since I bought that Dodge truck."

"Hey, I can save you some time. Let me call them up and I'll get them to pick the car up and you won't have to bring it back to them. How's that?"

"That'll be great."

Immediately before lunch, the car had been returned to National Car Rental and Charlie had taken delivery of his new truck.

He drove out of the dealership and went to his bank. He walked into the bank and spied his contact, Stuart Travis. As soon as Mr. Travis saw Charlie, he got up and went up to him while extending his hand.

"Mr. Mackey. Nice to see you again. What can I do for you now?"

"Well first, I got married to a wonderful woman named Donna. I want to add her name to my account. She'll be joining me just after Christmas. I'll get her signature then, but I want her name on the account now. Is that okay?"

"It's a little irregular, but I can swing it. Anything else?"

"Yes. Did you receive the additional money I wired to the bank?"

In an enthusiastic voice replied, "Yes sir. We sure did!"

Next, can you recommend a good contractor who can build me a building and a house?"

"I sure can. Try Willard's Construction Company. They are over on Tenth Street. Talk to Willard Thompson - he's the owner and one of the bank's customers. He'll help you."

"Great. Now I need some credit cards for me and my wife and also some checks so I can spend some of my money. I might as well tell you now, I'm finally moving to that area I told you about - you know near the entrance to Crater Lake National Park. I know we'll like it there."

"That's great Mr. Mackey. I'm glad you decided to move up here. I know you'll be satisfied with our service. Now, I can have two Visa Cards ready in an hour and your checks will be ready about the same time. You can pick them up right after lunch."

"Let's make that about 3:30 this afternoon because I want to visit with Mr. Thompson."

"That'll be fine."

It was ten in the morning when Tony Andratti saw Clive driving up towards the house. He thought now I'll finally get that bitch for killing Uncle Joe. I wonder what rock she is hiding under."

Clive rang the doorbell and the door was immediately opened by Tony himself.

"Well, did you get some information as to where Donna is?"

"Yes and no. I talked to several people and I think Runt actually saw Donna. She had dyed her hair black though, but she couldn't hide her good looks and especially her body. It was her."

"Okay, where did she go?"

"There were seven planes which took off from that gate area that morning after Runt's plane. One was to Portland, another to Chicago, then Anchorage, New York, Atlanta, London, and even one to New Orleans. All of them were non-stop.

"My guess is she didn't go to Portland because that's so close to California. All the rest are possibilities, especially Chicago. If she went there, she could have caught a plane to anywhere in the world.

"Now for some more information about Donna. I persuaded a cop who knows Mike real well to talk to me. He's in the hospital now, but I'll be able to get any information I want from him in the future. I beat him up pretty bad.

"Anyway, he told me that Donna actually got married right after she was shot. This guy said Mike thought her death was faked along

461

with her husband's death. Now here's the kicker. If you take out Donna, you'll probably have to take out her husband."

"Why's that, not that it will make any difference?"

"You remember that independent hit man, the Iceman?"

"He's just a figment of Interpol's imagination."

"According to this guy, he isn't and he's for real. The name he was using was C. C. Duncan - the guy Donna married. And to make matters worse, he is supposed to be better than his press clippings. He's supposed to have taken out Deng and the Tong's hit squad. He didn't know how Mike knew this, but he said Mike definitely believes the Iceman and Donna are now married. He also said Mike doesn't believe they are dead either and neither does the guy from Interpol, one Pierre Richard."

"You've brought me some interesting information. Contact the other families in the Big Family and see if they can help. Offer a $100,000.00 reward for the family who finds Donna. We'll just have to take care of both Donna and this Iceman when the time arrives. Now get in touch with the other families and Clive, do some more investigation on your own. Maybe she did go to Portland and somebody saw her, but I agree with you, I don't think she would be that stupid."

CHAPTER 16

It was 2:15 when Donna finally said goodbye to Nadine and left Nordstrom's. She hurried back to the hotel where she crossed the street to go to the shopping center by the river to meet Ellen. She saw Ellen sitting on a park bench in front of the coffee shop where they had agreed to meet.

Donna spoke to Ellen as she walked up to the bench, "Hi! Glad you came. Let's go to that cute little coffee shop over there" while pointing towards the shopping center "where we can talk and not be disturbed."

"Okay."

The two women walked over to a small coffee shop and went in and sat in a booth that was in a corner of the coffee shop. Donna ordered some coffee for herself and Ellen ordered a cup of cappuccino.

Donna noticed Ellen was very nervous she thought because of her job, but anyhow she began, "I've noticed that jerk Lance give me the eye and I didn't like what another guy said to me, but I don't want to start any trouble. So after I checked in, I made some expensive arrangements. I have my room wired for pictures and sound."

Ellen started to giggle. "That would be fun to see him get caught with his pants down - literally."

"Will you help me, but if you say yes, you will do just as I say? I must add I am not after Lance to do him harm, but just to teach him a lesson which he will never forget. Also, I cannot have the police

called in on this. You may want to do him harm and that is out -
understand?"

"I'd do almost anything to see that jerk get what he deserves -
yes I'll help you."

"But I emphasize - you must do as I say. I am not out to really
hurt him, only teach him a lesson and that only if he continues on
with his ideas towards me. Understand?"

"I don't like not doing him big time, but I understand. What do
I do?"

"First, find out exactly where he and all members of his family
lives - you know, mother, father, brothers, sisters. Then be ready to
bring some tapes to his residence if I say so."

"The first part is easy. I know he lives in Vancouver,
Washington. I can easily find out his address. The addresses of the
rest of his family might take some time, but I'll find their addresses
also. How soon do I get to deliver the tapes?"

"Maybe soon or maybe never. We'll see. Now go back to work
before someone catches us together.

The sign on the front of the building read Willard Construction
Company. Charlie walked inside and was greeted by a secretary.
She was a pleasant looking woman in her late thirties with her hair
cut short.

"Hi! May I help you?"

"I'd like to see Mr. Willard Thompson. Mr. Travis at the bank
recommended Mr. Thompson to me."

"You must be Mr. Mackey. Stuart called and said to expect you
today. Have a seat. I'll get Mr. Thompson."

Soon a balding, robust man in his late forties walked into the
room and extended his hand.

"Mr. Mackey, I'm pleased to meet you. Now how can I help
you?"

They walked down a short hallway and went into Mr.
Thompson's private office that was a small room just off the
reception area. Charlie was seated in a very comfortable chair and
Willard Thompson walked around his desk sat in a high back,

executive type chair behind his desk.

"I would like you to build me a house and a restaurant near the entrance to the park. I already own the property and I'd like you to give me a ball park estimate as to the cost, then proceed with getting an architect to design the buildings, the exact price and then if everything is right, build the buildings."

"Well, first, I must have an idea what you want and several other things. But yes, what you ask is possible."

"Well to begin with, I want a house that has four bedrooms and a bath for each bedroom. An extra large bath with a hot tub for the master bedroom. A large kitchen, dining area, living area and family room. And oh, I'd like to have a log cabin appearance on the outside and modern on the inside. Next..."

Willard interrupted, "That one's easy. We have a log cabin construction division as part of my company. My guess is it'll cost about $150,000.00."

"That was almost painless. Now for the restaurant. I would like another log cabin type of building with room for maybe thirty tables, room for expansion to fifty tables, and room to move easily about the room between the tables. Another room should have a cocktail lounge, banquet area, and of course a kitchen. I know there would be enough land for a parking area. And I keep remembering things, a covered drive where customers can get out of their cars in inclement weather."

"You want sort of the rustic look I guess. That type of building should cost about $250,000.00 to $350,000.00 with equipment."

Charlie shook his head, then said, "That should be okay. Get me the exact numbers for the cost of the buildings. My wife and I will return sometime around the New Year. We will then look at what you have prepared for us. How soon can you get us some plans for us to see and approve? Do you need anything else to make your bid?"

"That'll be fine Mr. Mackey. I will need to see the property before the final design is made. Incidentally, we have log cabin designs for buildings also, so it won't take too long to obtain plans for your buildings. Now, when can I see the property?"

"You can see it today, if you wish?"

"I can't see it today. I have some other appointments, but how about tomorrow?"

"That'll be fine. I'll just put off going to the property until tomorrow. How about 9:00 AM?"

Willard Thompson got up, held his hand out to Charlie, and said, "Nine in the morning. Right here at my office."

"Great."

Ellen walked back into the hotel and straight to the elevators smiling all the time. She was happy because she thought Lance was going to get what he deserved at last.

While Ellen was returning to the hotel, Donna was walking over to an unmarked van which was parked in the park's parking area about three hundred yards from the hotel. Donna knocked on the back doors of the Ford van.

In less than a minute, the door opened and Donna got in the van. What she saw was plenty of electronic equipment including three TV screens and a tape deck for recording voices which was in addition to the VCR tape decks. A man named Timothy Browne had opened the door for Donna.

"Well Tim, are you set up?"

"Yes mam. And you're right about what you suspect. Some guy used a passkey and got in your room and went through all your things. Apparently, he didn't find anything he wanted and he left. I have him on tape. Do you want to see the tape?"

"Yes. Then I hope I'll know....I don't know what I'll know, but I want to see the tape."

Tim put a tape in the VCR and pressed the play button. The screen right above the VCR came alive with light, then snow, then the picture of a man entering Donna's room, obviously using a passkey.

Donna thought it's Lance, that jerk.

Lance closed the door and looked for her suitcase. Noting the suitcase was empty; he opened the dresser draws. He saw Donna's undergarments that he held up, shook his head, and returned them to

466

the draw. He looked everywhere in the room - in every draw and under the draws. He was careful not to disturb anything or if he picked something up, he would return it to the same position it had been in before he picked it up.

After a while, he just stood in the middle of the room and looked around the room.

He started to talk to himself, "Now where could she hide her money. I have to find it if I am to have a bargaining point to have her invite me up here. Damn, I bet she took it with her. I'll just have to get her to invite me another way."

With those words, he left the room and closed the door behind him.

The screen went blank.

"Tim, that was excellent tape. Are you sure you are close enough to the hotel to get that type of reception all the time?"

"Mrs. Mackey, this is the latest and best equipment on the market. I could be over a mile from your room and still get this type of reception or so the company's propaganda says."

"That's good enough for me."

"Mrs. Mackey, we should discuss payment of our fee for this surveillance."

"We agreed to $8,000.00 for the rest of the week - I believe that's correct."

"Yes mam."

Donna opened her fanny pack and withdrew some money; then said, "Good. Here is the $3,000.00 balance. I would appreciate a receipt."

"No problem."

Tim wrote Donna a receipt and gave it to her. Donna put the receipt in her pocket and opened the door.

As she left the van, she turned and said, "Thanks. But remember you are not to call the police or anyone if he returns to rape me or do anything else. And please, don't save any pictures of me just in my pajamas. I don't want my husband to get the wrong idea and I would hate to extract them from you."

Tim looked at Donna and saw something different - he thought

467

she was not a person to mess with. He knew he would not keep any of the pictures she didn't want kept.

Donna now walked across the street and into the hotel. Lance Hunter was behind the desk working on something when he saw Donna walk to the elevators.

He thought damn, I can't get away now. I'll just have to wait until I get off tonight. Maybe tomorrow.

Donna opened the door to her room, walked over to the TV, and turned it on. She found the 5:00 o'clock news on channel 4. She listened intently to the news to see if what happened on the train had made the news. It had not. When the news broadcast was over, she turned the TV off and left the room. She thought she would eat early and then get some sleep. She had made arrangements to go to Mt. Hood the next day just to see what was there.

As she got on an elevator, Lance got off another elevator. Immediately on seeing Donna going down in the elevator across from the one he was on, he all but ran over to the elevator Donna was on and just got on the elevator before the doors closed.

"Good evening, Mrs. Mackey."

"You just made the elevator. Did you forget something downstairs, Mr. Hunter?"

Lance thought quickly and seeing Donna was getting off the elevator on the third floor where the restaurant was located, he replied, "Yes. I forgot to tell the people in the restaurant something. Never a dull moment here."

Smiling, Donna replied, "No, never a dull moment."

Donna got off the elevator and walked to the restaurant. She selected a seat so Ellen could be her waitress.

Ellen walked up to Donna and introduced herself saying in a relatively loud voice, "Hi, I'm Ellen. I'll be your waitress this evening." And in a low voice, "I think Lance is making his move. He wants to see any money you give me. What's that all about?"

Donna continued to look at the menu and shrugged her shoulders to answer Ellen. Soon Donna smiled and raised her head to look at Ellen.

In almost a whisper, she said, "I'll bet it's the old counterfeit scam. You know, I gave the hotel a counterfeit bill and he'll save me for a price."

Ellen smiled back at Donna and nodded signaling Donna she thought Donna was right and said, "Try the fish filet, it's good."

Donna replied, "Sounds good."

After dinner, Donna returned to her room, leaving Lance in the restaurant. When Donna returned to her room, she turned on all the lights so the cameras would have no trouble filming the room and the people in it.

Less than ten minutes after she had turned on the lights, she heard a knock on her door.

CHAPTER 17

Donna peered through the peephole in the door to see who was knocking on her door. It was Lance Hunter.

She opened the door and Mr. Hunter asked, "May I come in? There is a problem with your room payment and I would like to discuss it with you."

Donna knew she was being recorded and taped as she let Lance Hunter into her room. He passed Donna and walked over to stand in front of the queen-sized bed. Facing the window and away from the door he heard the door close behind him and smiled.

He turned to face Donna. She was wearing a loose fitting blouse and a skirt which went down to below her knees. This was becoming fashionable according to Nadine.

He said in a very serious tone of voice, "Mrs. Mackey, you gave this hotel one thousand dollars in counterfeit money, ten one hundred dollar bills. It is the policy of this hotel not to report an event like this if the person can correct the problem and give the hotel good money. Can you do this?"

"Mr. Hunter, I know the money I gave you was good and not counterfeit. You must have me mistaken with someone else because I gave you only eight one hundred dollar bills."

Playing what he thought was his trump card, he said, "Mrs. Mackey, I am quite sure it was you who gave us the counterfeit money, but if you would rather I call the police or federal agents, I will oblige."

Donna sensing he was playing his trump card, but really having

471

no idea of calling the police, she replied, "Call them so we can get to the bottom of this."

Donna's answer surprised Lance, but he quickly recovered, "Perhaps you can tell me how you know the money you gave the hotel was genuine."

"My husband gave it to me and he got it from our bank." She noted to herself she liked the sound of our bank.

Lance Hunter now was sensing this was not going the way he anticipated, decided to just come out and tell Donna what was on his mind.

He walked close to Donna and said, "Mrs. Mackey, if I call the police, you will probably go to jail over the counterfeit money, but if we were to kiss and not tell, I would refund your money and let you stay here for the week without charge."

"Mr. Hunter, I think you have the wrong idea about me." Although Donna did not try too hard to put distance between her and Lance Hunter, she did make a small effort so the effort could be recorded.

Lance just followed her and put his arm around her and tried to kiss her. Donna just lowered her head and he kissed her on the forehead.

He pulled her to him and felt her breasts on his chest. His hand went under her blouse and pushed it up, exposing her bra. He grabbed her bra, feeling her breast under it.

Donna struggled just enough to give the impression she was struggling for the camera. Hunter now thought he could subdue Donna and have sex with her and he didn't think she would report him because of the counterfeit money scam.

He threw Donna on the bed and his right hand reached down under her skirt. As his hand groped farther and farther under her skirt, Donna thought this has gone far enough.

Moving her two arms quickly and having one hand on one side of his head and the other hand on the other side of his head, she cupped her hands and smashed them together over his ears. Although she could not hear his eardrums break, she did hear him scream in pain. She rolled him over and out of the bed and onto the floor.

472

Lance Hunter had not expected this turn of events, but now he was mad and when he got up, he looked at Donna, "You bitch, now you're going to get beat up and I'm still going to screw you."

Donna smiled, "Mr. Hunter, on your best day you couldn't come close to taking me on."

Lance hunter lunged at Donna, swinging a roundhouse right. Donna simply stepped to one side and as he passed her, she kicked him on his but as well as pushing him into the wall.

For the first time, he thought he might be overmatched, but he would make one more effort and if he failed, he would leave and call the police.

He again lunged at Donna. Donna again stepped aside and grabbed the back of his shirt and threw him against the other wall. Lance now knew he was no match for Donna and ran to the door and opened it to escape. Donna let him escape, but she immediately left the room to go down to the van. If Tim was able to get a tape of what went on in the room, she had what she wanted - tapes of Lance Hunter trying to rape her.

She went down to the lobby and seeing Mr. Hunter, walked up to him as he was now behind the desk, "Mr. Hunter, I am sorry things are not different, but I would advise you not to call the police or the feds. You know that money is real and you don't have enough funny money right now to show the feds or police, plus I will have something for you tomorrow morning."

Not understanding what she meant, he thought she was going to get in bed with him the next day because she did not want to involve the police.

Donna went out to the van and got in the van with Tim.

Donna was looking at a smiling Tim as Tim spoke, "You really were playing with that jerk, Mrs. Mackey. Why didn't you just take him out? No one would have blamed you. I have the entire thing on tape to prove your story."

"I don't take people out any more, but as you said, it would have been easy to do. I want the two videos spliced together so I can show it to him and then I'm going to have some fun. You know, I still think that jerk thinks he's going to get me in the sack."

473

Tim thought I wonder what she meant by she doesn't take people out anymore? No matter, he then replied: "How many copies do you want?"

"I think five would suffice and after tomorrow, I won't need your services anymore. However, I'll need two copies in an hour."

"Mam, I'll have your five tapes in half an hour, but I have to say it again, I like your style."

"Thanks."

Donna left the van and returned to the hotel.

Lance Hunter was waiting. He walked up to Donna and said, "You want to see me tomorrow morning?"

"I sure do. Nine o'clock."

Donna left Lance Hunter and went to find Ellen. When she met Ellen, she said, "I have what we both want – a tape of a babbling fool trying to rape me. He couldn't have come close, but he tried."

Ellen replied, "You mean he actually tried to rape you?"

"Yep. But now to what I want you to do. I will have several copies of a very interesting tape in about an hour or maybe a half hour. I will give you all but one and I will deliver the other one to his mother and I hope she will agree with us and help us."

Forty-five minutes later, Donna left the hotel, picked up the tapes, gave all but one tape to Ellen, and hired a taxicab. The cab took her to an apartment complex in Vancouver where she got out of the cab and walked up to the door. She rang the doorbell and when the door opened, she saw a nice looking woman in her mid sixties.

Donna said, "Mrs. Hunter?"

The woman answered, "Yes."

The sun rose in the east sending bright sunlight into Donna's room, waking her up at 7:35. She immediately went into the bathroom and turned the switch to turn the cameras off in the bathroom, got dressed and turned the switch back on. She then went down to the ground floor and saw Tim waiting in the lobby for her.

"You got them."

"I have the videos you ordered and I have a TV with a built in VCR for you to play them. As soon as you give the signal, I'll close down the shop."

474

"Thank you so much for your help, Tim."

"It's been my pleasure."

Tim carried the TV up to Donna's room and left the hotel. Donna walked back to the elevators and went to the third floor. She walked over to the restaurant and signaled for Ellen to come to her.

"We definitely got him. Remember don't let anyone see any of the tapes and don't tell a sole what you have or what happened, understand?"

"I do, but I know some people who would like to know."

"Remember what you promised."

In a disgusted manner, "I remember and I won't tell anyone - at least for right now."

"Ellen!!!"

"Okay, not unless you tell me it's okay."

"You won't be sorry. Now make some excuse and come to my room for 8:45. Okay?"

At 9:00 AM, Lance Hunter knocked on Donna's door. Instinctively she knew who it was and opened the door.

Lance came in the room expecting to see Donna undress, but he saw Ellen sitting in the chair near the window.

He thought wow, two of them - then he realized this was something else as he saw the TV screen of him coming into Donna's room.

Ellen had turned the VCR and TV on. Lance sat down on the bed and watched the entire video. For the first time, he realized he was in no position to bargain for anything, but he could try.

"Mrs. Mackey, I will cancel your bill and return your money and Ellen, I will see to it you get a big promotion to head the convention department. You know we lost the head man yesterday."

Donna and Ellen smiled. "Donna, do you think we should give the tape to his wife?"

"I don't know. I think it's fun to see a weasel squirm."

"I do too."

"What do you think Mr. Hunter? Should we give the tape to your wife?"

"No - please don't do that. It would wreck a good marriage.

And I have two children, you know that Ellen."

"Yes, but do they know what you do here?"

"I promise I'll never do that again - please."

Donna was satisfied to see him squeal and squirm for the twenty minutes they were playing with him. She now walked over to the bathroom and opened the door. Mrs. Sally Hunter walked out of the bathroom.

Lance Hunter was surprised and shocked all at the same time. "Mother!"

"Yes, and I heard and saw it all. You rotten jerk. You have a lovely wife and you do this to her. When Donna came to me last night with her story, I didn't want to believe her, but even though it was probably the hardest thing she has ever done, she convinced me to watch her tape and to come here this morning just for the purpose of saving your worthless hide.

"When I saw the tape, I was absolutely...If you were in the room when I saw you on tape, you would not be standing. Now I agree with Donna as to what you are going to do."

Ellen now spoke, "I agree also."

Lance Hunter had never seen his mother this angry, but he was now listening to every word being said by everyone.

Donna said, "Lance, we all know you have been a very naughty boy, but we are going to give you a second chance. Your mother has one of the tapes and Ellen has more tapes. If you ever try this again, one or both of these tapes is going to be delivered to your wife. Do you understand what I have just said?"

In a meek voice, "Yes mam."

Sally Hunter said, "Good. Now get back to work and oh, what you said about the free week for Donna and giving Ellen that job, it had better be done by tomorrow, understand?"

Ellen interrupted, "Mrs. Hunter, I think we should give him at least one week to give me that raise, don't you Donna?"

"That would be all right."

"If both of you say so, I guess it'll be okay, but no more than a week."

Lance Hunter walked out of the room like a beaten man, but

476

still a married one.

And the important thing was he would go home and do everything in his power to love and honor his family.

CHAPTER 18

Charlie was up at the crack of dawn. He drove to the Cascade Trailers, Inc. As he drove through the gate, he saw trailers of every description - recreational type trailers, home trailers which were meant to be placed on a lot and used as a home, pop up trailers, and even motor home RV units. He pulled his new brown Dodge pick up truck to the office, got out and walked in the office.

He saw a man in his early fifties sitting with a woman in her late forties and obviously his wife.

When Charlie walked in, both the man and woman got up and the man greeted Charlie: "Hi. My name is Zachariah Kathman. People call me Zack though and this is my lovely wife, Hope. Now, what can we do for you sir?"

"My name is Charlie Mackey and I would like to buy a double trailer if you can install it on my property for Christmas or at the very latest, New Years Day. Can you do it?"

"I don't know, but I sure will try. First thing, is the property where you want the trailer placed close by?"

"It's within fifty, no maybe seventy five miles."

"That's great. Does it have water, electricity, and sewerage?"

"I don't think so, but I am willing to pay a little extra to have it done."

"Let's go to your property so I can see what needs to be done."

"You can come with me and Mr. Thompson. He's going to build me a permanent home and business on my property with a log cabin motif for both buildings."

479

"Willard is a good contractor. Now if you are going to have him build you a home, why don't you rent one of our trailers in the trailer park for a couple of months? It'll be a lot cheaper."

"I thought about that, but I want another home for possibly an employee to live in after I move into my home - I should say our home. I just got married a short time ago and I just haven't got the hang of saying our home yet." Charlie smiled.

Hope responded, "I know how you feel. It took us maybe two or three weeks to start saying our home, etc. Of course we have been saying our now for twenty eight years."

"I hope I can say that twenty eight years from now. But can you place the trailer and have it ready for Christmas?"

"You're in luck. This is a slow time of the year, but I would expect New Years Day would be a better bet."

"Well, let's go meet Mr. Thompson."

"Hope, can you watch the store for me?"

"Sure. Go with Mr. Mackey and Willard."

Charlie and Zack got in Charlie's truck and drove to the Willard Construction Company where Mr. Thompson was waiting for them just outside his office. He got in the back seat of the king cab pick up.

"This is a pleasant surprise, hi Zack. I was going to recommend Charlie rent a trailer from you while I build his home. Hey, this is nice. Nice truck, Charlie."

"Thanks, Willard. I just bought it."

Charlie drove on a two-lane highway with the mountains all around them. Crater Lake was to the north of the highway. Finally, Charlie came over a small hill and stopped. He pointed ahead of them and down at the bottom of the hill. There were pine trees on both sides of the highway, but on each side of the road behind the pine trees were cleared areas. On the north side of the highway was a relatively large cleared area and on the south side the cleared area was just a little smaller than on the north side.

"That's it. I want the house built on the south side of the highway and the restaurant on the north side. Willard, see that little rise in the land over there and just behind it a little stream bed. That's

480

where I want the restaurant. The parking area can be between the restaurant and the highway right behind that little rise in the ground. I plan to have the delivery door there and a hedge row to hide the parking lot from the delivery area."

"Sounds like you know what you want and I kinda like your idea. Of course, before I start construction, you will furnish me with a title to the land."

"I would need a copy of the deed before I bring a trailer onto the property, also," added Zack.

"No problem. I had Stuart Travis get two copies of the deed for me when I saw him. Your copy is in this envelope and yours is in this envelope," Charlie said as he handed each of the men an envelope.

"Now for my - oops our home. Willard, you see where that stream goes under the roadway - that bridge over there."

"Yes."

"Follow the stream for about two hundred yards down stream from the bridge and you'll see a little finger of land coming out from that small hill. I want our house on the front of that finger of land."

"Good choice. Sometimes that stream floods, but I have never seen water to the top of the hill. A good place for your driveway to come in right over there by that grove of pine trees, don't you think so?"

"That would be a good place Willard. Now Zack, I want you to place the trailer about three hundred yards west of the main house. You and Willard can get together on things like a water-well and who builds the road, but remember I want the trailer to be ready for my wife and me to begin using it no later than New Years day."

Zack looked at Willard who replied, "Zack, I can get the road finished a couple of days after Christmas. Can you get a big well drilled and operational before then?"

"I think so. Our driller isn't very busy now, so I think he'll do it. I think it'll be ready for New Year's Day. If it isn't, I'll pay for you and the missus to spend a couple of nights in the motel where you're staying now. Is that satisfactory?"

"Sure is. Let's go down and walk over what we have just

481

discussed so there are no mistakes."

The three men nodded in agreement.

After the three men had walked over the land and both Willard and Zack knew exactly where Charlie wanted the buildings, they got back in the truck and drove back to the bank where Mr. Travis was waiting for them.

"Come on in Charlie. Nice to see you," speaking to Willard and Zack. "Now what can I do for you?"

"Well first, guarantee the price of the trailers I am buying from Zack. We haven't discussed the price yet, but perhaps you could tell him that I own the property and my credit is good."

"Zack, Charlie's credit is good up to...let's see would $250,000.00 cover it. And Willard, the bank will guarantee whatever the cost of building his restaurant and home is – let's say up to $1,500,000."

Zack and Willard looked at each other. Both men thought, but now they knew Charlie was rich.

After Charlie returned Willard and Zack to their businesses, he ate some long overdue lunch and returned to the Holiday Inn for some rest. However, he went to his room and changed into a swimsuit and went to exercise and then for a swim. He now went back to his room, showered and changed into some street clothes. It was now 4:30 in the afternoon. He thought he would rest for a while and then get some dinner.

After Donna had her meeting with Lance and the others, she was happy as a lark. She didn't have to kill or beat up Lance to get the desired results and she would have a place to stay until Christmas, then she would go to Mt. Hood and meet Charlie and they would really become husband and wife. She was absolutely ecstatic.

She went downstairs to pick up her rental car - a blue Ford Mustang. She was going to see Mt. Hood and Timberline Lodge. She decided to drive along the Columbia River and see the waterfalls, which she had heard were beautiful. These waterfalls were along the interstate highway that ran along the river or close to it.

She saw several waterfalls and a dam. She now noticed it was getting late and she wouldn't be able to see Mt. Hood tonight so she turned around and returned to her hotel. Donna resolved she would leave the hotel early next morning and see Mt. Hood and Timberline Lodge.

Donna was up very early the next morning and was driving along the Columbia River towards Hood River. It took her almost three hours to arrive at Hood River where she turned south and towards Mt. Hood. The first part of the drive was through a typical farming area, mostly flat, but she could see the mountains and she was reasonably sure she saw Mt. Hood standing above the rest of the mountains towards the south where she was heading.

The highway started to climb and she was in the mountains at last. It was beautiful especially with the sun shining in a clear blue sky. It was going to snow late that day or that night. The weather was to turn nasty so she had to be back in Portland by 4:00 o'clock to be safe. It would be only two days later and she would be with Charlie and be a married woman. The thought was pleasing to her - very pleasing.

She saw a road sign, US 26, 5 miles. She knew she was close to turning and less than ten miles from the turnoff to Mt. Hood. Donna turned onto US 26 going west towards Portland. A short distance from the turnoff, a sign said Timberline Lodge and an arrow pointing to the right. She turned north and traveled on a relatively narrow, but good road that soon became snow packed. As she approached the lodge she saw a large parking lot and several relatively large buildings.

After parking her car close to the lodge, she went in hoping to eat in the restaurant. She was in luck. The restaurant was still open. She only had a salad, but the view from the restaurant was fantastic. Mt. Hood was out the window with people skiing down the ski slopes. She hoped she could learn how to ski as well as the skiers on the slopes. Maybe Charlie could teach her or they could both take lessons.

After lunch, Donna walked around the lodge; then left and drove down the road towards US 26. She thought she would take the highway to Portland instead of going back to the Columbia River. The clouds were closing in by this time, but she was able to see several mountains peeking above the clouds in the distance. The sight was beautiful.

Charlie thought of one more thing he forgot to tell Zack. He dialed his number.

"Cascade Trailers," came the answer over the telephone.

"Hi. This is Charlie. May I speak to Zack?"

"Sure. Just a minute."

In less than thirty seconds, another voice came over the telephone. "This is Zack. What can I do for you Charlie?"

"I forgot to tell you to furnish the trailer. I don't know what to get and I don't really have the time to buy furniture, so could you buy it for me?"

"Sure. I'll let Hope buy the furniture. We'll keep the bills for you."

"Good. How are you coming? Do you think you will make Christmas or New Years?"

"Christmas is not possible, but I think New Year's Day is almost definite."

"That'll be fine. See you then."

Charlie hung up the phone and drove the Dodge pickup out of the Holiday Inn parking lot. He would drive north on Interstate 5, then follow the Columbia River to Hood River and then to Mt. Hood.

Charlie was secretly hoping to see Donna before the second day after Christmas so they could be together sooner. He passed through Portland, but did not see Donna.

As he drove along the River, he noted the waterfalls he had seen before which were still beautiful. He did not stop to look at them, but continued towards Mt. Hood. He had lunch in a little cafe just before he turned south towards Mt. Hood.

He thought the road towards Mt. Hood was beautiful, but the clouds were now gathering to dump snow on the area. Charlie turned west on US 26 and was soon turning north towards Timberline Lodge. As he drove up the highway, a blue Mustang passed him going down the highway. He parked in the lodge's parking lot and went in to the lodge's desk.

"Hi. My name is Charlie Mackey. I just want to confirm my reservation for December 27th for seven days and do you have a room open before then?"

"I'm sorry Mr. Mackey, but we are booked. We do have your reservation for the 27th though."

Charlie nodded and returned to his car. He left the lodge and returned to the highway along the Columbia River. He would return to the Holiday Inn and spend Christmas waiting to be with Donna, never realizing he passed her going up to Timberline Lodge.

CHAPTER 19

Donna woke up early on the second day after Christmas as this was the day she was to join Charlie at Timberline Lodge and she wanted to get there early so she would be there waiting for him. He might even be there before her - that would be even better she thought. What if he didn't show - no that was not an option - she put that thought out of her mind.

She hurriedly packed the few things she had not packed the night before and called for the bellboy to come to get her luggage. Since shopping at Nordstrom's, she had acquired three suitcases and many stylish clothes.

She had laid out a very stylish ski outfit which was supposed to be worn around the fire and not on the slopes. The trousers were bright red and the blouse was more like a sweater. It had a turtleneck, long sleeves, was principally yellow, but had a red trim down the arms. Donna just looked stunning.

Donna's thoughts were interrupted by a knock on the door.

Donna opened the door and let the bellboy in to take her luggage downstairs. She kept her heavy parka so she could wear it when she got to the Timberline Lodge where it was a good deal colder than here in Portland.

As Donna was leaving the hotel carrying her parka, Lance Hunter came out from behind the reception desk.

"Mrs. Mackey, may I have a word with you."

Donna looked at Lance and replied, "Sure."

"I just want to thank you for not turning me in to the hotel and most of all, not telling my wife who I really adore. I know my mother won't tell unless I don't behave. Again, thank you very much."

Donna extended her hand as she said, "I hope you get some help if you need it and I certainly hope you won't ever try what you tried again."

"I won't, I promise."

With those words Donna turned towards the hotel door and walked outside. As she was walking, she thought I hope he'll keep his word, but it will take a few years for him or anybody else to find out if he will keep that promise.

As she got in a taxicab to go to Mt. Hood, she noticed the weather was anything but sunshine - it was cloudy, drizzly, windy day and colder than what she had anticipated. It was in the mid twenties. The cab pulled out on to the street and began the trip to Mt. Hood.

Donna directed the cab to take the highway along the Columbia River. Since Donna was not driving, she looked at the river and the many waterfalls along the highway as they approached Hood River. After turning towards Mt. Hood, Donna could appreciate the beauty of this portion of the ride to a greater extent than when she first went to Mt. Hood. This time, however, she could not see Mt. Hood because of the clouds.

As the cab climbed to a higher elevation, the mist changed into light snowfall and the road became covered with a thin skim of snow with auto tracks tracking through the snow and removing the snow on the highway so one could see the road in the tire tracks.

It was a pretty sight with all the snow on the ground - with the streams on the side of the road partially frozen. The pine trees green standing in the background with a good deal of snow on the needles.

The cab now turned west on Highway 26 and after a short ride turned onto the road to Timberline Lodge. Soon she could see the Lodge through the falling snow. The cab pulled into the parking area for the lodge and stopped.

Donna had put on her parka in the cab and now got out of the cab into a respectable snowfall. The cab driver retrieved her luggage from the trunk of the cab and placed it on the sidewalk.

Donna asked, "Could you help me carry my luggage into the lodge?"

The cabby expecting a large tip replied, "Sure."

Donna and the cabby carried her luggage into the lodge where it was warm.

Donna reached into her purse and retrieved her money. She gave the cab driver a substantial tip over his charges for driving her to the lodge.

Donna now walked up to the desk. It was a relatively small desk tucked away in a little cove.

"Miss, My name is Mrs. Mackey. My husband made reservations for us a couple of months ago."

The woman looked at Donna as much as to say, *"Yeah, your husband. I wonder if you are really his wife."* She then replied with a smile, "Yes mam. In fact he was in here a couple of days ago checking on the reservations."

This relieved Donna who was getting nervous because she really did not know Charlie would show up. She now knew he would at least show up.

"May I go to our room now?"

"It will cleaned up in less than twenty minutes. Please have a seat over there on one of the benches."

Donna turned to walk over to the benches, but turned back to the woman behind the desk.

"You know, I'm a bit nervous. My husband and I were married less than two months ago and we were immediately separated because of circumstances beyond our control. This will be our first night together and I'm so nervous."

The woman thought, I wonder if she's telling the truth. Anyway, I have to play it straight. "Well congratulations. I'm sure you will calm down when you see him."

"I sure hope so."

Seeing the cleaning maid, she said, "Your room is ready. It is up those stairs and to the left. It's room 208. Here's the key."

"Thanks."

Charlie was up early and very excited. He had to call Willard Thompson, the contractor and especially Zack to make sure the trailer would be ready for Donna and himself. He looked out the window and saw nothing but a light drizzle and clouds. He thought, damn, the weatherman was right this time - drizzle and then snow. The trip to Timberline Lodge should only take five hours from here, but with this weather, it might take longer.

Charlie dressed in his blue jeans and woolen shirt, left his parka out, and then packed the rest of his clothing in one suitcase. After packing, he went down to the coffee shop. He ate hot cakes and bacon with three cups of coffee - black. He returned to his room, prepared himself for the five-hour drive to Mt. Hood, then went to the phone. After dialing a number, he waited for the phone to answer.

After two rings, a voice came over the phone, "Cascade Trailers, Hope speaking."

"Hope, this is Charlie. Is Zack around?"

"No, but he thought you would be calling to check on the progress of placing the trailer on your property and everything, so I am to tell you first, your trailer will be ready New Year's eve morning, Zack thinks about ten or eleven. The reason for this is the furniture will have to be delivered and placed in the trailer, then the trailer must be checked. Second, the water well is pumping water better than the driller anticipated. There will be enough water to supply the trailer and the house and even the small pond you wanted with a stream coming from the pond. Third, the septic tank is in and he is checking it now. And fourth and last the trailer will be installed two days before New Year's day and the final checking will be done the next morning. Any questions?"

"Hope, you have answered all of my questions. Now I have to call Willard. If I don't see you and Zack before New Year's Day, hope you had a Merry Christmas and have a great day. I also hope it will be a great year for both of you. See you after New Year's Day. Bye."

"Bye Charlie. Hope everything goes right for you and your

490

wife. Take good care of her. Bye."

Charlie hung the phone up and dialed another number.

A voice answered the phone, "Happy New Year. Willard Construction. How may we help you?"

"Hi, this is Charlie. Can I speak to Willard, please?"

"Sure can. Just a minute."

Within twenty seconds, a man's voice came over the telephone, "Hi Charlie, this is Willard and before you talk, I will have the complete plans for your house and restaurant ready for you and the Mrs. to look at them on January 4th. What time do you want to look at them?"

"Let's see, it'll take us about two hours if the roads are clear, but a little longer if there are any detours....let's say 1:00 PM. That'll give us enough time to get there and not rush."

"Fine, 1:00 PM it is on January 4th at my office."

"Great, now I must get on the road to pick up Donna. Take care, Willard."

"Take care, Charlie and be careful, it is slip and slide time on the highways."

"I will."

Charlie hung the phone up and walked to the front desk and checked out. He had one stop to make before he left Eugene. Stop at the bank and pick up a Visa card for Donna.

He left the bank with everything in order and Donna's card in his wallet. He entered Interstate 5 and began the trip north to Mt. Hood. If everything went right, he would arrive at Timberline Lodge somewhere between 1:30 and 2:30 that day, depending on road conditions.

It was 11:30 and Donna was getting anxious and that was feeding her empty stomach. She thought she would go down to the restaurant and eat a light lunch, then wait for Charlie in the room.

Donna walked down the stairs and went into the large open room. The restaurant was on the other side of the room and as she walked to the restaurant, her beauty turned several heads. She was absolutely beautiful in her ski clothes.

She sat down to eat a salad with some iced tea. She ate her lunch and was finished by 12:45. She signed the bill and got up to go to her room.

Just then, a waiter bumped into her and spilled the food that he was carrying all over Donna. The waiter was all apologies and the female maitre de started to wipe the gravy from her outfit.

She said, "We're so sorry. Let us pay for your lunch. It's the least we can do. And also, send us the bill for cleaning your clothes."

Donna being more and more relaxed, replied, "No problem. I'll just go upstairs bathe and change. It was really my fault. I should have looked before I got up."

What Donna had said surprised herself because before her out of body experience and her marriage to Charlie, she probably would have blown her cork and maybe even beat the waiter to a pulp. Instead she walked across the big room and then upstairs.

She thought I like doing things this way better. A lot quieter and less stressful...I'll order some champagne; the best the house has, and be ready for Charlie when he shows up. Golly, I hope he shows up soon.

Donna called room service and ordered the champagne. Room service told Donna the champagne would be there by 1:45, chilled. That was what Donna wanted. It was 1:12 and that would give her enough time to take a shower and get dressed so she could prepare the room for Charlie when he arrived.

Donna had finished taking her shower and had one of those large towels wrapped around her when she heard a knock on the door. Thinking it was room service and not thinking about how she was dressed, went to the door, and peeked through the peephole.

Standing there was Charlie smiling.

Donna screamed with joy. "Charlie."

She opened the door and leaped into his arms. Charlie came into the room and kicked the door shut with his foot.

After they had kissed, another knock was heard on the door. Donna said, "Leave it outside. I'll get it in a while."

The towel slipped down her body revealing a muscular, naked female body.

492

As Charlie was taking off his clothes, he said in a kidding manner, "I hope this is just for me and nobody else."

Donna replied, "You know it's only for you!"

Soon the two muscular bodies were joined as one. Thus began Charlie and Donna's life together.

CHAPTER 20

The champagne stayed outside Charlie and Donna's room until 4:45 PM that day when Charlie opened the door and retrieved it. Charlie poured two glasses of champagne and they both drank the bubbly. A short time later, they got dressed and went down to eat dinner. After eating, they walked around the lodge, then went outside. It was dark by then, but the sky had cleared and it was a beautiful night with the stars beaming their light down to earth. The moon was only a half moon, but it had enough brilliance to light up the snow, which was all around the lodge and up Mt. Hood. Charlie and Donna thought the night was just made for them.

The next day, Charlie and Donna found the shops in the building below the lodge. Even though they shopped until noon, they only bought two pull over warm shirts with a picture of Timberline Lodge and the name on the front of the shirt.

That afternoon, Charlie and Donna went for a ride to explore the surrounding area. They drove down the snow packed road leading to and from the lodge down to Highway 26, then turned left. Highway 26 had patchy snow on the roadway so Charlie did not take the pickup out of 4-wheel drive. The Dodge truck turned right to go down a dirt road only to discover it was closed a short distance from the main highway. There were four vehicles parked at the gate. It appeared the people in the vehicles got out of them and hiked in.

Donna said, "Charlie, let's come back here tomorrow and hike in. It must be a nice hike with four cars parked out here."

"That would be great, honey."

That night as they were getting ready for bed, Donna turned to Charlie and said, "Charlie, I had some experiences - I mean really experiences - after you left me in Jasper. Did you have any experiences?"

"Do you mean did I help some people?"

"Yeah, something like that."

"Well I met this minister and his family in Calgary and I believe I helped save their daughter's life. Later after we entered Montana, I probably saved the minister and his other daughter and another woman who ran a B & B. But you know I almost had a disaster happen."

"What happened?"

"There was this (skin head) who was the root of the trouble there. I knew him from Idaho. I don't think he recognized me, but it was close. I somehow think I will see him again and I will regret not taking him out."

"Charlie, you know that's not good. Let me tell you what happened to me. I met a very nice couple on the train. They were with the Resistance during the war."

"Korea?"

"Donna smiled and replied, "The only war, World War II. Anyway that's what they said it was. To continue, there were four jerks on the train who were going to kidnap a boy and I stopped the kidnapping and I beat one of them to a pulp, captured another one and shot a third one. The man, Philip, shot and maybe even killed the fourth man. I left the train before I found out if he made it.

"When I shot that man, Yvette knew I was a good shot and started to ask questions, but I didn't tell her too much. They put me in touch with some friends of theirs and they helped get me back into the states.

"As I was about to get on my plane, I think that maybe I might have been recognized in the Minneapolis airport."

"You too?"

"Yes. When I was in the Minneapolis airport going to get my flight, I saw a man named Runt. I don't know his real name, but he was a runner for the family. If he saw me and recognized me, we might be in for big trouble."

Charlie was sitting on the bed and paying absolute attention to what Donna was saying.

"You know the man I killed in Seattle was named Andratti. Louis and Frank had ordered me to take him out because he was going out on his own and skimming from the family. Well, I read in the paper that Louis had trouble with the IRS and was expected to plead guilty to tax evasion and then in about a week, he was going to tell all to the police about the family's operation.

"I know Louis wouldn't do that unless he had set everything up so that what he told the police would have little or no effect on the family and had the approval of the new godfather. That is where we might have trouble."

"How's that?"

"The heir apparent is Tony Andratti, nephew of Joe Andratti and he is hotheaded and a very revengeful man. He wants me dead and he wants to be the one who kills me. My guess is if he gets wind that I am alive, he will make every effort to find me - and Charlie, he has contacts everywhere."

"That could be bad. We will have to watch ourselves. I've been thinking about what would happen if we were ever recognized and I have a plan, but I don't think we should use the plan unless we have to because it is very risky. It involves a super plastic surgeon in Switzerland who is used by most of the governments of the world. Anything else happen?"

"Now that you mention it, I guess I blackmailed a sex mad jerk into being a good family man. I don't know if it will work, but I thought it was worth a try. I spent a good chunk of my money setting him up and getting him on film trying to climb in bed with me. I wanted so to really beat the jerk up, but I didn't - well I didn't completely beat him up, just a little bit though."

"You really had some experiences, didn't you?"

"I sure did and just like you." Then Donna looked straight at Charlie and asked, "Charlie, are all men after only one thing - sex?"

"You have to admit that's one of the basic drives of man."

"I guess so. And I guess the same can be said of women also.

497

But to get back to my experiences after Jasper. I had several visions of Martha and each vision gave me valuable information like maybe a guardian angel would. Did she appear to you?"

"Yes - several times and I feel the same way you do about her appearances. It was like she is our guardian angel."

With those words, Charlie leaned over and kissed Donna who responded with vigor.

The next day, Charlie and Donna drove to the area where they saw the cars the day before. They got out and walked down to the lake. The lake had a skim of ice on it and there was snow all around the lake. It was a beautiful sight. After staying there for almost two hours, they returned to their car.

On the ride back to the lodge, they saw several mountains that were snow capped.

Donna remarked, "Those peaks are beautiful aren't they?"

Charlie replied, "They sure are."

Several days later, they left the lodge and began their drive home - to their new home near Crater Lake. The drive was uneventful even though it was an overcast day and it looked like it would snow any minute. As they drove up to the trailer house, Charlie stopped the pickup on a hill overlooking his property.

"That's our temporary house over there. Our permanent home will be just over the hill from the house. I've ordered it, but I want your input so the contractor won't start it until you see the plans and you have a chance to tell him what you want."

Charlie slipped his hand from holding Donna's hand to gently moving his hand up her thigh, but stopping and holding her thigh.

Donna playfully slapped his hand and said, "Didn't you get enough of that last night."

Charlie smiled and replied, "All I wanted to do is to touch you. Anyway, I also want you to remember what happened last night."

"That's different. I was in bed with you and I wanted to touch you."

They bent over and kissed.

Over the next two days, Donna and Charlie set up their house

498

the way they wanted it - moving the furniture to different places in the house, checking the water and electricity – generally doing what families do when they move into a new house. During this time, Charlie had called Willard Thompson and changed their appointment for them to look over the blueprints of the restaurant and the house he was to build.

At 9:00 AM on January 8th, Charlie and Donna walked into Willard's office.

When Charlie saw the secretary, he said, "Hi! We have an appointment to see Willard. Is he here?"

"He sure is Mr. Mackey. I'll get him."

In a short time, Willard came out into the reception area.

Charlie, with a bit of pride in his voice, said, "Willard, this is my wife, Donna."

Willard extended his hand to Donna who took it and shook his hand.

"You didn't tell me your wife is so beautiful. It's a pleasure to finally meet you, Mrs. Mackey."

Donna replied, "First, it is a pleasure to meet you also and second, flattery will get you everything."

Willard smiled and replied, "That's what my wife told me many years ago when we first met. Flattery got me married and believe it or not, I am very happy man. Now let's go into my office where I have the blueprints laid out on my drawing table."

Donna and Charlie followed Willard into his office and stood in front of his drawing table where the blueprints were. Willard went around to the backside of the table.

"First, here is the plan for the restaurant. I must tell you this - I can't start the restaurant for four months. I have a problem - my supplier of logs doesn't have the logs I require to build the restaurant, but he has assured me he will have them ready in four months. I will lay the foundation and pour the concrete immediately so when the logs come in, the framework can go up immediately. I hope that's all right with you two."

Charlie looked at Donna who nodded.

Charlie responded, "That'll be fine."

"Now to the plans. The parking lot will be here and the service entrance will be in the rear with the road to the service entrance coming in behind a little rise in the land...."

Charlie interrupted, "Much like a levy?"

"Yes. I was thinking you could put some shrubs on the hill to block any view of the service road, which will have an entrance to the main highway. There will also be a trail or walkway as you may call it from your house to the restaurant that goes under the little bridge and up to the service entrance. The trail will be hidden from view.

"Next, the entrance to the restaurant will be here and ..."

Willard Thompson continued to describe the plans with Charlie and Donna nodding in an approving manner where appropriate.

After he finished describing the restaurant, Willard asked, "Is that about what you wanted?"

"Charlie spoke, "That's about what I think I want. What about you, Donna?"

"Charlie, I couldn't have done a better job if I were drawing the blueprints myself, but what I really want to see is the plans for my house."

Charlie turned to Donna and said, "Our house."

"You say what you want – it will be my house. It's going to be my first home and I hope my last home, but if you insist I'll let you live there too."

Before Charlie could reply, she added, "You know it's our house, but I like to think of it as my house. Okay?"

In a sarcastic tone of voice, Charlie replied, "Anything you say, honey."

Willard was smiling at both Charlie and Donna and interrupted their conversation, "Charlie, you are a wise man to let your wife say what she wants and anything else she wants to do. Now that is settled, I just need for you folks to sign the authorization right here by the x mark to build the restaurant and I'll spread the house plans on the table."

Charlie and Donna signed the authorization and Willard removed the restaurant plans and placed the house plans on the table.

"Now, I thought about it and I think you would like a house based on the house in Bonanza, the TV show. As you drive up to the house, the first thing you see is the porch. You enter into the formal living room and the formal dining area is to the left of the doorway next to the kitchen.

"To the right is the master bedroom and on the other side of the wall in the middle of the house is the large den or family room. The breakfast nook is next to the kitchen. There are four bedrooms upstairs with an open hallway over looking the formal area of the house. Your bedroom will be on the ground floor. You have a three car garage and a hot tub inside next to your bedroom and a computer room off the bedroom also...."

"Charlie, I'd like it much better if he would change some things."

"What do you want, honey."

Willard looked a little disappointed, but asked, "What changes would you like?"

"First, I think we should have a four car garage, but even more important, I would want the hot tub outside in a - what do you call it, a small building?"

Willard responded, "A gazebo?"

"That's it and change the hot tub room into a small bedroom for our children when they are small so we do not have to go upstairs to see what is going on. Also, could you install an intercom so we can hear what is happening in all parts of the house?"

Charlie was nodding his head as much as to say I never thought of those things. I like them. Donna sure has a good head on her shoulders.

Willard replied, "Those changes won't hinder me at all. In fact, I think they are good suggestions. I'll make the changes and bring you the corrected plans in a couple of days for your approval."

Charlie nodded and said, "That'll be fine. Are you ready to go to town Honey? I want to show you our bank and some other things."

Willard got up and walked them out of his office and after they were out of hearing range, he turned to his secretary and said,

"They're really nice people. I'm glad they are moving here."

Four months passed and the house was on schedule. Donna had not been feeling too good so she had made an appointment to see a physician in Eugene who had a good reputation. As she walked up to his office for her 11:00 AM appointment, she looked at the physician's sign, which read Dr. Ralph Cameron, Obstetrician and Gynecologist.

That afternoon as Donna walked into the house and saw Charlie sitting down, looking over some plans, she said, "Want to know what the doctor said?"

"I do, but I need to know something. How do we order the cooking equipment for the restaurant? I don't know anything about that kind of stuff...."

With a little snap in her voice, Donna said again, "Do you want to know what the doctor said?"

Having already learned when she spoke in that tone of voice, it was wise to stop what you are doing and thinking and pay attention to her.

With very little enthusiasm, he replied, "Now, what did the doctor say - a little flu?"

"Well, it's a virus. A nine month virus, daddy to be," she said as she was smiling.

Charlie's mouth dropped open, then he recovered and said, "Here sit down. You won't do anything around here that I can do...."

"Look, honey, I'm just pregnant and I don't intend to be incapacitated by being pregnant. Understand?"

"Yes, but if you want anything, all you have to do is ask and I'll get it for you, understand?"

"Yes, but that's only part of the news. I'm due in seven months - that's October - and we'll have to double up on everything. I'm going to have twins. The doctor says the ultra sound indicates it's a boy and a girl."

Charlie now sat down and whistled. A boy and a girl the first time. He now thought of what Sam had said - he and Donna were walking towards Sam and Ruth and they had two children walking beside them. Everything in Sam's and Ruth's dreams was coming true.

"Donna, I couldn't be happier. But we have a problem."

"Is it the same problem you've been talking about for the past few days?"

"Yes. If we are to have a restaurant, we need to hire a cook and I believe I know where we can hire a good one – possibly the best in Louisiana!"

THE END?

www.ingramcontent.com/pod-product-compliance
Lightning Source LLC
Chambersburg PA
CBHW050019030726
47506CB00001B/22

* 9 7 8 1 8 9 3 8 9 2 0 8 8 *